Crossing Jordan

Born and raised in Glasgow, Jack Dickson is very much the product of his home town. Since gaining an Honours degree in English from Glasgow University, he has had several trial runs at a variety of careers including fashion designer, model, roadie and bouncer. His short fiction has been published widely in the USA. His previous novels are *Oddfellows* ('A reflection of the darker side of our desires, making it a compelling but uncomfortable read,' *Gay Scotland*) and *Freeform* ('A weaver of intricate plots which cunningly combine the most gripping elements of the hard-boiled thriller and most stimulating of erotic fiction,' *Gay Times*). His fourth novel *Banged Up* will be published by GMP later this year.

Crossing Jordan

Jack Dickson

Millivres Books
Brighton

First Published in 1999 by Millivres Books (Publishers)
33 Bristol Gardens, Brighton BN2 5JR, East Sussex, England

A CIP catalogue record for this book is available from the British Library

ISBN 1 873741 41 3

Typeset by Hailsham Typesetting Services, 2 Marine Road,
Eastbourne, East Sussex BN22 7AU

Printed and bound by Biddles Ltd., Walnut Tree House, Woodbridge
Park, Guildford, Surrey GU1 1DA

Distributed in the United Kingdom and Western Europe by Turnaround
Distribution Ltd., Unit 3, Olympia Trading Estate, Coburg Road, Wood
Green, London N22 6TZ

Distributed in Australia by Stilone Pty Ltd, PO Box 155, Broadway,
NSW 2007, Australia.

Thanks to Tom, co-conspirator and confidente; to Placebo for 'Bruise Pristine'; to Charlie, for transatlantic support, and in memory of Greg.

Also, thanks to the skinny redhead on the top of a Number 38 to Garthamlock, for inspiration.

No thanks to Adidas for the Black Banshees, which are not stocked by the Glasgow *Schuh*– does this mean I get a free pair, please?

This is for all the Dannys and all the Kels.

And Cosimo.

Prologue

"Nae bitin', nae ticklin', nae usin' two hands – an' nae tellin' onywan. Total...secrecy!" Palms rubbed together, business-like.

The bedroom was cold. The wallpaper was hideous. Danny blinked.

Explanatory grin. "'Sa game – a kinda contest. Like seein' who can pish the highest."

Danny hugged himself. "What's the point?" He stared from bright green eyes to where their knees were touching.

A sigh. "The point..." One hand reached across, fingers curling.

He gasped.

"...is that whoever comes first has gotta dae somethin' fur the other wan..."

Danny dragged his eyes from the hand around his knob. "What sort of something?" His voice sounded like someone else's voice. He watched his own fingers leave shivering forearms and shorten the distance between their bodies.

Shrug. "Onythin' – but nothin' daft, eh?" Centre-parted red hair skirted pale shoulders. "Nae jumpin' aff bridges or nothin'."

Words which had hovered at the back of his throat for two hours sprinted forward to his lips. "If I win, can I kiss you?"

Snort. "No way, hombre – nae poof-stuff!"

His palm curved around the length of flesh. It was warm and sticky and thicker than his own.

A low sigh.

"Can we...cuddle, then?"

Snort. "Christ, that's no' much o' a...prize..." Words lower, longer. "...an' ah'm no' intae fuckin', either, so ye can forget that!" The fingers of one pale hand swept a hank of hair from a furrowed forehead. "It's gotta be somethin' like..." Fingers tightened.

"You didn't say we'd started!" He wrapped his fist more

1

tightly around a corresponding length.

Hoarse laugh. "We huvney – no' til you understand the rules."

Fingers reluctantly uncurled. Tacky skin stuck to sweating palm.

Resigned sigh. "Want me tae decide – since it's yer first go? You kin pick next time."

He lowered his eyes. On the thin chest inches from his, a tiny clump of ginger hair sprouted between two hard nipples. He nodded. The shivers had moved lower, tingling over his balls. Danny watched a droplet of clear liquid ooze from the tiny slit in his knob. His head dropped forward in a nod.

"Okay..." Pause. "If you win, ah buy the chips..."

Red hair tickled his face.

"..an' if ah win..."

His heart thundered in time with slow, thoughtful words.

"...you eat ma spunk."

Chapter One

"Aye?"

"Aye...what?"

"Aye ye're no' gonny let me doon?" The toe of Kel's trainer nudged the remains of an unofficial bonfire.

Danny frowned. "Of course not!"

"Cos ah've never brought onywan else wi' me." Kel pushed charred sticks towards what was left of a melted Irn Bru bottle and arranged them around it.

Pride swelled in his chest. "Not even Frank or..." The name stuck in his throat. "...Gibby?"

Snort. "That paira wee kids? No way, hombre – it wid be aw' roon' Glasgow in nae time – an' Jordan widney like that."

The crack of a firework, in the distance.

Danny jumped. His eyes left the dim outline of Kel's pale face and darted around the deserted patch of land. "I can... keep my mouth shut."

Inside a Puffa jacket, thin shoulders rose then fell. "Ah ken – ah wis jist checkin'."

"Well, you don't need to – you can trust me." Danny echoed the shrug and looked beyond to a rusting, tripod-shaped structure. "Who would I tell, anyway?"

Snorting laugh. "Aye, that's a point!"

Danny blushed. He dragged his eyes back to where Kel was still arranging semi-burned sticks and spent bangers with a trainered foot. "So...who is this...guy?"

Kel's foot paused, mid-prod. "Just a guy – a mate o' Jordan's."

"Why can't...Jordan meet him?"

A pale face pulled itself from scrutiny of the grey sunburst on the ground. "Cos that's no' how things work." In the half-light, one green eye winked. "Man, for somewan doin' five highers yer affy thick, sometimes!"

A grin twitched his lips. He fought to keep it to a twitch.

"Jordan's got other things tae dae – he takes care o' the...paper-work. Ah dae the..leg-work." A size ten Nike

3

blocked out the sunburst, then squashed it into ash-muddy ground.

"He must trust you a lot." A familiar resentment tugged at his lips.

"Jordan an' me ur like that..."

Two fingers crossed in front of his face. Danny stared at them.

"...bin workin' thegether fur nearly a year, noo. Ah've done aw' sortsa stuff, wi' him."

Danny moved his eyes from the fingers to the face beyond. "Like?"

"Like..." Snigger. "...ah'll tell ye mair later, when ye've proved ye can keep yer mooth shut." He squinted in the gloom.

Danny rolled his eyes. He looked up into a grey sky which had been threatening all day. A large rain drop hit his cheek. Further wet splatters pattered his face. He sighed: it always poured on Guy Fawkes' Night. Danny thrust hands into Wrangler jacket pockets, glancing at his wrist: nearly eight. "They set the fireworks off soon..." He nudged a Puffa-ed shoulder, eyes sweeping the four corners of the waste-ground. "How long is this going to take?"

The shoulder nudged back. "No' long – we'll drop-aff the merchandise at JB's an' get there in time fur yer precious fireworks!"

Merchandise...

...he picked his way through assorted rubbish to a stack of splintered pallets. "What sort of merchandise?" Underfoot, trainers sunk into the pile of a drenched and long-abandoned carpet.

Shrug. "Sometimes H an' stuff – other times it's plastic, or letters. Wance it wis jist this lista numbers."

"Numbers?"

"Aye, numbers."

Danny shook a foot free from rotting carpet. "What sort of numbers?" He hoisted himself onto the pallets.

"What sort of numbers? What sort of numbers?" Sniggering mimicry. "Jist...numbers...ah, fuck – ma Nikes

4

are aw' dirty!" Annoyed. Foot drawn from the remains of the fire and wiped on soggy carpet.

"So you just...take this merchandise to Jordan?"

Nod.

"And...that's it?"

"Usually we exchange merchandise, but Jordan's no' dealt wi' this guy afore."

"Mmm..." Danny gripped broken pallet-slats. "I see." He didn't, but it didn't matter. Head swivelled over shoulder.

Fenced on four sides, the only access to the waste ground – apart from a loose railing – was a locked gate. He stared past the shadow of the tripod thing he knew was part of the drains' renovations. Dim light drifted over from the motorway to the north and the Securicor depot west. Fifteen minutes earlier, they'd scrambled down the steep incline from Townmill Road.

His gaze inched along the perimeter then spiked upwards. He tried to get his bearings. Beyond the M8, the Roystonhill flats glared down at him. On the opposite side, he could see the dark shapes of the factories at the bottom of Whitehill Street, and the back of the Iceland frozen food shop.

Four bangs and a burst of stars erupted somewhere over the Parade.

Danny flinched.

In the distance, cars roared past, the sound slicked by the increasing rain.

The middle of nowhere...

He stared up through the fence.

...yards from the main road. He lived less than a mile from here – they both did. The closeness was half-exciting, half-unnerving. Danny tore his eyes from civilisation and remembered earlier. "About what we were talking about..."

"No' this again..." A groan. Kel was wiping the toe of the Nike on a tuft of grass, hands deep in Puffa jacket pockets.

Danny watched the process and bit back a frown. "It's important..."

Sigh. "Says who?"

Danny echoed the sound. "Says...everyone."

Snort. "Ye mean they books ye've eyeways got yer nose stuck in?"

"Not just them." Danny drummed his heels against the pallet-stack.

Another snort. Kel stopped wiping the trainer's toe. "Ah dunno whit it is, wi' you an' they books." The muddy side of a Nike carefully stroked over wet grass. "Ye should git oot mair – live a little."

Danny frowned. "I...want to." The rain was getting heavier. He turned up the already wet collar of the Wrangler jacket. It felt cool against his hot skin. He watched rain splatter off the melted Diet Irn Bru bottle, then turned his face to the dark sky. "It's even called...coming out."

Snort. "Comin' oota where?"

Danny frowned. "I told you, 'member?"

Another snort. "How could ah forget?"

The frown tightened.

"But whit dis it matter?"

"It matters." Danny stared over at clouds illuminated by motorway lights. Puffs of orange/grey stared back at him.

"That's no whit ye usually say..." Mimicking. "They're idiots – I don't care what they think!"

"I don't! But it's better to be honest – you can't have a...relationship with someone if you're not honest with them." The words rolled from his mouth, gathering meaning.

Laugh. "Aye, right! Get real, eh?" Snort. Pause, then: "You're no' honest, aw' the time, wi' me..."

"Yes I am!" Danny stared at Kel.

"No ye're no' – you tell me ye liked Quentin Tarentino, an' ye don't."

"That's different – and I do like...bits of his stuff. You..."

"Telt me *Pulp Fiction* wis yer favourite film..." Kel talked through him. "...an' ye must looked at the screen fur aw' o' ten minutes, when we got it oot the vid-shop!"

"I was...willing to give it another chance."

6

Hoot. Hand held up, fingers counted off. "Telt me ye liked Tarentino; telt me ye liked no' huvin' ony friends; telt me ye didney care whit everywan else thought; telt me they wur a buncha losers onyway – an' then, aw' of a sudden, ye wanna... tell folk what hauf o' them think they've worked-oot awready?"

Danny's face flushed up. "That's different – I'm talking about telling mum and dad – just them."

Victorious laugh. "Seems like it's aw'...different, 'til it's somethin' you..." The words an accusation. "...wanna be honest aboot."

Danny sighed. "I hate...lying."

Snort. "'Sno' money that makes the world go round, it's lies." Pale face shining through gloom.

Danny pulled his gaze back to the sky. "I just think..."

"Aye, that's yer problem – ye think too much." Philosophical sigh. "It's none o' onywan's fuckin' business, an' ah dunno why yer makin' such a big deal oota this." Snort.

Danny's eyes reached beyond the clouds.

Six months ago it hadn't been a big deal.

Six months ago it had been just him. Alone. With the thoughts. And the books.

Then the Polo Lounge.

Trying to look older. Trying to blend in...

...and almost managing it. Until someone had stuck a nobbly elbow into the back of his Wrangler jacket and hissed: 'Ask'em tae turn that fuckin' juke-box doon so's we can hear MTV, eh?'

Now?

Suddenly irritated. "Life's too short tae get aw' riled up ower whit other people think – ye said that, ages ago."

"I know..."

Other people...

Warm, wet hands gripped his knees. His gaze flicked downwards.

Kel was crouching between his legs, freckled face illuminated yellow by sodium motorway lights. "So ah'm right, eh?"

7

Danny looked at pale face.

'...whit other people think...'

His stomach tightened. He shoved Kel backwards and stood up. Feet squelched on the carpet, mind searching for a change of subject. "This friend of Jordan's obviously not coming – we might as well just go down to the bonfire and..."

A yelp obliterated the end of the sentence.

Danny looked down at where the slim shape was sprawling on muddy grass.

"Aw' man, ma jeans ur fuckin' soakin'!" Long fingers plucked at mud-smeared denim. "Spent fuckin' hours ironin' them." Green eyes glared up, half-angry, half-frustrated.

Danny stuck out a hand. "Get up..."

Wet fingers tightened around his. And pulled back. Kel's laugh cut through the driving rain:

"Naw, you come doon!" Hand wrenching forwards.

'...whit other people think...'

He tried to brace one elbow for the approaching fall, but his wrist was seized in a scrabbling grip. Then wet Puffa-padded arms were around him and Kel was biting his neck.

Danny buried his face in a nylon-coated shoulder, hands slipping under Kel's arms and holding on. A groin bucked upwards. Something hard dug into his thigh. A shiver darted over his body. He could hear his own blood pound, feel Kel's breath warm and wet on his skin.

'...whit other people think...'

Hips moved against the hardness. Then they were rolling and Kel was heavy on top of him. His face was in wet red hair and the thought was words. "What would Frank and Gibby think if they could see you now?"

The mouth paused on his neck.

Danny regretted the question as soon as it formed in the air.

"Ah wis jist in that pub tae try an' shift CDs, right?"

The voice was stiff, harder than the outline against his thigh. Danny squirmed, tried to move away.

8

Strong hands grabbed his wrists, holding firmly. "Right?"

Danny looked up. He wanted to agree. Couldn't. Kel's pale face floated before his eyes, the black-attired rest of him too dark to see. Then hands darted downwards, gripping his waist. And tickling.

He howled.

Long fingers tickled more determinedly.

Danny gripped wrists, stuck a thigh between wet denimed legs and rolled again. Pinning Puffa-jacketed arms above a red head, he laughed down. "Stop it!"

The pale face thrashed from side to side. A snigger in the dark. "You gonny make me?"

Then a crunching sound.

Further away.

Danny looked up.

The movement registered. "Whit's wrang?" Sudden panic.

Danny continued to stare, slowly levering himself off the hardness in the CKs.

On the other side of the waste ground, an outline was making its way down the incline.

Beneath him, Kel was struggling to his feet. Pale hands brushed wet mud from from the back of wetter jeans. "Whit a mess..." He moved forward.

Danny staggered upright, watching the figure approach. The rain had eased to drizzle. His jacket was drenched, sticking to his back like a half-sloughed skin. Beneath the sweet/sour smell of Kel's breath, he could taste his tea and the edgy flavour of excitement. "This him?" The words low, aimed at a wet ear.

"Keep yer knickers oan..." Low laugh. Puffa-ed outline turning.

A muddy finger against his lips:

"...an' don't let me doon."

His lips quivered against the finger. Over black, padded nylon, he could see the man's face, now.

Older. Thin. Rodenty. Cheeks pink with exertion. Woolly hat pulled low over ears. From below the zipped neck of a leather jacket, a prominent Adam's Apple illuminated by a streak of motorway sodium. Over one shoulder, a JCB ruck-sack.

"Mister Lennox?" Hank of hair flicked behind ear.

"Aye – you Jordan's boy?"

"Aye." Grin. "Ye're late." Matter-of-fact.

Rain wiped from forehead. "Got held up..."

Laugh. "No' literally, ah hope!"

The man had an accent. Not a Glasgow accent: east coast. Danny focused on the exposed ear. He tried to look nonchalant.

A ferret face peered past the Puffa-jacketed figure. "Who's this?"

"Just a pal..." More matter-of-fact. "...that it?" A pale hand moved towards yellow JCB letters.

Danny's skin reddened under the scrutiny. The guy's eyes were boring into him. He tried to think of something to say. And failed.

"The package, Mister Lennox?" Kel's tone was low, even.

Something large and solid had wedged itself in Danny's throat.

Lennox moved one hand to the straps of the rucksack, the ferret-face wary.

Danny tried to swallow the thing in his throat. It refused to move. As did his legs.

Kel was talking again, just general stuff about the weather. Casual stuff. I'm-part-of-this stuff.

Lennox had removed the rucksack from his shoulder, but was still holding it. Watery blue eyes flicked around the waste ground, then resettled on Danny's face. "You another of Jordan's boys?" One hand beckoned.

Danny watched. Shock solidified the thing in his throat. With supreme effort, he moved one foot. Backwards.

Two pairs of eyes focused on him. Kel just stared.

Lennox did more. "Eh?" Something different in the tone. "C'mere..."

Danny was mesmerised by the man's accent. He managed another step into the background. Soggy carpet squelched underfoot. He opened his mouth. Nothing came out.

"Whit's up wi' him?" Eyes from Kel to Danny and back again.

"Nothin'..." Kel was scowling. "...he's no' the full shillin'."

Now Danny couldn't take his eyes off the ferret-face.

Lennox's turn to flinch under scrutiny. "C'mere so's ah can git a better luck at ye, son."

Kel's responding laugh was thin.

Danny continued to stare. His mind searched for a clever response, and came away empty-handed. Then a claw-grip grabbed his wrist:

"Ah said c'mere!" The voice dropped an octave.

His arm was twisted up and back. Danny yelped.

Lennox drew him closer, scowling into his face. "Pretty wee thing, eh?"

Danny could smell the man's breath. Behind:

"Jist geez the merchandise an' we'll get aff..."

Pain jolted up his arm. Danny felt his eyes water. He tried to pull away, but the man held on. In seconds, Lennox had twisted his wrist behind his back, forcing him around. "Some operation, this!" Wheezing laugh. "Whit's Burns thinkin' of, lettin' kids work for him?"

Danny stared into Kel's paler-than-usual face. Words finally came. "I'm not a kid!" Tears prickled hot behind his eyes.

Low, wheezing snigger. "An' ye're no' Jordan's!"

"Let him go, eh?" Kel was staring past him, at a face Danny could no longer see.

Lennox twisted Danny's arm higher. "Ever bin tae Edinburgh, posh-boay?" Another twist.

Danny almost screamed. His head was forced downwards. "No..."

"Ah didney think so..."

The man's legs pushed against his.

"...so whit you doin' wi' the likes o' this wee toe-rag?"

Breath stung the back of his neck. He stared at the blurry toes of Kel's Nikes, trying to make sense of the question.

11

"He's jist a mate, pal – let him go, eh?"

"Whit ye say me an' you take a wee walk, posh-boay?"

He couldn't speak. Something in his arm was stretching. It felt warm rather than sore, like a burn-pain. Fireworks zipped and sizzled in the distance.

"Fuckin' let him go!"

On the ground in front of him, Kel's right trainer moved, planting itself two feet away from the left.

The grip on his wrist increased. Through blurring vision, everything began to swim. Through the noise in his head, Lennox's ferret-wheeze.

Then a banger exploded and Kel screamed.

Danny fell forward onto grass, the hold on his wrist suddenly slack. Sulphur spangled in his nostrils. He curled into a ball and cradled his aching arm. Rolling onto his back, Danny stared up at a leaden sky...

...and the dark silhouette in the Puffa-jacket, hopping around and holding the gun.

"Ma haun'! Ma fuckin' haun'!"

"Where did you get that?" Danny's brain wouldn't work.

Kel was sucking fingers, then spitting onto the ground. "Bought it aff a guy doon Paddy's – hundred and twenty quid and it blows up in ma fuckin' hand!"

The pain in his arm had vanished. Danny leapt to his feet. "You okay?" He pulled Kel's fingers from his mouth, stared.

Pink and silvery patches dotted the pale flesh. Heat seeped into his own fingers.

"A hundred and twenty quid! Fuckin' thing's lethal..." Kel wrenched his hand away, stuck it back between lips and resumed the sucking.

Danny sank to a crouch, patting the dark ground for a darker object. And finding it. He picked up the gun gingerly. It was heavier than he'd thought a gun would be.

And warmer. It looked old.

Holding the weapon between thumb and forefinger, he peered.

12

Kel had stopped sucking his fingers.

Danny stuck the gun into his pocket and took a step forward.

An ashen face. Beneath two auburn slugs, ginger lashes batted like birds trying to take off.

His trainer impacted with something soft and solid. Danny scowled down, drew back a foot to kick the soggy carpet.

"Oh fuck..."

Two sets of eyes stared downwards.

Danny's foot hovered, mid-kick, then prodded gently.

The shape didn't move.

Kel sank to a crouch. "Mister Lennox? You okay?"

The only sound was a distant whizz then fizzle as a rocket streaked across the sky.

His stomach followed it. Clammy fingers tugged at a padded arm. "C'mon..."

Kel wrenched the grip away. He leant over the prostrate form, ear pressed to where the mouth should be.

"Oh please, let's just..." His voice cracked.

"Shhh!"

His legs gave way. The knees of Danny's jeans sank into mud. Beside the crouching figure, he strained to hear breath. The blood pounding in his head obliterated everything else.

"He's deid!"

"No he's not." Danny's eyes acclimatised to the dark. "He's just..." A cylindrical smear of mud clung to the man's brow. He tried to brush it away. One finger sank into a mushy indentation. Danny leapt back, staring from the thick liquid which coated the tip of his index finger to the man on the ground. The crack in his voice split wide open. "Come on – please, let's go!" Danny stood up.

Everything had slowed to a crawl. He couldn't drag his eyes from the deep gash in the middle of Mr Lennox's forehead. Pelting rain pooled in the furrow then spilled over and dribbled pink down a ferret face.

Kel was on his feet. "We canny jist...leave him here." He turned. Red hair plastered to head. Nose wiped on the sleeve of his Puffa-jacket.

"We could phone an ambulance?" His voice sounded weird.

Then Kel was talking and everything speeded up.

The carpet was heavy. And smelly. It took ages to unfold and spread out on the ground. Hot sweat mixed with cold rain and ran into Danny's eyes. He blinked it away and stepped back. "Do we really have to...?"

"Ye wanna go to jail?" Kel was breathing heavily.

Danny paused at the other end of Lennox. The shoulders of the leather jacket greasy against his palms. He took a deep breath. "It was an accident." He watched Kel's ashen face.

"Think the polis'll believe us?" Skin paled further. "Think Jordan'll believe us?"

Danny looked away.

"Wan, two..." Kel re-gripped.

They heaved together.

Fingers slipped. He grabbed lower. "Why did you shoot him?"

Kel staggered backwards towards the carpet. "Ainly meant tae scare him, stoap him hurtin' ye." Voice was low with effort.

Danny's stomach lurched. Terror cooled on his sweating skin. Underneath, Mr Lennox's last words swam through his veins.

In silence, they manoeuvred the man sideways.

"Bastard weighs a ton!" Kel groaned. "This why they ca' it deid weight?"

Danny paused. "What?" He couldn't believe how little his arm hurt – it was like it had never happened.

Kel was gripping the legs just above the ankle. "Cos things dae weigh more deid than alive?"

He could see an inch of yellowing white towelling sock protruding from under well-cut trousers. "That's a fallacy."

"A whit?"

"Nothing..."

At the edge of the patterned blue square, they let go.

Mr Lennox hit the carpet and rolled a little.

Kel gripped CK-ed thighs, breathing hard. "You're doin' biology – is there no' somethin' aboot the distribution of weight, when somethin's relaxed?"

Danny stepped off the carpet. It clung to the soles of his trainers like chewing-gum. "No idea – we've not covered the 'Disposing of Dead Bodies' part of the syllabus yet."

Kel didn't laugh.

Danny leant his foot against the dark shape and pushed.

Mr Lennox rolled over. The woolly hat fell off. It was full of what looked like mud but wasn't. Something acid-tasting rushed up from his stomach and hovered at the back of his throat. Danny swallowed, picked the hat and crammed it back on.

"The bullet!" Kel fell to his knees and began to search.

"Leave it – if we're moving him anyway..."

Kel looked up at him. Sudden panic gave way to confusion. Then understanding. "Good thinkin'!"

They grabbed an end of the carpet each and began to roll. Ten minutes later, Mr Lennox was no longer visible. Kel leant on Danny's shoulder, panting at the sausage-shaped tube on the ground:

"So, any suggestions how we get him oota here, Mister Five Highers?

Chapter Two

Wire dug into his hands. Legs flailed, trainers slipping and skidding on rusted mesh. Danny clenched his teeth and threw himself over the top of the fence.

Green eyes darted in the half-light. Questioning green eyes.

He landed a foot from the Puffa-jacketed figure. Impact shivered up through the soles of his feet into rubber legs. Danny ignored the jolting in his stomach and began to jog up Whitehill Street.

Every footfall was titan.

Splashes behind told him Kel was following.

As they rounded the corner into Iceland's car-park, Danny sprinted towards the bank of shopping trolleys which sheltered under Kwik-Save's blue/yellow canopy. Grabbing the first, he pulled then saw the chain.

Kel skittered to a halt beside him.

Danny's heart was trying to break out of his chest. He thrust a hand into the pocket of his jeans, withdrew a fist of change. "We got a pound?" Silver and copper-coloured coins quivered dark against off-white skin.

"Whit?"

Danny yanked demonstrably at the row of secured wire trolleys with his free hand. "You need a pound to get one loose." His gaze returned to the copper-coloured coins on his sweating palm.

"Ah always use a basket, maself..."

"Look and see!"

"Okay – haud oan..." Pockets searched. "...two ten pees an'..."

Danny released the front trolley and began to search the slots of others.

"Whit ye doin'?"

"If they're in a hurry, people sometimes forget to collect their money, when they put their trolleys back." He made his way up one row, then down the other.

Snort. "No' roon' here, they don't!" The sound of money

17

being counted.

Hope dashed itself against his forehead. He turned his attention to the red-mesh security-screen which cloaked the front of the Iceland Frozen Food shop, then remembered Iceland kept their trolleys inside.

"Twenty seven pee..."

Kel's voice cut through thoughts which were going nowhere anyway.

"...how much you got?"

"Seventy." He thumped the bank of trolleys, then pulled at it and tried to think.

Metal rattled noisily. Somewhere close by, a banger exploded.

Danny flinched. His brain was back on the waste-ground. His head was full of wet carpet. He wanted to be anywhere else, apart from here.

"Oh man oh man oh man!"

His head jerked up from the security-locks.

Kel was pacing, rubbing his face. The Puffa-jacket was streaked with mud. Trainers slapped wetly on dry asphalt.

The sight kick-started thought down a more productive road. "You got a knife?" His eyes zeroed back to the slot-device.

"Naw, but you've still got the gun."

Something made him almost laugh. He glanced up, patting pockets and feeling only keys and the hard outline of a weapon he didn't want to feel. "The wee spring from a pen would do – anything thin to slip into the lock and..."

"Shoot it." Low words.

"What?"

Kel's hair framed the pale face like a liquid balaclava. It was so wet it looked black. He tilted his head. "Shoot wanna the locks." A long index finger patted the plastic-encased mechanism.

Danny shivered. "Too close to the road – someone'll..."

A firework sang solo in the distance. Kel stared at him. "Oh aye, like another bang the night's gonny be noticed!"

Then Danny was holding the gun, two handed, aiming at a blue plastic slot-mechanism.

The weapon was less warm now.

And wetter.

A finger curled over the trigger. Arms out-stretched, he watched shivers ripple up over drenched denim.

The gun twitched.

Danny tried to relax.

The gun twitched more violently.

He moved closer to the trolley-bank, wedging the end of the barrel against a plastic-encased slot. Arms rigid, he closed his eyes.

And squeezed.

The trigger didn't move. Voice at his shoulder:

"Jist dae it!"

Danny's eyes shot open. "I did!" He squeezed again, staring at the lock.

Nothing. The trigger remained jammed. A sigh at his shoulder:

"A hundred an' twenty fuckin' quid..."

Danny's left hand dropped. He returned the gun to jeans' pocket, could still feel its hard shape against his sweating palm. Staring at the bank of trolleys, he tried to will one free. Then Kel was talking again:

"Haud this."

Danny turned.

Kel tipped coins into his palm, nodded to a rectangular shell of light on the other side of the street.

Danny peered through sheets of rain, watching the Puffa-jacketed shape lope across the car-park towards the steps leading up to pavement level.

He only realised how wet they were when they stood beside dry people.

The bus-shelter housed five figures. Two moved outside as soon as he and Kel entered. The other three watched them curiously from the opaque back-wall.

Danny looked from left to right, scanning the road outside and trying not to meet eyes.

"Onywan gotta pound?" A hopeful voice cut through his panic. "Ah've only got ninety seven pee, but it's really important."

Silence.

Danny opened a clenched fist, re-examining the coins and hoping they had miraculously clubbed together and made another. His hand smelled of metal and sweat.

"Whit aboot you, pal?"

Kel was bobbing beside a man in an earring and a donkey-jacket.

The man thrust fingers into pockets, fumbling. One green pound note and two blue fivers produced.

"Naw, it's gotta be a pound coin."

Danny looked back to the road and caught the froggy eyes of a woman in an Adidas jerkin. They bulged at him. Whiplash tingled as he jerked his head left.

The soaking figure in the Puffa-jacket moved on to an elderly man in a stained overcoat who was trying to sidle back out into the rain:

"Pound coin, mister?"

Danny thought about Mr Lennox. The longer that carpet lay in the rain, the heavier it was getting. The heavier it got, the more difficult it would be to move.

The more difficult it was to move...

"Whit aboot you, missus?"

The woman in the red Adidas and the froggy eyes shook her head. "Sorry, son."

Danny frowned: she hadn't even looked.

"Fuck it!"

Kel's fingers hauled the hard object from the back pocket of his jeans:

"Money! Noo!"

The words echoed in his head. His eyes followed the barrel of the gun as it flicked between the shelter's occupants.

Then everyone was tearing their pockets and bags apart. Kel loped outside, herding two more figures into the illuminated shell with jerks of the gun.

Something coated his teeth. Danny tried to remove the film with his tongue. It stuck like glue. Kel bobbed about behind him as Froggy-Eyes, Earring and a woman with a

20

Farmfoods' bag offered him wallets and purses.

The old guy in the stained overcoat was waving a cellophane-encased Travel-Card.

A dribble of rain fell from the shelter's roof and dripped down Danny's neck.

Kel thrust the gun into his hand, snatched the offerings and rifled. Frustrated sigh. "Christ, huv they withdrawn pound coins from circulation or somethin'?"

No-one answered.

Someone was holding out a twenty-pound note.

Danny blinked. His feet had taken root. His tongue stuck to the roof of his mouth. Through double-glazed vision, he watched Kel toss two wallets and a velcro-fastening purse onto the ground, laugh at the twenty-pound note then slump back against him:

"Whit we gonny dae?" The question hissed into his ear.

Danny stared at the gun. It drooped at a puddle. He opened his mouth. It stayed open.

"Here..."

A voice broke him free from suspended animation.

The woman in the Adidas and the froggy eyes held a small, mustard-coloured coin. Danny just looked at it.

"Ah asked you nicely, missus!" Annoyed. "Why did ye no'...?"

Danny stuffed the gun into his back pocket. "Thanks!" He grabbed the coin, tipped ninety-seven clammy pence in change into the woman's hand and hauled Kel out of the shelter.

A Number Fifty One sprayed a tidal wave against his back as they sprinted back into the car-park.

The rain had stopped.

So had time.

The carpet refused to bend.

Sweat drenched Danny's body, flooding from pits and adhering a soaked tee-shirt to stomach.

"Why did she no' hand it over in the first place?"

Danny shoved for a third time, jamming a foot against the trolley's front wheels.

21

The sausage-shape carpet flopped across the breadth of the basket-section but refused to do much else.

"Ah mean, even if she needed it fur the bus, they woulda let her off wi' bein' three pee short."

Which end of the carpet was which? If he could find the knees...

"Ah dae it aw' the time."

Keeping one foot in place, he inched round to Kel's end and stuck a hand inside the tube of mouldering rubber and fibre. At elbow's length, fingers met something soft and slimy. Danny wrenched his arm out, wiped palm on wet jeans and inched back to where he'd started.

"If ah've only got...say, ninety two pee, ah shove that in the machine an' ask fur a pound fare."

"You going to help, or what?" He patted up from the bottom of the carpet until he reached what felt like a knee-joint.

"Ah wis jist wonderin'..."

"Well, don't!" Danny pushed downwards.

A castor moved against his foot but the carpet remained straight. His eyes were wet and stingy. He leant over the sausage shape and tried to breathe normally.

They'd been here for hours. Days. The carpet's perished rubber backing stuck to everything and smelled like old, unwashed clothes.

They were going to die here.

"Think he let hur aff wi' the three pee?"

He raised his head.

"Eh?"

Danny picked remnants of carpet-backing from his cheek. He didn't want to think at all.

"Think the driver let her aff wi' the three pee?"

"Fuck the three pee!" He felt a hundred years old. Two hundred. He'd always been here, with this carpet and this shopping-trolley and this guy who wouldn't stop talking, and always would be.

"Christ, whit's that smell?"

Danny turned his head.

Kel was raising one trainered foot, then the other,

22

scrutinising the soles of the Nikes. Forehead wrinkling. "See if ah've trod oan dog-shite ah'll..."

"Bowel evacuation." Danny sighed. He'd forgotten about that.

Kel was staring, both feet back on the ground. "Whit?"

Danny straightened up. "You...lose control of your bowels when you..." He couldn't say the word. "Afterwards." Suddenly, mushy carpet-backing didn't seem so bad.

Kel goggled. "He's...shit himself?" The Puffa-jacketed shape took a step back.

Danny nodded wearily. "And he'll have an erection too."

"Ye're kiddin'!"

He returned his attention to the sausage-shape.

"That why they call it a...stiffy?"

Danny swallowed something between a snigger and a sob. "No idea." He was shaking again.

They were never going to manage it.

This was never going to work.

Tears rolled down his face.

"So he's lyin' there, inside that carpet, wi' a big hard-on?" Kel's voice was closer, awe-filled. "That's amazin'!" Low whistle. "Maybe that's whit's stoppin' the carpet fae bendin'."

Danny spun round. "Shut up!" Even the words was shaking.

"You okay?" The voice was gentle. Too gentle...

Danny lowered his head. A tear dripped off the end of his nose. He sniffed.

A sigh. "Lemme think a minute."

He rubbed his face and tried to pull himself together.

Then Kel was nudging the sausage-shape from its position across the wire basket section and tipping the trolley onto its side.

Danny shrieked: it had taken hours to get the carpet onto the trolley in the first place.

"Sit on him!"

He stared. Tears fled, pursued by anger. "You're not

funny."

"No' meant tae be funny! You're heavier than me. Get in behind this..." Kel had grabbed one end of the carpet and was dragging it up from muddy grass. "...an' sit on him when ah tell ye tae."

Danny hesitated. Then began to move.

The ground was a quagmire. He kept slipping.

Kel hauled one end of the carpet up and forward.

Danny staggered into position behind it.

Gripping the edge of the vertical section, Kel moved out of the way. "Noo!"

He sat down hard.

The sausage creased beneath him. Danny winced. An image of a hard-on, squashed between a leather jacket and wet trousers danced before his eyes. Danny swallowed another sob.

"Jump up an' doon a bit..." Kel had released the carpet and was now pulling the trolley towards the centre bend.

Danny wriggled. Carpet-backing rose in damp, puffy farts. He coughed.

"Harder, man! Squash it right doon!"

Danny bounced more vigorously, watching as Kel positioned the still-on-its-side trolley at the fold. Beneath his legs, the carpet was deflating like a pricked balloon.

"Noo, get aff slowly an' get behind it."

Danny did as he was told. Amazingly, the sausage stayed doubled over, and remained like that while he and Kel eased it, bend first, into the trolley's basket section.

"Nae sweat – see?"

He was choking on carpet-backing. "I see a trolley we're never going to get upright." He wiped dusty lips on the back of a dustier hand and tried not to think about Mr Lennox's head pressing into Mr Lennox's ankles.

Snort. "Trust me, eh? Ah've seen this done..."

He wondered vaguely where. Danny sank to a crouch and rubbed stinging eyes.

Kel scanned the waste-ground, grabbed a length of not-quite-burnt wood and stuck it under the trolley.

It snapped.

He grabbed another.

It didn't.

"You git roon' the other side..." Kel gripped a charcoaled end and started to lever. "...make sure it disney topple."

Staggering to his feet, Danny picked his way around the trolley and gripped.

The wheels skited once.

He shoved a brick behind them and they didn't skite again.

Minutes later, the trolley was upright and Mr Lennox was in it.

Danny stared in disbelief.

Kel was slapping the arms of the Puffa-jacket. Head cocked questioningly towards the motorway.

Danny nodded, amazement ebbing away. "Take it slow..."

Each gripping an end of the trolley, they started across the waste-ground past the rusting tripod.

One wheel squeaked.

Danny stared at the back of Kel's head, listening to the rhythm. It gave him something to concentrate on. He pushed wordlessly, watching the opposite bank of trees move towards them.

The incline leading back up onto Townmill Road was more rock than grass. Danny shoved hard and up.

Wheels impacted on something solid. The squeak changed to a jarring groan.

He wrenched sideways and pushed on. Castors spun in all directions, rebelling against the uneven surface as they wove between trees. Rain-drenched lilac bushes whipped against his face and cooled it.

Kel turned, grabbed the front of the mesh basket and hauled, climbing backwards over a heap of burst bin-liners.

After a lifetime, they were clearing the trees. Danny paused, breathing through his mouth. The lights from the motorway back-lit the pale face in front of him.

Kel's eyes were huge, shining down from a face the

colour of sour milk. "Put yer back intae it, eh?"

Shoulder-sockets were about to release arms. He pushed one final time, half-lifting the trolley over the last of the burst bin-liners.

Four wheels hit grass again. One squeaked. Then squeaked again. And continued to squeak across the final ten yards, through the hole in the railings and onto tarmac.

Kel was breathing heavily. "Feels like we should plant a flag or somethin'!"

Danny could only pant. Eventually, his lungs returned to something near normal. "Which way?" He glanced in both directions.

Right led towards the motorway and a dead end. For a dead man? Too open, too...

Under his hands, the trolley was wrenched left. Low words:

"Wanna catch they fireworks?"

Danny stared at the pale face. Glasgow Green was miles away, down endless, very public streets and full of masses of people and...

Green eyes slitting. "Nice big bonfire – everywan watchin' the pretty lights in the sky while we..."

"Oh, God – all right...." He could almost smell the sulphur, nostrils tingling with the stench of burning carpet and worse.

"Ah'll steer, you walk beside him an' watch he disney fall oot."

His fingers had soldered themselves to the trolley's handle. Danny wrenched them free.

Kel pushed past him, knuckles curling white around the blue grip. He set off at a brisk pace.

Two sets of footsteps echoed in Townmill Road. The castor squeaked in time with their progress.

Everyone was already at the fireworks display. The Parade was wet, carless and peopleless...

...as was Hanson Street and Craigpark Drive.

On the grass at the foot of Ark Lane, a gaggle of pre-teens unloaded wood from another trolley onto a small, unofficial bonfire.

Too small.

Danny's hand was rigid on the V-shaped bundle projecting up in front of him. Eyes moved from flames and fixed back on the carpet. The fingers of his other hand clenched tightly against his palm.

He listened to the squeak and the slap of their feet over crackling wood.

Across Duke Street, the rhythm took over again.

Danny stared through the V. On the other side of the road, living-rooms winked at him through half-shut curtains: normal people doing normal things. Over the wheel-squeak, the *Brookside*-music drifted into his ears. He wondered if the programme was starting, or finishing.

Then something was syncopating with the squeak.

A beeping-something.

Danny stared down at the trolley.

A snigger. "It's fur you-oo..."

The sound of a mobile-phone continued to pulse from inside the carpet.

Danny looked at Kel. "Make it stop..."

"Ah'm no' fumblin' aboot in there!" Scowl towards the V. "It'll stoap in a minute..."

They pushed on.

It didn't.

The sound filled his head, amplified itself and boomed out into the night. Danny moved his fingers gingerly, trying to locate the pulse. Carpet-backing crumbled beneath his palm.

A jolt refocused his thoughts. The front of the trolley dipped, bumping off the pavement and onto the road.

The beeping stopped.

Relief drenched his body. He released the bent-sausage, moving to Kel's end to help lift it onto the approaching kerb.

The rhythmic squeak sang solo. Then:

"Danny?"

The word was too loud. His head flipped round. "What?"

27

"Why dis that happen?"

"Why does what happen?"

"Why dae ye get a hard-on when ye're deid?"

"How should I know?" He increased his grip on the V-shaped sausage.

"Ah thought, whit wi' you doin' biology..." Words tailed off.

The wheel squeaked on.

He tried not to think further than the next minute. Then:

"Must be somethin' tae dae wi' the blood-supply..."

Danny chewed his bottom lip. Shut up.

"...or muscle-control..."

Danny stared at the V-shaped sausage. Shut up.

"Dis it always happen?"

Shut up..

"How long dis it last?"

Shut up...

"Ah mean, when stiffs go tae the mortuary, ur they still...?"

"Fuckin' shut up about hard-ons, willya?"

"Ainly askin'! Ah – oops!"

Danny caught the change of tone, following Kel's gaze to the group of men walking up Tobago Street. Something cold trickled down his spine. He slowed.

Kel walked faster. "They've seen us, onyway..." Voice a whisper. "Keep goin'..."

Danny lowered his head. If he didn't look, they weren't there.

If he closed his eyes, it wasn't happening. He leant on the V-shaped cargo like his life depended on it.

The four men were silent. Even the wheel had stopped squeaking. There was a spotlight on the trolley. The four sets of approaching feet were a drum-roll. Beneath a soaking tee-shirt, his skin flushed cold then hot again. Danny wanted to crawl into the carpet beside Mr Lennox.

Then more beeping.

Outside the fire-station, four sets of footsteps were almost parallel with two. Danny's brain was on wheels: if they tried to swerve onto the road...

"Better answer yer mobile, son!" One mock-sober voice, then three others laughing.

His eyes shot open. Danny released the V-shaped sausage, joined Kel at the handle.

Then they were running across London Road and the men were laughing. But walking on. Not stopping.

The phone was still ringing as they pushed the trolley down a rough gravel path towards green railings and on through the gate.

Chapter Three

Brightness.

Everywhere. After dim streets, it hurt his eyes,

Huge floodlights illuminated Glasgow Green. The grass was crushed to a mushy soup, mashed semi-liquid by thousands of feet. The air was thick with metallic-coloured balloons and the smell of hamburgers. Somewhere, a sound system was belting out the Spice Girls.

Danny knew what he wanted, what he really really wanted...

...side by side, they negotiated the crowd. Wet leaves and litter slapped underfoot. Memories of previous years told him the bonfire was over the far side. Danny stared through a now-floppy V at the thickening mass of families between them and their goal.

They needed to get off the grass and onto the walk-way beside the river. Then they could cut back up and..

"Sorry, missus!

The handle of the trolley stabbed into his stomach as Kel manoeuvred it backwards. Danny looked up into a pair of annoyed eyes.

A small girl with a metallic coloured balloon hit him in the face with it. Somewhere near, a man in a Parks Department jacket was talking into hand-held radio.

Somewhere in the distance, a siren squealed.

The sound pierced his brain. Fingers tightening, Danny pushed faster, guiding the trolley round groups of people eating chips and drinking juice. Someone waved a luminous green hoop in front of his eyes.

"Comin' through! 'Scuse us!"

Danny cringed. Kel's shouts of warning only drew more attention to them. But at least people were getting out of the way, and the floodlights were fading.

Then new light.

Orange light.

And heat.

The far side of the bonfire...

...and the wrong side of a waist-high crash-barrier. Danny sighed. At his shoulder:

"Fuck!"

They followed the temporary fence, searching for a break. Each section was encased in concrete and overlapped the previous by a good six inches. Heat blasted his face.

Yards – feet – away, an inferno blazed. He wondered about hauling the carpet from the trolley and trying to hurl it over the crash-barrier.

Then he remembered the struggle to get it off the ground in the first place. Sweat ran down his forehead.

The trolley stopped.

Danny tore his eyes from the blaze and looked at Kel.

Bathed in fire-glow, the face matched the hair. The frown matched his own. Then an orange-shadowed fist hit the handle:

"Let's jist lea' the fuckin' thing here an'..."

"Oi! You pair!"

Danny froze.

A figure in a Parks' Department jacket was striding towards them. Squawks issued from a radio clipped to waistband.

"Can we put this oan the bonfire, pal?"

Laugh. "Whit ye got there?" Wet footsteps. Louder squawks.

Danny stared at the ground.

"Whit dis it look like – 'sa carpet!"

The footsteps stopped. Danny focused on the toes of muddied wellies.

"Gonny let us, eh?"

Another laugh. "Ainly official material, son – you shouldney even be round this side, onyway..."

"Aw', go on – we've pushed fur it miles."

Danny's heart threw itself against his ribs. He risked a look upwards.

"No can do..." The Parks Department guy was shaking his head. "It wid break Health and Safety regulations." The voice became more official. Arms out-stretched. Herding movement. "Noo, move oan back round where ye should be an' watch the fireworks like everywan else."

"Whit we meant tae dae wi' it, then?" Protesting.

Danny's fingers curled around the handle. He dragged the trolley backwards.

Wheels protested, sinking into squashy ground.

Less friendly. "Ah don't care whit ye dae wi' it, son – it's no' official material, so jist get it an' yersels oota here!"

Snort. "No much o' a bonfire if ye can ainly burn... official stuff oan it."

Danny tried to manoeuvre the trolley. It rejected his efforts. He seized the rapidly-drying sleeve of a Puffa-jacket.

The arm dragged itself free. "Ma auld man pays his council-tax – it's oor bonfire tae, an' ah wanna put this carpet oan it!"

"Go on – get oota here!"

A strong hand grabbed his shoulder. Danny flinched, watching another fist tighten on a Puffa-jacketed arm. Then they were both pushed back towards the walk-way and the trolley was squeaking in front of them, on its own.

They caught up with it just before the railings.

Danny's lungs were full of burning air he couldn't expel. He launched himself onto a wilting V-shape.

Kel grabbed the handle.

Metal clanged off metal.

Somewhere below, wings flapped and something hissed. Somewhere in the distance, distorted music continued to belt from speakers.

Danny exhaled into a crumbling mass of grey. Heavy breathing at his side:

"Bastard thing's gotta life o' its ain!"

Breath continued to gush from his lungs. Dragging his head up, he stared around.

They were standing on the semi-circular tarmac platform which stuck out over the Clyde. The carpet was half-resting against a curved railing.

On the other side of the river, security-lights from the

flats loomed down, squinting into fuzzy zig-zags in the dark water.

He moved from the floppy V to beside Kel.

Back up on the Green, he could just make out an orange glow. The Parks Department guy had disappeared, replaced by dribs and drabs of dark, strolling shapes, some of whom waved green glowing circles.

Danny looked left into other glowing green.

Kel was frowning, rotating Puffa-jacketed shoulders and rocking slightly.

"What do we do now?" The words were staccato, through suddenly-chattering teeth. He gripped the railing and tried to stop shaking.

No response.

Danny stared at the side of a pale face.

Yards away, shouting.

His head flicked right.

A group of dark shapes raced down the incline and ran on towards the bridge beyond the Life-Saving station.

The music was a distant din over the thump of his heart. Exhaustion draped his limps in an iron shroud. "What do we do?" Words aimed bonfirewards.

A sigh. "Ah need a pish – ah canny think when ah need a pish..."

He watched a Puffa-jacketed figure stagger onto the walk-way in the direction of a huddle of leafless trees. Dark merged with darkness...

A frisson of electricity shot up his spine.

...then panic. He was alone. His head swivelled right.

He was alone with...

...the trolley sat there, its drooping cargo drooping further. The grey V splayed outwards like the wilting leaves of some neglected plant.

Danny edged away. His thigh contacted with an iron railing-spar. In his back pocket, other metal contacted through denim. Eyes darted back to the walk-way. Heart pounding, he searched for a Puffa-jacketed shape amongst leafless tree-shapes.

A pale face emerged from the darkness...

34

Relief drenched his skin.

...and a voice. "Hey, Kelston!" More voices. Laughing voices...

...voices he recognised. Danny slumped over the railing. He tried to blend in with the metal and night.

An explosion above his head, followed by a communal gasp from the Green. The distorted music had changed to something classical. Last year, it had been the *1812 Overture*. Kel's gruff tones squeezed through the memory:

"Doon tae watch the pretty fireworks, Frank?"

"Aye, right!" Scornful. "Bin ower at Gibby's brother's place."

"Hoose-warmin'..."

Different voice. Danny shivered. Kenneth Gibb's sneering face projected itself onto the dark water below the railings, edging Frank Drysdale's beefy features aside.

"...it's gotta balcony – great view! We left when the hash ran oot..."

"...came ower the bridge, see if there wis ony action." Laugh. "'Member last year? Bent-Boay MacIntyre an' his fuckin' sparklers?"

Danny stared into dark water. They spoke in tandem. Acted in tandem. Monkey see, monkey...

"Fuck all happenin' here – whit you up tae?"

"Nothin' much."

"Comin' up the road, then?"

"Naw..."

"Whit you dain' here, onyway? Fireworks ur fur wee kids!"

"Hey, check that..." Gibby's nasal tones. "There's some auld coffin-dodger ower there wi' a trolley..." Giggle. "Wanna push him in?"

Danny shivered.

Disdain. "No' here fur the fireworks, am ah?"

Curious. "You goat ony money?" Gibby's attention re-taken.

Gruff voice lowered. "No' yet..."

Danny's ears strained.

"...goat a bitta business tae attend tae..."

35

Danny's ears fizzed.

"...wi' Jordan."

"Oh aye?"

Silence.

"Mebbe the coffin-dodger's goat money..."

Danny clenched fists around metal railings.

"...wanna...?"

"Whit sorta...business?"

Another overhead explosion made him gasp in sync with the crowd back on the Green.

"Canny tell ye, boays..." Low, conspiratorial. "...but ye ken Jordan's bin havin' trouble wi' they toe-rags fae Barmulloch an'..."

The words obliterated by a series of screaming, sulphurous rockets.

Danny's head slumped sideways, met a fold of wet carpet. Fury and frustration spangled through his veins.

They'd come over – Gibby had a nose like a ferret.

They'd come over, and they'd...

...then his hands were scrabbling on a grainy surface. Fingers sinking into crumbling mush, he hauled the carpet from the trolley and pushed it over the railings.

If there was a splash, he didn't hear it over the sound of metal hitting metal. Fury taking over from frustration, he heaved the trolley into the air.

"He's gonny jump! The coffin-dodger's gonny jump!"

Danny's arms trembled. One wheel caught on the edge and whirled, squeaking desperately. He wrenched it free and hurled the trolley over the railings.

Somewhere in the distance, a plaintive beeping.

Then he was running. He slid on something, almost fell. Danny kept running. Distorted cannons boomed in his ears, under the deafening thump of explosions above his head and rapid gun-fire in his chest.

He ran on, past the Life-Saving Station...

It was over.

...and on, narrowly avoiding two women with prams at the iron bridge...

It was over.

...and on, feet slapping on tarmac...

It was over.

...he was sprinting up the embankment towards a hedge when a hand grabbed his shoulder and pulled him down onto wet grass:

"Ya beauty!"

Danny's mouth was full of leaves. Chest heaved. The same hand wrenched him onto his back. A pale, admiring face fluttered before him:

"Shouldda thought o' that in the first place..." Gulping in air. "...the current'll carry it away an'..."

"Where's your...friends?" He spat the word.

Kel slumped beside him. Breathless. "Who cares? We aw' ran after you, but Frank's that fuckin' oota condition he an' Gibby gave up at the auld rowin' sheds." Slumping onto back. Green eyes cloudwards. "Man, that wis some stunt!" Snigger. "Ah couldney believe it – ye wur standin' there, holdin' that trolley above yer heid like ye wur gonny...deliver some sorta thunderbolt doon intae the water! Ah jist hope that mobile's battery runs oot soon." An arm slung itself around his shoulder. "But at least it's no' oor problem, ony mair."

His brain began to work. Danny levered himself onto an elbow. He stared down at a pale face. "Did they see it was me?" He needed to pee.

"Naw...ye wur movin' that fast aw' we saw wis a streak."

"They'll not...go back there?"

Snort. "Frank? Climb railings? In his fuckin' dreams, mebbe...

An image of Frank's flabby body scrambling over the metal fence flashed into his mind. Danny giggled.

Then a Puffa-jacketed torso was on top of his, legs pinning him to the ground. "Lemme in oan it, next time ye huv a brain-wave though, eh? Ah didney ken where ye wur aff tae!"

Danny stared up. The need to pee was getting stronger.

A hank of damp hair fell over the pale face.

He pushed it behind a pink ear.

A flinch. Then a sigh. "Pity we missed the fireworks..."

Sparks of a different variety soared through his body. Danny's fingers lingered, slick with scarlet hair. "Doesn't matter..." Cold wetness was seeping up from the grass.

Then footsteps – dozens of footsteps.

Danny turned his face from Kel's.

Legs...

The Bonfire Night Display was finished and people were making their way home.

It wasn't over.

Not yet.

Danny lowered his voice. "You'll need to go and see..."

"Ah ken." Sigh.

"What are you going to say?" Inches from his face, a brow creased. A hand released his shoulder, a finger thrust into mouth:

"Nae fuckin' idea..."

Almost everyone had left. The Green was empty.

The space had helped clear his mind and take it off the fact he needed to pee desperately. "Okay, one last time."

They were leaning against the wall of the derelict tennis pavilion.

The arse of his trousers was soaked through. Danny peered from the tall structure that was JB's Health Club into a frowning face.

A cuticle nibbled. Words by rote. "Ah say we – you an' me – waited til nine, an' no-wan showed up."

Danny nodded. "What did we do then?" He glanced at his watch.

Curious look. The chewing paused. "Why will he want tae ken that?"

"Cos it's nearly ten and it wouldn't take us an hour to get down here."

Understanding. "Oh, right..." Forehead creased in concentration. "The roads wur really busy, cos the fireworks had jist finished an' it took ages tae get through."

Danny nodded again. It was plausible. Sort of.

"Aw' man..." Kel was chewing again, red sceptical head

shaking slowly. "Jordan's no' gonny buy this..."

"Yes he is – why shouldn't he?"

"You don't ken Jordan..." White teeth tugged at a sliver of skin. "He's no' stupid."

"Neither are we!" Danny grabbed a bony wrist, wrenching Kel's hand from his mouth. "That's why we don't make a big deal out of this. Mr Lennox could've...changed his mind, been mugged, got lost – a thousand things."

Pause. Then: "You don't ken Jordan."

"You're his partner. He trusts you." Kel's wrist was warm and damp in his fingers.

Hesitant. "When ah said...partner, ah didney mean that – no' exactly..." Kel pulled his hand free.

Danny stared. Now didn't seem the time to confess he'd not exactly bought all the partner-stuff anyway. "But he still must trust you – if he lets you handle the... merchandise."

"Aye..." Head lowered, cuticle nibbled more vigorously. "...but that jist makes it worse, ken?"

Danny tried to find something positive to say. Failed. He stared at hunched shoulders.

Kel's head remained lowered.

"It's going to be okay..."

The shoulders slowly relaxed. Turning.

"...if we just act normal, no-one'll suspect anything."

Head raised. "Ye think so?" Finger-gnawing again.

"I know so." He looked back at the health club, wondering what time it closed.

"Ye...wanna wait here?"

Danny refocused on the shuffling, Puffa-jacketed figure. He wanted to pee. He wanted to go home. He wanted never to have left the house. The reason the trigger had been pulled at all exploded in his mind. "We're in this together."

Voice lower still. "Then we dae this thegether." Words slow, like slowness might make them believable.

"Right." A vague satisfaction hovered in his mind, nudged away by pressure in his bladder. "But I need to use a...toilet first."

They waded through piles of litter towards the brick outline.

Kel lounged, side on, against a pine reception-counter. He peered through a perspex window at a girl in a leotard with scraped-back hair and orangy-looking skin. "Jordan in?" Nonchalant.

The girl peered back at him. "Who wants tae ken?"

"Tell him Kel's here, eh?"

"Kel who?"

Less-nonchalant. "Jist tell him Kel, okay?"

Danny looked away from the interrogation. Eyes swept the walls of the foyer for possible lavatories.

A door marked 'Private'.

Double doors.

A staircase...

..and a wall. Timetables of aerobics-classes.

'Lose Weight Now!'

'Gain Weight Safely with the Hi-Pro Performance Regime.'

A poster for the live satellite relay of Scotland's World Cup qualifying match with Lithuania, next Tuesday.

Danny sighed. He didn't even know Lithuania had a football team. In the kitchen, at home, a Free with Today's *Record* chart hung above the fridge, the result of each match neatly filled in by his father.

"Fancy the weight-trainin'?"

A voice at his side shattered the thoughts. A bitten finger stabbed at a hand-drawn sketch of two men – one grinning and muscled, the other slope-shouldered and looking like Kel with shorter hair. "Where's the toilets?"

Sigh. "Can ye no' haud oan?" Eyes back on the notice-board.

From speakers above his head, low music changed to something equally familiar and instantly forgettable.

"Wednesdays six to eight. Beginners welcome..." One pale finger moved along a printed line, beneath the sketches of Muscle Man and Kel-Man. "...they've got MTV an' everythin'. Ah keep meanin' tae gie it a try, but ah never get the time, know whit ah mean?" Cuticle chewed.

He didn't: Kel had never expressed an interest in anything more strenuous than a wank. Danny glanced from the finger-gnawing and looked over to where the girl with the orange face was talking into a telephone.

Kel thrust hands into Puffa-jacket pockets and sat down on a row of white metal seats.

Danny continued to stand. He stared at a collection of framed and signed photographs on the opposite wall:

Steve Davis the snooker champion, Kenny Dalgleish and some guy in a JB's warm-up suit with a face as orange as the girl behind the reception desk stared back at him.

Everyone knew Jordan Burns owned this and two other health-clubs – one in the centre of Glasgow, the other up the West End.

Danny crossed his legs.

Behind, a tuneless whistle tracked the musak. Then stopped. Resigned voice from the metal seats. "Ye really desperate?"

"Yes..." He tightened thigh muscles.

More resignation. "Through the double doors, second on yer left..."

Danny spun round, eyes brushing stairs and following a cocked red head. Then he was sprinting past the girl with the orange face, through swing doors and down a silent corridor.

The toilets were empty...

Danny moved quickly to an end cubicle, locked the door and hauled his jeans down. Relief poured from his body with the contents of his bladder.

...a door opened. Voices. And moaning.

His bowels clenched, halting the flow:

"Neat job..."

The sounds of running water. More moaning. Another voice:

"Should we no' git him tae a hospital?"

The sounds of splashing. Then slapping. "Aye, but he's gotta be conscious..." More slapping. Louder voice.

41

"...c'mon, Patrick – it's all over..."

Louder moaning. The first voice again:

"Christ, man – whit a mess!"

"He had it comin' – ah warned him..." Footsteps.

Danny wrenched jeans up and leapt onto the toilet bowl.

"...the boss huz eyes fuckin' everywhere." Sounds of paper towels ripped from dispenser. Footsteps receding. Laugh. "Aye, mair eyes than he kens whit tae dae wi'!"

More moaning. Then sobs.

Danny's stomach lurched. Soothing voice:

"Ye're aw' right, Pat – take it easy, man."

Louder sobbing. Then a shriek.

The sounds of crying made his clenching bowels churn.

The first voice: "We takin' him?"

"Naw, there's a taxi ootside – driver kens tae keep his mooth shut..."

Shriek subsiding into sobs.

"Haud this against it, Pat..." Rustling. "...aye, that's it, pal..."

Then the sound of a door opening. And shuffling. The first voice again. Fading:

"Whit did he dae, exactly?"

Dragging, stumbling sounds. "Ken that wee guy fae Motherwell the boss is tryin' tae set up a deal wi'?"

"Aye..."

"Well, Patrick – c'mon, Pat – help me here! Ye weigh a fuckin' ton..."

The door closed on the explanation.

Danny remained crouching on the toilet bowl. Ears buzzed in the silence. The sole of his left trainers slipped on the wet rim.

Then he was zipping up, bolting past urinals and the smears of red decorating a row of sinks.

Chapter Four

In the foyer, Kel was exchanging mock-punches with a huge man in a JB's warm-up suit. "How ye doin', Maxie?"

A hoarse, grumbling sound shook the enormous frame. "Jist fine, Kel son..." Giant head lowered, blocking mock-blows.

Danny shrank past the huddle.

"Ye met Danny, Maxie? Maxie, this is Danny – Danny this is ma pal Maxie!"

He felt himself grabbed, wrenched forward.

The man's eyes were tiny. They stared down at him...

He tried to look blase.

...at least, one eye did. The other focused over his head at the wall of photographs behind.

Danny found his voice. "Hi, er...Maxie." He couldn't pull his gaze from the man's artificial eye.

The greeting ignored. Voice lowered with head. "Ye got the merchandise, Kel son?" Blue raised lines pulsed on the side of a huge neck.

Danny's mind was back in the toilets, with the contents of someone else's veins.

"Jordan around?" Studiously casual.

One eye focused on a red head. "Problems?"

"Jist tell Jordan ah wanna talk tae him, eh Maxie?"

A sigh.

Then a huge arm around both their shoulders, manoeuvring through the door marked Private into a red-carpeted corridor.

Dwarfed by the massive man in the JB's warm-up suit, he tried to check Kel's expression but couldn't see over the vast chest.

Half way along the corridor, Maxie released them. One eye continued to stare over Danny's head. A mammoth, hair-covered fist turned a handle and pushed open the door. "In ye go – an' don't touch onythin'."

"Thanks, Maxie!" Kel loped into the room.

Danny hesitated. Then followed.

"Notch oaffice, eh?" Kel threw himself into a swivel chair. "Eh?"

Sweat trickled from one armpit. Danny stared around. "Yes, it's..." The Wrangler jacket had half-dried and smelled terrible.

Three walls lined with bookshelves. On the fourth, more framed photographs of a man with dark hair shaking hands with other men in either suits or sportswear. And a certificate.

"Ah love this chair..."

The voice dragged his eyes away.

A desk. Two leather couches. A computer. A really complicated-looking telephone. A smell...an expensive smell.

Kel leant back, muddy trainers propped on top of the desk. "This is the...nerve-centre." Leaning forward, grubby fingers hovering over the multi-buttoned telephone. "Jordan dis aw' the business fae here." Grubby fingers picked up the telephone receiver, listened, then replaced it.

Business...

Danny feet sank into deep-pile carpet. The arse of his jeans was wet against his skin. He plucked at soaking fabric, fingers contacting with metal heaviness.

Business...

...the toilets.

Sobbing.

Smears of red flowing over a hand-basin...

...for a fraction of a second he considered slipped the gun down the side of one of the leather couches. Then his eyes noticed a darker, wet stain on the right thigh of his jeans and he remembered fingerprints.

The room was plush, posh...

...another carpet thrust its way into his mind. He walked quickly to the edge of the desk and pushed Kel's feet off.

"Oi!"

Danny wiped muddy trails from the polished surface, then perched. From the other side of the desk, a pale face beamed at him:

"Ye're impressed – admit it!"

44

Danny stared back at yards of bookshelf.

His gaze was followed. Kel leapt from the chair, trainers squelching. "Jordan's read almost as many books as you huv..." Fingers pulling a volume free. Eyes scanning spine, then returning the book. Another withdrawn.

Danny joined the Puffa-jacketed form in front of the display.

"...an' he's bin tae university!" Said with pride.

He ran a finger over leather bindings, thinking about the tattered paperbacks in his bedroom. Too new, too unread. "The university of...life?"

Snort. "Naw, the...Open University – it's in Milton Keynes!" A third volume removed. "Did English – like you wanna dae – an'..." Thoughtful pause. "...history, ah think..."

Danny took the book, read the title: *Paradise Lost*.

"...when he wis in the jail."

Expensive, leather binding dampened against his fingers. Danny brushed wet smears from the front cover. "Kel, when I was in the toilets, I heard..."

Proud voice talked through him. "Says he's gonny dae another...degree, wanna these days – when he's got mair time. Law, ah think..." Snigger. "...save himsel' a fortune oan solicitors!"

Danny's eyes flicked to the framed photographs. "What did Jordan go...to jail for?" He peered at the broad figure common to all. At his side, the sound of Puffa-ed shoulders shrugging:

"Ach, it wis ages ago – he wis 'boot oor age..."

Danny examined the handsome, dark-haired man, moving his gaze from a smiling face to the framed certificate.

MA (hons).

Ordinary MA (hons) took at least four years, in ordinary universities – he wasn't sure about open ones.

He was sure about a row of sinks smeared with blood. Behind:

"...got intae a fight, lost his temper an'..."

"Kel, someone was...hurt in the toilets."

The door opened.

He dropped the book.

"Hi Jordan!"

Danny sank to a crouch, fingers scrabbling on leather and thick carpeting.

"How you doin'?"

"Fine, Kel – just fine..." Expensive, accentless voice, to go with the smell and the furnishings. Not a toilet-voice.

"That's guid, Jordan...that's really guid..."

"Running off with my Milton?" Expensive, vaguely-amused voice now directed downwards.

His knees had locked. Danny looked up.

A ringed hand extended.

"Er, sorry..." He held out the book and managed to stand. And stare.

Bigger than the photographs. Broader. Taller. Hair longer and blacker, swept back into a ponytail. One gold earring in the right ear. White shirt, blue tie slightly askew.

He was still staring when the hand took the book. Ringed fingers brushed his, lingering:

"Do you read poetry, Danny?"

He was vaguely flattered the man knew who he was. He couldn't take his eyes from the face. "Er, not much..."

Other, darker pupils rapidly swept his own face, making contact with his eyes...

Danny's heart thumped.

...before scanning the rest of him. Then the fingers moved away and Danny was staring at a dark ponytail:

"You should, you know..." Volume replaced on shelf. "...especially JM. A great poet – one of the greatest."

"Went blind, did he no'?" Over-eager gruffness from his side.

The remark roused him from the trance.

Kel was perched on the edge of the desk, eyes focused on the back of Jordan's head.

"Sadly, that's true, Kel – but it did not impede his genius..."

As Danny returned his attention to the bookcase, he caught the one-eyed stare of the huge figure in the JB's warm-up suit. Maxie stood in front of the door, preventing anyone entering. Or leaving.

"...but sight is also an internal process."

"Oh..." Confusion. Then confusion quickly disguised. "Right!"

Danny concentrated on the source of the voice and tried not to think about why they were here.

Kel was picking up things from the desk, looking at them then putting them down again. "So whit happened tae Mister Lennox?"

He heard the edge, wondered if Jordan heard it too.

"Me an' Danny waited around for ages, in the pourin' rain..."

"Maxwell, get the boys a can – Coke okay, Danny?"

"Er...yes, fine. Thanks." He searched the words for some coded message, then became aware of something large moving behind as Maxie left the room.

Jordan walked to the recently vacated swivel-chair and sat down. "Lennox didn't show?"

"Nope – me an' Danny waited fur ages in the..."

"Shut up, Kel."

The tone was even, matter-of-fact. Tanned hands picked up a mobile phone, punched buttons. The chair swivelled round.

Danny could hear words. A high, padded back obscured most of the meaning. He risked a look at Kel.

The pale face was fixed on the back of the swivel-chair.

Then the chair swung back round and Jordan Burn's clear brown eyes were fixed on green.

"Did ye get holdda him?" Kel cocked his head.

"How long did you wait?" Mobile clutched in a tanned fist. "And don't say 'ages' again."

Theatrical tilt of head. Thoughtful pause. "We got there ...quarter to eight-ish, wasn't it?" Confirmation glanced.

"Yes, quarter to eight..." Danny hoped he sounded convincing.

"An' we hung aboot 'til nearly nine – missed the fireworks an' everythin': nae sign o' him. Did he get held up, Jordan?"

Danny watched the tanned face frown:

"He's not answering his mobile..." Jordan stood up, walked to the window and stared out.

"Mebbe it's switched aff."

No answer.

The image burst into Danny's mind...

...of a telephone beeping from within the rotting folds of an old smelly carpet floating seawards. He blinked the vision away.

"No' fae aroon' here, is he?" Kel was talking again. "Mebbe he...got loast – want us tae go back, huv a hunt around fur him?"

Danny glowered left, eyebrows raised. .

Kel made a motion with his hand, nodded towards the figure at the window.

Jordan was on the telephone again.

Danny strained to hear.

The phone lowered. Another number dialled.

Behind, the door opened. Then something huge was at his elbow.

"Cheers, man!" Kel accepted the can, popped the ring-pull and drank half of it in one gulp.

Danny held his, feeling cold seep through into his sweating palm. Wet, dirty fabric clung to his clammy skin.

They should have dumped their jackets...

Kel was talking to Maxie in hushed tones. "Will Jordan want me tae fur onythin' else, the night? We got fuckin' soaked, hangin' around there an'..."

"Maxwell?"

The huge man moved to beside the window. More murmured words. Maxie left the room again.

Danny took a step in a similar direction.

Kel held back. "So dae ye want me tae...?"

"Not tonight, Kel. I'll let you know."

Apologetic sigh. "We really did wait for ages – ah mean an hour an' ah quarter. Did we miss him? Christ, ye ken ah..."

"I know, Kel..." Jordan moved out from behind the desk, stuck a hand into the pocket of expensive trousers and produced a wad of money. "...you did your bit."

Danny watched ringed fingers peal off two notes, fold them deftly then hold them out.

Paler fingers grabbed the money. "Thanks, Jordan – you got ma number, yeah?" Two twenties stuffed into pocket.

Laugh. "Yeah, I've got your number!"

Danny looked to where Kel was nodding and grinning and thanking. He sat his can on the desk and stuck out a hand. "Nice to meet you, Mr Burns."

"Nice to finally meet you." Cool brown eyes regarded the gesture. "And it's Jordan, Danny." A cool hand gripped his fingers firmly. Squeezed.

Danny forced a smile and returned the pressure.

"Any friend of Kel's..."

His fingers were released. "Ditto." A voice at his shoulder:

"If you dinny need me fur onythin' else, we'll get aff."

A nod. Jordan stared at Danny.

Behind, the door opened. A cool brown gaze moved to over his shoulder.

"Seeya, then – oh, hi boays..."

Danny turned, following Kel past three men only slightly smaller in stature than Maxie. One held a briefcase.

"Seeya, Jordan..."

Danny held his breath.

Jordan didn't reply.

Maxie moved as they approached. Then Kel was pushing him through the doorway, dragging him back down the corridor and Danny's brain was full of the dark stain on the thigh of his jeans and the smell of rotting carpet-backing.

It took hours to find a taxi.

"Your dad's definitely out for the night?" In the small kitchen of Fifteen Priestview Road, Danny struggled out of the Wrangler jacket.

"Ah said aye, did ah no'?" Mildly irritated.

Cold erected the hair on his arms. The denim was slimy in his hands.

49

Kel was rifling through cupboards. Minutes later, pale hands were tearing at a roll of black polythene sacks.

Danny grabbed one, thrust the Wrangler jacket inside.

Feet away, the Puffa-jacket was going the same way.

The kitchen filled with the sound of crinkling plastic. Danny didn't mention the toilets again.

Neither of them mentioned Jordan.

"Whit you gonny tell yer mum and dad?" Kel was kicking feet free of filthy Nikes. "Aboot yer clothes, ah mean."

Danny fumbled with his zip. "I'll say someone pinched the jacket – they'll not notice anything else." It was a lie: they would, but he'd deal with that when it happened.

Half-laugh. "Ah ken whit ye mean. Ma auld man widney notice if ah lost an arm!"

Danny stopped thinking. He wrenched jeans over feet, hauled off trainers and socks then thrust them all into the black sack. He rubbed his thighs. Gooseflesh stiffened beneath his fingers.

Kel moved to the cooker, turned on and ignited a gas. "Better?"

Danny stared at the skinny back, noticing a fresh bruise just above Kel's kidneys. His own body felt like he'd wrestled an alligator. "Yeah – thanks." He seized his bin-liner, squashed it down then knotted the neck.

The mouth of Kel's sack still yawned open. A pair of mud-caked Nikes sat a little away. Danny peered. "Trainers, too." He crouched, picked up the shoes.

Kel turned, snatched. "Ainly got'em last week." Anguished. "Ah'll gie'em a wash an' they'll be guid as..."

"No..." Danny stared at the Nikes. The black tick was invisible beneath a thick layer of brown/black goo. "...it's got to be everything."

Sulky. "Ah don't see why." Fingers tightened around grubby white leather.

Danny was too tired to argue. He turned back to his own bin-liner.

Behind, silence. Then the sound of shoes dropping into polythene. A sigh. "Fuck, ah really liked them..."

50

Danny grabbed, squashed air from the bin-liner, knotted a second neck then stood up. Lifting the two sacks, he walked through to the hall and dumped them by the front door.

Kel followed.

"Another bin-liner..."

The sound of ripping polythene.

Danny took the sack, leant against a wall. He tried to slow his thoughts. "Matches – or a lighter. And paper."

Kel was rubbing a mud-smeared face. "Yesterday's dae?"

"We're not gonny be reading it." He was shivering convulsively.

"Okay..." Nodding upwards. "You find something tae put on, ah'll get the rest o' the stuff..." He padded back down the hall.

Clutching his arms to keep warm, Danny took the stairs three at a time.

It was raining again.

He jogged up the hill towards the semi-demolished church. A pair of too-big trainers flapped about on his feet like flippers, stretching further with each wet step.

The windows of boarded up and abandoned tenements flashed past like closed eyes, conveniently ignoring them.

Danny trudged on. The cuffs of Kel's Nike jacket hung down over his wrists, scratching at knuckles.

In front, a figure in an Umbro warm-up suit paused, waiting for him.

Danny caught up. They passed the smoking remains of three more unofficial bonfires and a burnt-out car. He gripped the bin-liner more tightly and stared up at the blackened tower which was all that was left of the church. It looked more weird than usual, stretching skywards from a patch of waste ground. A wet, off-white banner was tied to railings. Fluttering letters read: 'Save our...' Wind whipped the banner over. Danny tried to read upside down then gave up.

It was almost over. Anticipation made him light-headed.

Kel was sprinting on in front, heaving at a Made Secure by Reicht sign over a padlocked gate.

On the other side of the road, a group of kids ran down the hill in pursuit of a dog.

Danny froze, suddenly conspicuous...

The kids only had eyes for the dog.

...then hauled himself on towards Kel, who had got the gate open and was waiting inside. They jogged round the back, to the open innards of what was left of the church.

Danny moved his eyes from a snake of red tail-lights on the M8 and stared at a rough circle of blackened rubble on the ground in front of him.

Someone had already lit a fire here. Recently.

Kel was tearing a hole in both bin-liners, arranging the contents of the sack within the rubble circle.

Danny separated double sheets of yesterday's *Evening Times*, scrunched them up into crumpled balls and stuffed them in between his Wrangler jacket and Kel's CKs. "Matches?"

A box produced with a flourish.

He struck one, held it to a ball of newspaper and watched the yellow flare.

Kel sank to a crouch, warming his hands.

Danny struck another match, igniting four other crumples.

Two shadows sprang huge on the wall opposite.

Heat glowed on his face. Shivers subsided to a convulsive ripple. Danny stood behind Kel's crouched shape and stared up. There was enough of a covering left to keep the area dry. Then the glow ebbed away:

"It's goin' oot!"

Danny stared at the fading flame, scrunched another newspaper and threw it on.

It burned for a minute or two, then joined the first.

Danny frowned. The area was dry...

...but the clothes were wet.

Then they were both tearing at newspaper, draping sheets over the soaking pile of clothes. Smoke billowed black. The smell of burning paper filled his head.

But not burning clothes. "We need petrol – or paraffin..." Danny sat down hard on a pile of rubble. He looked at Kel.

The pale face was smeared black, eyes alight. "You wait here." A pair of Umbro-ed shoulders moved swiftly back round the front of the church.

Danny rested chin on hands and stared down at the burnt paper mess. The shivers were back.

He should go after Kel.

There was no petrol station up here, and all the shops would be shut, even if any did sell paraffin.

A vision of gnawed fingers and lips trying to siphon petrol from someone's car flared in his mind.

He should go after him.

Danny continued to focus on blackened paper, fists clenched against a growing chill. He looked down at the ripped bin-liners...

...the gun. Danny's stomach lurched. He knelt, scrabbling in ash and blackened paper and Kel's CKs.

All the pockets were empty.

His blood ran cold.

Footsteps interrupted the panic. A figure in an Umbro warm-up suit belted into view, bottle in hand. "Oota the way!" Bottle-top unscrewed, contents shaken over the heap.

Danny stared at the partially-visible red label.

More shaking.

The air was filled with a honed odourlessness. Danny stifled a sneeze.

"Matches?"

He stuck hand into the bin-liner, produced the box and held it out.

Stepping to one side, Kel struck then tossed the flaring stick onto the clothes.

A whoosh of flame.

Danny staggered backwards. The space stank of heat and burning fabric. He stared at the inferno. Mock-hurt voice at his side:

"Well, don't thank me – ah thought the vodka wis inspired!"

Hope cooled as the blaze intensified. Danny's mind was elsewhere. "We've lost the gun."

Green eyes blinked firewards. "No we've no'. It fell oota yer jeans, in the kitchen – saw it when ah went back tae get this." Empty bottle waved, then tossed over shoulder.

Vague smashing sounds.

Danny stared at the side of the angular face. "You've got it?"

Long fingers patting pocket. "Ah wis thinkin' it'd be better tae chuck it doon a drain or somethin'."

Danny blinked through thickening smoke. He could smell the trainers burning. "Yeah – good idea!"

Kel's face shone orange through black. "Seems a shame – a hundred and twenny quid's worth an'..."

"Get rid of it!"

Sigh. "Okay..." Kel slumped against him.

Danny returned his attention to the blaze. Four vaguely trainer-shapes poked up from a mass of blackened clothing remains. The Puffa jacket had melted, smearing everything else with a shiny, silvery-looking film.

"Whit noo?"

Danny sighed. So much to remember...

...fooling Jordan had become the least of their problems.

The carpet was bound to be washed up somewhere.

The police would be called...

...he sat, watching until yellow flame became a red glow which slowly dulled until he could no longer see it.

The clothes hadn't burned completely, but he doubted they'd be recognisable or traceable – or connectable to either he or Kel, even if anyone did find them. He turned. "Now we find somewhere to dump the gun, then..."

"The rucksack..." Slow words, speeding up. "...the fuckin' rucksack!"

It was the longest night of his life.

In the shadow of Iceland Frozen Foods, Danny sank to a crouch, hand snaking towards the bright yellow letters which shone like a beacon amongst wet, flattened grass and pallet remnants. Fingers tightened around wet straps.

He stood up, the back-pack clutched to his chest. It was heavy.

Roving green eyes settled on the shape. "Thank fuck!"

Danny looked down at the top of the rucksack, easing the bag away from his chest.

"Wanna huv a look?" Kel's voice was closer.

Danny's fingers hovered on the metal fastening. "No..." He turned, thrust the back-pack at the Umbro-ed shape. "Just get rid of it – and the gun!"

In the distance, a bus stopped then moved off. Danny listened to wet wheel sounds over the echoes of his last words and wondered that the two could exist in the same world.

Kel slung straps over a shoulder.

Danny stared into green, grinning eyes.

It was over.

Almost over.

He gazed at black-streaked skin and returned the grin. "You should see your face."

"Mine?" Snigger. "You look like...zebra-man!"

Danny wiped a cheek with his sleeve, then rubbed. "How's that?"

The snigger increased. "Worse – lemme huv a go."

Danny stood, motionless, fists shoved into pockets. The right curled around keys, reminding him of one last obstacle.

One grimy hand held his shoulder. The fingers of the other had produced a handkerchief from somewhere, and were pawing at the skin around his nose. "Ah suppose this means we canny...dae it, the night?"

Danny closed his eyes, tilting his head up to the attentions and gave up thinking about anything except the feel of Kel's fingers on his skin.

Chapter Five

One finger jammed against the snib. Danny closed the door slowly.

A loud click. Then:

"Daniel?"

"Yeah..." He waited for his mother to appear.

She didn't. "Still raining?" The voice was coming from the living room.

Relief soaked his body more than any downpour ever could. "Pouring!" He slunk past the half-open door then walked quickly into the bathroom, unzipping the Adidas top as he moved.

Behind the locked door, he tore off Kel's warm-up suit and t-shirt, kicking the too-big trainers into a corner beside the laundry basket and stuffing the rest inside. As he turned to switch on the shower, a black-streaked face glanced at him from the mirror.

Zebra-man was an understatement!

Hauling off his underwear, he stepped under hot jets and rubbed his face vigorously. Over the sound of pounding water:

"Want a coffee?"

Danny tilted his head towards the door. "Yeah – I'll be out in a minute." He reached for the soap and began to wash.

Grey rivulets streamed from his hands and face. He dipped his head, enjoying the feel of the water as it coursed over neck and onto scalp. The smell of old carpet, shit and charred clothes left his nostrils, replaced by a lemony odour. Danny blinked, staring at the smoky-grey swirls which curled around the plug-hole and carried away every trace of the last three hours.

He soaped under arms, thought about another body under another shower in another bathroom less than a mile away.

The idea made his stomach knot all over again. He reached up, turned off the control-knob and stepped out of the cubicle. Feet sank into fluffy blue bath mat.

Unexpectedly, the strength left his legs. The bathroom lurched, began to spin.

He sat down hard on the toilet. Water dripping from wet hair and ran down his burning face. Danny gripped ankles and shoved head between legs.

The sharp stench of disinfectant drifted up and into his lungs. Something high pitched whined in his ears. Danny swallowed down vomit. A fluffy blue bathroom mat floated inches from his face. The whine in his ears changed pitch. Fists tightened around ankles, digging in as he fought to stop himself either fainting or throwing up. His head hung limply between thighs. Eyes fixed on the pale blue underside of the toilet bowl, Danny waited for the feeling to pass.

Eventually it did. When it felt safe enough to do so, he released an ankle and fumbled for a towel. Danny draped the soft fabric round his shoulders. He stood up.

The bathroom had stopped swaying, but was full of steam. Danny drank in silence and warmth. He could have stayed there all night.

Logic dictated he didn't.

Danny rubbed his hair, tucked the towel around his waist and headed for the door.

The television was on.

Two mugs sat on the table at the side of the couch. He lifted one and perched on an arm. The late news was starting.

"I was getting worried." Trying to sound un-worried.

"We got talking, and I forgot about the time." He watched the screen and let his mind fill with something about council budget-cuts.

The news-reader talked on. The picture cut to a bald man with a face like a moon. Danny peered at the giant features. Then the volume lowered.

"We don't see so much of Frannie, these days..." The voice now trying to sound casual. Pointedly so.

The TV screen cut back to the studio. Danny focused on

the newsreader's mouth and tried to lip-read.

"How is she?"

"Fine." The news switched to an outside broadcast report and a group of smiling councillors. He looked away from the screen and made a mental note to talk to Frannie, tomorrow at break.

His mother was staring up at him from the couch. "Did you two have a falling out?"

Danny cocked his head. "What?"

His mother aimed the remote, pressed.

Light died at the other end of the room.

"I mean, you used to be thick as thieves..." His mother's face creased with concern. "...but you hardly ever mention her, these days..." Trying to be casual. Again. "It was a surprise when you announced you were going round to her house, to study."

Not now...

Danny looked beyond his mother's head.

The library.

The resource-centre.

The drama-group which had folded sometime last term.

The chess-club...

...Frannie was a new addition to four, rotated lies. "No, we've not fallen out." He groped for justifications. "She's just doing different subjects, this year – we're not in so many of the same classes."

"Ah..."

Danny heard dissatisfaction, badly hidden. He stood up, ignoring the coffee. "I'll just get off to bed, I'm..."

"So you two are still friends?"

The word was loaded. He tried to ignore it the way he ignored the coffee. Then his mother was on her feet too, looking at him that way she did when she wasn't about to allow a subject to be dropped. "Yes, we're still friends." He looked at the floor.

"Good – that's good. She's a nice girl, and I'm glad you two are being...sensible."

Danny's head flicked up.

His mother was trying not to blush and failing. A sigh.

59

"I think these are yours..." A hand into cardigan pocket, then a palm held out.

Danny stared at the packet of condoms.

"...now, don't explode!" Trying to stay calm. "I found them when I was making the beds."

Danny peered at the silver-grey packaging. Heat spread over his face. His mother talked on:

"You're fifteen, you're obviously mature enough to know what you're doing..."

Danny's eyes moved from the packet to the shag-pile.

Embarrassed laugh. "...which is why I'm not going to make a big deal out of this."

Danny cringed.

Pause, then: "Frannie's planning to go to university too, isn't she?"

He nodded.

"Edinburgh?"

Danny shook his head. "Strathclyde, I think..."

"Right..." Smiling words. "...well, remember you two can do your studying round here, too. Can't have you drinking Frannie's mother out of coffee, night after night, if this is going to be a...regular thing."

Danny sighed. He'd been using the condoms for a month, trying to get past fifteen minutes. The first time, his hands had been shaking so much he'd stuck a thumb through the circlet of latex before it was even out of the foil packaging.

The second had felt slippery, and warm. He'd read the instructions four times, in between bouts.

Using them had set his endurance back seven minutes.

"Now..." His mother wouldn't shut up. "...I don't know where you and Frannie have been..." Awkward. "...getting together, and..." Embarrassed laugh. "...I don't know that I want to, but I'm going to ask you to be even more mature than you've already shown you can be, and not get together when Nicola's home, okay?"

Danny raised his head. He had to say something.

His mother had her school-teacher's face on. A bright, artificial smile painted itself on her lips. "Remember, she's only eleven and..." Eyes raised exaggeratedly. "...you know what she's like!"

Conspiratorial.

Adult-to-adult.

Danny's stomach knotted. He had to say something. "Okay?"

He twisted wet towelling between sweaty fingers. "Frannie an' me are..." The whole conversation had been cliches already. "...just friends. Really just friends." He stared at the strained face and watched it stray into surprise. Then confusion.

"Oh..." Laugh. "Well, why didn't you say so!" His mother placed the condom-packet on the coffee table, then sat down.

Danny was glad she'd done so. People should sit when important things were discussed. He opened his mouth, but she was in there first:

"Have I met her?" Memory searched. A slight frown. "It's not that...person with the pierced eyebrow, is it?"

Danny sighed. "No, not Moira..."

Relief smoothed the concerned features. Mrs MacIntyre re-arranged the collar of her blouse. "Well, I'm sure if you like her, she's a..."

"Mum..." Danny's voice cut through the babble. His legs felt wobbly again. One hand gripped the back of the sofa. He stared at the confused face, ignored the churning in his stomach.

Panic. "What is it? She's not pregnant, is she?"

Danny shook his head. He was going to be sick.

He was going to be sick, or pass-out or cry or explode if he didn't say something. "Er...nothing. I'm tired – goodnight." Danny grabbed the remaining condom and walked quickly to his room.

The alarm buzzed, just as a naked Kel ran off with the shopping-trolley towards a wall of crumbling carpet.

Danny bolted from sleep, heart pounding. He hit the button on top of the radio-alarm, winced. Every inch of his body ached. He slumped back down into warmth. And silence. It was short-lived.

Beyond the bedroom door, Nicola's voice shrilled through his mother's harassed tones.

He pulled the duvet over his head and tried to block out the day. Bits of last night floated around in his mind.

A thump on the door. "Get up!"

He groaned. "Go 'way!"

Another thump. Then: "You playing with your wee man again?"

Danny buried his face in the pillow.

"Nicola! I told you what would happen if you didn't stop using that silly phrase, didn't I?"

"Well, that's what he does in there – I've heard him."

"Now, don't tell lies..."

"I'm not! He does it all the time!"

Danny wriggled free of the duvet and smiled at the conversation on the other side of the door. Usually, it drove him mad. Today it was reassuringly normal.

Nicola thumped again. "It'll fall off, Daniel..."

He staggered out from under the covers, grabbed his dressing-gown and wrenched the door open. "If it does, I'll keep it and put it in your bed!" His arms hurt most of all. He glowered at the small, bespectacled girl in the brown skirt and yellow Alexandra Parade Primary sweat-shirt.

"You're disgusting!" Nicola squealed, punched his stomach and ran into the bathroom.

Danny staggered then followed, catching the door before she managed to lock it. "You're...disgusting-er!"

A yellow arm pawed at him from inside, giggling.

He put his shoulder to the door and heaved, snatching at the arm.

The figure in brown and yellow squealed again, dashed past him and thundered down the hall.

Danny rubbed his shoulder. "And you look ridiculous with those stupid things on." He walked into the kitchen, trying to ignore the ache in his thighs.

His mother was standing beside the toaster, eyes focused out of the window. She didn't turn.

Nicola sat on a chair, swinging feet encased in huge,

thick-soled shoes.

"They make your legs look like match-sticks..." Danny kicked a club-like foot with a bare one, lounging against a worktop.

His sister snorted. "No they don't!"

"Yes they do – you're the sixth Spice Girl, all right – Skeletal Spice!"

Nicola lunged viciously with a huge foot. "Shut it!"

Danny pulled a face. "No, you shut it, Skelly Spice, an'..."

A thump. "Both of you shut it! Now!"

Two sets of blue eyes darted to the trembling toaster.

A figure in a faded pink dressing-gown was hunched over the worktop, hands clenched into fists.

The sound of toast popping free punctuated sudden quiet.

Danny looked at his sister.

Nicola looked back, magnified pupils staring from behind glasses. She shrugged.

Four pieces of browned bread appeared in the middle of the table. Danny took two, dropping one on Nicola's plate.

They buttered and ate in a silence filled with unspoken words.

Under the table, an oversized foot kicked his.

He looked up.

Nicola was all eyes, darting between his face and a dressing-gowned back in front of the window.

He frowned, shrugged again and continued to chew. His mind moved onto Kel, and the rucksack and gun...

...and a carpet floating down towards the sea.

The sound of a door slamming.

Nicola jumped from her seat and raced into the hall. "Dad, can I...?"

Distant laugh. "Let me get my coat off, first."

His mother moved from the window and joined the reception-committee in the hallway.

Danny pushed his chair back and stood up. Ears strained:

"Dad, everyone's got one! They're only fifteen pounds

63

an'..."

"Go and brush your teeth, Nicola."

"Aw, mum – I just want to tell..."

"Now, Nicola!"

Danny listened to the sound of large feet pounding, then low words he couldn't make out. He waited for his father to appear and the usual shouted greeting.

Neither materialised. Just more low whispering sounds.

He moved to the doorway, in time to see his parents enter their bedroom. Danny watched his mother's dressing-gown sleeve disappear behind the closing door.

Something cold formed in his stomach. Danny frowned, walked slowly through to his bedroom and began to dress.

Nicola had finally finished brushing her teeth.

Danny stood in front of the bathroom mirror, fighting a rebel fringe. Another renegade pulsed in his biceps. His arms had grown at least two inches overnight. His mind reached past his reflection...

...onto another, darker glassy surface.

It had been daylight for at least two hours.

Had the carpet sunk, or was it still floating?

If it was still floating, where had it reached – Clydebank? Port Glasgow?

He pressed harder, flattening with the heel of his hand. Then behind:

"What do you have, first period?"

Danny stared at his mother's now-dressed reflection. "Er, English. What...?"

"Can you miss it?"

Danny blinked.

His answer wasn't fast enough. "Just this once?" Her face looked different. Older.

"I suppose so." Kel would be waiting, at the place he always waited. "But..."

His mother was gone.

Danny stared into the mirror. He listened to the sound of the telephone being lifted from the hall table and carried into the living-room. Then the sound of a door shutting.

"Bye..." Nicola's shrill tones pierced his ears.

"Seeya, Skelly!"

"Try an' leave your wee man alone today!" Giggle, then another door opened and closed.

Danny looked at his watch: twenty past eight. He slumped against the bathroom wall.

A door opened. "Daniel?"

Stomach tightened. He stuck his head out of the bathroom.

His mother was replacing the phone on the hall table.

Danny watched her unhook a coat from the coat-rack:

"I've phoned the school-secretary..." She struggled into sleeves, wouldn't look at him. "Your dad's in the kitchen." She grabbed a bag.

He struggled to make a connection between the two facts as she moved past him towards the front door.

She paused parallel, pushing sliding shoulder-straps further onto shoulder. A look.

The pause stretched out, widening to a gulf.

Danny looked away. "Bye." He waited for the door to close behind her, then walked slowly in the direction of the kitchen.

The radio was on. *The Record* lay, unfolded beside the milk. And a white-shirted arm.

Danny's mind reached towards the newspaper. Then shrank back: no way would the carpet have been found in time to make that edition. But it might have been found, all the same, and if it had, the police would know. A neatly cut head flipped up at his entrance:

"Mornin'!" A smile. A normal smile.

Danny smiled back, hands resting on the back of a chair. "How was...the shift?"

Surprise. "Fine."

"Anything...interesting?" He tried to keep the words casual and the smile in place.

Surprise increasing. "Only three mass-murderers, this time!"

The attempted joke made his stomach curl into a tight

ball. They'd had conversations like this, years ago. Then for some reason, he'd stopped asking...

...and his father had stopped volunteering.

"Sit down, son."

Danny's fingers tightened on the chair-back, eyes everywhere except his father's now-sober face.

He knew...

He knew...

...how did he...?

A sigh. "Anything you want to...tell me, Daniel?"

Fingers tightened on the back of the chair. Danny stared at the football chart on the wall above the fridge and tried to find Lithuania.

How did he know?

How could he know?

Danny's brain was racing again. Fizzing in his ears.

Someone had seen them...

...or maybe just him.

Someone had seen him push the carpet over the railings and into the river.

Only him...

"Anything about...johnnies?"

Through the fizz in his ears, Danny heard the blush in his father's voice. He lowered his eyes from the football chart. "Johnnies?"

Another sigh. "The ones your mum found in your room. She's ...worried, Dan and..."

"Oh, them!" He tasted toast at the back of his throat. "I use them when I'm...you know..." He sucked air into his lungs, held it, then let it gush out. "...having a wank!"

A face in need of a shave stared at him. Sceptical eyes narrowing.

Danny frowned. "It's less...messy – you know? Stops the sheets getting..."

Slightly-less-sceptical eyes. "This whit all the boys are doing, these days?"

Danny felt the urge to giggle. "I...don't know, but it's what...I do!" For some reason, this was more awkward than having used the condoms for what his mother

66

presumed.

Relief. "She was imagining all sorts!" Gruff laugh. Head shaking. "Wanking into johnnies..." Standing up. "...that's a new one on me, Dan!" Sly smile.

Danny cringed.

Man-to-man smile...

...like his mother's adult-to-adult words, last night.

Curious. "Does it not work-out a wee bit expensive?"

His skin was getting hot again.

"Or do you...re-use them?"

The idea made his skin crawl. "No..." He fumbled for justification. "...if I...you know, wank, in the toilet, I use toilet paper. The...condoms are for...in bed..." Danny glanced at his watch, hating the way his voice sounded. "...I'm going to be late."

A hand patted his shoulder.

Danny flinched.

"Good practice too, eh? By the time you come to...er... have sex with a girl, there'll be none of that..." Awkward. "...awkwardness..."

The hand removed itself.

Danny moved away, groping for his duffle-bag.

Laugh. "Jeez, I remember my first time – couldn't get the damn thing on!"

He didn't want to hear any more. "I've really got to go." he backed towards the door, hearing the camaraderie in his father's voice and wishing he would shut up.

"Okay, Dan – but any time you want to...talk about anything, you just say."

As he continued to back out of the room, Danny could only nod.

67

Chapter Six

He bought a *Record*, a *Scottish Sun* and *The Scotsman* in the newsagent at the corner of Cumbernauld Road and Onslow Drive.

It took less than ten minutes to scan all three.

Nothing...

At the gates, Danny paused, staring beyond railings into the deserted playground.

On the second floor of Whitehill Secondary, his English class would be discussing Hamlet's dilemma. He stuffed the sheaf of newsprint into duffle-bag and looked at his watch.

Quarter past nine.

Danny slid through the side gate, head down. He walked quickly across the carpark and ducked round the side of the building.

Nothing...

...the carpet-smell exploded in his head. As he jogged down the steps to the boileroom:

"At fuckin' last! Whit happened tae you?"

A hand grabbed his blazer sleeve, hauling him into the alcove:

"Ye've made me miss home-eccy, an' we wur doin' flans the day." Anxious. "Nothin' oan the news – ah hud the TV oan since six..."

'I know...'' He stared at the bundle of newspapers in Kel's hand, then leant against a warm wall and looked up at a greying sky.

"Man, ah thought...somethin' had happened – whit kept ye?" Panic replacing anxiety.

Danny's eyes focused sideways. "My mum thinks I'm having sex with Frannie."

Kel stood side-on, one arm braced on the warm wall behind Danny's head. Snigger. "Frannie? Frannie wi' the tits?"

He stared at the freckled face, then at the bruising around the left eye. "What happened to you?"

Frown. "Musta hit it aff somethin' last night – man, every muscle in ma boady's throbbin'!" Pale, tentative fingers patted around the area. "Dis it look affy bad?"

He rested one hand on Kel's skull, tilted and peered. The bruise was fresh, but already starting to yellow. The skin was warm beneath his fingers. "No...it's fading already..." He stared at the mottled area, then removed hands and shoved them into his pockets.

They weren't talking about...it.

Why weren't they talking about..it? "Did you get rid of the...ruck-sack and stuff?"

Nod. "Nae worries, man!" Kel continued to finger a purplish cheekbone. "So how come they think you an' Frannie Big-Tits ur an item?" Grin.

"She found my...condoms."

Curious. "Whit you doin' wi' condoms?"

He wasn't going into all that again. "Nothing – I've had them for ages. She found them, and she just...assumed..."

Kel nodded sagely. "Aye, folk make...assumptions." Lolling against the boiler-room wall.

Danny smiled at the word, eyes flicking left.

Kel wasn't smiling. "They assume...everywan's like them, as if bein' like them's the ainly way tae be..."

Danny stared at the pale, angular face, counting freckles around the blue/purple skin above Kel's cheekbone.

Laugh. "He keeps offerin' me drinks."

"Who?"

"Ma auld man!" Snort. Slow head-shake. "He says it's no'...normal, me no' drinkin'..." Another snort. "...aye, like mumblin' rubbish fur hours then fallin' asleep in a chair an' pishin' yersel's the height o' normality!" Sigh. "Smoke wan joint in front o' the auld fucker, an' he goes aff the deep end!" A trainered foot kicked a shower of gravel across the playground.

Danny watched it patter back to earth, yards away.

"So how come they think it's Frannie ye're huvin' sex wi?"

"Cos we...used to be friends."

"Ye didney tell me that!" Nudge. "How come

70

you're...no' friends..." The word stressed. "...ony mair?

Danny frowned. "We are, but..."

Another nudge. "But whit?"

Danny nudged back, suddenly irritated. "She got upset that I didn't want to...kiss her."

Snigger. "She tried to kiss you?"

The memory still made him feel bad.

Nudge. "When wiz this?"

"Oh, ages ago – last year."

Another nudge. "Did ye get a feel o' her tits?"

Danny nudged back. "No!"

Disappointed. "Shame..."

Danny cocked an eyebrow. "You...like tits?"

Laugh. "They yissed tae sorta fascinate me, when ah wis a kid."

Danny's eyes moved downwards. "Just big...lumps of flesh – for feeding babies with." An Umbro-ed arm pressed against his:

"Aye, but they're sorta...nice, onyway."

His face flushed. He didn't want to think about tits, because they reminded him of Frannie. And he didn't want to think about her. Danny sighed, remembering his alibi for last night and knew he had to.

A bell rang in the background.

He levered himself off the wall. "I've got to go – you?"

Kel grabbed a Head sportsbag. "Gym, then fuckin' Life-Skills – some guy's comin' tae talk tae us aboot..." Snort. "...relationships, an' ah'm no' sittin' through that!" Sigh. "Goat ma Encounter Group in the efternoon." Cuticle nipped. "Ah ainly came in the day cos we wur doin' flans in Home-Eccy." Nike-ed feet took the stairs in two giant strides. "After dinner-time – you hangin' around?" Studiedly off-hand.

"Not sure..." Danny chewed his lip and jogged to the top. Double library then biology. He liked biology. "Meet you back here, one-ish?"

They walked back round the side of the building towards the main door. "Okay – don't be late again, eh?"

A thundering of feet on corridors greeted his ears.

Danny watched Kel lope off left into a sea of rushing figures then walked in the direction of more stairs.

The first thing he noticed was the relationships-guy was a woman. With a flip-chart. The words Trust and Respect glared at him from within an arrowed red love-heart.

The second thing he noticed was a pair of Nike trainers propped on a desk...

...beside two others. He wondered what had prompted the change of mind. Danny looked away from the Kel-Frank-Gibby triumvirate and scanned the crowded classroom.

Two rows from the back, an empty chair. He threaded his way towards it.

Behind, leaning on the window-sill, he caught the eye of his English teacher, Mr Cooper, evidently here in the wake of last week's discussion of birth-control and the Case of the Missing Plastic Womb.

Danny sat down. The last two hours had passed at a crawl. He'd tried to concentrate, but his mind was stuffed with stuff that shouldn't be there...

...and stuff which should, but they hadn't talked about.

He opened his bag, took out a notebook and pencil and stared at it.

At the front of the room, the relationships-woman was audible.

Through the jumble in his brain, a thin, feminine voice asked questions and received the usual scoffs and giggles by way of response.

How far would the carpet float?

Would it float at all?

Who would find it?

Would anyone find it?

His mind skimmed the surface of answers, then dived deeper...

...into a fathomless sea of variables he didn't even want to think about. Then sniggers...

...and Big Frank's scornful tones: "Ye mean poofs, miss?"

More sniggers.

Danny's head shot up. Eyes darted towards the triumvirate.

"We don't use terms like that, these days..."

Danny stared to where the woman was fiddling with the flip-chart:

"Trust and respect are the key words in all relationships. Gay and lesbian people have relationships too. We must be tolerant of..."

A familiar snort. "Respect?"

Danny stared at the back of a red head.

"Whit's respect goat tae dae wi' poofs?"

Gibby and Frank were grinning. In between them, an Umbro-ed figure leant forward:

"Poofs don't huv...relationships!"

Danny's back was drenched with sweat. The sniggering had stopped.

Placating. "Many gay people form stable, loving partnerships which last..."

"That's no'...love! That's...disgustin'!" Kel was on his feet.

"That's enough, Michael Kelston! Sit down..." Mr Cooper was making his way from the window to the front of the class.

The woman with the flip-chart held out a restraining hand. "Now let's talk about this in..."

"It's fuckin' sick, that's whit it is!" Spit sprayed from full lips.

Danny tried to look away. Couldn't.

"It's no' love – it's no' a...relationship. It's just folk takin' whit they want an' no' giein' a fuck aboot onywan else!"

"That's it, Michael..." Mr Cooper had a hold of an Umbro-ed arm. "...outside!"

"Get yer fuckin' hands aff me!" Kel shook the grip free.

Heart hammering, Danny looked to where Frank and Gibby sat grinning.

"They should be loacked up!"

Mr Cooper had regripped and was now hauling a furious Kel towards the door.

Unfocused eyes brushed his:

73

"Loacked up! Then they'd ken aw' aboot it! Loack'em up an' throw away the key!"

The sound of a door closing. Shouting drifted in from beyond, filtering through the silence in the room. Sweat cooled on icy skin. Danny barely heard the last twenty minutes of the talk.

He bumped into Frannie on his way to the boiler-room.

She smiled. "Hi, stranger!"

Danny sighed. He had to get last night ironed out...

Kel's spitting words exploded in his mind.

...and now was as good a time as any. "Got a minute?"

Curious nod.

They walked in silence along the corridor and out the main entrance into the carpark.

Cold air stung his face. Wind whipped his tie over his shoulder. Danny let it stay there. Eyes scanned, settling on the back of a lowered ginger head.

A set of Umbro-ed shoulders was hunched in conversation with a Nike and an Adidas-clad set. Gruff words drifted over from the other side of the forecourt.

He slowed for Frannie, listening to her shoes on tarmac and watching Kel.

"What's up?" Intrigued.

A gruff voice negotiated the distance between them:

"Aye, Jordan an' me goat jumped – three o' them! Big bastards..."

Danny tried to catch the rest of the words but the wind swept them away. As Kel embroidered one alibi for last night, Danny started on another: "Frannie, I need you to..." A gale of laughter hurled itself against his ears and cut short the request. He looked at the discreetly made-up face. "If anyone asks, I was round at your place, last night."

Smile. "Really?" Teasing. "And what were we...doing round at my place?"

He almost returned the smile. They'd been friends for five, six years – since primary. He liked Frannie: clever, funny, pretty Frannie. Why didn't they hang around together, any more? His eyes slipped from her face to the

74

two raised areas in her regulation navy-blue-but-fashionably-tight jumper, and glanced away.

A year ago – long before Kel. Someone's party – he couldn't remember whose, or if he'd even known in the first place. Frannie and he had commandeered the stereo-system, the way they always did, laughing at their host's musical taste and playing all three Dinosaur Junior albums one after another in the face of drunken opposition.

She had three Moscow Mules and most of a joint.

He'd drank four cans of Tennents and could only think about peeing.

Their faces were very close, the smell of Giorgio and ginger-beer mingling in his head. One minute they were laughing at a room full of swaying couples, the next her mouth was searching for his and her tits were pressing into his chest...

Wind stung his face, Danny frowned.

...he really had needed to pee. There was a queue for the bog. Then he got talking to someone in the kitchen. The someone who's party it was. The talking became arguing – first time in his life Danny had picked a verbal fight.

He would have torn his own arms off and eaten them, rather than go back into where the stereo was and face her.

Snorting normality from the other side of the tarmaced space brought him back to the present.

And present favours sought. "Last night, we were doing homework, okay? I mean, you weren't...down at the fireworks or anything?"

"No..." Laugh. "...I actually was doing homework." Mascara-ed eyes narrowing, mock-inquisitional. "The question is, what were you doing, Danny MacIntyre?"

He attempted a smile. It stuck somewhere miles from his mouth.

An extra-loud guffaw jolted across the playground.

Danny's head flicked round.

The movement noted, the eyes followed. Sudden animation...

...and change of subject. "You're in rent-a-ned's life-skills class, aren't you?"

He returned his gaze to her face, nodded.

"It's all over the school." Lips pursed. "Did he really lose the rag completely?" Fascinated.

Danny looked away, eyes settling anywhere not-Kel and not-Frannie. "Will you say I was with you – if anyone asks, I mean?" He turned and began to walk slowly back to the main entrance.

She followed. "I might..." Curious. "...if you tell me what you were really doing." Pause. "God, look at him!"

Out of the corner of his eye, Danny watched Kel's arms spin like windmill sails, demonstrating some vital point in his version of last night.

Frannie stopped at the bottom of the steps, leant against a metal railing and stared past him. Disapproving sigh. "He shouldn't be here..." Matter-of-fact. "You know they had to take him into care – his father couldn't control him..." Matter-of-record. "And he still goes to the...special school!"

Danny frowned, grinding the toe of his shoe into a pot-hole and watching. "So?"

"So?" Dismissive. "So he's..." Finger tapping forehead. "...not all there!"

Danny's eyes drew a line from the toe of his shoe to the heel of Kel's Nike, twenty five yards away. The frown deepened. He didn't want to argue. He did want her to cover for him. Danny shrugged. "It's not...fair to say that. His mum's dead – it's just him and his dad. He's got to do all the housework and..."

"Oh, come on!" Her laugh echoed around the playground. Everyone looked round. "You're not sticking up for him, are you?"

Including three figures in expensive sportswear. Danny met a pair of green eyes, then looked away. "Will you do it?"

She stared beyond, oblivious. Another voice:

"Hey Frannie?"

She looked back at him, rolled her eyes and moved onto the first step. "I suppose so – but just this once, and you owe me, right?"

He nodded. "You're a pal..." He saw the word register on her face and hoped she understood about the party. Other voices, sing-songing from across the playground:

"Fran-nee, Fran-nee!" Hoarse laughter.

Danny heard Kel's voice amongst the shouts. He jogged to the top step, waited for her and the chance to end the conversation on neutral ground. "You done that essay for English?"

"Fran-nee, Fran-nee..." More hoots. Getting closer.

She paused.

He could see she was half-appalled, half-flattered by the attention from Kel and his mates. Suddenly he envied her.

"Fran-nee, Fran-nee..."

Danny watched her cheeks flush up. Three voices were now chanting.

"...show us yer fan-nee!"

She spun round, eyes blazing. "Away an' play with yourselves!"

Exaggerated gasps of astonishment. Then: "No' wanna dae it fur me, Frannie?"

"I wouldn't touch you with lead-lined gloves!"

"Aw'..." A chorus of mock-disappointment

Danny turned slowly. Stared.

Frank was leering. Gibby mock-fondled a Nike crotch. They lounged at the bottom of the steps, grinning at each other. Kel stood to one side, staring at tarmac.

"Keepin' it aw' fur Bent-Boay, eh?" Gibby.

"Leave him alone!"

More chortles. "He wouldney ken whit tae dae wi' it!"

Danny stared at Kel, cringing at Frannie's unwanted defence. The bruise on the left cheekbone was almost completely yellow.

"Wid ye, Bent-Boay?"

Frank's face leered into his.

Danny took a step back...

...and collided with Gibby. A fist thumped his shoulder:

"Git away fae me, ya poof!"

Danny fell forward.

"Shut up! Leave him alone!" Frannie was shouting now.

The shrill voice hurt his ears.

Then hands grabbed the bag from his shoulder.

Danny snatched. Frank was quicker. Bag tossed:

"Come and get it, Bent-Boay!"

His face flushed. Danny moved towards the Nike-clad Gibby, who hurled the bag back to Frank.

In the background, Frannie continued to shout. Another mouth was ominously silent.

Danny's arms were aching again as he tried to catch the bag. He knew he should just walk away.

"Bent..." Bag thrown. "...Boay!"

"Bent..."

Danny leapt, missed.

"...Boay!"

The bag hurled past him, dropping to the ground at a pair of trainered feet.

Danny stared at a scuffed toe. Behind:

"Get it, Kelston!"

Danny watched the toe nudge the duffle bag:

"Ah widney touch onythin' o' his..." Low, gruff words.

Danny snatched the straps and ran towards the side of the building. Shrill voice in the distance:

"Now look what you've done! Danny? Hold on..."

He kept running, swerving round groups of people until he reached the back gate.

Ten minutes later, an Umbro-ed figure with a Head bag was standing beside him.

Chapter Seven

"Yon Frannie's okay..."

The first words in fifteen minutes.

"Gibby an' Big Frank fancy her like mad – annoys the hell oota them that she'll no' gie them the time o' day."

Danny sighed. "Would you?"

"Never really thought aboot it." Thoughtful. "But noo ye mention it..." Snigger. "...Big Frank's got a knob like a horse!" Nudge. "Eyeways wavin' it around, in the bogs – why ye think he gets called Big Frank?"

Danny could have lived without knowing. He'd been tying a knot in it or using a cubicle for the past nine months. Something about standing at the urinal, holding himself so close to others doing the same, made him uncomfortable.

"Disney get that much bigger when he's hard, though – weird, that..."

A car swerved round from Finlay Drive. They paused.

Snigger. "Hard, he's only half an inch bigger than me. We measured."

Danny's guts lurched. His mind pictured Big Frank – greasy haired, chubby, rotten teeth – holding his Big Knob...

...his stomach turned over.

"Haud oan..." An Umbro-ed figure loping into a newsagents'.

Danny yanked at his tie, unknotted then thrust it into the pocket of his blazer.

He'd bunked off only once before.

Last spring. To queue for Dinosaur Junior tickets.

He peered into the doorway of the shop.

Furtive – exciting. Like the act itself was satisfying, regardless of the reason behind it.

Now?

A mild curiosity about Encounter Groups tingled on his skin.

The shop-door opened. Kel walked out, head lowered,

fingers flicking through the *Evening Times*. And kept walking.

Danny moved in behind, peering over the Umbro-ed shoulder. Women's Page, TV-bit...classifieds...back to the front page and starting again. Then a hoot. And a pause. Then:

"Muggers use gun tae obtain pound coin!" Laugh. "Allright!" Finger pointing. "Man, we're famous!"

Eyes sprinted to where a badly-bitten nail was stabbing at the newspaper. A small paragraph on Page Four. Words jumped in front of him.

Kel was hopping around from one leg to the other.

Danny grabbed, steadied. Then began to read. Kel was quicker:

"Last night, two teenage muggers threatened a group of passengers at an Alexandra Parade bus-stop. The four men an' a wuman were terrified tae find themselves held at gun-point, fur what appeared tae be a pound coin. They escaped ontae a bus, unharmed, but police ur reluctant tae treat the incident as a prank, as the fire-arm involved may or may not be a replica..." Snort. "Replica, ma arse!"

"Officers are appealing for witnesses..." Danny took over, steering them both in against a shop-window. "...to the incident, and for anyone who may have seen the muggers after they fled the bus-stop for the...Milnbank area of Dennistoun." He stopped, letting the words sink in.

Another snort. "Christ, aw' this fur three pee!" Then a grin. "You ever bin in the newspaper, before?"

Danny scanned, re-reading. "There's no descriptions, so..."

"Fuck descriptions!" The newspaper was ripped from his fingers. Then Kel was tearing a jagged rectangle from page four. "We ken it wis us." Beam. The rectangle brandished. "Wanna get another copy? Then you can huv wan tae?"

Danny shook his head.

Rain.

Panic.

A carpet and no way to move it. He re-ran last night in

his head, comparing it to the newspaper report.

No-one had been hurt, and none of the people at the bus-stop seemed to remember what they looked like, but it was still wasn't good. He leant back against the wall and stared.

Kel was re-reading silently, lips moving slightly.

"Put it away, yeah?"

Vigorous nod. "Aye, ah'll put it somewhere safe..." Rectangle carefully folded, slipped into side pocket of the Head bag.

Danny frowned. "Anything...else there?"

Stare, then more flicking.

Danny tried to reign-in his brain.

Just a paragraph.

No description of the muggers.

No description of the gun.

No connection made between the hold-up and the discovery of a body wrapped in a...

The newspaper closed:

"Nothin'!" Almost disappointed. *Evening Times* folded, shoved into back pocket.

His mind was racing. "He must have floated right down the river..."

They moved to the edge of the pavement, waiting for the green man.

Beeping. They crossed Duke Street and turned down towards the railway line.

Danny moved parallel. They strode on, side by side. Danny peered left.

Kel's forehead was creased.

Danny nudged him. "This is good..." He didn't know if it was good or not. He only knew it was easier to handle one problem at a time.

"It is?"

"'Course it is..." They jogged up the steps to the iron railway bridge. "Means, if anyone asks, we can...honestly tell'em we've no idea where Mr Lennox is!" The logic was comforting.

Two sets of feet slapped on welded metal. Danny waited

for Kel to say something – anything.

"Christ, get a move oan – they go daft if ye're late!"

Then he had to run to keep up.

They crossed the Gallowgate. Half way down Abercromby Street, he recognised houses from last night, then remembered their present destination. "How come you've got to...?"

Shrug. "Condition o' ma release."

"What do you...do at it?"

"Jist talk." A trainered foot kicked a Coke can. "Me an' the counsellor an'...coupla other boays."

Danny listened to the skittering sound of metal on tarmac and scrutinised the side of a ginger head. "About what?"

Another shrug. "Aboot...bein' part o' a trumpet."

Danny stared. "Part of a...?"

"A trumpet – ye ken whit a trumpet is." Bitten fingers wiggled in front of full lips, blowing an imaginary instrument.

"Of course I know what a trumpet is!" Danny giggled.

They walked on.

He registered the turn-off down to the Green. They turned up towards the old St Mary's Primary, which now housed Glasgow District's Outreach Unit. "Why just...part of a trumpet?"

Kel paused in front of a newly sandblasted building. One ginger-slug raised.

"I mean, why not a...whole trumpet?"

Slope-shouldered shrug. "We aw' pretend we're different parts o' the trumpet, an' the trumpet can ainly work properly if we aw'....work thegether – get it?"

Danny blinked. "Sort of..."

Kel pushed the gate open and walked into the courtyard.

He followed. "Why a trumpet, though?"

At a metal security-door, Kel paused. "Nae idea..." A bitten-finger hovered over a buzzer. "..ah've bin the moothpiece, an' the second valve. Bein' the bell's the worst – ye canny dae onythin' until everywan else is workin' properly." Buzzer depressed.

Danny tried to imagine the process.

More buzzing. Kel pushed at the door.

He hesitated. "Is it okay if I come in?"

"Sure!" The red head flicked back, green eyes surmised him. Sigh. "But lose the school blazer, eh? Ah got ma rep tae think of!"

Danny struggled out of the black jacket, draped it over one arm and followed Kel into a hall which smelled of linoleum and old school dinners. A group of chairs lined one wall. Posters decorated others.

"But why a trumpet? I mean, why not a clarinet?"

"Ah don't fuckin' ken, dae ah?" Kel walked to a door, knocked, then turned. "Wanna ask the counsellor?"

"Come in, Michael..." Voice from beyond the door.

Danny shrank back towards the wall of chairs. "No thanks!"

Kel opened the door, grinned at him and nodded to the wall behind. "Well, you go an' think aboot why it's no' a clarinet – ah'll be oot in an hour." A hand lightly slapped his cheek. Kel disappeared into the room.

He sat for ten minutes, thinking about the carpet.

A woman with very short hair came down the stairs, eyed and asked him if he was looking for someone.

Danny explained his presence.

The woman with the short hair smiled and walked away.

Danny stared at the door of Kel's room, thinking about the carpet and the gun.

Ten minutes later shouting from behind another door.

Danny moved his eyes to the floor as the woman with the short hair emerged from behind the other door, one arm around a very young kid.

The shouting continued in the room she'd just left.

Danny got up, thinking about the carpet and the gun and the way his arms still ached. He read a printed poster about the Needle Exchange at Ruchill Hospital, then a photocopied one about a support group for the parents of

ADD children. The acronym defeated him until he read a third, detailing the symptoms of Attention Deficit Disorder.

A guy with glasses asked if he could help him.

Danny explained again...

...after the fourth enquiry he moved outside. Leaning against a recently sand-blasted wall, Danny fiddled with his duffle-bag and thought about the carpet, the gun, his aching arms and wondered if there was a Reverse Attention Deficit Disorder.

He peered at his watch: thirty five minutes had passed. He walked out of the gate, scanning the area.

North led up to Duke Street.

East led back to Abercromby Street.

West stretched towards town...

...Danny gazed south, beyond London Road to the Green. He couldn't see the river, but knew it was there. He moved to the end of the wall, craning his neck towards the brick outline of JB's.

He stared.

The sound of a car engine seeped into his ears.

Danny continued to stare. A good-looking, tanned face appeared in his mind's eye.

Jordan Burns had seemed convinced by the story, but what had happened, after they'd left?

A memory of an iron grip on his wrist, twisting his arm behind his back...

Danny shivered.

...did Lennox have...family, people who were worried about him?

What were they doing now?

What was Jordan Burns doing now?

What had happened to the guy in the toilet?

What...?

"Danny?"

He jumped. The blazer slipped from his hand.

A tanned hand reached down, picked it up.

Danny stared from the good-looking face to the car behind and its one-eyed driver, then back again:

"Thought it was you." The tanned hand held out the blazer.

Fingers rigid, Danny took and wriggled into it.

Jordan Burns was wearing a dark blue suit and a light blue shirt. Collarless. It made the tan deeper, his eyes browner. Dark tufts of hair were visible beneath two, undone buttons.

Danny's face reddened.

"Shouldn't you be at school?" Mock-reprimanding.

He swallowed. "I...er..." Eyes darted behind to the recently-sandstoned building. "I've..." Words stuck in his throat.

Surprised eyes following the dart. "You attend the...?"

"I've got a free period and I'm waiting for Kel." Words gushed forth. His head flicked back.

"Ah, free period..." Understanding. "...of course – well, that's saved us a lot of driving around." Jordan turned back to the white car. Head lowered to the open window: "I'll walk back, Maxwell..."

Smooth engine-revs. The car glided off along Stevenson Street. Danny wondered vaguely if people with one eye were supposed to have licences.

Silence.

Danny braced himself for an interrogation.

Jordan propped himself against railings. "What do your parents think about you and Kel?" The question came from nowhere.

Danny's heart hammered. His throat was a desert. Rigid fingers twisted blazer-fabric. He stared at the toes of highly-polished shoes.

Soft laugh. "Not the most expected friendship in the world, is it?"

Danny found himself relaxing. "They...don't know."

"Ah..." More understanding. "So what do they think you were up to, last night?"

Danny sighed. "They think I was with Frannie..." He raised his head. "...she's a girl I know, at school." He stared into the interested face. His mouth moved on its own, bypassing his brain. "Me an' Kel were supposed to go to the fireworks display – I told my mum and dad I was round at Frannie's doing homework because if I...told them

85

about Kel, they'd want to meet him – they want to meet all my friends – and if they met him they wouldn't..." He ran out of breath.

"They wouldn't understand." Understanding.

Danny nodded into the good-looking face.

Silence, then: "Shame you missed the fireworks – they were spectacular. We got a great view from the top-floor weights room."

Memories of overhead explosions as he pushed a smelly carpet into the river crackled in his brain. An expensive, more pleasant smell drifted into his nostrils. Danny refocused on the pavement.

"Kel tells me you're going to university, next year..."

The expensive smell moved closer.

"...you're doing five Highers, you read a lot – in fact, he never stops talking about you, Danny. I'm pleased you two are friends – you're a good influence on him..." Pause. "I wonder if Kel's going to prove an...influence on you?"

"Oh, I can take care of myself." Danny smiled: he'd never had a conversation like this with anyone before. His head was full of sweet scents and warm words.

"I'm sure you can – said as much to Maxwell, last night. I said, there's someone who can look after himself – someone who knows where's he's going..."

Danny looked up.

Jordan's mouth smiled. "...someone I can trust."

Something cold trickled down his spine.

"How old are you, Danny – seventeen, eighteen?"

He nodded.

The mouth continued to smile. "Don't lie to me, Danny – never lie to me..."

The shiver reached his bowels.

"...you're fifteen and you live at Flat two, Eight Kennyhill Square. Your father's a sergeant with Strathclyde Police, 'G' Division, and your mother's a primary school teacher. You have a sister – Nicola – who's eleven and..." Pause.

A hand lightly patted his shoulder.

86

"...I'm sure you have no free periods this afternoon, so I'd keep that blazer off, if you don't wanted lifted for dogging school." Low laugh.

Danny shrank back against newly-cleaned sandstone.

The hand lingered. "Know what I was doing, at your age?"

His bowels churned. Danny shook his head.

"Eight years." Low laugh.

Danny tried to make sense of the words.

"Three in Longriggend, the rest in Peterhead." No laugh. The hand pressed.

His bowels spasmed.

"One mistake, Danny, that's all it takes." Words soft. "Interesting experience, prison. But one I do not intend to repeat." Pause.

He raised gaze from scrutiny of highly-polished shoes.

Jordan was staring a spot behind his head. The hand patted his shoulder again then removed itself. Dark brown eyes consulting wrist. A sigh. "I must go..." Moving away.

The churning in his bowels eased.

"...drop into JB's any time, Danny – I have quite a library. If you want to...borrow any books, just ask."

"Yes – thanks. I mean, thanks a lot..." Danny stared at a neatly-tied ponytail which swayed gently against the back of a dark blue suit.

No mention of Mr Lennox. No mention of the JCB rucksack – hardly any mention of the early part of last night.

The churned melted away. He watched the figure amble across the road, then turned and pushed at the gate leading back into the Outreach Unit.

"Oh, Danny?"

Cramp gripped at his bowels. He froze, one hand gripping the metal gate.

"Tell Kel to give me a ring later."

"Yes, of course, I'll..." His voice cracked. "...tell him." Danny turned slowly.

"And enjoy your illicit afternoon." The blue suited figure raised one hand in salute and continued to walk.

87

"How come you talk to Jordan – about me?" It made a change to be mentioned in conversations.

"Whit?" Kel was pealing cling-film from a half-inch square he'd bought from the trumpet's third valve. Bitten fingers raised the block to snub nose. Sniffed. "Guid stuff, this."

As they walked towards the bridge at the town end of Glasgow Green, Danny explained.

By the time he'd finished, they were under the bridge and Kel was skinning up.

Danny stood in front, blocking the wind.

Bitten fingers tipped tobacco into Rizla papers then sprinkled light brown flakes with darker, mud-coloured crumbs. "Ah never telt him nothin'..."

The sound of rushing water from a nearby weir gushed into his ears. "Well, someone did!"

"Mebbe ah..." Pink tongue licked paper. "...mentioned the readin' an' university, but that wis it." More licking, then fingers twisting the end. "Jordan likes tae find oot stuff aboot folk – it's nothin' personal or nothin'. Lighter produced from pocket. Crouching. Pale hands shook. "He disney like... surprises – likes tae ken who he's dealin' wi'."

Danny gripped a wrist, held it steady as another hand wafted the disposable lighter under the twisted paper end.

Lips tightened, paler-than-usual cheeks hollowing with effort. Sloped-shoulders rose, hovered there.

The familiar herby, burning smell seeped into Danny's nose. He released Kel's wrist, sat back on his heels.

Traffic thundered overhead, joining with the sound of falling water.

Words through an exhaled cloud: "Did he say onythin' else?" Pale fingers quivered once, and relaxed.

"Just that he wants you to phone him. Later."

"Nae sweat..." Kel extended the joint.

Danny shook his head. He stood up, knees cracking, and moved to beside the crouching figure. "Does that mean he's... suspicious?" Smoke exhaled near his knees:

"That means he bought it!" Kel was leaning forward, staring at the river. "Listen, if Jordan thought we'd crossed him, you widney be standin' here noo!"

Danny laughed. "Oh yes – he's going to...abduct me and take me to the basement of his health club, then pull my fingernails out, one by one!"

Eyes flicked up. "No' yer nails..."

Danny frowned. The strange smile of half an hour earlier. And the blood in the toilet, last night.

"...no' your onythin' – officially, you dinny work fur him, so ye canny cross him. But ah'd get tae see Gaza." Kel's lips parted around an increasingly soggy roach.

"Paul Gascoine?"

Kel took another long drag. Longer pause. Then slow, deliberate exhale. "Naw, Gaza fae Milton." Fingers grabbed trouser fabric, pulling him down.

Danny's back hit the arched wall of the bridge. "Milton... up by Bishopriggs?" Car-vibrations tingling up his spine.

"No' that Milton! "Laugh. "Milton – the poet that went blind?"

"Say all that again..." His head swam with herby smoke and the moaning man in the toilet.

"Forget it." Kel took a long draw, then held out the joint again.

Danny shook his head, mind full of footballers. "I can't go home stinking of dope."

Wink. "Ye'll stink o' it onyway..." The grin widened. Kel took a slow drag of the sagging, singeing length, then held it away and slid a hand behind Danny's neck.

He moved back a little, watching the wide green eyes and feeling the warmth from bitten fingers. "Last night, when I had to go and pee, I..." His stomach leapt.

Then Kel's lips were an 'o', inches from his and his mouth was full of herby smokiness.

Danny coughed. His lungs were on fire. He coughed again, choking on the smoke. "Get off!" He pushed Kel away, trying to clear his throat.

Sniggering from the ground. Kel took another drag, sniggered again. "Chill-oot, man..."

A familiar fuzziness tugged at the back of his brain. The frown sank into a smile. "Let's go back to your place and try for...twenty." It was easier, stoned. It lasted longer.

"Canny..." Sigh. "The auld man'll be in." Deep inhale. Roach flicked weir-wards.

Danny swallowed disappointment with the last gulp of herby breath. "Fancy a walk, then? Round the shops?" He looked at the blurring face of his watch: almost three.

Kel continued to stare into the river. "Where ye think it is noo?"

Danny followed the train of thought. "Miles away..." He watched frothing water thunder over the weir.

"Think so?"

Danny rubbed his forehead. There was no point worrying. He nudged Kel's trainer more vigorously. "Yeah, let's go look round the shops."

The nudge returned. Kel bounded to his feet, staggered slightly then grinned. "Wanna go tae that wee place in Virginia Street again? The wan wi' the whips an' stuff?"

Danny laughed. "Okay, but leave the magazines alone, this time."

Mock-innocence. "Me?" Kel hauled a rolled-up *Evening Times* from back pocket and aimed a whack at the side of Danny's head.

Danny dodged away. "Yeah, you..." He struggled into the blazer.

Snigger. Umbro warm-up jacket unzipped, *Evening Times* thrust inside. "The guy'll no' remember us, you wait an' see." Kel rezipped the jacket, lurched from under the bridge and headed for the path.

Chapter Eight

The guy did.

Danny could feel his eyes following their backs, past the Accessories section. Low music flowed from speakers hidden somewhere. The shop was empty, apart from himself, Kel and the guy behind the counter who had been eating a Marks and Spencer sandwich.

It now sat beside the cash-register, back in its wrapper and ignored.

Kel walked on past an array of leather objects and paused at the magazines, Umbro-ed back to the guy behind the counter.

Danny twirled a carousel of paperbacks. Titles flashed by. He stopped the display rack at a novel by an author he recognised. From a little away:

"Aw', man – c'mere!" Awe-struck.

"Hold on..." Danny removed the book from its place, turned it over and read the back. Eyes moved down to the price.

Theatrical wolf-whistle. "Aw' yeah!"

Eyes flicked up and left.

A snub nose inches from coloured pages.

He wandered across. "What's so...?"

"Look at the knob on that!" Magazine thrust out.

Danny stared at the too-large, glistening length. He frowned. "That's been touched-up."

Snigger. "Aye, well ah'd touch him ony day of the week!"

Danny continued to stare at the gleaming rod of flesh. He'd bought three similar magazines, last year. They were still there, under the carpet beneath the wardrobe. "No, I mean they...do things – with airbrushes and the like..." Eyes narrowed, taking in every detail of the immaculate shaft.

Flawless.

Too flawless...

...and too big. He'd wanked over the magazines for two

weeks. Then got bored. And frustrated. Danny's hand moved automatically to the front of his school-trousers. "No-one's knob's that size."

Another snigger. "Big Frank's is." A nail-bitten finger traced the ridge of skin just beneath the spongy purple head. "Only he disney huv that." The finger paused at a nub of scar-tissue. "Whit is that, onyway?"

Danny stared. "That's where he'd been cut..." Eyes moved to a pale, fascinated face.

Fascination soured into horror. "Cut? Whit ye mean...cut?"

"Circumcised – like what Jewish people have done."

Ginger slugs sprinted upwards form above eyes. "He's Jewish? Didney think ye could get...blond Jews."

"Sure you can! But he's not Jewish – at least, he doesn't have to be. In America, lots of guys have their foreskins cut – it's meant to be more...hygienic."

Kel was turning pages, staring. "Sounds fuckin' barbaric tae me..."

"It happens when they're babies – they don't remember it." Danny was wondering if it did hurt.

Hands paused at another page of beigy flesh, then flicked back to the blond. "Aye, well cut or no', that's some knob!"

Danny's frown returned with a vengeance. "It's not real, though – nobody's that..."

"Hey, pal? Gonny settle an argument?" Kel was loping towards the guy behind the counter, waving the magazine. "These photies bin touched up?"

Danny walked behind, eyes fixed on the sales-assistant's face. The man's expression was a mixture of amusement and apprehension:

"Touched up?"

"Aye..." Kel slapped the magazine down on the counter, stabbing with a gnawed finger. "This real – ah mean, this aw' his – or has it bin air-brushed?"

The sale-assistant had pink-rimmed eyes, very short hair and a West-End accent. And a prominent Adam's Apple which was, at the moment, bobbing about in his throat.

Danny tried to close the magazine. "It doesn't matter..."

Irate. "Aye, it does!" A pale hand slapped down, holding the pages open. "Ye could git done under the...Sale o' Goods Act, if these knobs huv bin interfered with!"

Amusement winning out over apprehension. "As far as I know, all the men in..." A hand flipped the magazine up, eyes glanced at the cover. "...*Honcho* are..." Cough. "...true to life."

Kel turned, glaring. "See? Telt ye – thanks, pal!" He grabbed the magazine, walked back to the shelf. Ginger head shaking slowly. "Touched up, ma arse!"

Danny looked at the sale-assistant, who was still watching Kel. "Sorry, I..."

"Do you want to buy that?"

Danny remembered the book in his hand. He raised it. "Um, I'm not..."

"You want it?" Kel was back at his side, snatching the novel from his hand and flicking. "Whit is it, onyway?"

"Just a book." Danny sighed. "It's nine ninety-nine – maybe I'll get it at the weekend..."

"We'll take it!" Kel slapped the paperback down on the counter.

The sales-assistant's eyes moved from the novel to Kel, then Danny and back again.

He frowned. "No, it's okay – I'll buy it next..."

"Ye want it or no'?" Pale fingers held out a now-crumpled tenner.

In the background, another figure entered the shop.

The sales-assistant ignored it, eyes now focused on the front of Kel's Umbro warm-up jacket.

Danny noticed the tell-tale bulge. His head flicked round, scanning the shelves.

"Eh?"

His stomach jumped.

"C'mon – the guy's no' got aw' day!" Tutting. An Umbro-ed elbow leant on the counter. Head cocked. "See some people? Canny make their minds up aboot onythin'!"

"Okay, but I'll give you the money back when I..."

"Ma treat!" Magnanimous wave of the tenner. Kel

93

straightened up. Jacket unzipped.

The sales-assistant lifted the book and moved to the cash-register, eyes fixed on the unzipping.

Danny stared, waiting for the familiar beep of the till. It didn't come.

Then Kel was hauling an *Evening Times* from inside the warm-up jacket, unfurling and opening the newspaper. "Fancy seein' a film later on?" Flicking past a page with a rectangular-shaped hole in it to the *Entertainments* section.

Danny could feel the salesperson's relief join with his own. "What's on?"

Beeps in the background.

He leant an arm on the Umbro-ed shoulder, scanning cinema-listings.

"The new *Alien* film's good." Now-friendly voice over the beeping.

Danny glanced to where the guy was sliding the novel into a brown paper bag. "Is it?"

Nod. "Worth seeing – nine ninety nine, please."

Snort. "Thought she snuffed it, at the end o' *Alien Three?*" Kel held out the tenner.

Tenner taken. "She did, but they clone her and bring her back..." Sound of cash-drawer opening.

Danny watched Kel take in the movement, then return to his examination of the cinema-listings:

Thoughtful nod. Then nudge. "Ye fancy that wan, then?"

Danny smiled. "Yes, okay – when's it start?"

"One pee change." Copper coin and brown-papered package held out.

Kel took both, shoved the book at Danny. "Er...five fifteen or seven thirty five – whit time is it noo?"

Danny glanced at his watch. "Nearly four – you got money?"

"Aye..." Kel closed the *Times*, moved towards the door. "Seeya pal!"

The sales-assistant smiled. It was a nice smile. "Bye..."

Danny nodded, following Kel from the shop and out into Virginia Street.

They were almost at Ingram Street before Kel thrust a

94

hand down the front of the Umbro warm-up pants and produced a rolled up *Honcho*.

He was walking, eyes focused straight ahead. Behind:
"Oi! Slow doon..." Breathless.
He jogged across George Square, scanning for a break in traffic.
Idiot!
Fuckin' idiot!
He paused because the man was red, opening his shoulder-bag to stuff the novel inside.
Kel caught up. "Whit's up?"
Danny scowled. "Don't ever do that again!"
"Dae whit again?"
The man changed to green. Danny darted across the road, up Frederick Street towards the bus-stop. A hand on his shoulder brought him to a halt:
"Whit's up wi' you?"
Danny turned, glared. "What would have happened if he'd called the police? They'd have wanted to know why we weren't at school, where we'd been – where you got the dope...everything!"
A Number Forty Two stopped yards away.
Danny lunged for it
The hand held his shoulder. "He wouldney have called the polis." Frown.
"You don't know that!" The bus pulled away. So did Danny.
"Man, you're gettin' paranoid..." Kel bobbed in front of him.
Danny stared. "It was still... risky – why did you not just buy it? You had the money."
Grin. "Eight quid fur a coupla big knobs? Nae chance!" The pale face sobered. "The book looked better value – whit's it called, onyway?" Rucksack grabbed, drawstrings tugged open.
Danny leant against the bus-stop.
Long fingers wrenched the book from the rucksack, then the brown-paper bag from the book.

"*Babycakes.*"

Snort. "Whit kinda name's that?"

"It's just a name." He scanned the darkening street for buses.

"So whit's it aboot?"

"It's about…" The bit on the back said it was the third in the series. "…it's just a story."

Pages tilted upwards, catching orange from a nearby street-light. "Whit sorta story?"

"'Bout people – in San Fransisco…" Danny grabbed the novel, shoved it back into his rucksack and tried to get the conversation back on course. "Listen…" He tightened the drawstring and looked up. "You know what I mean, don't you?"

Kel was leafing through Honcho again. "Aboot people in San Fransisco? Earthquakes an' stuff?"

"No!" Danny lowered his voice. "About…attracting attention."

Eyes narrowed, still pagewards. "If these knobs are air-brushed, ah canny see where they've been…"

"Listen to me!" Danny grabbed the magazine.

Howl. "You've fuckin' ripped it, man!" A snatch towards him.

"Shut up and listen!" Danny moved back, holding the magazine out of reach.

Kel stared, hand hovering.

Danny's stomach clenched. "We've got to be careful."

Stare, then slow nod.

"And we've got to be able to trust each other."

Sigh. "Aye, ah ken…"

Another bus drew level. A fifty one. Danny let it pass.

They moved back into a doorway, away from the bus-stop.

"Can ah huv it back?"

"In a minute." Danny moved in front of the figure in the Umbro warm-up suit. He wanted to rip the stupid magazine into shreds and make Kel eat them. "We have to be sensible about this."

"Aye…" Reluctant. Words directed at the ground.

"Didney even want the fuckin' magazine that much – dunno why ah nicked it, really…"

From above, a security-light illuminated the patch of yellowing skin on a pale cheekbone. "Best behaviour – act normal…"

Snigger. "Well, ah normally…"

"You know what I mean." Danny held out the magazine. "Don't do anything that will attract attention."

Ginger head raised. Green eyes focused over his shoulder.

Danny flinched. Head flicked round.

From the bus-stop, four sets of eyes were fixed on the two boys huddling in a doorway.

Heat drenched his face. The magazine grabbed. Breath on his neck. Then an over-loud voice:

"No' ye canny play wi' ma knob fur a fiver, pal!" Kel loped from the doorway, grinning and scanning the street.

The thought made the crotch of his trousers tighten. Danny frowned through the blush. Head lowered, he joined Kel at the edge of the pavement just as a Number Thirty Eight swerved into view.

One of the four people stuck out a hand.

Breath on his neck:

"Seeya later? After ah've phoned Jordan? We'll go see that film…"

"Dunno – I've got homework." He watched the bus approach and wanted to be on it and away from here so much it hurt. "…and it's a school-night and…"

Excuses swept away. "Ah'll wait ootside fur ye…"

Then more breath on his neck. The shiver sent arrows of heat from his face downwards. Danny turned, smiled. He fumbled for change.

Then Kel was loping backwards up Frederick Street, waving the magazine. "An' bring yer…airbrush!"

Pneumatic doors wheezed open. Danny let the other four people on first and watched Kel's smile disappear into evening darkness.

The food was cardboard.

Danny chewed methodically at a fried egg. Behind, his mother washed dishes silently. Somewhere further behind, his father was getting up, getting ready for work.

Nicola pinched a chip from his plate, waiting for a response.

Danny raised another forkful of egg to his lips, munched then swallowed without tasting.

Small fingers seized two chips.

Danny continued to eat. He listened to the sound of dishes rinsed and placed in dish-rack.

Another two chips disappeared.

Then three...

...under the table, a foot impacted with his.

Danny looked up.

Nicola was stuffing chips into her mouth. Face pulled. "Playing with your wee man make you lose your appetite?"

Danny waited for the automatic reprimand...

Sounds of cupboards opening and closing.

...it didn't come. Nicola stared, all eyes. "What've you done?" Giggle.

Danny shook his head, refocused on the plate.

"Mum? What's Danny done?"

He kicked in the direction of her foot.

Over-large shoe snaking out of the way. "Mum..." Whining. Curious. "Tell me..."

"Eat your tea, Nicola!" Sharp. Tired-sharp.

Danny forced down more food.

"I've finished." Smug.

"Then go and get changed." Said too quickly.

The speed was seized upon. "I'm still hungry – any biscuits?"

"Go and get your changed – then you can have a biscuit." His mother's voice was closer.

Danny didn't look up. The fried egg was taunting him, daring him to eat more of it.

Studiedly casual. "I'll just have a cup of tea first and..."

"Get changed, Nicola! Now!"

The tone made him jump. Fingers tightened around the fork.

"But..."

"Just do it, Nicola!"

Resigned sigh. "Okay, but I'll find out anyway..." Chair-legs scraping. The sound of small feet in too-large shoes reluctantly leaving the kitchen.

Then more scraping.

Sitting-down scraping.

Danny gripped his plate and stood up. A hand on his arm:

"How was school?"

Danny paused. "Fine." Meaningless answer to meaningless question.

"You didn't miss too much?"

His heart pounded. How did she know? Who had...?

"Your dad says you and he had a...nice talk." The hand on his arm relaxed.

Danny flinched at the word. He moved away from the hand, trying to feel relieved. "Er, yeah..." He walked to the sink and sat his plate on the draining board. He stayed there, looking for something to concentrate on.

A sound. A sparking sound. Then a smell.

He turned.

His mother inhaled on the cigarette.

Danny frowned. She'd given up two years earlier. They'd thrown out all the ashtrays. He opened a cupboard above his head. Eyes settled on an egg-cup no-one ever used.

"This is an important year, Daniel." She didn't look up as he sat the egg-cup on the table.

He hovered behind her chair.

"You've got your prelims in December. I know next year seems a lifetime away, but time passes quickly, and your Highers'll be here before you know it."

He watched her draw on the cigarette. Two sets of eyes focused on the growing length of ash.

"Your dad and me want you to be able to give school your full concentration. You don't need...distractions, at this stage."

His mother talked on.

99

Danny gnawed at his bottom lip, half-listening. Why was it always 'your dad'? Why did she say that? His eyes moved to the Free with Today's *Record* football chart above the fridge.

He could only remember...two other occasions, in the past few years, when his father had talked to him – really talked – about anything.

The first was the drugs-lecture.

The other had been the sex-lecture.

Danny cringed at the memory. In the background, his mother's voice tugged at his ears.

His father had been scarlet-faced, talking about girls and the proper way to treat them when making love, in between the stuff about condoms and diseases. He remembered the questions which had half-formed on uncomfortable lips and stayed that way as he watched his father's mouth.

'How do boys make love?'

'Do boys make love, or is it called something else?'

'What does it mean when your knob's like a rock and you want to kiss someone? And the someone's not a girl?'

Recall made him shiver all over again. Danny refocused on his mother's voice and bit back resentment:

"...so you don't want to be worrying about girls or anything, Daniel. Next year, when – if – you go to Edinburgh University, you can...get your own flat, do what you like, but for now it's best you concentrate on school-work, yes?" She looked up.

Why did she think he'd do anything else? Nothing had changed between yesterday and today...

He sighed. One thing had changed, but not the thing she presumed.

...he still wanted to go to university; he was still going to work towards his Highers – school-work was a dawdle, anyway. He was the same as he'd always been.

"Daniel?"

The name hauled him back. He had to say something. "Aye – er, yes." He looked away. "I told...dad this morning – I'm just..."

100

Sigh. "Oh, Dan..." Cigarette stubbed out in egg-cup. "...you'll be careful with...whoever it is, won't you?" Sounds of chair-legs scraping. Then the voice was closer. "You know what I mean, don't you?"

He hated the familiar heat on his face. Something twisted in his stomach. He had to say something. "I'm not doing anything."

She talked through him. "You're too young, Daniel – there's enough time for...that sort of thing later, when you've got your Highers under your belt..."

"I'm not doing anything with anyone!" His head was going to burst. "Which part of that sentence don't you understand?"

She flinched.

He had to say something. "The condoms are for wanking into!" Danny lowered his voice. "I. Am. Not. Having. Sex..."

"Who's having sex?" Nicola's delighted squeal cut short the tirade.

Two sets of eyes focused on a now-changed figure.

"No-one's having sex – go and watch TV, Nicola." Frustration made the words strangely quiet.

Tone ignored. Mouth gaping. "You're having sex? Oh... excellent!"

Danny almost smiled.

"Go and watch..."

Nicola was grinning at him. "Is it nice? What does it feel like?"

Then his mother was grabbing Nicola, shoving his sister into the hall. "Go to the living-room and stay there 'til I come and get you." Door closed. Ominously.

"Mum..." He had to say something. If he didn't say something, this would go on and on and... "I'm gay."

Two short words floated between them.

His stomach stopped churning. Skin cooled. Blood made its way back to his brain.

Mrs MacIntyre stared at him, school-teacher's face frozen in place.

"I'm gay, mum." Danny said it again, to make sure she'd

101

heard. He leant against the cooker.

Her mouth opened. Then closed. Then opened again. "What do you mean...exactly?"

"You know what 'gay' means!" Danny found himself laughing. He felt as if something huge and heavy had been removed from his chest. "I like...other boys, I..." He pushed a hank of damp hair out of his eyes and remembered a phrase in one of the books. "I'm...oriented towards men."

Mrs MacIntyre stood up, walked over to the sink and began to wash more dishes.

The laugh died. This wasn't going the way it should. She was meant to say something – anything! He racked his brain for a prompt. "I've known for...ages – wanted to tell you months ago." Another phrase from a book flitted into his mind...

There was never a right moment.

...and another.

There was never a predictable reaction.

Sounds of splashing filled his head. "Mum?" He walked to the sink and grabbed a dish towel.

"Leave them."

Danny lifted a plate from the rack and began to dry. This wasn't going the way it should at all. "Mum, I..."

"Leave them." Soapy fingers pulling the dish towel from his.

Danny pulled back. "Oh, mum – I know about Aids and stuff, and the condoms are really just for wanking and I'm not..."

"Leave them!"

The plate smashed on the floor between them.

Danny stared at it, blocking the sound of her voice from his mind. He threw the dish towel onto the worktop and ran through to his bedroom.

Chapter Nine

Quiet...

..too quiet.

Danny re-read the last sentence he'd written on Hamlet's dilemma, then scribbled two more to round it off and closed the jotter. He got up from the desk, walked over to the door and pressed his ear against it.

Vague television sounds. No voices.

He looked at his watch: seven twenty two. An hour ago, his mother and Nicola had left. Fifteen minutes later, his mother was back. Half an hour after that, his father had left for work.

He walked back to the desk, lifted his English and History homework and replaced both jotters in the drawstring rucksack. He switched on the radio, listened to a minute of something by the Spice Girls, then switched it off and shoved on the first Dinosaur Junior CD. After half of 'Out', he switched that off too.

Danny threw himself onto the bed and stared at the ceiling. He could re-categorise the CDs.

By musical catagory, rather than alphabetically...

...or maybe chronologically...

Beyond the door, the phone rang. Stopped ringing. He could just hear his mother's voice. He jumped from the bed, walked to the door and opened it a crack. Words drifted in:

"Christine, I was going to phone you – Daniel's..."

He closed the door, glanced at his watch: almost half-past seven. He switched the radio back on, searching the waveband.

Radio Clyde news was on the hour: Clyde One FM was the half-hour.

He sat down on the edge of the bed, lowering the volume and moving his head closer to the speaker.

Something about a pile-up on the M8.

Something about a proposed strike of Cleansing Workers.

103

Something else about Operation Hawk and Strathclyde Police's planned initiative to crack down on drug-dealing in the East End.

Nothing about...

...Danny listened until the voice on the radio bled into a commercial for Pantene Pro-V, then sank back onto the bed. Staring at the light fitment, he thought about the carpet and wondered if Kel was thinking about it too.

Thinking about it didn't help.

Sitting around, waiting didn't help.

On a shelf above his head, CDs stared down at him.

What time did the film start? Eight? Ten two?

Danny leapt from the bed, grabbed wallet from the desk and stuffed it into pocket. His blouson jacket hung behind the door. He paused...

Another school night.

...then grabbed the jacket.

In the hall, his mother was still on the phone. Danny met her eyes, then snatched keys from beside the phone and walked briskly to the front door.

"We've missed the beginnin'." Kel thrust hands into pockets and kicked at the edge of the pavement.

Danny gulped lungfuls of air. He'd waited for a bus, then tried walking between bus stops and had ended up running the whole way into town. "There's commercials first – perhaps we've not..."

"Aye, we huv." Sulky. "Nae point goin' in noo."

Danny sighed, ribs heaving.

A group of girls pushed past them into the cinema.

He edged back against the wall.

Kel moved to lounge beside him.

Warmth seeped from an Umbro-ed hip into his. He glanced behind at screening-times. Eyes focused on the start-time for *Alien Resurrection*: seven twenty-five.

Kel had waited over an hour.

Voice at his side:

"Wanna go fur a burger?" Unenthusiastic.

Danny shook his head: he could still taste the fried egg.

104

"Wanna go see..." He looked back at the programme-schedule. "...*George of the Jungle?*"

Even less enthusiastic. "Naw..." Toe of one Reebok rubbing the heel of the other. "Don't fancy it."

Danny raised eyes from Kel's trainers and watched people watching them. He looked away. "What do you want to do?"

"We could go doon tae JB's, get in a coupla frames?"

"You mad?" Danny frowned at the side of a pale face.

Slope-shoulder shrug.

A tanned, handsome face thrust itself into his mind. Danny chewed his bottom lip. "I don't think it's a good idea, hanging around there when..."

Sigh. "Ye're probably right..."

Last night had become something which dangled at the end of sentences and didn't need a name to be recognised. "What did Jordan say – when you phoned him?" A couple were trying to peer past them, to start-times.

Kel moved away.

Danny followed.

"Nothin' much – ah'll tell ye, efter."

Anxiety tingled on his skin. He remembered the toilets and the blood and a good-looking tanned face. "What did you mean, about...Gazza?"

"Nothing – sorry ah mentioned it noo..." Less sulky, more enthusiastic. "So...wanna get a vid an' go back tae mine?" Kel levered himself off the promotional poster.

Danny swallowed, mind full of Jordan and toilets and carpets and guns. "Okay."

"Seen it...seen it...seen it...don't wanna see it...seen it..." Snort. "These ur aw' auld wans!"

Under harsh, fluorescent lighting, Danny moved back from a bank of titled boxes. "Just because they're...old, doesn't mean they're not worth watching."

Sceptical eyes were skimming the selection.

Danny pointed a finger. "That's meant to be good."

A pale hand snatched *Killing Zoe* from a shelf and read the back. Green eyes raised. "You dinny like stuff wi' lotsa blood in it."

Danny shrugged. "I can watch it."

Red head shaken slowly. "Ah wanna get somethin' we both like..." Box returned to the shelf, another picked up.

Danny leant sideways, peering at the spine. "That looks okay..."

A snort. "Bet it's got blood in it."

Danny smiled. "But it's got Jean-Claude Van Damme too!" An elbow poked his ribs:

"Since when wur you intae aw' that..." Kel executed an off-balance high-kick. "...martial arts stuff?"

Danny grabbed a nearby cardboard display unit before it toppled. "I'm not – I just like Van Damme."

Wink. "Ye like his knob, mair like!"

Danny's face flushed. "No, it's..."

"Oi! This got ony knob-shots in it?" Kel was waving the video-box at the Asian guy behind the desk.

He cringed. "Shut up!"

The request ignored. "Well? Has it?"

Danny thumped an Umbro-ed shoulder. Sweat was dripping from already clammy armpits.

Snort. "Ah'm just askin' a simple question, man..." Kel walked up to the counter. "You got any films wi' knob-shots? Fur ma pal here?"

Danny slunk behind the bobbing form, conscious of stares from three women, a guy on his own and two giggling girls.

Bewildered look from the Asian guy.

Kel nodded to the top shelf near the cash-desk, and the row of Adult-rated films. "Ah can see the tit-stuff – where's the knob-stuff?"

Hysteria rose in his throat. Danny wasn't sure if he was going to laugh or cry.

"Ye keep it under the counter?" Arms braced, Kel levered himself up and peered over the formica desk.

The brown face creased into a scowl. The Asian guy moved protectively towards his cash-register.

Tutting behind.

Kel spun round. "Whit's wrang wi' you, pal? You

106

lookin' fur a nice big knob tae take hame tae?"

Danny moved in between Kel and the man-on-his-own, facing the former.

Kel stared past him, pale face contorted into confrontational scowl.

Danny stuck a hand in Kel's pocket, fumbled for the video card and placed it on the counter beside *TimeCop*. He couldn't look at the Asian guy's face. Keyboard beeps exploded in his ears.

The tutting man-on-his-own had moved away to mutter with the three women.

Kel just stood there. Then a laugh. "Ah see we gettin' Van Damme, then?"

Danny risked a look at the Asian guy, who pushed a non-pictured box toward him, eyeing Kel's back:

"Before six tomorrow."

Danny nodded, tried to smile. Voice from over his shoulder:

"An' make sure ye get some knob-films in – ah'll be back tae check!"

Face on fire, Danny manoeuvred a once-more grinning Kel out into the street.

They were sitting on the carpet, eating crisps and watching the trailers.

Trainered feet crossed at skinny ankles. Kel leant back on the floor. "Ah kin dae hauf an oor!"

Danny stared down. Stomach dissolved. "Since when?" It had only been a day.

Hand raised above face, one crisp dropped into mouth. "Since...last night." Munching.

Danny watched the process, then stared at a darker area on the carpet where someone had spilled something. Last night was the first night in months he'd not practiced. "On your own doesn't count."

Mock-sulk. "Aye it dis!" Snigger. Subject changed. "Geez the doo-da, eh?"

Danny grabbed the remote from the sofa behind them and handed it over.

Something silly with Steve Martin froze to a quiver on the screen. "You want juice or somethin'? Before it starts?"

Danny shook his head. Half an hour...

...even alone, he'd never managed more than twenty five minutes, and that was with lots of breaks. With Kel, he was lucky to reach fifteen.

"Sure?" Kel leapt to his feet.

"You having something?" Danny dragged his mind from The Contest.

"Naw..." Grin. "...but don't change yer mind half way through – ah'm no' pausin' it fur ye."

Danny grabbed the remote and fast-forwarded. "Let's just watch it, eh?"

Grin. "Okay..." Sitting back down, leaning against the edge of the couch. "...but ah'm callin' ye fur afterwards – hauf an oor!"

Danny stared straight ahead. He pressed 'play' when the titles appeared and felt Kel's shoulder relax against his.

He tried to lose himself in the film.

Kel took control of the doo-dah. He paused half-a-dozen times to point out things and warn Danny about incipient blood-letting, re-wound another half-dozen to watch fight-sequences again.

Danny smiled, nodded and ignored the way his knob pulsed against the zip of his jeans every time Van Damme removed his flak-jacket.

Sometime during the subsequent hour and a half, Kel moved from the couch to lie stomach-down on the floor.

Danny edged forward, resting a hand on the back of an Umbro-ed leg.

Kel let it stay there.

So it did.

Heat from a warm thigh seeped up into his palm. He closed his eyes..

...an on-screen explosion blasted them open, sometime later. Danny kept his hand where it was, staring at the back of a red head and watching the way Kel's shoulders flinched in parallel with the video-action. He'd lost the story somewhere around the time Van Damme had gone back to the past to alter the present.

Danny frowned. He pushed The Carpet out of his mind and inched his hand further up Kel's leg. His knob was getting sore.

Thirty minutes was too long – no-one could last thirty minutes and...

...he became aware the film had finished when his hand slipped off and the view of Kel's back was replaced by one of a grinning face:

"Guid choice, man! Ah take it aw' back. San Fransisco looks great..."

"Los Angelos." He poked at a matted tuft of carpet.

"Whitever!" Thoughtful pause. "You ever think aboot gettin' oota here?"

Danny looked up. "I'm going to Edinburgh next year, remember?" The idea suddenly wasn't as appealing.

Half-frown. "Aye, so ye are..." Frown swept away. Grin. "Well, ah'm goin' tae San Fransisco!"

Danny flinched. "When did you decide this?"

Laugh. "Ah'm no' goin' the morra, or anythin'!" Shifting onto side, one pale hand holding up a paler face. "But ah like the look o' San Fransisco."

"Los Angelos."

"Whitever – when the time comes, ah'll be oota here like a shot." Eyes moving round the small living-room.

Danny followed the gaze. "This place isn't so bad." He thought about his own, constantly full house. "At least you have it to yourself, most of the time."

The half-frown again. "Aye, well most o' the time isney enough." Moving onto back. The grin again. "You bin abroad?"

"Greece...." He sighed. "...with my mum and dad, and Nicola. It was horrible – too hot..." He stared at the skin in the hollow of a pale elbow. In the background, a voice was enthusing about restaurants, clubs, shops and flats. Behind that, film credits rolled up the screen. Danny's eyes were filled with pale skin.

Half an hour.

It wasn't possible.

...especially tonight. "Kel..." The pounding in his ears blocked out end-music.

"Whit?" Sitting up. Moving closer. Curiosity stained the previously-grinning face.

His chest was as tight as his jeans felt. The thought of his hand wrapped around Kel's slender knob made his heart pound faster: the thought of Kel's hand on his made it stop. "Nothing..." Danny frowned. His voice sounded strange.

"Whit's up?"

"Nothing – really!" Danny's ears were full of fizzing. He looked beyond the pale face to the TV, which had switched itself off, then back to Kel. "It jist feels...different, tonight."

Sagely nod. "That's cos ye're wired, man – ah've bin wired aw' day."

Kel was looking at him. His eyes seemed very big and his face seemed different...

...even the grin was different:

"Ah wis kiddin' aboot the half an oor, man – ah didney even manage five, last night..." Words lowered. "But we can dae it properly noo, eh?"

His stomach flipped. "Your dad's...?"

"Ach, he'll be oors yet." Kel stood up.

Danny's leg had gone to sleep. He staggered upright, flexing his right calf.

"Sure ye don't wanna try fur hauf an oor?"

His head was full of stupid things and the desire to say them. "Twenty..."

"Twenny five?"

Danny shivered. "Okay – what do I get if I win?

Laugh. "You've no' won fur weeks!" Kel walked to the door, opened it then switched off the light.

Brain reeling with carpets and guns and Jordan Burns, Danny stared at the back of a red head and limped upstairs.

The carpet was gone. The gun was gone. Jordan Burns was a vague memory...

110

...warm fingers relaxed then re-clenched around his shaft.

Eyes darted from flashing red digits. Danny bit his lip, echoing the movement with his own fist. His other hand twisted in bed-clothes. Heat flared in his stomach. He tried to fill his mind with carpet.

Couldn't.

A grunt. Kel was staring at the radio-alarm.

Knees sank into rumpled bed-covers. Danny's gaze was everywhere except the figure inches away. He squinted in harsh light.

The flaring in his stomach ignited something in his brain. He focused on the wall behind a red head and moved his fist faster.

Another grunt. Kel regripped, cupping Danny's balls.

Fingers stuttered. Lightening shot through his stomach. Eyes sprinted from wall to overhead light fitment to the rumpled covers on the dipping bed.

Then a curled hand was back on his shaft and moving faster.

Danny's fingers turned to rubber, bending and flexing in all the wrong places. He could hear his breathing over the sound of a hoarse laugh:

"Telt ye!"

A thumb rubbed the moist head of his knob:

Gasping snort. "Ye're no' even gonny manage ten!"

His breath was a white fog, condensing in the cold air. His mind was a carpetless blank. Danny raised his eyes and stared at Kel's stomach. A hot fist clenched in his own.

Jordan.

A bloody sink.

The Carpet..

"You..." Fingers tightened. "...think..." Squeezed. "...so?"

A sharp inhale.

Kel's knob was warm and slightly sticky. And flexed back against his palm. Danny watched his hand curl reflexively around the rigid length of flesh.

"Aye..." A rush of released air. "...an' then ye're gonny

huv tae..."

Danny moved his hand. Bristling ginger hair brushed the side of his pinkie. The fist in his stomach clenched more tightly.

"...lick ma pits!"

His heart leapt, taking his knob with it. He slumped back onto heels.

Hoot of satisfaction. "Man, ye're leakin' like fuck..."

Danny concentrated on each rise and fall of Kel's chest.

Jordan...

He watched two pink nipples reach out towards him, then shrink away.

...blood everywhere...

The fist in his stomach moved lower. He tried to think about the carpet but his mind was full of bushy pit hair and the smell of their bodies. On the periphery of his vision, pale fingers tugged triumphantly.

Rasping laugh. "C'mon – ye're no' tryin'!"

Danny looked up.

Green eyes still focused ceilingwards.

The clutching increased, twisting inside. Danny scowled. His leg had gone to sleep again. Sharp stabs of cramp tingled in his wrist. He ignored both, hand moving faster.

Paper-thin skin dragged against his fingers.

Jordan...

A pinky velvety head sprouted from between his thumb and forefinger, then ducked back down again.

...The Carpet...

His balls spasmed.

"Fifteen..." Hoarse chuckle. "Ah'm lookin' forward tae it – ah'm gonny make ye lick both ma pits an' then..."

Danny's mouth was opened. His throat was dry.

"...ye're gonny..."

Fist paused at the root of Kel, hauling the flexing shaft forward and down until it lay parallel with a quivering thigh.

Kel made a noise in the back of his throat, half-sigh, half-howl.

Pressing with the heel of his hand, Danny rubbed the

pulsing length of flesh against thigh flesh.

"Cheatin'..." Half-word, half-moan.

"No..." He gripped the bed-clothes. "...it's..." Danny's palm moved in circles, trapping Kel's knob. "...not." He watched a muscle twitch in a pale thigh as he continued the massage.

Blue-veined flesh pulsed under the less densely veined skin of his wrist.

Inches away, the grip on his shaft slackened.

Danny raised his head.

Kel was sitting up, one arm braced behind him on the mattress. Back arching. Mouth open. Eyes shut.

His wrist was going to snap. Danny stared at the pale face, feeling flesh swell further beneath his hand.

Kel's forehead was creased and sweaty. Damp red hair hung against closed eyes. Full lips tightened upwards, forming an open-mouthed smile then moving past smile.

In a slack grip, his knob twitched. Danny stopped the circular massage and dragged paper-thin skin downwards, flexing the length back.

The slack grip tightened.

The fist in his stomach tightened in response. Breath hissed into his lungs.

Full lips narrowing over white teeth.

He could see the tip of a pink tongue flicking around inside Kel's mouth and longed to feel it flicking around his. His arm was getting sore. He paused, hand lingering at the root of the taut, quivering length.

Narrow lips hardening.

Danny's pinkie contacted with hairy fullness.

A groan.

His pinkie stroked once. He let his fingers lie there. Shivers trembled up from Kel's balls.

Cramp shattered the moment. Danny yelped, tearing his hand away and shaking it.

A howl. Flesh slapped off stomach-flesh.

He flexed cramping muscle, feeling other muscle shudder within rigid fingers. His palm was clammy and warm and he could smell his own sweat.

Then Kel was lurching forward, grabbing Danny's wrist and thrusting his hand back into place.

First rule broken...

...the clutching in his stomach pulsed in sync with the twisting in his balls.

A hand covered his. They were sitting side by side, now. Sloping shoulders hunched forward, pale face aimed downwards.

Danny stared at the back of a pink neck. He hauled on the knob furiously, wanting to feel Kel come and never wanting to stop.

Fingers dug savagely into cramping knuckles. He yelped again, moving his fist faster.

Kel's shoulders were rigid.

Danny's head flopped forward, colliding with bone. Sweaty skin met sweatier skin. Every tug of his fist echoed in the body which leant against his. Danny regripped cool, clammy skin.

Kel was moving now, little jerky movements of skinny hips.

Danny's fist tightened.

Jordan...

His arm ached.

...a tanned hand...

He buried his face in Kel's neck, spitting hair from his mouth and hauling on the flexing flesh.

A loud buzz blasted his brain.

Twenty-five minutes!

A foot lashed out, kicking the radio-alarm onto the floor.

Muffled buzzing drifted up over the thump of his heart. Bitten nails scraped his knuckles...

...another fingers scrabbled through bed-clothes, pawing his.

Then he was holding Kel's hand tightly and his mouth was open on Kel's neck and liquid warmth was oozing between two sets of cramping fingers as two bodies shattered in tiny, pulsating spasms.

"A draw?" A new heat spread over his slowly-cooling skin.

114

"Aye, ah suppose so..." Kel was draped over the side of the bed, hauling the radio-alarm from the floor.

Danny stared at a pair of pale buttocks, remembering how it had felt to hold Kel's hand.

Red, non-flashing figures back on bedside table. Snort. "So...whit dae we dae?" Legs splayed, fingers extricating gingers hairs from slowly wrinkling knob-skin.

Danny tucked rubber legs under himself. He was sleepy and limp with the new heat. "It's your...contest – you get to... say." A yawn stretched the word into infinity.

Frown. "Ah cheated – ah used both hauns." Fingers flicking a limp hank of hair from a freckled face. "You won fair an' square." Snub nose rubbed. "Whit dae ye want?"

"It doesn't matter." Danny crawled up the bed towards the pillows. He leant against a bony shoulder.

It flinched. "Aye, it dis! Ah gotta stick by ma ain rules."

Danny sighed and resettled. "Honestly – it doesn't matter." He looked sideways at the frowning face. "I told you tonight would be different."

Scowl. "Aye, but that's nae reason tae throw the rule-book oot the window!"

Danny giggled. "Fuck the rule-book!" Raising one hip, he tugged a pillow from beneath his thighs. Squashed softness contacted with a frowning face.

A snort. "Quit it!"

Danny drew back his arm and hit Kel a second time. "Will I tell you what I want?"

A gruff giggle. "Whit ye really, really want?"

His arm was rigid, mid flail. What he'd wanted for weeks, months...

The look on his mother's face froze itself in his mind.

...pale hands snatched the pillow from his. Kel-scented fabric smashed off his face:

"Well? Tell me..."

Danny scowled into softness. "I want to sleep with you."

The pillow hauled away. Red-head cocked. "Whit ye mean?" Tangled hair flopped over one curious green eye.

"What I said..." He didn't know if he could say it again.

One ginger slug raised. "Ye wanna...sleep ower?"

115

"No..." He looked away from freckled curiosity and watched the way his knob was rehardening. "...with you. Here." He nodded at the crumpled sheets around them.

Snigger. "Will it no' be a bit o' a squeeze?"

A twitch between his thighs. Sleepiness made him brave. "I won, and the rules say I..."

Resigned sigh. "Okay, okay...you go doon an' phone hame an'..."

A door slammed.

Danny jumped.

Kel groaned.

The thump of two hearts filled his head. Over the sound, vague bangings downstairs.

A sigh. "Haud oan." Kel threw the pillow at him. "Fuck, ah hope he's no' steamin' again..."

Danny sat, motionless.

Kel staggered from the bed and grabbed the Umbro warm-up pants. The faint outline of a bruise at the top of a pale bum disappeared beneath a drawstring waistband. He turned. "Back in a minute..." Weary grin.

Then the bedroom door was closing.

Chapter Ten

Danny slipped under the covers, burrowing down into the bed. A heavy warmth filled his stomach. He buried his face in the pillow.

Knob chafed against the inside of one thigh.

He closed his eyes, replaying the last fifteen minutes over and over in his head. He paused, freeze-framing at the best bits, then fast-forwarding.

All night.

Lying with Kel all night.

Going to sleep with Kel.

Waking up with Kel...

...complications edged into sticky afterglow.

He'd say he was staying at Frannie's.

Did she have the number...

A frozen face and two words shattered in his mind.

...would she check?

Eyelids inched open. Danny stared at the door: he never wanted to go home again. Under the covers, one hand fiddled abstractedly with drying spunk. He pulled a damp sheet over his head and burrowed back down into Kel-scented warmth.

Maybe they could have a bath together...

...did Kel's bathroom have a shower? He closed his eyes, visualising waterproof wallpaper patterned with blue, long-legged birds. He remembered a shower-attachment – maybe that was just for rinsing your hair? Maybe...

A muffled thump.

Eyelids shot open.

Then another. Then shouting. Two voices. One he recognised.

The other made his stomach twist. Danny hauled head from covers. Skin flushed hot and cold by turns. He couldn't make out words. It was the type of conversation drunks had in the street: belligerent and flaring from nowhere, words all vowels from the back of the throat.

Fists gripped bed-covers.

Another thump.

Less muffled.

Draping a sheet around his shoulders, Danny moved off the bed and crept towards the door.

Formless shouting again...

Fingers hovered above the handle. Then made shaking contact. He turned slowly, easing the door open. A voice roared in:

"Whit did ah tell ye?"

Danny flinched.

"Think ye're the big man, don't ye, ya stupid wee bastard!"

Danny leapt back from the door. A thump. Then the voice again:

"Did ah no' warn ye?" Another thump.

Danny's legs crumpled. He hung onto the door-handle.

Then the sound of a door banging back against a wall, then the same – or another door – banging shut. Ears strained for Kel's voice...

"But oh, no – you widney listen! Ye ken it aw', don't ye?"

...another thump. Then mumbles, and:

"...fuckin' bum-boay!"

The sound of something falling.

Danny couldn't move. Terror draped his body, soaking the sheet around his shoulders. His heart was a solid weight, slamming itself against his ribs. His stomach was jumping, churning fear into something sore and hot.

Then footsteps.

Lurching footsteps...

...on the stairs. Another thump. Against a wall. Footsteps back on course.

The weight suspended itself, hovering in his chest. Danny backed away from the door. He kept moving until his spine impacted with flowered wallpaper. Danny continued to move. Downwards. At the side of the bed, he slumped to a crouch. Fists twisted in damp bed-sheet.

The footsteps paused at the top of the stairs...

He stared at the door.

...then lurched left. The final thump of a slamming door echoed in his head, sending shivers up and down his arms....

...and restarting the weight in his chest.

Ice melted on his skin. Danny fumbled for his clothes. He dressed quickly, pieces of the shouts overlapping with Frank and Gibby's sneering tones.

Stomach tightened along with trainer laces. He sat on the rumpled bed and stared at the door.

One minute passed. Two.

Five minutes later, he opened the door as quietly as he could.

Downstairs, the living-room door was half-open. Inside, dark.

"Kel?" The name was a whisper.

No answer.

The kitchen was also in darkness. Back in the hall, Danny nudged the living-room door further open and fumbled for a light-switch. And stared.

A pale shape trying to merge with flowered upholstery.

Danny's heart stopped. He moved quickly into the room, pausing beside the couch. He touched a shaking shoulder.

It pulled away.

Danny knelt, regripped clammy skin. "What's..?"

Words muffled by cushion. Shoulders rebelling against the grip.

He sat back on his heels. Hand slipped, hung limply at his side.

The hunched figure raised its head. "Go home, eh?" Voice cracking.

Danny stared.

Blood smeared Kel's chin, and still leaked from a cut at the corner of his mouth. One green eye was already half closed, pale skin puffy and purpling. The other was wet and red-rimmed. A sniff. Pink nose on the back of a shaking hand.

Danny's chest hurt. "Kel, let me...?"

"Just...fuckin' go home, eh?" Face thrust back into cushion.

He stared at the back of the ginger head. Muffled sobs and ragged breathing filled his brain. Something without a name solidified in his chest...

...Danny grabbed his jacket from the back of a chair and ran from the house.

He was still running when he reached Kennyhill Square.

"So Hamlet is faced with a not one, but several dilemmas..."

He gazed out the third floor window. Mr Cooper's voice droned on:

"When he returns to Elsinore, the situation has changed, and continues to change as he receives more information about the way things actually are, as opposed to the way they appear..."

Danny watched a line of shorts-clad boys dribble out from the PE block onto the football pitch. Eyes focused on a tall, loping figure, red hair secured behind a sweat-band. His heart thumped.

The figure turned.

Danny sighed.

The bespectacled boy kicked a ball to another boy, then jogged off up the pitch.

He rested his chin on one hand.

Last night.

Last night.

He raised his eyes from the football game and focused beyond the chain-mesh fence.

Two women with a pram were making their way up Onslow Drive towards Whitehill Street.

He followed them with his eyes.

Last night filled his head like a slowly inflating balloon he wanted to burst but didn't know how.

Danny narrowed his eyes, concentrating on the two women with the pram.

His mind forked with the Van Damme film.

What if he had arrived at the Odeon in time to see *Alien Resurrection*?

What if they hadn't gone back to Kel's?

What if he hadn't won?

What if...?

Danny chewed his bottom lip.

Last night.

Last night.

...skin in his mouth. He wiped away fragments of lip and refocused on Onslow Drive.

The women with the pram had gone, replaced by a crocodile of kids in yellow-and-brown, waddling their way towards Whitehill Pool.

Danny stared at a moustached man in a sports-jacket who was herding the last of the kids through the gates.

Kel's house.

Kel's dad...

...Danny's heart thumped. Sweat trickled down his back, sticking his shirt to his shoulders.

Two nights ago. A claw-like grip on his wrist. Hurting. Then Kel pulling a trigger because...

"...perhaps Daniel can drag himself away from morning meditations long enough to share his musings with us." Mr Cooper's voice boomed.

He jumped. "Sorry, I..."

"No need to apologise, Daniel." Good-natured sarcasm. "Just answer the question, please."

He glanced around.

A room full of amused faces stared at him.

Danny looked away.

Theatrical sigh. "Hamlet: young guy, Scandinavian. Bit of a problem in the old decision-making department."

Someone giggled.

Danny tried to focus. "Maybe he was scared."

Mr Cooper folded his arms. Staged fascination. "Pray tell us more."

Someone else giggled.

Danny's face was hot. "Maybe he was just...scared to do anything – about his fa...Claudius." Danny stared at Mr Cooper's sceptical face.

"So you subscribe to the theory that Hamlet was a coward?"

"No!" Danny was on his feet. Fingers clutched the edge of the desk. "He just needed time to think about things, that's all! Christ, just 'cos he didn't rush in and off his uncle straight away, doesn't mean he was a coward, does it?"

Silence.

No-one giggled.

No-one made any sound at all. Then Mr Cooper's hand was on his shoulder:

"It certainly doesn't, Daniel."

He stared at Mr Cooper's face.

"Classic dilemma: a choice between what one ought to do, and what one wants to do. Hamlet was an intelligent, educated – modern – man: the codes he was obliged to follow were ancient."

Danny looked away, met twenty other pairs of strange eyes. He stared at his desk.

"Good thing he was the thoughtful type, too! If he wasn't, the play would be over in one act and there would be nothing for you lot..." Forced laugh. "..to write essays about."

Still no-one giggled.

Heat behind his eyes. Danny blinked it away. The hand on his shoulder patted:

"Sit down, Daniel." The hand removed itself.

He sat.

Mr Cooper walked slowly to the front of the classroom. "Right, let's have the female perspective." Joking normality. "Shirley: you're Gertrude. Your better half's just kicked the bucket, and you've jumped into bed with his hunky brother."

Giggles.

"Your only son – your pride-and-joy – comes back from university, clocks that daddy's demise might have not been altogether natural and goes all moody on you. Calls you names, argues with his best friend and gives his childhood sweetheart the heave-ho. How do you respond?"

More giggles.

Danny fiddled with his pen and prayed for dinner-time.

Ten minutes later, a bell rang and his prayers were answered.

At the corner beside the steps to the boiler-room, a hand grabbed his arm:

"We've got a problem."

Danny stared at the discreetly made-up face and pulled away. "Later, I..."

"No, now!"" The hand re-gripped. "Your mum phoned my house, this morning."

Danny froze.

The discreetly made-up face frowned at him.

"What did she want?"

Frown deepening. "Something about you leaving a jacket at my place..." Eyes rolling. "My mum didn't have a clue what she was on about."

Danny sighed: the Wrangler jacket.

Arms folded over jumper-bulges. "I covered for you, and I think mum bought it but..." Staring at him. "...I don't ever..." Finger in his chest, emphasizing word. "...want to be put in that position again!"

Danny slumped back against a breeze-block wall. His head was starting to hurt.

She leant beside him. "What's going on, Danny? I don't mind you using me as an alibi..."

The word was like a slap.

"...but it would be nice to know..." Sarcastic. "...when I'm expected to cover for you."

Something thick and sticky was coating his brain. Thoughts tried to push their way through. And failed.

He had to see Kel.

Before he did or said anything else, he had to see Kel. Then:

"Aye, five o' them – The Barmulloch Del..."

His head flicked left.

Emerging from the top of the steps, a group of four.

Big Frank.

Gibby.

Someone else he didn't know, in white-and-red Le Coq Sportif.

All silent. All agog. All walking backwards in front of...

Danny couldn't look at the fourth.

"Waitin' ootside the hoose fur me, when ah got hame."
Hoarse laugh. "Fuckin' five against wan, but ah got a
coupla o' them ontae the ground afore the other two held
me doon an' wan big bastard tried tae smash me in the
mouth wi' a baseball bat."

Then he had to look up.

"Whit happened after that?" Big Frank.

Danny stared at the bruised, animated face. The cut at
the corner of the mouth had scabbed over. The left eye was
still puffy and purple, ringed by a border of greyish skin.

Laugh. "Fuckin' knee-ed the bastard in the nuts, didn't
ah? Man, he fuckin' howled! The rest wur shittin'
themselves by that time."

The thick stickiness dissolved. Danny stared at the
battlefield of a face.

"Whit happened then?" Gibby.

Grin. "Fuckin' legged it intae the hoose, didn't ah? Ah'm
no' fuckin' daft, man – five against wan? Ah wis lucky tae
git aff wi' jist this..." Bitten fingertip tracing the outline of
an eye-socket. Nonchalant shrug. "'Course, it's aw' cos me
an' Jordan gave their boays a doin' last week." Head
rotated slowly.

Blue eyes met green. Danny watched his presence
register.

Shock, embarrassment then fear fluttered across the less-
than-pale face.

Danny's stomach turned to mush. He looked away.
Then:

"Hiya Frannie!" Big Frank.

A groan at his side. "Hi yourself, Frank Drysdale!" Then
Nike:

"Still wastin' yer time wi' Bent-Boay MacIntyre?" Snort.
Big Frank again:

"Danny an' Frannie...it rhymes! Whit else rhymes wi'
Danny, boays?"

More snorting. Mock-suggestions from Gibby:

"Tranny...janny...nanny...fan..." Then a hoarse voice:

"Lea' him alain, eh?"

Big Frank. Surprised. "Whit's wrang wi' you?"

124

"Nothin' – c'mon, ah'm hungry. Let's go tae the chippy..."

As Frannie continued the exchange of insults with Big Frank, Gibby and Le Coq Sportif, a tall figure in an increasingly grubby-looking Umbro warm-up suit was striding off alone towards the school gates.

Part of Danny wanted to follow. Another, larger part wanted to walk in the opposite direction and keep walking.

Frannie extracted a compromise. She gave the gruesome threesome the finger then steered him towards the dinner-hall and food.

Somehow, he secured Frannie's continued complicity without actually telling her anything.

Somehow, the afternoon passed.

Somehow, three different teachers accepted spur-of-the-moment excuses as to why he'd forgotten that day's homework.

Kel's bruises burned into his brain, superimposing themselves over a sobbing figure on a couch.

Bum-boy!

Bent-Boy!

Danny frowned.

The strained silence which had been tea echoed in his head. Kel's hoarse, bragging voice throbbed in his ears and made him feel hurt and annoyed and embarrassed and sick all at once.

He's ducked out to the boiler-room at each period-break. Nothing...

...Danny stared at his CD collection then got up from the bed and opened the door.

His father was in the bathroom, shaving.

His mother and Nicola were in the kitchen, arguing about pocket-money.

Danny lifted the phone, punched in a seven digit number.

It rang twenty two times before he replaced the receiver and walked into the living-room.

The TV was on. Sound low. He grabbed the remote, increased the volume and listened to a recap of the headlines.

Something about budget-cuts.

More about the strike by Cleansing-Workers.

Nothing about...

"Since when were you interested in current affairs?"

The voice made him jump. Carpets and guns and bruises swam in his head. He managed a smile.

His father was sliding the knot of a tie closer to the slightly-frayed collar of a blue shirt.

Danny scrutinised the process. Carpets and guns faded, leaving only bruises and a cut lip.

The news cut to a weather-forecast.

"How do you know?" Tom MacIntyre tucked the tail of his tie into the waistband of the trousers-which-didn't-match-the-jacket and half-watched the screen.

Danny stared at a tiny nick on his father's neck. "What?" On the TV, a woman was going on about the weather. He concentrated on her voice and ignored the question. "Dad, I... er...I know this boy, and his father's..."

"Your mother told me what you...told her." Remote grabbed. Eyes never leaving the now-mute weather-forecast.

Danny sighed: last night was a lifetime away. "I was going tell you too, but..."

"So how do you know?"

The question took him by surprise. His skin was on fire. "What..er...what do ye mean, exactly?" He cringed: he was sounding like his mother!

"I mean, how do you know you're...homosexual? Are we talking...feelings? Or...?"

He didn't want to think about this now. Danny's stomach churned. His throat was a desert. Hearing his father use the words made his chest tighten.

"Dan? Talk to me!"

Danny stared at the side of his father's face and thought about another, damaged face. Eyes prickled. He wiped palms on the thighs of jeans then thrust fists into pockets.

126

"It's no big deal." He continued to stare at where his father had been. Kel's bruised skin exploded in his mind. Something wet rolled down his face. "I'm the same as I was yesterday..." He knew it wasn't true. "...everything's the same as it was yesterday..."

"You're right..."

His father's voice was very close. Danny flinched, spun round and blinked into a white shirt. And stepped back.

"...it's no' a big deal..."

Danny sniffed. His nose was running: he wanted to follow it to the ends of the earth. And he wanted his dad to hug him, like he used to do, and tell him everything would be all right. He raised his head.

Tom MacIntyre's face looked like it always did. Broad. Strong. Laughter lines furrowed the sides of his mouth. "...as long as you don't...do anything." His father wasn't laughing now.

Danny blinked. His eyes stung.

Kel...

Angry words...

Running away when...

"Lots of boys have...feelin's..."

His father's words were worse than his mother's silence. Danny's skin flushed icy.

"...it's a...phase, that's aw', son..." His father stuck hands into pockets.

"It's not a phase." Tears dammed themselves, drying on his face. Danny glowered at his father.

Frannie would have been welcomed with open arms.

Even Moira would have been tolerated. Eventually.

He could have been doing anything with any girl the length and breadth of Glasgow and his mother would have smiled the school-teacher smile, and his father would have winked.

Nails were biting into palms. "It's not a phase, an' I know what I'm doin' so..." He scowled. "...just leave me alone!"

In the hall, he pulled the telephone into his room.

127

He dialled the seven-digit number eight more times in the next three hours. He only stopped dialling when his mother asked who he was phoning.

Chapter Eleven

He waited at the boiler-room until five past nine and was late for Biology.

At break, he searched every room on every floor and phoned the seven-digit number from the phone outside the secretary's office.

Lunch-time was a three-way split between boiler-room, chip shop and pay-phone. Back in the playground, Frannie waved at him from a group of girls he didn't know.

Just before the start of the fifth period, a fist thumped between his shoulder-blades.

Danny staggered forward, spun round and stared into Big Frank's big, mocking face.

Gibby.

Le Coq Sportif.

He almost asked them, then turned away and ducked into a classroom which wasn't his.

The afternoon dragged its feet.

Seconds after the half-past three bell he sprinted out of the gates, up Armadale Street towards the Parade and the footbridge across the motorway to Roystonhill.

In the front garden of Sixteen Priestview a burly, bald man was padlocking the chairs of a white plastic patio set to a white plastic table.

Danny peered left through the venetians of Number Fifteen then rang the doorbell for the fourth time.

Nothing.

He dragged his duffle-bag from his shoulder, sat on the doorstep and stared at cracked paving.

Six months.

Six months of listening to stories about fights with half an ear.

Six months of admiring battle-scars and bruises...

...which came from a source closer to home than the Barmulloch Del.

His eyes narrowed, focusing on a patch of gray/green moss. Voice from the patio-set:

"Is it the boay ye're after?"

Danny's head flicked up.

The burly bald man was staring at him.

"Yes, I..."

"No' seen him fur a coupla days, noo..."

The news made his heart lurch. Danny stood up. "Er, thanks..."

The burly bald man was still staring at him.

"...if you see him, could you tell him to phone Danny?"

Scowl. "Ah'm no' his answerin'-service, son!" Wandering back to the patio-set, hauling once at the chain.

As Danny walked away, a handsome, tanned face superimposed itself over the burly one.
"Again?"

At least she was talking to him. Danny shovelled a last forkful of macaroni into his mouth and nodded. "Prelims next month – 'member?"

Another frown. "Don't speak with your mouth full!"

Danny scowled. "Don't ask me questions when I'm eating, then!" He got up from the table.

His mother followed. "I thought Frannie was doing different subjects from you?"

"She's still doing English..." In his bedroom, Danny removed the blouson jacket from behind the door and shrugged it on. He turned, walked past his mother into the hall. "I might be late, so don't wait up for..."

"Won't you need this?"

Fingers tightening on keys, he turned. Eyes focused on the duffle-bag which dangled from her hand. Danny snatched drawstrings. "Thanks..." He walked quickly towards the door and wondered why lies were accepted more easily than the truth.

Another girl with an orange face frowned at him. Four scarlet nails over the mouthpiece of a telephone. "Who?"

"Kel – Michael Kelston?" He raised his voice over the sound of the muzak.

More frowning. "Is he a member?"

Someone in shorts with a squash-racket pushed it through a space at the bottom of the perspex window.

Danny shrugged duffle-bag onto shoulder and moved left. "I'm...not sure: could you just put a call out for him?"

The girl with the orange face took the squash-racket, placed it in a rack behind the pine counter then opened a drawer. A ten pound note slid back through the gap at the bottom of the perspex window. Smile to the customer, frown to Danny. "What was the name again?"

"Kel – Michael Kelston." Danny shoved hands into jeans pockets, took a step back and stared at the signed photograph of Steve Davis. Muzak filled his ears. He was wondering how long someone had to be gone before they technically became a missing person. The muzak stopped abruptly. Tinny, tannoy voice:

"Would Kel – Michael Kelston – come tae reception, please. That's Kel – Michael Kelston – tae reception. Thank you."

An instrumental version of some song started playing again. Danny's eyes flicked gratefully to the girl with the orange face.

She stared at him once, then went back to her telephone conversation.

He sat down on the row of metal seats and hugged the duffle-bag. Eyes circled between two sets of swing doors and a flight of stairs.

Three sweaty women in leotards.

A couple with badminton rackets, in JB's warm-up suits.

A man in a leather jacket and very short blond hair carrying a snooker-cue case.

Danny's gaze followed the latter to the pine-counter...

...and the large figure in a cap-sleeved tee-shirt who had somehow appeared behind the perspex window and was now talking to the orange-faced girl.

Three eyes regarded him through perspex.

Danny flinched.

One eye was unfocused somewhere behind his head.

The man with the snooker-cue case slipped money through the gap.

Danny blinked, stood up. The duffle-bag slid to the floor. Then the huge figure in the cap-sleeved tee-shirt was standing beside him, blocking out light and muzak:

"Kel's busy right noo, Danny son, but Jordan says tae go oan through an'..." Behind, the sound of doors opening. Then a familiar smooth voice:

"Thank you for coming..."

"Thank you fur calling us, Mr Burns. Your lockers look secure enough..."

Danny inched closer to Maxie's massive body as Jordan escorted two police officers holding hats towards the exit.

"...but ah'll pass the call on to Crime Prevention – they'll drop in tomorrow, provide you with posters and the like."

Danny stared at the floor. Jordan's tones seeped into his ears.

"Thanks again – sorry to have bothered you."

"No bother..." More doors opening. "...better to be safe than sorry. Good night."

As the doors closed, he expelled a breath he didn't know he'd been holding.

A low laugh. "Didn't see you there, Danny..."

Light and sound poured over him as Maxie moved away. Danny picked up the duffle-bag and raised his head. "Er...is Kel around?" He inhaled, lungs filling with the expensive smell.

The tanned face smiled. "He's been doing a little bit of business for me, but he should have finished by now – come on through."

Eyes darting once through the main doors and out into the night, Danny found himself walking between a huge shape and less huge, but more powerful figure through double doors and down a carpeted corridor.

Trainered feet crossed at ankles. On table. Kel was eating peanuts in a corner of the half-empty bar. Three empty packets filled the ashtray. One, less-puffy eye focused on a soundless, large-screen TV in another corner.

Danny stared to where Jordan and Maxie were now talking to a group of men, one of whom had a pad over one eye. He dumped the duffle-bag on a padded seat and sat down. "I put a call out for you..."

"Ah wis...busy." Shrug. Both eyes fixed on screen.

The bar was dimly lit. Through the gloom, Danny examined the still-swollen face. His stomach flipped over. "You okay?"

"Fine – ah jist had tae dae somethin' fur..."

"No, I mean..."

"Ah'm fine." Peanut-bag jiggled.

Danny let a handful pour onto his palm, looked at it then a dark patch on a cheekbone.

Bitten fingers thrust into mouth.

Danny looked back at the peanuts. "I tried to phone you."

Munching. "Ah wis oot."

"All...night?"

"Ah disconnected it, so's ah could sleep..." Munch then swallow. Then: "You gonny eat them or no'?"

Danny tipped the peanuts into an out-stretched palm.

Bitten fingers brushed his. Then more munching.

His stomach turned over. "Kel I..."

Voice lowered. "Ah had it oan CNN a minute ago but him behind the bar changed it fur this." Sigh.

"What?" Danny moved his gaze from the bruised face to the opposite corner. Thin women swaggered down a catwalk to the accompaniment of flashing cameras.

"CNN – Cable Network News." Eyes continued to stare at the large-screen TV. "Nae mention o'..."

"They only cover international news – wars and stuff." Danny refocused on the face. "Has Jordan...said anything else? About...?""

Slow headshake. "He's fuckin' pissed-aff wi' Lennox, but..." Peanut-bag tilted upwards. Remnants of salt and browny-red skins shaken into mouth. Peanut-bag scrunched and tossed into ashtray.

Danny watched the packet slowly unfurl. His mind was back with floral-patterned sofa and a curled, crying shape. His mouth opened. "Kel, I..."

"Whit's this?" The duffle-bag between them nudged.

He frowned. "That's my...alibi."

Snigger. Then mimicking. "Couldn't have been me,

133

officer – I was wi' ma school-bag, at the time!"

Danny scowled...

Green eyes stared at him, rolling. Ginger slugs waggled above puffiness.

...then giggled.

Kel grinned. Full lips twitched downwards. "Oh, an' ah huvney forgotten ah owe ye, fae Tuesday."

The groin of Danny's jeans twitched in response to the memory. "Double or quits?"

Scab-cracking grin. "Ye're oan!" Ankles swung from table.

Danny shrank back against plush upholstery. "Now?"

Kel was on his feet. "Aye, c'mon..." A hand slapped the duffle-bag. "Don't forget yer alibi."

Smeary bloodstains on white enamel filled his head. Danny snatched the duffle-bag and followed a loping figure towards a door marked 'Men'.

Weaving between huddles of figures drinking and now watching televised snooker, he caught a pair of vaguely-amused brown eyes.

A toilet-roll dispenser scraped at the small of his back. The duffle-bag hung from a hook on the back of the door.

Opposite, Adidas warm-up pants and pale purple jockeys bagged around knees.

Danny moved along the wall, jeans and underwear tight around thighs. The flesh in his fist flexed.

"Oi! None o' that!"

"Sorry..." He stopped, focused past a bruised face to blurring red pen grafitti and remembered other red. "Tell me about Gazza..." His voice was a hoarse whisper. Thumb and forefinger re-forming a half-hearted ring. Danny slid his fist upwards.

Sigh. "'S'a place, really..." Nail-bitten fingers mirrored the movement.

Danny inhaled sharply.

"...in a poem, by the Milton-guy..."

The hand around him faltered for a second, then got back on course. Danny tugged harder.

"Ken Samson? The wan in the bible, wi' the lang hair?"

134

Danny's ears were full of words which made no sense. He nodded. Peanut-salty breath brushed his face. Underneath, another saltier odour.

"Efter he let whit's-her-face cut it aff an' he loses aw' his strength..."

A door opened, somewhere behind them. Laughing voices.

Kel moved closer. Words softer, more hoarse.

"...the...Philistines take him tae Gazza an'..."

The flesh in his fist was damp. The fist around his length was damper. Danny's legs buckled. Eyes slid down the wall behind a red head.

The movement mirrored. "...blind him...an' that's when Samson really starts tae see properly, get it?"

"No, not really..." His knee struck another. His right hip impacted with the toilet bowl. The lurching in his stomach was moving higher, churning the macaroni he'd had for his tea into a sour-tasting, semi-digested soup. Somewhere in the distance a door closed and the laughing stopped. Danny glanced at the hand which tugged between his legs...

...and up to a puffy, bruised face.

Green eyes stared back. The hand paused. Then one gnawed finger from another hand flicked back a hank of dangling hair. "That's..." Tugging resumed. "...whit..." Pause. "...happens ..." Tugging faster. "...if..."

A clammy film drenched his face. Danny's balls clenched. Fist slackened. Coldness clutched at his stomach.

"...ye're caught..."

Words ebbed and flow in his ears. The coldness rushed downwards, warming. His heart pounded. A fiery heat tingled deep inside him.

"...crossin' Jordan..."

Then the rushing was boiling and someone was gasping. Danny fell forwards onto the hand around his shaft. Over distant, victorious hoots and a spreading warm wetness, all he could see was the green of Kel's blazing irises...

...and the man with the pad over his eye, back in the bar. A hand had clamped itself over his forehead, underneath

135

his damp hair. It felt cool.

Like the surface beneath his fingers. Danny gripped the sides of the toilet-bowl and dry-heaved.

The hand was pressing gently. "That's it, man..."

He concentrated on the voice and the hand. In the distance, the sound of a door opening. Then a thump on the stall door:

"You okay, Danny?"

Laugh from his side. Kel stood up. "Aye, he's fine, Jordan..."

A hand patted his back. Danny scowled, open-mouthed. He'd not been sick for years.

Concern. "Bring him through to the office, Kel..."

"I'm all right – really." Danny wretched, wiped his mouth and raised his head. The hand remained on his back. His empty stomach spasmed.

"If you're sure..."

Danny pressed his cheek against the cool rim of the toilet-bowl. Jordan wasn't going to go away – none of this was. An odour of macaroni and disinfectant filled his head.

A memory of smeary blood and recent words made him want to throw up again.

He lurched to his feet, hauled open the cubicle door and stumbled in the direction of the sinks. Hands fumbled for taps. "I'm okay."

Nail-bitten fingers were wiping his face with wet paper-towels.

Danny turned, leant back. The rim of a sink was digging into his spine. His vision slowly focused...

...on a tanned, unamused face.

He wanted to close his eyes. Couldn't. Soggy blue paper dabbed at his skin.

Kel reached around him, soaked another paper towel and continued the clean-up.

Memories of another clean-up in another toilet swam in his head. Slow words across him:

"Have you given him anything?" Accusatory.

"No' me, Jordan – ah widney dae onythin' like..."

"Something I ate, I think." Danny stared at the tanned face.

136

Unconvinced brown eyes gazed past his face. Jordan turned to the mirror behind them, ran a tanned hand through immaculate dark hair.

The patting on his face stopped:

"How ye feelin' noo?" Low voice.

Danny could still taste semi-digested cheese sauce. He couldn't get the Gaza-story out of his mind. "Fine – I'm fine! But I need to go..." He scanned the toilet for his duffle-bag, then noticed Kel was holding it. As he eased it from an Umbro-ed shoulder, mirror-directed brown eyes met his. Danny looked away.

Throat clearing. "Ye need me fur...onythin' else, Jordan?"

Low laugh. "You get a taxi..." Hand into pocket, bundle produced. Notes pealed off. "...take Danny home."

"Sure, Jordan – thanks, Jordan!" Notes gripped by bitten fingers.

His eyes sloped downwards.

"Don't forget about tomorrow."

"Ah won't, Jordan."

He watched a pair of highly-polished shoes move out of his line of vision.

A door opening. "Good night, Danny."

"Er...good night..." As the door closed, his face was a clammy mask of relief.

They got chips and walked. Cold air and light rain helped. Greasy fried potatoes didn't.

He passed his bag left. "What's happening...tomorrow."

"Nothin'." Fingers accepted the unwanted chips.

Danny watched Kel eat. "I don't believe that Gaza-stuff..."

Kel continued to eat. "Jordan's really intae the guy – quotes bits o' the poem as he dis it." Chewing. "Eyeless in Gaza, at the mill wi'..." Pause. "... somethin'-somethin': canny remember the rest, but there's lines an' lines o' it!"

Danny's heart stuttered. "You've...seen him do it?" He'd heard the aftermath.

"Jist wance." Kel blew on a chip, then popped it into his mouth. "Disney happen that often..." Chewing. "Ah mean, folk've jist gotta look at Maxie an' ony ideas aboot bein'...disloyal go right oota their heids." Something like a laugh.

Something like pain formed in his empty stomach. "What did Maxie...do?"

"He...considered anither offer. Jordan fun' oot." More chewing.

Danny's stomach gurgled. "How come you're so...calm about it?"

Shrug. "'S'a fact o' life – jist the way Jordan is...."

Other facts of other lives refused to leave his mind. Danny looked at the bruised face.

"He's okay, maist o' the time..." Chip-paper unfolded, licked. "...an' folk gie him...respect." Chip-paper balled, tossed into the air and kicked.

Danny looked away from a green-and-yellow cheekbone...

Respect.

...more questions burbled at the back of his throat. He hoisted the duffle-bag further over his shoulder and walked faster.

Ten, silent minutes later, they were standing at the foot of the motorway bridge. Danny glanced right, along the Parade, then refocused beyond a red head.

From Roystonhill, the new houses glared down at him. Drunken, angry words reeled about in his skull. Other, hesitant words, close to his face:

"Thanks fur...jist leavin', the other night..."

His eyes slid from red tiled roofs to purplish skin.

White teeth gnawed at the side of an index-finger. Green irises aimed pavementwards.

"Does your dad...do that a lot?" He tried to sound casual, then waited for the question to be deliberately misinterpreted.

It wasn't. "Ainly when ah annoy him." The voice was low, un-Kel-like and directed at the ground.

Danny aimed his question in the same direction. "How did you...?"

"Ah forgot tae replace his vodka..."

138

Danny remembered a heap of damp clothes which had refused to ignite.

"...an' there wisney ony lager in the fridge..." The voice lowered until it was almost inaudible."...an' ah'd finished the bread an' he didney like *Timecop* an'..." Sigh. "But he wis steamin' – he's eyeways worse when he's steamin', an' ah shouldda replaced the vodka."

Bum-boy.

Bum-boy.

Danny opened his mouth. Nothing came out. He tried again. "Will you be...okay, tonight?"

Snort. "Aye, the morra's Child Benefit day – he'll be in a guid mood."

Danny examined the pavement. Somewhere behind, cars roared past.

...then a foot nudged his. "Double or quits, ye said?" Grinning voice.

Danny flinched.

Movement. "Can ah huv overnight tae think aboot it?" An Umbro-ed arm half-Nelsoned his neck from behind.

Breath on his ear. Danny leant back into the movement, one hand reaching to grip the arm half-heartedly. He closed his eyes. "Okay."

A heart thumped against his shoulder blade...

...then Kel was pulling away and loping up steps. "Seeya the morra..."

Danny spun round. "At school?"

"Naw..." Words carried on the wind. "...come up the road, after!"

"Okay..." Danny watched the figure take steps two at a time, then break into a run. He continued to watch until Kel disappeared from sight.

Chapter Twelve

Only ten-thirty.

The house was silent.

In his bedroom, Danny undressed through mud. Kel and an older, red-haired man slow-waltzed in front of his eyes...

He sat on the bed, hauling at trainers which refused to leave his feet.

...joined by men with eye-pads and unseeing, glassy stares. Danny pushed them away and gave up with the trainers. Around him, his bedroom was the same as always. He stared at *Babycakes* on the bedside table, gaze panning on past orderly rows of CDs and books to the wardrobe, chest of drawers and the desk by the window.

The same as always...

Danny stood up. He grabbed two note-books and *Babycakes*, thrust the trio into the lolling mouth of his duffle-bag then hung the bag behind the door.

Not right...

He jammed a foot between the bed and the floor, wrenching one then both feet free of the trainers. Trembling fingers opened the wardrobe and replaced sports shoes beside school shoes.

The same as always...

He closed the wardrobe door. Something got in the way. Danny dropped to his knees, fiddling with the section of loose carpet.

Not right...

Fingers trembled more violently. Danny stuck one hand under the wardrobe. He nudged already-rumpled carpet aside, scrabbling for...

Soft knocking.

Danny froze, fingers rigid in empty space.

More soft knocking. Then: "You awake?"

He dragged his hand from the empty hiding-space and opened the door.

Darkness surrounded the small, bespectacled figure in candlewick. Nicola smiled at him.

Danny stared at the magazines in her hand, then grabbed a dressing-gowned wrist and pulled her into the room. "Where did you get those?"

"The bin..." Magazines held out. "...they yours?"

He snatched the crumpled, tea-bag stained *Honcho*s and fell back on the bed.

"Where did you get them?" Giggle.

Danny scowled at the ceiling. "In a shop, of course – where do you think?" When had they searched his room – before his father left for work? What else had they found – what else was there to find?

Another giggle. "Well, I've never seen anything like that, in John Menzies!"

He dismembered the room mentally, trying to remember if there was anything else he'd forgotten about. Part of him was surprised his mother hadn't waited up for him. His face flushed. He could visualise her sitting there, in the living-room, producing the *Honcho*s with the same flourish as the condoms.

"Danny?"

The magazines slipped from fingers. He'd forgotten Nicola was still in the room. "Thanks for...bringing them back."

"Danny?" The subtle 'go' message ignored. "Are you gay?"

He dragged his eyes from the ceiling and stared at her.

Nicola sat on the edge of the bed. Thoughtful. "Are you?"

He frowned. "What do you know about...being gay?"

"I'm not stupid!" Indignant whisper. "Sam in *Casualty*'s gay..." Sigh. "He's gorgeous – and Simon in *Eastenders*'s gay ..." Pause. "...there's no gay people in *Neighbours* or *Home and Away* – don't think they have them, in Australia..." Voice lowered. Thoughtful again. "... Yvonne says Mr MacKay who takes the Primary Twos is gay, but I think he's too old."

Danny blinked. Bespectacled eyes scrutinised him:

"Who are you having sex with?"

Danny groaned. "No-one..."

Concerned. "Have you fallen out with your boyfriend? Sam in *Casualty* fell out with his boyfriend cos he started going out with a girl and..."

"We haven't...fallen out." *The Joy of Gay Sex* leapt into his mind. Danny scrambled off the bed, opened the bottom drawer of the small pine chest and rummaged between the folds of spare blankets. Fingers contacted with reassuring shininess. Danny relaxed, pushed the book back down. He closed the drawer, turned.

Nicola was sitting cross-legged in the middle of the bed, leafing through a tea-stained *Honcho*. "These are much better than the ones Yvonne's dad keeps in his sock-drawer." Small mouth curling with distaste. "Those're just all women with really big chests and mushy pink fannies! No boys in any of them." Middle pages held vertically. "This what your wee man looks like when you get excited?"

Danny shook his head.

Giggle. "Ronnie Gilmour's is like that..." Index-finger crooked around the side of the page. Wiggled. Magazine lowered. Wiggling finger now pointing. "Your boyfriend's wee man looks like this?"

Danny tried to remember the centrefold without actually picturing it. "No..." He wondered vaguely who Ronnie Gilmour was.

"Hmmm..." Philosophical. "Yvonne's mum's chest's nowhere near as big as the women in the magazines her dad has."

Danny walked unsteadily to the bed, eased the *Honcho* from between his sister's fingers and rolled it up with the others. "Put them back where you got them and go to bed..."

"I'll just keep this one..." Fingers snatching one magazine free, opening and flicking. Then careful tearing.

Danny stared at her choice.

A dark haired figure.

Full frontal, not just knob.

Thick covering of chest hair...

Jordan Burns' undone shirt-buttons filled his mind.

143

...he grabbed the magazine from small, determined fingers. It tore just below the dark-haired man's thighs. "You've got to put them back – they'll notice if you..."

"Okay, okay..." Nicola stuffed a ragged section of coloured paper into dressing-gown pocket. Owl eyes gazed at him hopefully. "You got any more – of men having sex? With each other?"

Danny remembered the line drawings in *The Joy of Gay Sex* and shook his head.

Disappointed sigh. "My pocket money's spoken for 'til Christmas, but maybe after that we can club together?"

Danny stared past the owl face. "It's too risky – they'll just...find them again."

Christmas.

Christmas...

...would the Carpet have been found by Christmas?

A hand touched his shoulder.

His eyes darted back to the owl face.

"So who's your boyfriend? Can I meet him?"

Danny found himself smiling. "Is...Ronnie Gilmour yours?"

Appalled. "Him?" Finger into mouth. Mock-gagging sound.

Danny laughed.

A noise from beyond the door silenced them both.

He listen to the sound of a toilet flushing. Minutes later, his mother's footsteps retreated back down the hall.

Whisper. "Can I tell Yvonne?"

Danny surveyed the animated face. His skin prickled. He shook his head.

"She'll not tell anyone else – honest."

Lies, secrets, carpets and a bruised face whirred around in his brain. Danny frowned. "Not yet – okay?"

Understanding nod. Legs unfolding, slipping off bed. *Honcho*s under one arm. Small fingers gripping door handle, then pausing. "This is really notch..." Owl eyes reverential. "...it's like living with someone off the television!" Giggle.

He listened to slippers padding towards the kitchen,

then closed the door and pulled off his jeans.

Time hung around his shoulders, weighing him down like the daily quartet of newspapers in his duffle-bag. He'd considered feigning illness: a day at home would pass equally slowly.

Breakfast had been a serious of parallel glances.

Nicola looked at him.

He looked at Nicola, knew without looking that his parents were exchanging similar looks for unsimilar reasons.

No-one mentioned the *Honchos*.

No-one mentioned last night.

No-one mentioned anything...

...he hadn't known eating could be so noisy.

At school, he ended up at the boiler-room three times, just in case.

He avoided Frannie.

He skipped dinner to get the early edition of the *Evening Times*.

A bell rang.

Danny folded the newspaper, slipped it into his bag. He avoided thinking about anything except...

"Oi, MacIntyre!"

Danny sighed. He levered himself off the railings, hoisted his duffle-bag onto his shoulder and walked towards the main entrance. Sniggers behind. Three sets of footsteps behind. Then:

"Poof...poof..."

He changed direction, swerving across the playground. Not now...

"Poof...poof..."

Threading between parked cars, Danny lowered his head and concentrated on later.

"Poof...poof..."

He speeded up.

"Poof...poof..."

So did three sets of footsteps.

He chewed his lip. Later...with Kel...

145

"Poof...poof..."

Four sets of feet...

"Poof...poof..."

...and two words in sync. A hand grabbed his shoulder. A snigger.

Danny twisted away.

"Poof...poof..."

The hand regrabbed. "Whit ye got there?" Big Frank.

A single, repeated noun throbbed beneath the question, pounding in his chest. The duffle-bag hauled from his shoulder.

Danny gripped the drawstrings and tried to keep walking.

The hand on the bag pulled him back.

He released the drawstrings. Ahead, the last few stragglers slipped through the doors into the building.

Behind, sniggering. And rummaging.

Danny turned slowly. "Give me my bag." He held out a hand.

Three sets of eyes stared at him. "Give me my bag! Give me my bag!" More sniggers. Gibby continued to haul jotters and newspapers from the duffle bag.

Danny scowled. "Give it to me!"

"Give it tae me! Give it tae me!" Another high-pitched parody from Le Coq Sportif.

His face reddened. His hand remained out-stretched.

Big Frank's big, dirty fingers curled around the smooth, colourful covers of a paperback:

"Ya swotty wee poof!"

Danny snatched, fingers closing around air.

More sniggers. *Babycakes* flicked away. "This a poofy book, Bent-Boay?" Volume held high, pages flicked.

His throat was dry. Tingling shivers swept over him. Not now...

Somewhere close, the sounds of newspapers and note-books crumpling.

Big Frank's big stupid face peered at pages. "Kelston should be here tae see this..." Snorting guffaw. "Hey, boays – the poof's goat a book aboot poofs!"

146

He snatched again. Someone knocked his hand away. Someone else thumped his shoulder. Danny staggered, waited for them to start tossing the contents of his duffle bag over his head while he tried to catch. More sniggers, then:

"This is...disgustin', Bent-Boay!"

He blinked. A harsh, drunken rasp superimposed itself over Gibby's cracking voice.

The scab at the side of a full mouth hovered in front of his eyes. Danny found himself thinking about Hamlet.

Big Frank's big hands were folding back the book's covers, bending and breaking the spine of the book Kel had...

...Danny launched himself at the large figure in the Nike warm-up suit.

They both fell.

The book flew from a fist which slammed into the side of his head.

Danny grabbed for the fist as the arm pulled back for a repeat action. His other hand scrabbled for purchase. Missed. One knee contacted with something soft.

A hoarse yelp.

A trainered foot in his side.

Danny held on to the yelping form, kneed Big Frank in the balls again.

Two trainered feet, one each side.

The fist wrenched itself free from his grip, smashed off his ear.

More feet...

...and shouts. Something loud and hot and Kel-flavoured was rushing through his veins. Someone was screaming.

Heaving beneath. Hands on his shoulders, hauling him upwards.

Danny clung on, fingers finding greasy hair and pulling. The sole of his shoe caught the inside of an ankle. He kicked.

Kicked again...

...and kept kicking. Panicky roars through the pounding in his ears:

147

"Get him aff me! Get him fuckin' aff me!'"

Then the hair in his fingers slackened. And a loud crack. Then lightening.

Danny slumped sideways. The impact of the top of Big Frank's big skull throbbed against his forehead.

Someone was gripping the collar of his blazer.

Danny lunged downwards, fingers curling around Big Frank's big thighs as he crawled across the playground.

Tightness under his arms...

Ripping.

...and more kicking. Through a haze of feet and flashing Nike ticks, voices echoed in his head. He threw himself forward, grabbed retreating shoulders and began to haul himself up Big Franks's big legs.

Voices.

Shouting voices.

Adult voices...

...then two pairs of legs were sprinting out of the gate onto Onslow Drive and the janitor was hauling him off a snivelling shape.

"So what was that all about?"

Danny stared at the floor of Mr Cooper's office. His nose was running.

"Frank?"

A sniff.

"Daniel...?"

He wiped his nose on his hand and stared at red smears.

"...this isn't like you." A sigh. "Come on – I'll find out anyway..." The sound of chair-legs scraping.

He raised his head.

Mr Cooper was sitting on the edge of the desk.

Danny avoided angry eyes and looked to where Big Frank was still nursing his balls.

A knock...

...the janitor's eyes were swivelling between his, Mr Cooper and the top of Big Frank's big, greasy head. One hand held a duffle-bag, the fingers of the other tight around a book and a pile of muddy school-jotters. "Nae sign o' the other two, but ah found..." Cargo extended.

"They're mine."

Mr Cooper nodded to the janitor, refocused on Danny.

He stared back at the floor. Sounds of a door closing.

"What happened to your books, Daniel?"

He sighed: it wasn't worth it. "Dropped them."

Snigger at his side.

Stern tones. "You'll be laughing on the other side of your face when I suspend you, Frank."

"Ah didney dae nothin'..." Protesting. "He...attacked me, man! Ah wis helpin' him tae pick-up his..." Snigger. "...dirty books an' he jist...jumped oan me!"

"Now why don't I believe that?"

Danny plucked the duffle-bag from the desk and began to re-pack its contents.

"'S'the truth – tell'im, Ben...MacIntyre!"

Two sets of eyes bored into his lowered head, each wanting different answers. Danny frowned: it wasn't worth it – none of it was. He talked to the floor. "Thought he was...trying to steal my stuff. I over-reacted."

"See? Wisney ma fault – wis his. He...over-reacted!"

Sceptical. "So what happened to your blazer, Daniel? Did it join in this over-reaction?"

"Oh, ah did that – tryin' tae get the bastard aff me! Ye canny fault a guy fur tryin' tae defend himsel', can ye? He should be locked up, that wan!"

"Wait outside, Frank..."

"Ah'll be late fur ma class an'..."

"I doubt you were going anyway, Frank – just wait outside. And don't be skulking off anywhere."

Sulky. "He's fuckin' mad, he is!"

"Outside, Frank..."

Fingers tightened around duffle-straps. He continued to stare at the floor.

Limping footsteps. The door opened then closed.

Silence. Then: "Want to tell me about it?"

Danny's eyes inched across the floor into the dark space under Mr Cooper's desk.

Tell me about it...

149

He frowned. "That is what happened."

Tell me about it...

Tell me about it...

A sigh. "I can't do anything about whatever's going on here unless you help me, Daniel."

Help me...

Help me...

...he didn't need help. Danny peered into the dark space until it was filled with a bruised, freckled skin.

Tell me about it...

Tell me about it...

"The other two – who ran away when..."

Words formed in the back of his throat. "This is...in confidence?" Eyes tracked upwards.

Encouraging nod. "Of course."

He tried to order sentences in his head.

"Take your time..." More encouraging nods.

He took a step back, looked away from the open, concerned face and saw another face. Then the words came. "He'll kill me if he finds out I'm telling you this, but it's not right. Kel's..."

"Kel?" Mystified.

Danny moved his gaze back to Mr Cooper. "Michael Kelston. His father's..."

"Stop right there, Daniel. I had a feeling Kelston would be at the back of this somewhere – Drysdale's not capable of doing anything on his own." Mr Cooper walked to the telephone, lifted the receiver. "Jenny? Get me Michael Kelston's address and home number. Oh, and send Frank Drysdale back to wherever he should be."

Danny opened his mouth. Nothing came out.

Mr Cooper talked on, a broad palm over the mouthpiece. "Who was the other one – Gibson?"

Danny blinked.

"Don't matter – I've no doubt Kelston's the ring-leader. If we can get him..."

"No..." The word leaked from his lips. Danny stared at the telephone.

Mr Cooper was talking into the receiver again. He

150

plucked a pencil from a holder and wrote something on a pad. "Thanks, Jenny." Receiver replaced.

A muscle in Danny's right leg spasmed convulsively.

Mr Cooper was frowning. "I'm going to stamp this bullying out, once and for all. Maybe a quiet word from the police will..."

"No!" Sweat poured down his back. "Don't call the police -Kel wasn't there! He's at home! I wasn't talking about..." Throat tightened, cutting off words. His face was wet. Danny brushed burning eyes. "...that."

Mr Cooper's face swam in front of him. "Take it easy, Daniel."

The muscle in his leg pulsed through his entire body. Danny clenched his fists and tried to make it stop. The muscle pulsed more violently. Voice close:

"Maybe Kelston wasn't involved this time, but he's part of it, isn't he?"

Danny flinched. "No."

"Yes he is." Voice closer. "It's affecting your school-work, Daniel – God knows what it's doing to the rest of your life."

The police...

...questions...carpets...guns...Gaza...

Somewhere outside, a bell rang. Danny moved away from the hand. "Don't do anything – if you do anything, I'll deny everything." Spine impacted with a bookcase. Danny wobbled.

Outside, thundering feet signalled the start of the last period.

He met frustrated eyes and looked away.

A sigh. "Think about it, Daniel – come and see me tomorrow."

He nodded. His neck was one of the few parts which didn't hurt. Legs moved past him, opening the door:

"Go and get cleaned up, then get off home – I'll clear it with your teachers."

Danny nodded again and somehow managed to leave the office.

The house was empty.

He hid his torn blazer in the bottom of the wardrobe, changed into rugby shirt and jeans. Tearing a page from a muddy English jotter, he scribbled a note and sat it on the kitchen table.

Chapter Thirteen

"A party. Ah tried tae phone ye..."

The woman on the radio was recapping a headline about school-closures.

Danny re-tuned to Clyde FM and lowered the volume. "At Jordan's?" That afternoon circled in his head. He glanced to the figure at the ironing-board.

Bruised features twisted in concentration. "Ye don't need tae come." Cuffs pressed.

Danny blinked. "I want to." He watched the process, registering the garment. "Is it...formal?"

Bottom lip chewed. "Naw..." Nail-bitten fingers deftly spread out a collar, applied the iron one final time then tore off the Nike warm-up top and slipped arms into the shirt. "...ah've jist bin dyin' fur the chance tae wear this."

Bare legs slipped past him to the mirrored wardrobe. Danny tried not to look at the yellow-purple patch of skin which taunted him from beneath a flapping section of unbuttoned green linen.

Kel plucked a dark-covered hanger from inside, hung it over the back of the mirrored door. Non-existent creases brushed from sleeve with a pale palm. "John Rocha, this is. Four sleeve-buttons..." Kel sat on the bed, dragging off warm-up pants and pulling on socks. "Ye should see the way it drapes..."

A socked and shirted figure edged past him, carefully easing suit trousers from under a jacket.

The bedroom was too small for both of them and the ironing-board. Danny sat back down on the bed. He stared at the dressing figure.

The John Rocha wasn't black – more a really dark green. Kel's red hair curled over the narrow collar. Danny knew he should say something about what happened at...

"See whit ah mean?" The mirrored door closed. The figure took a step back. Jacket unbuttoned, image scrutinised. Jacket unbuttoned, image re-scrutinised.

Danny watched the reflection do the same.

Nail bitten fingers finally shoved into pockets. Weight thrust onto one leg. "See whit ah mean..." A little sway. "Eh?"

Danny gazed at a reflected Kel. What had happened that afternoon didn't matter. "What's it made of?"

The face in the mirror paused, mid self-scrutiny. "Whit?"

Danny's eyes roved away from the bruises. "The fabric?"

One hand from pocket, left side of jacket opening. Green eyes peering. "Fifty-five purcent viscose, forty purcent polyester, five purcent silk. Dry Clean ainly..."

"It'll be the viscose."

In the mirror, one ginger slug raised. "No' the silk?"

Danny shook his head. "My mum's got a viscose blouse – it hangs really well too." The reflection turned. He stared from slope shoulders to his own jeans and rugby shirt.

"Ah..." Sounds of wardrobe-rummaging. "...but silk'll go' wi' it okay?"

A narrow, sludgy-green tie dangled in front of his face. Danny fingered rough, slightly nobbly fabric. "That'll go great." He levered himself off the bed.

Kel was fastening the shirt's top button, the knobbly tie slung around his neck.

"You sure I'm okay like..." Danny peered down at a spot of grease on his jeans. "...this?"

"Ye don't need tae come.." Fingers flipping thin over thick end. The scab at the corner of the full mouth had half-fallen off.

Danny examined new, still-slightly-bloody skin: after the fight with Frank, there wasn't a mark on him.

"Got something for ye..." Fingers paused, mid tie-knotting. The voice was different, softer. "...haud oan." Kel dived under the bed, emerging with a long, white object.

Nail-bitten fingers poked the envelope towards him.

Danny stared.

Self-conscious laugh. "Ah didney nick it! There's a receipt aroon' somewhere if ye wanna check."

Danny took the envelope. It felt light, empty.

Nudge. "Go oan – open it."

Danny tore, tipped the white rectangle upwards. A slim,

silver-coloured chain poured onto his palm. Low voice in his ear:

"Ah ken ye dinny like flashy-stuff..."

Delicate links flowed like water across his hand.

"...an' silver's sorta...unnerstated."

The gesture drenched him in a warm glow.

A gnawed nail was pointing to a tiny link. "Really subtle – that's where it opens..."

Danny's brain was back in Mr Cooper's office with Mr Cooper's assumptions.

Suddenly uncertain. "Ah can take it back, change it fur somethin' else if ye...?"

"No, it's..." He looked from palm to worried green eyes. "...it's...thanks – I really like it."

The bruised face creased with relief. "Gonny put it oan, then?"

He'd never take it off. Carefully undoing the tiny catch, he clasped ends around his neck, lowering his head and allowing nail-bitten fingers to re-secure the chain.

They both stared in the mirrored door. Danny watched the way the slender links shone dully against his skin. It didn't go with the rugby-top.

Bitten fingers tucked the chain beneath stripes. "It's that fine, ye can wear it underneath stuff an' nae-wan'll see..."

A frown hovered above his mouth. Danny sighed. No-one...like Gibby, like Big Frank, like...

The chain brushed his collarbones. He could smell the newness of the John Rocha, and beneath that, the sweet-sour scent of Kel's body. Danny reached up, sinking his fingers into a dangling hank of red hair. He pushed it back from reflected-Kel's bruised face.

A flinch. The reflection moved away.

Danny stiffened, fingers curling around nothing. "Thanks..." He listened to the sounds of an ironing-board dismantled. In the mirror, a suited-figure darted around in the background. The chain was cool against hot skin. "So who else is going to the party?" He turned.

Kel was sitting on the bed, pulling on a pair of highly-polished shoes. "Jist us an' Jordan – mebbe Maxie."

155

Blending into the background, in a room full of people was one thing: being the only one in jeans – Jordan wasn't the jeans type, and Danny doubted they made denims in Maxie's size – when there were only four, was something else. "I can't go like this..."

Snort. "Jordan's no' gonny care whit ye're wearin'!" Red head raised from lace-tying.

Danny stared at an expression he couldn't read.

Kel stood up, brushing more imaginary dust from the John Rocha. "Ye wanna change yer mind, it's nae sweat." Voice low, studiously casual. "Ah'll pass yer...regrets on tae Jordan."

Danny's groin tightened...

Jordan.

Jordan Burns.

...as did his stomach.

Two days ago. JB's. Cool brown eyes staring at him. Appraising him. Smiling at him. The tightening in his jeans increased, matched by a stomach-flip.

"Ah'll tell him ye had...hamework the night, an' ye couldn't..."

"I want to come." Danny stared at Kel.

Green eyes narrowing. "Ye sure?"

Danny nodded. The carpet tossed itself into a brain cluttered with silver chains and eye-pads. He shoved it into a dark corner, with the bruises.

Sigh of resignation. "Okay..."

Danny's mind was skipping ahead. "Jordan gives...lots of parties?"

Kel was back at the mirror, frowning at his hair. "'Pends whit ye mean by a lot." Hair finger-combed, frown increasing. "Weeks go by – nothin'. Then he'll feel...sociable, three nights in a row." Sigh. Hand through hair a final time. Then another sigh. "You definitely sure ye wanna come?"

The thought came from nowhere. Danny's face flushed up. "Don't you want me there?" He stared over a dark-green shoulder into green eyes, looking for more green.

Kel moved away from the mirror. Shrug. "Makes nae

156

difference tae me if ye come or no'..."

He frowned at the shrug. "We're in this...together, right?"

Frown. "Aye, ah suppose..."

Danny laughed, pushed the suited figure backwards.

"Oi! Mind the...!"

Then they were rolling on the bed and Kel was grumbling about creases and Danny could feel the slender silver chain flop and shimmer against one nipple as he ground his face against a faintly-rough neck.

The phone rang.

Kel heaved. Sighed.

Flipped onto his back, Danny smiled up. "That'll be the coach and horsemen to check the address!"

Snigger. "Well, lemme answer it, Cinderella..."

A hand mock-slapped his cheek. Kel bounded towards the door.

Danny leant back, staring at the ceiling and thinking about Jordan Burns. From downstairs:

"Aye?" Off-hand.

Parties...with Jordan Burns.

Talking...with Jordan Burns...

...crossing Jordan Burns. A hot shiver rippled over his scalp.

"Aye, Michael Kelston lives here..." Less off-hand. "Who wants tae ken?" A million miles from off-hand.

Jordan vanished. Danny leapt from the bed and ran downstairs. In the hall, he stared at the phone and the nail-bitten fingers which clenched around the receiver. Panic-stricken green eyes answered the unspoken question.

His mind was blank. Hand on automatic pilot, he grabbed the receiver and held it between his and another ear. Unwanted identification seeped from the instrument:

"Stewart Street Police..."

The words filled his head, superimposed over Mr Cooper's threat from earlier.

"...we've got an Archie Kelston here, wants Michael Kelston to come an' get him..." Weary sigh. "... that your dad, son?"

Danny slumped against the wall. Relief unblanked his mind and made room for irritation.

"Aye..." Wearier words from a still-healing mouth. "...how bad is he?"

Laugh. "I've seen him worse."

Danny tried to catch Kel's eye.

Green focused on the phone's push-buttons. "Ah'll be up..." A ragged fingernail traced a circle of dust on the 'monitor' button. "...soon as ah can."

"He'll be in Reception."

Kel replaced the receiver.

Danny frowned. "You should have told them to keep him!"

Index-finger gnawed. "Disney like wee spaces. Goes daft in a cell – ah gotta go." Kel walked back into the bedroom, grabbed the warm-up suit from the floor and began to rifle through the pockets. "Fuck, why did he pick the night tae git lifted?"

Danny sighed, grabbed his own jacket from a chair and struggled into it.

"If you jist wanna go on..." Kel was examining a handful of coins. "...ah'll meet ye at Jordan's."

"We can get a taxi from the police-station, drop your... dad off here, then go straight to...wherever Jordan lives."

Eyes raised from palm.

He'd walked away, the last time...

Danny managed a shrug.

...and the idea of arriving alone at Jordan's party made the tightening in his stomach overwhelm the tightening in his groin.

Kel stared, blinked. Then shrugged back. Ten minutes later four-button sleeves were waving in front of taxis at the bottom of Roystonhill.

"Aw' Michael..." The large, tousle-haired man in a greasy More-Store windbreaker lurched up from the row of plastic seats and staggered towards them. "...kent ye widney let me doon, son." Gruff, slurring words.

Danny stepped back. He tried to forget this was a police-station.

158

One large arm thrown around long-suffering, John Rocha-clad shoulders. "This is ma boay..." Words hurled at a uniformed figure behind a plexi-glass screen. "...came aw' the way doon here, jist tae get his dad, eh Michael?" Greasy windbreaker sleeve tightening in mock arm-lock. "He's a guid boay, ma Michael..."

"Aye, he is that, Erchie." Chuckle from behind plexi-glass. Sympathetic glance from Kel to Danny and back again.

Danny moved quickly to the door, holding it open as Kel half-led, half-dragged the large man towards it.

Archie Kelston was at least six-four. Kel fitted beneath one arm, a crutch in designer green. A tattooed hand saluted the uniform behind the protective screen, nodding and smiling to other people then stopped to pat someone's dog on the head.

Danny gripped the side of the door.

Kel haul-pushed his father through.

"Sorry tae be so much trouble, son..." One side of the greasy windbreaker patted. "...loast aw' ma money..." Gruff-whine. "...fuckin' dug had three wooden legs..."

Reassuring. "'Sokay, dad..." Wearily urgent. "Geeze a haun, eh?"

Danny's skin crawled. He closed the door behind the staggering twosome, then ducked under a limp, flailing arm and slung his own around a damp-feeling waist. Kel's father weighed a ton. The sickly smell of vomit and a meaty odour filled his nostrils. He could feel muscle through the thin, cheap fabric. Slowly, they manipulated the mumbling, whining giant down the steps and out of the car park:

"This yer pal, Michael?"

"Aye, dad..."

"Aw', ye brought yer pal – tha's nice."

A yeasty wheeze in his ear:

"Whi's your name, son?"

"C'mon, dad..." A red head flicked around the back of a bull neck. "See if there's ony taxis."

Danny tried to ease away.

"Naw, don't go, son..." A greasy arm tightened around his shoulder. "Whi's yer name?" More whining.

"C'mon, dad...try tae move a bit, eh?"

The stench of sick and sweat rose in waves. "Danny." He wrenched himself free, darting out into the road and scanning.

No taxis.

No cars at all.

Slurring behind. "Danny...'sa nice name, Danny..."

He shoved hands into pockets, willing a taxi to appear. Palms were greasy against curled fingers.

A group of uniformed figures emerged from a side entrance.

Palms drenched. Danny slunk back to where Archie Kelston now sat on the edge of the pavement, head in hands.

Kel stood over him, griping a handful of windbreaker. Bitten-fingers hauled uselessly. The John Rocha unfashionably rumpled. "C'mon, dad...please?" Weary tone tinged with panic.

Danny joined the huddle. He stared at a damp patch between splayed, tree-like legs and listened to the tramp of regulation-issue shoes in the other direction.

Kel hauled a second time. "Come on!" Less-patient.

Pulling away. "Ah, ye're a guid boay, Michael...aw' this way tae git me...an' Danny tae..." Blearing eyes unfocused up at him.

Then Danny met other greener eyes. Together, they re-gripped elbows and heaved.

"Ah'm sorry, boays..."

Boneless legs dangled, feet trailed on tarmac as they half-carried a still-apologising Archie Kelston down towards the intersection with Cowcaddens Road.

The apologies only stopped when he passed out in the taxi.

Danny sat on the pull-down seat, back to the driver.

A tousled head lolled against the shoulder of the John Rocha. Kel's arm was still around a greasy back. Green eyes were focused out of the window.

The taxi hit a pothole.

A snore, snorting into a choking sound.

Green eyes flicked back. A Rocha-clad arm moved slightly, then tightened.

The choking sound reverted to a snore.

Green eyes refocused on the window and Townhead Interchange.

Danny sighed. Archie Kelston looked nothing like Kel – his mum must have had red hair. Eyes moved to a pair of thick wrists, which poked from frayed, elasticated cuffs. Bitten nails curled limply above home-tattooed knuckles. He concentrated on India Ink swirls and tried not to think about the bruises on the pale face inches away.

Then the taxi was swerving down into Royston Road and Kel was fumbling for change.

Danny sat in the bedroom. He fingered the slender chain and scanned a damp-smelling late edition *Times* Kel had pulled from the back pocket of his father's jeans. He listened to distant thumps and bumps...

...different thumps and bumps: sounds of son undressing father.

Grainy letters blurred in front of him. Danny closed his eyes, didn't like what he saw, then opened and focused them on a series of headlines.

None featured carpets.

None featured guns...

...the bus-stop story hadn't been re-run. He closed and folded the newspaper, placing it on the bedside table. Danny pushed his mind onwards.

Kel had said seven.

His watch said half-past.

His tightening stomach said a number of things he didn't understand...

Jordan. Partying with Jordan.

...then something he did. Danny turned his head, stared into the wardrobe's mirrored door.

Someone else looked back at him.

Someone who had caused a death then got rid of the body.

Someone who had sat here and done nothing while a man with bitten fingernails had beat the fuck out of the most important person in his life.

He frowned...

...someone who was going to a party. His stomach lurched.

With Jordan Burns.

At Jordan Burn's house.

With Kel.

Danny stared at the reflection, recognising fragments of himself. Voice from the doorway:

"Okay?"

Danny turned from the mirrored door.

One green eye attempted a wink. "Try an' drag yersel away – ye luck lovely!"

Danny laughed. "You look...okay too." It was true.

One hand brushed non-existent creases from a dark green sleeve. "Ye get whit ye pay fur." Both hands into pockets. "Come oan, then..." Red head nodding towards the front door.

Danny's stomach gave a final lurch.

Then Kel was switching out the light and grabbing keys.

Chapter Fourteen

He was still taking in the marbled hall when Maxie opened another door.

Kel strode into the room, hands thrust into pockets. "Hi Jordan. Sorry we're a bit..."

"Hello Kel. Like the suit. Don't recognise it."

The rich voice tore his eyes from marbled walls. Danny stared at Jordan.

Jordan stared back. Something like a smile played around his lips. Something less than a smile shone in clear brown eyes.

Danny's groin tightened. He looked past expensively-cut hair to more shelves lines with books.

"Aw', this auld thing?" Pleasure, badly-hidden. "Goat it fur court, ages ago..." Imaginary creases smoothed from thighs.

Rich laugh. "That explains it. Hello again, Danny..."

The voice was closer now.

"...glad you could make it."

The words rumbled in his ears, competing with the sound of his heartbeat. Danny tried to think of something to say. He remembered the last time he'd been unable to speak – and the results.

Kel rushed in to fill the void. "Okay if ah show Danny round?"

"If Danny wants the guided tour..."

Every time Jordan used his name, something clutched at his balls.

"...go ahead. I've got a couple of calls to make."

Then nail-bitten fingers were on his sleeve and his trainers were squeaking across a shiny wooden floor. "...an' this is the games-room!"

Several leather couches lined panelled walls. A full-size snooker-table dominated the low-lit space.

Kel perched on the edge, racking and unracking a flat pyramid of coloured balls.

"Notch place, eh?"

Danny reached over, fingering soft green baize. The house was a blur of subtle furnishings and enthusiastic adjectives. "Jordan lives here...on his own?" The tip of his finger moved slowly over the matt fabric.

The clacking of racking close by. "Dunno – ah think Maxie stays sometimes, but ah'm no' sure."

He looked up from the table. Gaze glossed dark panelling and heavy red velvet curtains, skidding onto a door in the far wall. "What's through there?"

"That's the...other games-room." A last clack. Then: 'C'mon...'" Shiny shoes slapped across shinier wood.

Danny's heart was back with the snooker-balls.

White...and green.

Plants.

Framed by a low jungle of foliage, a jacuzzi bubbled violently in one corner, next to a toilet and a shower. In another, something half way between a bed and a raised platform loomed at him. A clothes-rail clanked with empty hangers. Beside it, a giant water dispenser, like they had in offices. Next to that, a table holding a bottle of gin and a tray of glasses.

And tiles. Everywhere. On the walls, on the floor. The room was half-bathroom, half-hotel-foyer.

Low light lowered further, then brightened only to sink back into artificial dusk. "Dimmer switches an' aw' – fur the plants."

The sound of a door closing. He continued to inspect the room.

"Wanna see the toys?"

His head flicked up.

Kel had opened a small white metal cupboard and was now crouching in front of it. "Knobs R Us, eh?"

He walked over, stared at a row of vaguely-penis-shapes.

Nail-bitten fingers grabbed one less vaguely-shaped, fiddled with an attached control.

Soft buzzing.

Danny stepped back.

164

The vibrating shape held against palm. "Want a go?" The object extended.

Danny backed away. "No, it's okay..." His eyes focused past a pink, faintly shuddering shaft to other shelves. He recognised cans and tubes of expensive lubricant from the wee shop in Virginia Street. Other smaller bottles.

The buzzing stopped. Kel picked up one of the cans, fiddled with the cap. "Ah'm allergic tae this wan – 'member that rash ah had, at the end o' the summer?"

Danny was still staring at the smaller bottles. Massage oil? His gaze registered.

Disapproving snort. A bottle grabbed, cap twisted off. "These shouldney be here – ah telt Maxie they go aff if ye dinny keep'em in the fridge."

A sharp, chemically smell seeped into his nostrils...

Kel wafted the open bottle under his nose.

...then hit his brain. Danny's head spun. His heart developed wheels and raced off. A rosy glow travelled down over his face and exploded in his groin. He swayed. A steadying arm draped his shoulder.

"Beats the pants aff lighter-fuel, but it ainly lasts a coupla seconds." Cap replaced.

The surge of lust receded. Danny moved away from the arm. Kel closed the white metal door before he had a chance to examine the objects on the bottom shelf. "So...what happens now?"

Slope-shoulder shrug. "Want somethin' tae eat? There's eyeways pizzas an' stuff in the kitchen."

Fumes evaporated around him. Reality seeped back. Danny shook his head, clearing the last uncertainty from his brain.

"A drink?" Nod towards the water-container and the gin.

His throat was a desert. Liquid wouldn't help.

Kel was loosening his tie. "Ye gotta try this..." Jacket carefully eased from shoulders, then draped onto one of the wooden hangers. Red head nodded to the bubbling in the corner.

Danny tried to swallow. "Jordan'll not mind?"

165

"Naw – eyeways makes me wash first anyway." Tie-untied, shirt following suit-jacket. Off-white skin and a light green bruise appear from under darker green.

He leant against a wall, cheek pressed against the tiled surface.

Kel carefully looped trousers over the hanger's smooth bar. From beneath blue jockeys, a tuft of ginger hair poked free. Then a slender back was leaning across bubbling water, nail-bitten fingers fiddling with where taps should be.

Frothing water frothed more vigorously.

Kel grabbed Danny's shoulder and wriggled free of the blue jockeys. Eyes on a still-fully-dressed body. "C'mon, ye'll love it!" Arms folded across skinny chest, hands thrust into pits.

Danny's gaze moved from the half-hard length of flesh between ginger dusted thighs.

Kel cocked his head. Waiting.

The sight made his stomach ache. The thought of him and Kel naked, with Jordan made it lurch.

Before the thought could move lower he was kicking off his trainers and avoiding a splash.

Warm, faintly chlorinated water frothed between his thighs, buffeting his balls.

Danny braced arms against the edge and hoisted himself higher. He glanced down at the slender, nipple-skimming chain. Kel had said it wouldn't tarnish, but he didn't want to get it wet just in case. Flicking silver-coloured metal upwards, Danny stared across a bubbling sea.

Lashed and lidded eyes aimed ceilingwards. Scraped back from the pale face, red hair hung like seaweed onto the tiles behind his head. Freckles bloomed up through discoloured skin. Lips parted in a sigh.

Danny noticed remnants of the scab at the side of Kel's mouth were softening in the heat. Fingers gripped the edge. Taking the weight on his elbows and arching his back, he lunged forward.

Feet connected with wet pit hair.

A low snigger.

Danny twined soft strands between his toes.

Kel wriggled, slipping lower into the water.

Danny gasped. A large foot surfaced inches from his face. He glanced back to the other side of the jacuzzi, blinking at the empty space. Then water erupted at his side and a heat-flushed face was close to his. Green eyes shone.

"Notch, eh?"

"Yeah, notch!"

Kel's skin was pinkish, like dye had leaked from his hair. Beneath the churning surface, legs entwined with his. A slim thigh replaced the water-jet at his balls. Beyond waves and ripples, he watched his hard-on bob and shudder against a softer length of flesh.

A wet skull leant against his.

Danny pressed back with his forehead, still staring downwards. "Kel?"

"Mmm?" Through the froth, four nail-bitten fingers abstractedly fondled the half-hard length.

"You brought...anyone else, here?"

"Oh, aye..." Amused snort. "...Big Frank an' Gibby ur eyeways beggin' me tae bring'em back!"

"Seriously." Danny stared at where their noses were almost touching. A brow crinkled, then pealed itself from his:

"You jokin'?" The hand not fondling between pale thighs was fingering the slender chain. Green eyes focused on the activity. "Think ah'd wanna bring onywan else?" Pause, mid-finger.

Danny was looking at Kel's hair, marvelling at the way it shone almost black. He thought about this room, the toys, the bed...then back before he'd met Kel...

'... bin workin' wi' Jordan fur almost a year...'

"I don't know what to think, but..."

"Well, ah widney wanna bring onywan else – an' even if ah did, it wouldney matter..." Head raised.

Green met blue. Water babbled in Danny's ears.

"...cos ah didney invite ye..." Green moved from blue. Kel's eyes were ceilingwards again, pale shoulders

167

lounging back against the edge of the jacuzzi. The fingers continued to play with the silver-coloured chain. "...Jordan did."

The name did the weird thing to his stomach again. Eyes moved from hair to frowning mouth.

The frown cracked into a grin. Dark pupils peered up at him from beneath half-lowered ginger lashes.

Danny grinned back. The babbling water faded away and it was just Kel, fiddling with the chain...

...another hand gripped his shoulder and pushed him downwards.

Water poured into his mouth. Danny shut it before the shriek became a gurgle. His head bumped softly against white plastic. He grabbed for a snaking limb. It slithered away. A water-jet blasted his chest, another forcing air into his face. He felt Kel behind him, legs shadowing legs.

Then arms were under his. Knees hit the bottom of the jacuzzi. Danny was laughing when his head broke the surface.

The laugh faltered. Kel's hands were slack on his against his chest.

He stared at a pair of hairy, well-muscled legs, then up over a loosely tied, white-towelling dressing-gown to the tanned, handsome face.

It smiled. "You look like a pair of water sprites." A ringed hand held out a fluffy towel. Rich brown eyes bored into his.

Danny stared down at foaming water. Fingers left his chest. He was aware of Kel standing up behind:

"Thanks, Jordan!"

Splashing around him. The sounds of drying. And talking:

"Maxie's left the poppers in the cupboard, Jordan – want me tae...?"

"Enjoying yourself, Danny?"

His stomach churned faster than the water around his nipples. He nodded.

Jordan perched on the side of the jacuzzi, smiling.

Danny dragged his eyes from the handsome face to the

gap in the white towelling dressing-gown. And the swollen length of untanned flesh which lay parallel to a well-muscled thigh.

Photographs from *Honcho* floated before his eyes.

Unbitten fingers were slipping beneath the slender chain. "Very nice..."

Jordan's nails were smooth against his chest.

"...platinum?" The fingers lingered.

Snort in the background. "Jist silver."

The fingers inched along tiny links towards his right nipple.

Danny watched them. Each touch sent jolts along his shaft.

"It's nice, all the same – suits you..." The fingers removed, dried on another fluffy towel.

Something half-relief, half-disappointment replaced the jolts. Danny lowered his eyes to the gap in the towelling dressing-gown. It had closed. Kel was talking again:

"Did ye get those...calls made, Jordan?"

"You know I don't talk business in the games-room, Kel."

Awkwardly apologetic. "Aye, sorry – ah forgot."

Sceptical laugh. "Like you forget anything."

The change of tone sliced through the atmosphere. Danny's eyes shot from the lump in the towelling dressing-gown.

Back in the office at JB's...

...and outside the Outreach Unit.

Something about the voice tripped the early-warning system in the depths of his mind. "Can I have a towel, please?" He stood up.

Expensively cut head swivelling right. Brown eyes swept over his dripping body.

Then a clump of wet fabric hit him in the face. Danny gasped. The soggy towel broke the moment. He dragged his head free.

A snigger from a naked figure, lounging on the half-bed thing.

Before Danny could throw it back warm hands had

169

removed the wet towel from his and were draping a warmer towelling dressing-gown around him.

Jordan smiled, running palms over Danny's shoulders.

He stared at the tanned chest. Thick hair lapped around large nipples. His own tingled.

"Okay?" The voice was back to normal. False alarm.

Hands patted his arms, just above the elbow. Danny looked up. "Yes – thanks." The brown eyes were staring at him.

Heat-slackened balls tightened. Danny looked down, away from the eyes.

Jordan's knob was curving out towards him from a thicker bush of crinkly back hair.

Danny shivered, dipped his eyes to the tiled floor. Soft fabric brushed against his groin and moved the tingling lower.

Ringed fingers loosely tied the dressing-gown cord. "Good." The rich voice was very close.

Mintiness in his nostrils.

Then ringed fingers were under his chin, gently raising his eyes from the floor.

Danny stared at the tip of Jordan's nose. He examined the tiny hair follicles on the smooth upper-lip, then past the handsome face to the water-dispenser.

Kel was watching. One hand caressed a now-completely-hard length of flesh.

His chest tightened. He caught one green eye.

It darted away.

A stroke beneath his chin reclaimed his attention. Danny looked back at the handsome face.

Jordan's mouth was smiling. The brown eyes were doing something else.

His face flushed scarlet. Danny stared into dark brown iris and watched it eclipsed by black.

A hand moved down his back, pressing white-towelling against his skin and settling at the base of his spine.

The eyes were hypnotising, pulling him in.

"Assume the position!"

The words made no sense. The tone made his heart

170

pound. Air fled from his lungs. Danny's knees were water.
His face was fire. His knob was another, harder element.
From the other side of the room:

"Aye, Jordan!"

A hand lightly patted his arse. Disappointment flared in
Danny's groin and he was staring at the long muscles of
hairy thighs as Jordan strode towards the bed-thing.

The jacuzzi bubbled on, oblivious.

Danny focused on a patch of uneven grouting, high on
the far wall. He hugged himself.

Over the bubbling, sounds. Flesh-on-flesh sounds...

Like a slow-motion sport. Like action-play.

...flesh-in-flesh sounds dragged his eyes back to the bed-
thing.

Kel. On his knees. Elbows braced. Hands supporting
head. Bitten fingernails poking up through lank strands of
damp hair.

Jordan. Also on his knees. Between Kel's thighs. The
fingers of one ringed hand wrenching a red head upwards.
The other hand braced against a quivering white hip.

Cold tile seeped through the back of the towelling
dressing gown. Danny examined the thick tufts of knuckle
hair. The skin beneath whitened each time Jordan pulled
skinny hips back into his groin. Eyes moved to the tanned
face.

Pin-prick pupils telescoping. No smile.

No frown.

Something between a sneer and a perpetually-
postponed curse played around the thin lips.

Danny stared lower.

Dense chest-hair shone, sweat-soaked. A ridge of muscle
flexed...

The slap of body-contact. A yelp.

...then relaxed as tanned hips pulled back.

His stomach lurched. The yelp rang in his ears, over the
wet, rasping scrunch of Jordan's hairy groin against Kel's
arse.

Danny concentrated on the sound of frothing water and

171

stared back at the line of mortar.

The light was too bright.

He blinked, refocused. Grouting swam, a matt white line spilling over onto blinding white tile. His eyes stung.

He'd tried closing them.

That was worse. His mind's eye replayed fifteen minutes earlier.

Kel sitting on the edge of the bed, unwrapping a condom.

Jordan, inches in front, staring down.

Kel leaning forward, easing the condom over Jordan's knob while Jordan watched. And Danny watched.

Jordan gripping Kel's chin, forcing his head up and making him watch too.

Kel's face, bruised and scarlet. Kel's eyes darting everywhere and nowhere. Kel's knob stiffening further before Danny's eyes as nail-bitten, practiced fingers dragged a layer of latex down to meet Jordan's big balls. Then:

"Cunt!"

The word made the hair on his arms stand on end. Danny hugged himself more tightly. The towelling dressing gown itched against his skin.

"Fuckin' cunt!" The polished accent gone.

Danny's eyes released the uneven grouting. He squinted through blurring vision.

Jordan thrust back into Kel, hauling the red head further upwards.

A yelp. Yelp-sob.

Danny stared at parallel scalp-furrows between clumps of gripped hair.

Then two tanned hands gripped white hips.

A flash of bruised, wet skin. Then Kel's face disappeared beneath a veil of sopping scarlet.

His chest hurt. Stinging eyes moved from the re-cradled head down under Kel's stomach.

A quivering length of hard flesh bucked and jumped each time Jordan thrust forward.

"Cunt – ye're jist a...?"

172

"Cunt!" The word screamed bed-wards.

Danny's legs gave way. He slid down tiles.

Flesh-on-flesh.

Flesh-in-flesh.

Terror gripped at his guts and twisted them.

Cunt...

...bum-boy.

The tanned, hairy body was moving faster, now. Yelps less audible, wet formless mumblings over fleshy slaps.

Danny stared at Jordan.

Tanned arms gleamed in bright light. Sinew rippled across chest, making the hair ruffle. Each time Jordan's latexed knob slammed between Kel's arse-cheeks, he got bigger...

...and Kel seemed to shrink...

...a fetal figure trying to merge with sofa-cushions.

Threads of sound and vision jumbled in his ears, knotting together. Danny's eyes flicked between the broad chest and Kel's limp, curled form.

He caught glimpses of the thick shiny knob, then snatches of Kel's ginger pubes beneath a flexing, equally hard length.

Jordan's tanned stomach was curved against Kel's arse, like Kel was growing out of Jordan, like they were the...

...same.

Whimpering sounds rose up from the bed.

"Shut it, cunt!"

Danny flinched.

The whimpered sank to sharp, staccato sighs.

He wanted to run...stay...run...

...hands balled into fists, nails biting in. Then the flesh-noises were drowned by the thump of his heart. Danny looked down between his own splayed legs.

Muted sighs from the bed sent jolts into his stiff knob. The sight hurt his eyes.

A strangled sigh from the bed. Danny screwed them shut...

...and the film in his head was speeding on and his knob was buried in Kel and Kel was moaning and whimpering and tight around him and Danny was thrusting hard, hips moving like Jordan's hips, mouth twisting like Jordan's mouth and...

Something beeped against his calf. Danny's eyes shot open.

Inches away, Jordan wrenched a hand from Kel's shoulder.

Danny stared at four finger-shaped bruises. The beeping continued against his thigh.

Fingers snapping. "The phone, Danny – give me the mobile." Jordan leant over the pale mounds of Kel's arse.

A shaking hand plunged into a towelling pocket. Fingers contacted with vibration. Danny held out the slim rectangle.

One tanned hand grabbed it. The fingers of the other fumbled between tanned stomach and pale arse. Jordan held the condom in place, jerked his knob out of Kel.

A farting sound.

Pale shape slumping sideways, knees curled up to chest.

Mild irritation. "What is it, Maxwell?" Accent back. "I told you I didn't..." Pause.

Danny's eyes flicked between the ball-shaped form on the bed and the way Jordan's knob bounced as he turned away.

"...okay, hold on." Turning back. Brown eyes staring. Pulling off the condom one-handed. Tossing it onto the bed.

Danny flinched, wriggled out of the dressing-gown.

Brown eyes between his legs. Vaguely-amused smile.

He held out the dressing-gown then sat down on the bed and tried to cross his legs over his hard knob.

Less-vaguely amused. "Back in a second..." Arms into towelling sleeves.

Danny met the brown eyes, held them.

One narrowed in surprise. Then Jordan reached over, ruffled Danny's hair before walking towards the door.

It closed softly.

Snuffling sounds seeped into his ears.

174

Chapter Fifteen

A pale pink comma on a paler hip.

Danny knelt behind the curled shape and pealed off the condom. A flinch beneath his fingers. Words thrown at knees:

"So now ye ken..." Slow fury.

The johnny stuck to his fingers. He wiped his hand on the bed.

Low words aimed at the mattress. "Ma auld man's right!"

Danny leant over the uncurling shape to a tangled mess of hair. "Kel, it..."

"Ah'm his..." The curved shape twisted round. "...bumboay!" The bruised face was a patchwork of expressions. "Jist somethin' fur Jordan tae come in!"

Danny looked from scarlet skin to Kel's slumping knob. A still-molten white globule leaked from the head.

The look registered. "Whit dae ye think o' me noo, eh?" Barely restrained fury lowered the voice half an octave.

Danny's eyes flicked back. He could smell spunk and sweat and the rubbery odour of the condom.

"Ye hate me, don't ye?" Index-finger between crusted lips. "Fuck, ah hate me!"

His chest was a tightening web of muscles he didn't know he had. His brain seethed with tangled, alien thoughts. Danny stared from lowered eyelids over a tear-streaked face.

A thin trickle of blood from a gnawed cuticle wound its way down the index finger.

His hand hovered in mid air, then landed on a shaking shoulder.

It flinched. "Lea' me alain!"

Tuesday night careered back and hit him in the face. Something tore itself free from the tangle in his brain. Danny let his hand stay where it was. "I don't hate you – why should I hate you?"

Barely audible. "Whit's the difference between me an'

that?" Red-headed nod to the corner.

Danny blinked, following the eyes. A shiver beneath his palm.

Sob-snort. "Jordan's toilet disney follow him aroon', efter he's used it!"

The memory of Jordan inside Kel kicked him in the stomach. His softening knob twitched. Pity, fear and anger shrank to nothing in the face of feelings which had no names. "It doesn't matter." Beneath his palm, the shoulder was clammy.

"Aye it dis..."

"No it doesn't."

"Aye it dis! How can ye stand tae touch me?"

Beneath his palm, the shoulder was shivering. Something in his stomach was hurting worse than the kick did. Danny reached behind, hauling at the surface of the bed. Whatever was covering it refused to come loose. He frowned. "I don't care." He stared at the crown of a ginger head and plucked uselessly at the bed-covering. "I don't care what you are. I don't care what Jordan thinks you are. I don't care what...your father thinks you are." It was lies...more lies: he cared because Kel cared. He cared because...

A pale, bruised face slowly raised itself. Kel's eyes were red-rimmed and huge. Danny stared into tiny black pupils. They ripped off his skin and raked at the flesh beneath.

"Ye really don't, dae ye?"

Danny tried to make sense of the question.

"At school...everywan callin' ye a poof..." Snub-nose rubbed on back of hand. "Christ, day in day oot! Gibby, Big Frank an' the resta them – that's how ye get through it, isn't it? Ye really don't...care whit onywan thinks."

Danny winced.

Next year.

Edinburgh.

New city. New life. New people – who wouldn't care one way or the other.

It was easy for him.

Kel broke the gaze a second before he did. A shrug. Then knee-hugging.

Danny's hand slipped from the clammy shoulder to a damp leg.

So many questions answered.

So many others not even asked.

Legs rubber eased themselves off the bed. Danny padded across cold tile to a pile of towels. Throwing one over his shoulder, he paused at the dispenser-thing and filled a glass. He padded back to the bed.

Kel drank the water, wiped his nose on the towel. Bleeding fingers reached out, lightly flicking the silver-coloured chain. "Ye sure ye really like it?"

"I'm wearing it, amn't I!" Danny tried for a grin and got nowhere near.

Sniff-laugh.

He tucked his feet under himself and pushed a hank of hair back from the pale face.

No flinch.

He looked from still-swollen eyes to the corner of the room and back again. "How long's...he liable to be?"

The sound of a door opening half-answered the question. Maxie's huge form reduced the room to dolls' house size. One eye met Danny's...

He blinked.

...the other focused blindly above his head.

Maxie turned towards the small metal cupboard. Large knees bending. Bones cracking. Cupboard doors opened. One eye peering inside. One hand lifting the three small bottles. Then standing.

Danny's heart thumped.

Then turning. "Jordan's gonny be a wee while – yon Lennox's finally put in an appearance..." One bottle held out. "You pair want wanna these left?"

"Mister Lennox?" Breathy voice at his side.

Not dead...

Danny's heart had stopped, squashed by something heavy and immovable on his chest.

Not dead...

"Aye – widney tell me onythin'..." Hoarse cough-laugh. "Wouldney even tell Jordan onythin', oan the phone.

Insisted he had tae see him, in person. He's oan his way up..." Slow head-shake. "Ah telt Jordan that closet-case fae Edinburgh'd be trouble." Bottle extended. "You boays want wanna these left or no'?"

"Naw..."

Not dead...

Danny could hear the panic in Kel's voice.

"...we'll huv another shot o' the jacuzzi, okay?"

Huge-shoulder shrug. "Whitever." Then turning. The door closing.

Not dead...

...the snib clicked into the catch.

Danny leapt towards his clothes. Sounds of hanger-clanking told him Kel was doing the same. A shaking hiss:

"How come he isney...?"

"You must have just...grazed him." Danny shoved a foot through a leg-hole.

"But there wis so much blood!"

"Scalp wounds bleed like mad." Danny stuck another foot into underpants. The jockeys were back-to-front. He pulled them off and started again.

"So where's he bin fur the past...?"

"I don't know! I don't care! Does it matter?" Danny hauled a rugby shirt over his head and struggled into jeans. His brain was racing so fast he had to snatch at thoughts before they tore past him. "He's coming here!" The zip stuck. He yanked at it and heard ripping. Then rigid fingers were fastening the top button. Danny turned, searching for trainers.

Kel stood there in the John Rocha, one end of a green nobbly tie clutched between white-knuckled fingers. Full lips half-open. Wide eyes staring.

He grabbed the tie, shoved it into a John Rocha pocket. "Get your shoes..."

Wide eyes continued to stare.

Danny sank feet into his own, scanned for Kel's. Beside the bed, he spotted them. He kicked two polished objects towards the still-staring figure. Over the sound of bubbling water:

178

That's it, man." Slow words.

Danny raised eyes from laces which refused to knot.

Wide eyes stared past him to the closed door. "It's over." Slow words gathering speed. "When Jordan talks tae Lennox..." Words galloping. "...Lennox'll tell him everythin' an' when Jordan comes back..."

"We're not going to be here!" Danny gave up with the laces and grabbed a John Rocha-clad arm. It was limp in his grip:

"He'll come efter us..."

Danny hauled.

Kel had put down roots. The body swayed but bare feet didn't move. Words a blur. "...an' he'll find us an' he'll..."

"We'll...tell someone – he can't...hurt us if we tell someone what happened!" Danny hauled again.

Sniff-snort. "Then he'll definitely dae us – we've crossed him wance already! Nae-wan crosses Jordan an'..."

"Come on!" Heels braced against tiled floor, Danny hauled Kel towards the door. "We'll work-out the details later." The tiled room had no windows. He remembered thick red curtains in the other games-room. Before Kel could protest further Danny was gripping the handle and turning it slowly.

He stared at therma-sealed double-glazing. Disappointment damped the rich velvet between his fingers. His mind was full of warm stuffiness. Rapid breath breath behind erected the hair on the back of his neck. Details from the earlier tour crept into his brain. "Is there a back door?" Danny turned.

The down-lit pool table splashed green over a pale and purple face. "Aye, but it's miles away – in the kitchen."

Danny dragged his eyes from sickly skin to brass hinges in glossy panelling – the only sign in the seamless wood. "Do we have to pass the...where Jordan'll be?" Eyes flicking back.

Slow head-shake. "Naw, but Maxie'll..."

"C'mon..." He might, but the risk was better than standing here waiting for the inevitable. Danny's hands were still full of velvet. He reclosed the curtains, walked to the almost invisible door, then opened a crack and listened.

Nothing.

He widened the crack, reached behind. His hand flapped for a John Rocha sleeve...

...and found sweating fingers. They clutched at his wrist.

Then Kel was in front and they were edging down a carpeted corridor, hugging the wall.

Regrets buzzed in his brain over the sound of their feet. Danny focused on the back of a red head. Fingers tightened.

If they'd tried to revive Lennox...

Kel paused. Danny flattened himself against the wall. A red head poked past a corner, nodded onwards. They ran across the space. More wall-hugging.

...where had he been for the past two days? In the river? Inside the carpet...

Kel was slowing.

...sometimes, after a blow on the head, people lost short-term memory. Danny clutched at the hope.

It was dragged from his fingers.

Kel stopped.

Voices. One, two rooms away.

Danny's ears strained.

Jordan and...

...a weasly, east-coast accent. Kel tugged at his hand, pulling him across the hallway.

Danny glanced ahead to a lighted space. The side of a large fridge with a transparent door loomed at him. Words in his ears from one, two rooms away. Jordan's words:

"I hope this isn't some sort of joke." Cool.

"Ye see me laughin'?" Cooler.

"I see someone I haven't dealt with before who disappears and leaves me holding three kilos of heroin I'd rather not be holding, then reappears, two days later minus twenty K with some cock-and-bull story about one of my boys and a gun." Cold.

"Ah couldda fuckin' drowned!" Colder. "It was my twenty K, and..." Icy. "...those two wee bastards have..."

180

Then Danny was stumbling into the kitchen, wanting and not-wanting to hear more. His wrist was released. Eyes grazed a hob, marbled preparation-surfaces and a rack of cooking utensils.

In front, Kel tore at a double-locked door.

Twenty K...twenty K...the JCB rucksack...twenty K...

Danny tried to clear the voices from his mind. Seconds later a blast of air did it for him.

Seconds after that two sets of feet pounded on tarmac. An eternity passed before a taxi did.

The TV was on.

Kel paced in front of it. "Whit did we come back here fur? It's the first place Jordan'll..."

"Shush an' let me think!" His house was out of the question. In between the pacing, Danny stared at sections of *Crimewatch UK*. He fingered the slender chain around his neck. His brain wouldn't work. He tried to kick-start constructive thought with images of Maxie's glass eye and the process which had led to it.

The idea made a mockery of rational thought.

"Oh fuck!" Kel's voice leapt an octave. "This is a fuckin' nightmare! Whit we gonny dae? Whit we gonny...?"

"We go to the police." The shriek focused his mind.

A pause in the pacing. Then Kel was crouching. "Don't be daft – we canny."

Danny stared at the ashen face. "Yes, we can! We've not done anything wrong..." He knew it wasn't true, but there were degrees of wrong. "Think Lennox is going to press charges?" He waited for the words to sink in.

They didn't. "An' whit we gonny tell the polis, Mr Five Highers?" Scornful sniff.

Danny flinched. "Jordan's dealing drugs – you heard him yourself."

"Really?" A sneer of disbelief painted a ghost face.

Danny stared back at the screen. "There's...three kilos of heroin in his house at the moment. I think the police'll be more interested in that than..."

Another ghost face.

181

On the TV.

A smiling ghost face, above the collar of an Umbro warm-up top. Full lips moving at another figure whose face was blanked out. Low words:

"This cocky young man..."

Danny shot from the couch, grabbed the remote and aimed it. Too-loud tones filled his ears:

"...recently, paying for an unusual and highly-distinctive platinum chain at one of Glasgow's most expensive jewellers with money which was stolen in a wages-snatch at the Balerno branch of Asda in Edinburgh last month. The youth – aged between fourteen and nineteen, is five feet ten to six feet one inches tall, of slender build with distinctive shoulder-length red hair and freckles. He spoke with a broad Glasgow accent, and had several bruises and a cut lip, although these may, of course, have healed..."

Danny blinked.

The on-screen policewoman talked on. "The platinum chain is one of only three made by the jewellers. If you recognise this youth – if you have seen him or been offered such a chain – please contact the studio, or Lothian police on..."

The remote torn from his hand.

The screen was blank.

Danny spun round, brain reeling. Silence pounded between them. "What did you think you were doing?"

Kel was staring at the floor.

Fingers curled into fists. He yanked the chain from around his neck and hurled it at the crown of a lowered red head. "What the fuck did you think you were doing?"

A silver-coloured sliver collided with a rigid shoulder, hung there for a second then slid downwards. Kel continued to stare at the floor. The toe of a highly polished shoe nudged at a tuft of carpet.

Anger and frustration robbed him of further words. "Eh?" He wanted to understand.

The shoe continued to nudge.

"Kel!" He needed to understand.

A shrug.

182

The gesture was the last straw in a haystack he gave-up trying to search. Danny grabbed John Rocha-covered shoulders and began to shake. The action gave him back the power of speech. "You're a fucking idiot! The police think you robbed a fucking supermarket!" Spittle flew from his mouth onto a creased, freckled forehead. Danny shook harder.

Shoulders limp beneath his fists. Words whipped from beneath flopping hair. "Ah didney ken that's where Lennox's money came from, did ah?"

"Fuck where it came from!" Anger, frustration and fear churned in his stomach. "You told me you'd got rid of the rucksack – I trusted you and you lied to me!" Expensive fabric creased under his fingers. "That's where this came from too, isn't it?"

The body in his grip was a limp, stuffingless doll. Red headed nod-loll. "Ah didney think it..."

"You never fucking think!" Tears stung his eyes. "What we going do now? We can't go to the police!" Anger, frustration and terror exploded into rage. A impulse burst into his brain.

He wanted to hit Kel – he wanted to push his fists into the beautiful, stupid face until...

"Wha's goin' oan doon there?" Gruff, semi-sober grumbles in the distance.

Hands flew from slope-shoulders. Wednesday night singed fingertips and cooled the impulse to a freezer-burn.

Kel staggered back against the couch. "Aw' that money – ah couldney jist throw it away..."

"Well, it's all yours now – enjoy it!" An icy anger directed at Kel, at Jordan, at the police...

...at himself. It balled into a solid, sub-zero lump in his chest. Danny stared at the side of a pink face, then walked towards the door before he wanted to hit it again.

Bitten fingers plucked at his arm.

He wrenched himself free. "You want it so much, you fucking keep it!"

"Danny, ah..." Fingers re-gripped.

In the background. "Wha's that racket? Keep it doon, eh?"

183

He turned, stared into paralysed features.

Moving the carpet...moving the body...burning clothes...all for nothing – all for...

"Fuck off!" Then he was opening the door and it was Wednesday night again.

Only worse.

Running...

...past the small neat gardens with the plastic B&Q patio-sets, up the hill to the burnt-out car and down towards the footbridge over the motorway.

A group of girls laughed then swore as he tore through them. At the top of the footpath, two drunks wove in front of him. Danny swerved instinctively, slipped and fell. More laughing. Hands scrabbling on grass and empty lager cans, he scrambled upright and ran on.

Orange street-lights blurred into fractured prisms. Downhill was easier. His feet pounded on tarmac, sending shivers of reason into his sore brain.

Jordan...Kel's father...Kel's business...

...Kel's problem.

The police didn't know Danny MacIntyre at all. No-one knew he was with Kel, on bonfire night.

Jordan.

There was nothing to connect him with...

...half way across the motorway bridge his lungs gave out. Danny gripped the metal railing, eyes focused on the tops of lorries and cars. A roar filled his ears.

He slumped against metal bars, pressing his face to a cold wet surface. Danny stared until his eyes burned and the roar receded. Then he closed them...

...and saw a bruised face creased with confusion. Green eyes full of concern. Lennox's angry voice drowned out what was left of the traffic. The feel of a claw-like grip on his wrist. The grip twisting, hurting...

...then Kel pulling a trigger and making it stop.

Danny opened his eyes.

Below, the M8 was a never-ending stream of white and red. Against shimmering tail and head-lights, a skinny figure in an expensive suit bobbed up at him. His hand moved to his neck, to finger a chain that wasn't there.

Bonfire night, Kel had started all this...

...by making Lennox stop.

He had run, once before...

...and Danny was running again, tearing back across the bridge and up a deserted footpath. His chest hurt. The soreness in his head hurt more and let him run faster.

He only stopped when he saw the crowd around Number Fifteen Priest's View Road.

And the ambulance.

Chapter Sixteen

Flashes of blue sketched wet eddies on dark tarmac. An engine rumbled in his ears.

Danny pushed through a semi-circle of mumbling, stripe-faced neighbours.

The door to Number Fifteen was wide open. From inside, two low voices he didn't recognise. Then familiar gruff shouting.

His stomach jumped. Ears strained for the voice he wanted to hear.

Belligerent tones roared out through the open door, angrier than ever.

Danny's stomach jumped again. Wednesday night...

...worse than Wednesday night.

No...

He stared up at the ambulance's strobing roof-light. Mumbles at his side:

"Aye, ah kent it wid happen, wanna these days – treats that boay like a football, so he dis. Ah've heard him, through the wall."

No...

Danny pounded towards the path, avoiding the gathering dribbles of children and women with prams. As his feet hit the second concrete slab, a figure in a green jumpsuit moved through the open door. Then another.

One pushed a wheeled stretcher. The second held a squashy bag at shoulder-level in one hand, pressed a large white pad against the prostrate figure with the other.

No...

The procession made its way down the path. He sprinted onto greeny-blue grass.

They met in the middle. Danny stared down at the stretcher through swirling white/blue light.

An unshaven, tousle-headed face glowered up. Mouth curled in a sneer...

Danny leapt back. The wheeled stretcher hit pathside edging.

...then a howl, followed by a torrent of abuse.

One of the jumpsuited figures grabbed his arm:

"Do you know what happened here, son? Are you...?"

Legs pistoning, he raced through the doorway of Number Fifteen and stuck his head into the living-room.

An over-turned coffee-table. Cushions scattered everywhere. Pieces of a smashed lamp lay on the couch, beside that evening's *Times*. The TV was back on. A smear of red bisected the screen. A trail of wetness led from the TV-and-video unit to the door. A smell...

...a vaguely familiar smell. Danny belted upstairs to the bedroom, fo l lowing the trail...

Empty.

...and continued to follow it. Three other rooms equally lifeless.

Outside, the sound of an ambulance reversing. Back in the living-room, Danny re-scanned, pausing at a bright wink from the floor.

The slender chain lay in a curled heap, a sloughed-off metal skin.

Danny crouched, fingers snaking towards it.

Inches away, half-hidden by scattered scatter-cushions, something duller and heavier caught his eye.

He snatched the gun. It was still warm and smelly. Grabbing the broken chain and stuffing it into his pocket, Danny stood up and raced out of the house.

The crowd was still there. Had grown. He stared at it from the doorstep of Number Fifteen then darted left, bumping into a chained-up patio-set as he ran across gardens.

The gun scraped against his hip-bone as he leapt fences and avoided dustbins. Danny skirted round above Priest View and only stopped when his legs started to shake. Leaning against the side of a pebble-dashed semi, he watched the scene below.

The crowd of neighbours were dark ants. White faces focused up the curving street to where the ambulance had left...

Panic seeped through relief and fear.

188

...and from where the police-cars would come. Then he was running again, peering into back courts. Danny zig-zagged up the incline.

When?

What?

How long after he had stormed out had Archie Kelston staggered through from where Kel had put him to bed?

Why?

The barrel of the gun was pressing into his groin. Danny ignored it and its reappearance.

A dog barked in the distance and set off others.

Danny ignored that too. Stomach lurching, he searched back-court after back-court, climbing walls and slipping through spaces in fences.

Then there were no more back-courts to search. He stood on the patch of muddy waste-ground where they were building the new houses. Danny squinted under the powerful beam of a security-light and looked past onto Roystonhill.

The blackened spire of the old church poked up into a starless sky.

The dark shape shone like a beacon. Feet sinking into soggy dirt, he squelched past chained earth-moving equipment and out onto the road.

Yards from the shell of the burnt-out car, the sound of a functioning vehicle on the hill behind him. Wet trainers skidding on cracked pavement, Danny threw himself behind charred metal.

Engine sounds nearing.

He risked a glimpse over what remained of the bonnet. Couldn't see who was driving...

Fingers tightened on blackened metal.

...but the handsome, tanned face in the back seat was unmistakable. Danny watched Jordan's car sail slowly past the church and disappear.

He continued to stare at where the rear-lights had been. Then he was tearing across the dark street, hauling at the Made Safe by Reicht sign and plunging into darker innards.

Eyes acclimatising, Danny blinked at a row of formless, silhouettes.

One of the silhouettes flinched.

He stumbled towards it.

On a section of rubble, John Rocha-clad arms hugged a dark shape.

Danny stared at three yellow letters. He sank to a crouch in front of the hunched figure. "You...okay?"

Slow nod. Then: "Ma auld man. Ah..."

"I know. Ambulancemen were taking him out when I got... back."

Another slow nod. "He okay?"

Archie Kelston's all-too-lively howls of rage echoed in his mind. "You didn't kill him, if that's what you mean – but no-one would blame you if you had."

Red-head raised, huge eyes directed over Danny's shoulder. "That's guid."

Danny picked up a hunk of blackened rubble and stared at it. He tried to work out which fact the response referred to. Eyes flicked to the bruised face. Remnants of scab had fallen off the lip-cut and it was bleeding again. "You should've told someone."

Snort. "Like who?"

Like me. Danny looked away. Fingers dug into sandstone. 'The police' didn't seem a very constructive suggestion, given present circumstances. Social Services? He stared at blackened stone. "Anyone..." Part of a trumpet. "...your Outreach-worker."

Another snort. "An' git taken intae care again?" Kel stood up. The toe of a not-so-highly-polished shoe kicked at the remnants of the fire. "That wis fuckin' worse."

Danny clawed at sandstone. "Maybe you could get into a...hostel." He stared up at Kel. "Maybe we could get somewhere together and..."

"After ma mum left, he went tae court, fought fur me." Kel was staring down at the motorway. Voice tinged with pride.

Sandstone crumbled beneath fingertips. Danny looked up at a purplish cheekbone. "I though your mum was dead?"

190

The question ignored. "They wur both there – she wanted me tae go live wi' her an' her new guy. Ma dad got a solicitor – a real wan, no' wanna yer legal-aid joabs – an' went tae court five times, so's he could keep me wi' him."Sigh. "No' many folk would dae that, eh?"

People did all sorts of things for all sorts of reasons he was still working-out. Danny chewed his lip.

Green eyes turned. "So why dis he keep...hittin' me?"

Danny had no words...

The fury, the fear, the...frustration, the tangle of itchy irritation mixed with heat and other stuff he couldn't untangle.

...thoughts were something else. He shrugged.

The gesture returned. Then regret. "Ah've done it noo, eh?" A shadow of a laugh.

Danny pushed the truth away. Eyes focused on three yellow letters. He stood up, wiped a dusty hand on the leg of his jeans then laid it on top of the rucksack.

Embarrassed. "It wis gonny be ma..." A ghost of a laugh. "...runnin' away money – kept it here..." Nodding to a corner. "...wi' ma runnin' away stuff."

Danny followed the nod with his eyes, then feet. Behind a semi-demolished wall, a Head bag identical to the one Kel carried to school.

The ghost of laugh laid to rest. "Ah didney mean tae start spendin' it. He wanted his vodka replaced, fae the other night, an' ah remembered whit you said aboot no' nickin' onymair stuff..."

Danny turned and walked back to where Kel was still staring motorwaywards:

"Then the suit wis in the sale, onyway, an' efter ah'd bought that ah jist...wanted tae git you somethin' nice, tae..."

"It doesn't matter." Danny stuck a hand into his pocket. Fingers tightened around slender links. Another, less slender outline dug into his hipbone. "But why did you keep the gun?"

"Made me feel...big, huvin' it around." Sad laugh. "That's really funny, eh?" Kel sat down.

191

Fingers twined between strands of platinum.

Maybe if he'd stayed.

Maybe if he stayed none of this would have...

He pulled the chain from his pocket, looked at it. "I'm sorry I...walked out like that."

"Ah widney huv blamed ye if ye'd jist kept walkin'."

Danny frowned: blame was double-edge. He let metal links dribble through his fingers.

"Hey, notch!" Brightening. "'Sno broken."

Nail-bitten fingers plucked at his palm. Kel raised the length, peering. "Guid thing the catch is a wee bit loose, eh?" On the top of the JCB rucksack, ragged fingers fiddling with the fastening-device.

Danny knelt. "Put it back on." He lowered his head.

Surprised. "Sure?"

He nodded. "Like you said, no-one sees it when it's underneath..."

Clammy fingers fumbled under his hair, securing the catch behind his neck. He looked up.

Kel was looking down at him.

The expression on the bruised face made his stomach flip over. He moved his eyes from green oceans, hands resting lightly on John Rocha thighs.

"Thanks." The word a whisper.

Danny rested his head against the JCB rucksack. "What for?"

"Fur...comin' back."

He should never have left. Danny pressed his cheek harder against the rucksack's ribbed leather surface and found a laugh. "We're in this together, 'member?" Dampness seeped up through the knees of his jeans.

Hollow laugh. "Ah'm losin' track o' whit 'this' is, tae be honest!"

Attempted murder – twice?

Handling stolen money...

The chain warmed against his skin.

...wearing items purchased with stolen money? Money stolen from whom? The Balerno Asda or...

A tanned face in the back of a car flashed into his mind.

192

"I passed Jordan and Lennox. They were heading towards your house." Danny released John Rocha thighs and sat back on a hunk of rubble. The gun dug into his stomach.

"Ah telt ye." Reproachless. Fingers slackening.

Maxie's sightless eye shone in his mind. "We can...still go to the police – everything was...self-defence an'..."

"You fuckin' mad?" Kel was on his feet, pacing. JCB rucksack hugged, a lifebelt of ribbed leather. "Jordan'll go daft!"

"He can't...hurt you in prison."

Snort. "Git real, eh?"

Danny grabbed an arm. "The police can...protect..."

It wrenched away. "Every minute o' every day? Aye, right." Kel spun away, mid pace. "Jordan's got...friends, man..."

He caught a glimpse of scarlet skin. The chain cooled against sweating chest. Images he didn't want to see projected themselves into his mind. Danny grabbed a collar and dragged the pacing figure to a halt.

Slope-shoulders heaved inside expensive fabric.

Kel's steaming breath burnt his face. Danny stared into wild green eyes. "Take it easy..."

Ginger lashes blinked rapidly. "'Sno' your arse that's oan the line."

Danny frowned. Jordan's faintly-amused face swam in his brain, superimposed over the less easily entertained pupils of faceless figures. The thought focused his brain.

He released the John Rocha collar and stared at the JCB rucksack. "We'll go away..."

"Aye..." Sceptical snort. "Like...where?"

Danny's mind swept the map.

"Maxie didney even bother tryin' tae run – jist turned up at JB's an' took his punishment like a man."

Danny sighed. There was nothing manly about letting some psycho gouge out an eye. He looked up.

Somewhere big.

Somewhere far.

Somewhere no-one knew them...

...somewhere with a population bigger than the whole of

Scotland. "London."

A doubtful snort. "An' how dae we get there, exactly?"

Danny nodded at ribbed leather. It was a risk. He leant forward. Another risk dug into thigh. He wrenched the gun from jeans' pocket. "But first we get rid of this..." He raised his head. "...and I mean really get rid of it!"

Kel snatched the gun. "No way, hombre!" Weapon shoved into inside pocket.

Danny frowned. "Hand it over..."

Violent head-shake. "We might need it." Low voice. "We should keep it in case..."

The end of the sentence hung between them, an unspeakable possibility.

The frown slid from his face. Danny looked at Kel.

Kel looked back.

Then they were grabbing a Head bag from behind the semi-demolished wall and nudging at the back of a Made Safe by Reicht sign.

"Two singles to London, please. For tonight." Danny glanced over his shoulder.

A pale face was studiously peering in the window of a closed underwear concession. Bitten fingers pushed a hank of red hair behind a pink ear.

Danny frowned. His picture hadn't been on *Crimewatch*, so he had been delegated spokesman until they could do something about Kel's appearance. He scanned the rest of the station concourse.

No police – few people, full stop.

"Euston or Kings Cross?"

His head flicked back to the perspex window.

The woman in the tartan jacket was staring at computer screen, eight pink shiny nails hovering over a keyboard.

"Either."

The pink nails fluttered then paused. "Sleeper?"

"Yes." Danny's neck craned.

Kel had turned up the collar of the John Rocha.

"Double or single berth?"

Whiplash tingled down his spine. "What?"

194

The woman in the tartan jacket looked up. Smile. "Single berth's just double without the top bunk turned down, but you get more...space. More expensive, though."

Danny smiled back and tried to look like someone for whom space wasn't a consideration. "Double's fine."

Pink nails fluttered maniacally.

Danny half-turned.

Kel had moved on and was examining the contents of the concession next to the underwear one.

A final tap, then: "That's two single sleepers, double berth on the 23.35 to Euston?"

Danny refocused. "Yes. Thanks. Great..." He bit back a second adjective and refixed the smile.

"Sixty two pounds, please." A final pink nail plunging downwards.

Cheaper than he'd thought it would be. Danny fingered the bundle in his pocket. He peeled off what felt like four twenties and slid them into the metal tray at the bottom of the perspex window.

The machine attached to the screen was making printing noises. Danny urged it on.

The woman in the tartan jacket counted, re-counted the notes in slow motion.

Then a slot spat two orange and yellow rectangles at him and pink nails placed his a ten, a five and two pound coins in the metal tray.

The smile was stuck to his face. Danny left it there, snatched the tickets and the change then strode towards Kel.

The shop beside the underwear concession was a chemist.

It was still open.

Danny steered Kel inside.

Eyes speed-read the back of a box. "Quick and easy. That's too...complicated-looking." He replaced Recital Ash Blond on the shelf, grabbed Ebony and sat it in his basket beside the tube of InstaTan. Scissors...

"Notch colour..." Disappointed sigh. "Whit is it they say

195

blonds huv?"

Danny frowned. "Split ends, going by the amount of ammonia in that stuff." He moved along the gondola. Scissors...

A John Rocha-clad figure followed in his wake. Bitten fingers possessively through tangles of red. "Can we no' jist buy me a hat?"

"You can't always wear a hat – it'll look suspicious..." Danny located scissors in the foot-care section. He removed two pairs from the rack, turned and stared at the suit. "..and I don't know what kind of hat would go with that, anyway."

Snigger. "Wanna they big, broad-rimmed joabs – like De Niro wore in *Goodfellas*."

Danny walked on, shrugging the rucksack further up on his shoulder. "Do we...need anything else?" He turned.

Kel was fiddling with a packet of corn-plasters. "Ah dunno ..." Bitten fingers replacing packet. "Ah've already goat toothpaste an' soap an' stuff, an ye can share ma toothbrush..."

Danny almost laughed. The rucksack on his shoulder contained almost twenty thousand pounds and they were sharing a toothbrush.

Sharing.

His eyes settled on a display of small silver packets beside the cash-desk...

...and he was thinking about his mouth and Kel's mouth; his hands and Kel's hands: his knob and Kel's...

"Ah'll get some juice – an' sweeties, eh? In case we're hungry." Slope-shoulders jogged off towards the refrigerated cabinet.

Danny grabbed two packets of condoms, shoved them in the basket and walked to the cash-desk.

The toilets were surprisingly busy, considering the station was so empty.

People lingered, watching the process. Danny sighed: hadn't they ever seen hair-dye before? He avoided the eyes of a balding, middle-aged man for the third time and

196

guided a water-blind Kel to the hand-drier. Hitting the ON button, he ran plastic-gloved hands through two-inch Ebony spikes.

"This'd better look okay..." Grumbles directed floorwards, over the sound of rushing air.

It looked...different. Danny grabbed a fistful of wet hair and wafted it under the drier. He glanced around the tiled area, thought of another tiled area and met the balding, middle-aged man's gaze for a fourth time. He looked away.

Over the whoosh of the hand-drier, the sound of footsteps entering one of the cubicles.

Danny pealed off the plastic gloves, balled and tossed them into a bin. He leant back against a sink.

Bitten fingers were now coursing through matt-black inches. The shorn head shook dog-like under jets of warm hair.

He stared at the back of a pale neck. A dark wet patch stained the collar of the light green shirt.

The hand-drier stopped.

He hit the button again, brain rushing with the warm jets. His watch read eleven-oh-four. The train was due in at eleven-fifteen. Platform One.

They would get on it.

They would find their compartment, lock themselves in.

They would stay there until London.

Then they would...

"Oh, fuck!"

The hand-drier stopped again.

Danny stared into the mirror at the frowning, freckled face...

...and the crop of two-inch black waves which wriggled out from a skull. A smile spread over his face. "I didn't know your hair was...curly."

The frown hardened. "Neither did ah – bin ages since it wis this short." A pair of nail bitten hands clasped to the crown of an Ebony head, trying to flatten. "We shouldda boaght gel or somethin'." More futile flattening-attempts.

Danny continued to stare. The hair didn't match the face – wouldn't match anyone's face. Kel looked...

197

He sighed.

...like someone he didn't know.

"Well, don't jist stand there – dae somethin' wi' this mess!" Suddenly frantic. Then equally suddenly, the face in the mirror cracked into a grin.

The first grin all evening. It spread like a virus.

"This'll help..." Danny rummaged in the Superdrug bag for the InstaTan. ...keep still."

"Hope you ken whit ye're daein' – ah'm no' wantin' tae look like ah had a close encounter wi' a dodgy sun-bed on top o' the naff hair-cut."

"You'll not – now shut up!"

Bitten fingers gripping the edge of the sink, Kel continued to talk.

Danny unscrewed the top of the InstaTan tube and felt the gooey brown liquid smear the tips of his fingers. He transfered it to the tilted-back face, watching pale skin disappear and take freckles with it.

Kel babbled on.

Danny stopped listening, only hearing the lack-of-babble when his hands faltered on a bruise and the flesh flinched beneath his fingers. The skin was warm and slightly damp, which helped the InstaTan go on smoothly and made the groin of his jeans tingle.

The pale face was an almost uniform copper when slow bootsteps on tile made his heart hesitate. Head flicked into the mirror...

...then heart stopping. Another uniform.

As did the babble.

Skin tightened under fingertips. In the corner of his eye, the balding man scurried up the tiled steps, followed by another three men he hadn't noticed.

Two figures in white shirts with attached radios glanced at Danny. One smiled, then walked to the urinal and unzipped. The radio on the shoulder of the other squawked, disrupting the sudden silence as he strolled over to the row of three cubicles.

In the mirror, Danny watched the policeman's reflection sink to a crouch and peer under one locked door.

The face beneath his fingers was trembling.

The policeman stood up.

Danny met reflected eyes. Heart hammered over the sound of pissing.

Then the face beneath his fingers edged away and Kel was moving in slow-motion. Bitten fingers casually picked up the Head bag and the rucksack. A John Rocha-clad shape glided slowly towards the foot of the tiled steps.

Danny moved in its wake, hearing the pissing stop behind, and the sound of re-zipping.

Each step was an eternity.

Each time his knee rose and his foot fell, his heart thumped louder. He stared at the back of an Ebony head, aching to just run.

They were turning the corner on the last flight up into the station concourse when:

"Oi! You pair!" The deep voice echoed up from the subterranean toilet.

Danny froze. In front, slope-shoulders hunched up around dye-stained ears.

Footsteps behind. Covering the steps two at a time. A hand on his shoulder.

Guts were water. He turned through glue...

"Don't forget yer...make-up, boays!" Laugh.

...and stared at the Superdrug carrier bag in the policeman's hand. Somehow he found words. "Er...thanks."

Somehow he managed to accept the offered carrier.

Then somehow they were back on the concourse and Kel's feet were pounding in front towards Platform One.

Chapter Seventeen

Beyond a tiny shuttered window, whistles. Voices. Trains drew in, departed.

A minute past. Then Two. Then five.

Danny stared from the face on his wrist to the weird, coppery-coloured face opposite.

Green eyes continued to focus over his head to the door behind.

He gazed back at his wrist. Footsteps padding along the carpet. And more voices. Hands blurred at eleven-fifteen.

People trying to find their sleeping-compartment.

People asking if there was a luggage-compartment.

People asking if they could have coffee instead of tea, in the morning...

The tramp of countless pairs of shoes up and down the corridor beyond their room.

...people asking ordinary questions about ordinary things. A trickle of sweat made its way from his left armpit, dampening already clammy skin. His mind was a clock moving backwards, hands ticking over the events of the last twenty four hours...

Archie Kelston's storm cloud gaze...a bruised cheek-bone and a scabbed lip shining through the grainy dots of CCTV footage...Jordan's telescoping pupils...Maxie's cyclops vision ...his own eyes. A sea-green gaze...

...then pausing, in a tiled room with a jacuzzi. Watching. Seeing...

Danny's groin tightened.

...wanting...

Two blasts of a whistle pierced his thoughts. A jolt beneath his feet. The face of his watch came back into focus. Danny gripped a coat hook and stared at bronzed skin two yards away.

Green eyes met his. A smile in the wordless compartment.

Then they were both at the window, watching the Clyde drift under the train as it made its way southwards.

201

Two hours later they'd finished the sweeties. Engine-sounds drummed rhythmically up through the floor. And engine-warmth.

"'Slike a fuckin' oven in here..."

Danny drained the last can of juice and fiddled with the heating-control. It refused to shift from 'low'.

Below, on the single berth, bitten fingernails pealed off the light-green shirt. The John Rocha suit hung limply over a hanger. It had been there since Motherwell.

Danny shivered and banged the heating-control with a Sprite can. It remained at 'low'. A voice behind:

"Wanna try the windae again?"

Raising the tiny glass panel let in more noise than air. Danny sat down on the bed, shook his head. "Maybe it'll cool down when we speed up." Beneath his clothes, his skin itched unbearably.

"Aye, maybe..." At the other end of the bunk, bitten fingers laced behind a spiky black head. On a pale thigh, a darker object. Stubborn streaks of InstaTan lingered around the jaw-line, the rest washed away somewhere around Carlisle.

Danny stared at once-more bruised skin.

Kel fiddled with the gun. "Wonder if he's okay."

"Who?" He gave up the last intentions of remaining dressed and pulled the rugby shirt over his head.

"Ma auld man – ah shouldda phoned round the hospitals before we left..."

Danny hauled hands free from cuffs and leant back against the side wall. "He'll be okay..." The words were angrier than he'd meant them to be.

Gun tossed from hand to hand.

The platinum chain was ice against his chest. "Put that away..."

"Ah canny work-oot how onywan actually manages tae off onywan else, wi' wanna these things." Gun tossed into air.

Armies of insects scuttled across his scalp. "Put it away!"

"Okay, okay..." Kel caught the weapon by the barrel,

then leant across and slipped it into a John Rocha pocket. "Happy?"

Happier, but not by much. Danny looked down at the space between his feet. Every time he relaxed, something else occurred to him and ruined it. A bare foot nudged his thigh and the shiver cooled:

"You sleepy?"

Danny frowned down at the bed: he'd never sleep again. Eyes moved to four bitten fingers scratching a pale-blue groin.

The foot nudged again, flattening itself against denim and moving down towards his knee. "Me neither – ah feel aw'... wired-up..."

Danny raised his eyes from a lump in pale blue underpants.

"...like ah could run mile an' never get tired." Lashes lowered, green eyes aimed bedwards.

The crotch of his jeans was tightening by the second. He stared at the lounging figure. Light at the side of the bunk drenched streaky skin in an orangy glow. The planes of Kel's face were all angles.

"Wanna count the money again?" Green eyes flicking up.

He stared into pupils which matched the hair and shook his head. It was the last thing on his mind.

Shrug. "Jist wondered."

His stomach flipped. Engine sounds seeped in, punctuating the silence. Then:

"Ah've been thinkin'..."

Danny frowned. That made two of them. He hadn't been able to think of much else since the tiled room. Two silver packets he'd bought without really knowing why squirmed in the back pocket of his jeans.

"...aboot whit's the best thing tae dae first when we get tae..."

"I don't want to talk about it!" He didn't want to talk at all. He didn't want to think. He wanted to...

"Keep the heid, eh?" Huffy. "Jist tryin' tae be helpful."

His body swayed with the motion of the train. He let it,

listening to the soothing sync of wheels on track and trying to anticipate the next increase or decrease in speed.

A bare foot abruptly jabbed his stomach and pulled him from the rhythmic coccoon.

Snigger.

As it drew back to jab again, Danny gripped the ankle, hauling.

A mock-yelp. A head banged off the wall, jarring onto the pillow.

Then Kel was falling back against the wall and hands were delivering further jabs to his chest. Danny gripped both ankles, knee pushing between Kel's legs. Soft warmth.

Another yelp, less mock. Kel bucked upwards from the bed. A corresponding knee rammed back against his hip.

Wrists grabbed forearms, pushing forwards. The body bucked again and Danny's spine hit off the side wall.

Kel's breath was hot and laughing on his face. Then they were rolling. Danny grabbed for the side of the bunk, missed and seized a hand instead. He lunged in the direction of the wriggling form, inhaling the sweet-sour scent of Kel's sweat and the faint, non-perfumed odour of InstaTan. The smell filled his head. He paused, mid lunge.

An opportunity seized. Triumphant hoot.

Scrabbling hands gripped his arms and flipped him onto his back. A blue-covered hardness impacted with his knee...

...mirrored by pressure of his knob against a tensed stomach.

Danny heaved sideways and wrenched an arm free. Spine grated against formica panelling.

Kel re-gripped, keeping him there with his weight. A thigh sandwiched itself between his. Danny gasped into a staring face.

Then hardness against his hipbone and Kel's mouth was on his neck, nipping. Sharp teeth broke more than skin.

His head pounded with images from the tiled room. He grabbed a fistful of black spikes, hauling the face from his shoulder.

It wrenched free and bounced back against his neck. The

chest pushed more determinedly. The platinum chain dug into Danny's skin and he knew it was digging into other skin. The teeth on his neck moved down to throat.

Mock-gnawing sounds. And grinding against his hip. Grinding wetness...

...which found an echo in his groin. Danny's head, heart and body were going to burst. With immense effort, he pushed the skinny chest away from his. "Kel, I want to..." He stared at the bruised face.

Slick lips licked into a grin. Head cocked.

Spit cooled on his neck.

Curious. "Ye want tae...?" Kel sat back on his heels, knees apart.

Danny levered himself from the side wall and knelt between splayed thighs. "I want to...make love to you."

"Ye wanna...whit?" Slope-shoulders shaking. Then nail-bitten fingers hugging skinny forearms and falling sideways on the bunk.

"I want to make love to you!" His skin was hotter than ever. Danny frowned at the laughing face, avoiding a kick from a flailing foot. His stomach tightened.

Amusement slowly subsiding. Green eyes blinking in orange light. "Ye mean ye wanna gie me a hand-joab? Ye wanna suck ma knob?"

Face scarlet, Danny swung legs over the side of the bed and staggered to his feet. He wanted to leave but there was nowhere to go, even if his legs would work.

A hand grabbed his thigh.

The touch made his balls sweat worse than the rest of him. Danny turned.

A genuinely-confused face peered up at him. "Well? Whit is it ye wanna dae so much?" The hand moved against his thigh. Another abstractedly scratched at a hair pit. "Ye ken ah'm no' intae ony poof-stuff."

Danny's stomach clenched. He closed his eyes and saw Jordan's strong body tall and thrusting behind Kel. Into Kel.

"Right?"

Danny's eyes shot open.

Kel was sitting, legs splayed. A slender torso curled forward over thighs. The shock of black hair made the eyes look bigger, greener.

He sank to a crouch. "Right – forget it."

Sigh. "This is they books again, isn't it?" Exaggerated slump onto the bed.

Danny leant back against the opposite wall and stared at the floor. *The Joy of Gay Sex* had been consigned to a mental dustbin hours ago. He nodded because it was easier than explaining.

Thoughtful pause, then: "Ye wanna...try an' beat twenny-five minutes?" Kel was lying on the bed, one hand supporting face. Orangy skin streaked scarlet.

He shook his head. The movement jarred his brain into action. "Just forget it." Danny stood up, lurching with the train. "Let's try to get some sleep." Hands unbuckling belt, then fumbling with zip.

Inches away, a sigh. "If that's whit ye want..."

He kicked off trainers and socks, dragged jeans and underpants down over clammy legs. What he wanted wasn't important.

Sounds of rustling, skin against fabric.

Danny looked up.

Kel was squashed against the far side of the bed, holding up a crisp white sheet. A half-smile creased the corners of narrowed eyes.

He switched off the light to get away from them. Danny eased shaking limbs between cool fabric and tried to stay away from the slim body stretched parallel to his.

He lay on his back, staring up at the ceiling. His heart pounded.

He wouldn't sleep.

Couldn't sleep.

A snuffle near his shoulder. Then a whisper:

"Did ye tell the guard-guy tea or coffee?"

"Tea." He focused on one end of the strip-light's outline.

Approving sigh. "Guid – ah canny stand coffee first thing in the mornin'!"

A leg brushed his. "'Night, then..." Softer whisper.

Danny edged away and turned over. "'Night." His knee impacted with the bed-edge. He let it stay there, concentrating on the feel of cold metal.

Breathing near his ear slowed. The sheet over his itching body rose and fell slower still. The sound of the engine merged with the sound of Kel's breath.

He wouldn't sleep.

Couldn't sleep.

He...

...woke up because his hand had gone to sleep. A spiky head was heavy on his chest. Warm legs twined with his.

The covers lay around his ankles, kicked into a tangled heap at the bottom of the narrow bed. Danny closed his lips.

His mouth tasted horrible.

His throat was on fire.

He needed to piss desperately. Danny eased an arm from around the lightly-snoring form, flexed fingers then grazed the floor for something to drink. Knuckles brushed three empty juice-cans.

On his chest, a snuffle.

Kel's body was limp and relaxed against his. The knowledge made him smile and frown at the same time. He moved carefully, drawing a leg from over a skinny hip.

A snuffle-moan.

Tingles zipped up and down his arm, jarring around his elbow. He raised his hand and made a fist.

Irritated snuffle-groan. Kel turned, drawing up knees and facing the wall. Two slender mounds of flesh thrust towards him.

A patch on his chest felt cold and empty without the spiky head. Ignoring the tingling in his wrist and the pressure in his bladder, Danny mirrored the movement and curled around the warm curve. His half-hard knob fitted neatly into a narrow crevice.

Snuffle-sigh. More movement...

...against his groin. Danny scowled.

The sleeping shape began to undulate against him. He

buried the scowl in the back of bristly neck, lips grazing a black hairline as his body responded.

They moved like thick liquid, ebbing and flowing with the motion of the train.

Slender silver-coloured links pressed themselves into his chest. Knees found the back of other knees. His knob dragged down the crack of Kel's arse.

The curled shape rippled away, dragging back up each time the pale wave broke against his stomach. The sleeping arm fell lightly over the sleeping figure, numb fingers curling around another arm.

The waves were stronger, heavier. Danny's lips slipped from the bristly neck. He pressed his face against a nobbly spine, pulled back and down. Lips stiffened. His knob poked at then slid between slim thighs. Lips parted in a soundless sigh.

Soft hairiness dragged along paper-thin skin.

Danny moaned, easing away then plunging forward again. Fully-awake hands inched over skin, settling on hip bones. Something hurt vaguely in his bladder. He mouthed the skin on Kel's back, drawing himself in and out of the smooth space...

...the head of his knob was damp when the need to piss blanked out everything else. Face creased, Danny eased himself from between Kel's thighs and staggered towards the sink.

A snuffle-moan.

Holding shaft between thumb and forefinger, he aimed at the plug-hole then glanced over his shoulder.

Kel had rolled over onto his back, moving into the recently-vacated space. One leg sprawled towards the end of the bed. The other splayed outwards, knee raised.

Danny stared at Kel's swollen knob, watching the way it twitched lightly against a white hip-bone. The pain in his bladder made him gasp. Refocusing on the plug-hole, he tried to piss.

Nothing.

He scowled at the drop of moisture on the head of his knob and tried to will himself soft.

208

Behind, more moan-snuffles weren't helping.

Danny gave up. Turning, he knelt beside the bed, watching.

Ginger lashes fluttered against purplish-orangy skin, eyes moving beneath lids.

He wondered what Kel dreamt about. Then he covered the sleeping figure with a less-than-crisp sheet and began to search the floor for his clothes.

By the time he'd found them and dressed, he was soft enough to piss.

Thirst was taking the skin off his throat. Running the tap, he read the *Not Drinking Water* sign on the wall then bent his head and sucked in a mouthful of liquid.

It was more than luke-warm.

He swirled evil-tasting water around his mouth, spat into the sink.

The last traces of his piss spiralled towards the plug-hole. Danny let the tap run a while longer, then turned it off and raised the window-shutter.

He stared past his own face at the darkness behind.

More darkness.

Throat burned more than ever. Glancing at the bed, Danny patted his pocket and heard the change from four twenties.

Kel had turned over again, face buried in the pillow.

He stared at two, sheet-covered mounds, then quietly opened the door.

The buffet was miles away.

Lurching through three compartments of sitting-up-dozing people, he found it eventually and joined the queue.

The smell of microwaved cardboard hung in the air. Danny's nostrils followed a woman with very short hair and a tray back down the aisle of passengers.

He wondered if Kel was hungry.

He wondered what else the buffet sold. Danny peered ahead to the menu at the front of the queue. Eyes paused on the all-day breakfast. He tried to remember the last time he'd eaten, apart from the sweeties.

The person being served was arguing with the guy behind the counter about children's portions.

Danny chewed a dry lip. He only wanted a couple of cans of juice, and maybe an all-day breakfast. They should have two queues, one for five items and under, like supermarkets. Bracing arms against the counter, he turned back to survey the compartment.

Reading-people. People with personal stereos. A group of four men with a table full of lager-cans were playing cards. The woman with the very short hair and the tray was now talking on a mobile phone and eating the burger.

Sweat formed on his upper lip.

The whole train was like a furnace.

He stared at several passengers with coats draped over their knees and wondered how they could stand it.

Someone walked past carrying two polystyrene cups and the queue moved on.

Danny took a step back, closing the gap between himself and the next-in-line. He turned, gaze panning the entire compartment.

The sweat on his upper lip froze. So did his breath.

Half way down the left hand side. A window-seat. A large figure in a suit re-lowered one eye to a different page of the newspaper clutched between meaty fingers.

Another eye glazed past Danny, focusing somewhere behind him. A voice from the same direction:

"Next!"

The burning in his throat plunged lower, igniting a fiery pit in his bowels.

Then he was running, head down, past rows of high-backed seats, through compartment doors and past other rows into corridors towards the sleeper-section.

Chapter Eighteen

Green eyes instantly awake, pupils shrinking to full stops in harsh, overhead light. "Canny be..." Tiny black dots said otherwise.

Danny's sat down. "Think he's got a twin?" Fingers tightened on the edge of the bed. He stared at skin the colour of ash.

Kel rubbed his face, bitten fingernails raking black spikes. "How did he ken?" Words into sweaty palms. "How the fuck did Jordan...?"

"We've got to get off." Danny released the edge of the bed and stood up. "Next time the train stops, we get off and..."

"Maxie on his ain?" Pale face reappearing from behind palms.

Danny stared, re-visualising the large figure spreading over two seats of a table for four. "Not sure – I think so, but..."

"Did he see ye?" Bare legs snaked past him, dangling over the side of the bunk.

"Don't think so."

Calm words. "Then we're gonny go talk to him." Standing. A hand finding underwear.

A sheen of frost formed on his skin. Danny's mind tried to work-out where the conversation had gone.

Pale skin slowly disappearing beneath various shades of green.

"Why?" The word was a croak. He wished he'd hung around long enough to buy juice.

"Cos we've been followed – if Maxie's oan this train, Jordan kens we're here, an' he kens where we're goin'."

His spine clung to the compartment wall. They'd been careful. On the taxi-journey from Royston to the centre of Glasgow his eyes had been everywhere. He re-wound back at the station, searching the concourse-memories for lurking figures.

Maxie was hard to miss anywhere. "How did he...?"

211

"Ah telt ye: cross Jordan an' he'll eyeways find ye." Bitten fingers attempting to tie a length of nobbly green silk. And stumbling. Kel sat down. "We'll talk tae Maxie, see whit he's sayin' tae it." Fingers renewing the attempt on the tie.

"And what are we going to say when we...talk to him?" Something between a giggle and a sob escaped his lips. "Here we are, Maxie? Take us back?" He blinked at the suited figure on the bed.

Kel was staring across the compartment.

Blurring vision followed green eyes...

...to a ribbed leather shape and three luminous yellow letters.

"We buy him aff."

Whiplash tingled down his neck. Danny looked back to the bed. It was empty.

Kel was squeezing past him, grabbing the rucksack. "Twenny thousand here – we offer him half tae say he loast us at Euston. That still lea's us ten tae get...established."

Danny blinked, rubbed face on the sleeve of his rugby-shirt. "What if he doesn't...?"

Hoarse laugh. "Then we leg it aff the train!" Socked feet thrust into shoes. Green eyes shone. "It's worth a try, eh? He'll no be expectin' us tae come tae him – that'll gie us the...element o' surprise." A pale face glanced mirrorwards, scrutinising asymmetric ebony spikes.

Then they were edging out of the narrow compartment and padding down a carpeted corridor.

Surprise didn't do it justice.

Maxie's huge face rippled with a hundred expressions, before settling into shocked recognition.

Kel sat down in what was left of the empty seat. "Fancy seeing you here, man!" JCB rucksack placed on the table.

Movement behind.

Danny flattened himself against the edge of the table. The scent of passing burger made his bowels churn.

Low rumbling whisper. "Kel, son, ye..."

"Train's busy, eh Maxie? Ye wur lucky tae find a seat."

212

Danny's stomach stayed flattened. He edged into the narrow space between Kel and the table, avoiding two sets of eyes from two passengers opposite. The tinny shimmer of a personal stereo jangled on his ears.

One unseeing eye stared at him, joined by a second, more seeing. Maxie refocused on Kel. "Boays, ye..."

Kel leaned sideways, full lips very close to a large red ear.

Danny tried to hear the words. Rhythmic tinniness from across the table filled his head. He couldn't see Kel's face any more. His eyes zoomed in on the broad, ruddy expanse above the collar of Maxie's shirt.

No expression. Then the enormous head shook. Rumbling whisper. "Listen tae me, Kel son..."

More whispering. Softer.

Danny stared at the pale hand resting on the table. Four bitten fingers raked at the nail of a thumb.

Maxie couldn't do anything.

Not here...

Eyes panned around and met several raised heads.

...not in a carriage full of increasingly curious people. Danny refocused on the whispering duo of wild-haired boy and immense man.

John Rocha-clad knees nudged his, pushing him back into the aisle. Danny reversed up the compartment. He paused and turned sideways, watching Maxie smoothly manoeuvre his vast body across the double-seat.

Kel leant against the table, waiting.

Danny tried to read the expression on the broad face. Then he was staring at pneumatic doors and walking towards them. Legs swayed with the train. A yard behind, Maxie's laboured breathing.

Behind that, he hoped, Kel's.

The tectonic plates of a third carriage-join shifted under his feet. Reality had gone the same way, three compartments back. Over the sound of wheels-on-track, occasional rumbling words from Maxie too low to understand.

Pneumatic doors drew him into another compartment

213

full of people. Had Maxie agreed?

Danny walked on, legs and brain on autopilot. The whispering had obviously achieved something, but he had no idea where they were going, or why: Kel had the rucksack – there was no reason for them to go back to the sleeping-compartment...

The train curved, throwing him against someone's seat. Danny apologised and staggered on. The motion tugged a thought loose.

...except to get a heavy, dark object which had already been used.

Twice...

His blood froze.

...too often. Pneumatic doors wheezed in front of him, sucking the breath from his lungs. Danny spun round, opposite a toilet. He collided with a large shape.

Doors shutting.

He stared into Maxie's good eye. "Take the money!" His voice was a shriek. The train curved again, knocking him off balance.

Doors opening.

"Take it!" Danny fell back.

Door closing.

He flailed against an 'Engaged' sign, grabbed a beefy arm for stability. His other hand flapped wildly, seizing ribbed leather straps from a John Rocha shoulder and hauling open drawstrings. Through the chaos of wheezing doors and stumbling bodies:

"Whit the fuck ye doin'?" Nail-bitten fingers scrabbled for ribbed leather.

Danny wrenched the rucksack back. Luminous yellow letters strobed in front of darting eyes.

Then his hands were around bundles. He hauled banded wads free, waved them in front of a stunned eye. "Take it! Take it all!"

The train lurched.

Breath left Danny's lungs in a vast explosion. A heavy body rolled over his. The back of his skull hit off a window pane. Fingers scrambled for a grip, nails raking down

214

yellow paintwork.

Hands on his arm.

Danny pulled away, waving a fistful of pink twenties before a huge face. "Go on, take it! Please..."

The train lurched more violently. The acrid smell of brake-fluid hot in his nostrils.

Nail-bitten fingers around his chest, hauling him back. "Quit it! Lea' him alain!"

Danny lunged forward. Tectonic plates shifted beneath his feet. He dropped the rucksack, staggering sideways. Then fingers found something to grab...

...something which moved. Downwards. He was falling again, sliding over a convex stomach, still waving a wad of twenties. The moving something in his hand followed.

Head hit metal. Cold air was rushing past his face. The shock stopped the flailing. Danny released the door handle.

Nail-bitten fingers had slipped from his chest and were now gripping his waist.

Danny stared out into the night. Wind buffeted his eyes and made them water. He watched rushing air suck the last of the pink twenties from the paper band in his fist.

The hands on his waist tugged sharply.

Danny stared up, head full of rushing. Above him, Kel gripped the handle of the open door, hauling it shut.

Footsteps. The smell of burgers replaced icy air and the stench of brake-fluid. Though a haze, two pairs of heeled feet picked their way over him. Tutting:

"Drunk..."

Another voice. "...or drugs." More tutting. "Disgraceful!"

Danny closed his eyes. Tutting faded into the distance. Vibrations shivered up into his face.

Then arms were hauling him onto rubber legs, dragging him along a carpeted corridor.

Someone had managed to turn the heating down.

He couldn't stop shaking. On the bunk, skinny arms tightened around him.

Fists clenched against chest. The shaking subsided to a shiver. Over engine-sounds another heart thumped against his.

Maxie.

The JCB rucksack...

...an open door, sucking him out into pit-like night. Every hair on his body erected. Bone-jarring shudders crept from the soles of his feet to explode in his chattering teeth.

A John Rocha-clad vice squeezed the breath from his body. "'S'okay...'s'okay..."

His jaw was rigid, raw throat swallowing down sobs. They backed-up somewhere in his chest and jolted against trembling fists.

"'S'okay...'s'okay..."

Maxie.

The JCB rucksack...

...syllables melting to little soothing noises. Vice-like arms slackened a little.

Danny pushed fists up inside the John Rocha jacket. Warmth from Kel's body slowly seeped into his. The shivers ebbed to shudders.

They had confined themselves to a grumbling in his stomach when he noticed Kel was shaking in parallel. Syllables re-solidifying from little soothing sounds:

"Fuck, ah thought you wur gonny go tae – when ye opened that fuckin' door an' you an' Maxie..."

"Think he...?" Danny raised his head. Words wouldn't come.

Didn't need to. One ginger slug raised. Green eyes narrowing. "He's got a lotta paddin', right enough. Mebbe if he landed in a...field, or somethin'..." Scepticism, badly hidden.

Danny wiped eyes on sleeve.

"Wanna cuppa tea? Hot sweet tea's meant tae be guid fur... shock." Legs uncurling beside him, arms moving away. "Want me tae nip doon tae the buffet an'...?"

"Don't go!" Danny frowned. He sounded like a wee boy, scared of the dark. The frown intensified.

Lying in the dark.

On railway line.

Other carriages thundering over a vast, suited shape. Other trains, wheels churning bits of Maxie southwards to...

Danny lurched from the bed, swayed in the direction of the wash-hand basin. The last thing he remembered was the sound of the engine hammering in his head and the acid taste of sweeties.

Eyelids flickered.

Hunger flared in his stomach. He stared at the wall opposite, searching for the CD shelf. His bedroom looked different.

A stranger with black hair and a black Adidas warm-up suit was sitting on the end of his bed, staring at a window.

Danny focused on narrow white sleeve stripes. Wisps of a dream in which he'd killed Jordan Burns' right-hand man by pushing him out of a moving train drifted away. Light from the window drifted in. The stranger with the black hair turned.

Worried smile. "Feelin' better?"

Danny nodded. The movement hurt something at the back of his head.

Kel stood up, walked to the top of the bed and sat down again. "Watford..." Nod towards lights beyond the tiny window. "They're off-loadin' the post. Takes ages. Ah've bin watchin' the mail-vans pullin' in an'..."

He opened his mouth. A croak came out.

Kel darted to the fold-down table and seized a polystyrene cup. He held it out. "Dunno how long this stuff holds heat fur..."

Danny pealed off the plastic lid, drenching his throat with too-sweet luke-warm liquid. He drained the cup, then looked at Kel.

Furrowed pale face. "You wur oot fur hours – ah nearly went an' got the guard..." Forced laugh. "..tae see if there wis a doctor on the train! Ye gave yer heid some crack against the edge o' that door."

He smiled. "I'm fine."

Unconvinced frown.

"Really." The back of his head throbbed, his chest felt like he'd taken a huge breath he couldn't expel, and everything swam a bit. Grumbling in his stomach. Different grumbling. "I could go something to eat, though."

Apologetic frown. "The buffet closed ages ago, but ah got ..." Reaching back to the fold-down table. "...these wi' the money that wis in yer pocket." Three packets of crisps, two giant chocolate chip cookies and a can of Coke tossed onto the bunk. "An' the tea an' biscuits'll be comin' soon, if ye can haud on."

Danny opened one of the crisp packets, popped a ring-pull.

Green eyes watched the process. The brow gradually unfurrowed.

Beyond, a whistle.

Another whistle. Movement.

He was on the third packet of crisps when Kel opened one of the giant chocolate chip cookies and leant back against his legs. "Ah ken the money's gone, but ah've got an idea..."

"She'll not...mind?" Danny swallowed the last of the crisps. Images from grainy CCTV replayed themselves in his clearing mind.

Kel was draining the Coke can. "She's eyeways writin' me these letters, askin' me tae come doon an'..." Coke can crushed between bitten-fingers. "...visit her." Eyes directed fistwards.

Words low, off-hand. Through the mists of a headache, Danny groped beyond them. "Why did you tell me she was dead?"

Slope-shoulder shrug. Coke-can squashed further. "Walked oot on me an' the auld man when ah wis ten." The sounds of crumpling aluminium. "Might as well be deid."

Danny licked cheese-and-onion flavour from his lips.

218

"But she keeps in touch?"

"Ainly since she goat married again." Snort. "Goat an invitation tae the weddin'..." Fingers abstractedly rubbed a now-greenish cheekbone. "...but ah didney fancy it."

Danny watched the movement.

Another snort. "Wanted me tae wear a fuckin' kilt!"

Danny grinned at the thought. "When was this?"

"Aw', ages ago..." Fingers rubbing from bruise into hair. "...when ah wis thirteen." Coke-can aimed floorwards. "Onyway ..." Face raised. Expression changing with the subject. "...we can go stay wi' her 'til ah get a joab an' we find somewhere proper tae live."

"I can get a job too!"

Slow head-shake. "You're gonny go back tae school, get they five highers."

"I can do both – get a part-time job at night, or something."

Head shaking more determinedly. "Ye'll need aw' yer time tae...study an' stuff."

His head hurt too much to argue. Danny leant back against the wall. "Where does she live?"

"Fifteen All Saints Road, Westbourne Park, London double-u nineteen, three are bee." Words committed to memory.

"Whereabouts is that?" Danny folded the crisp-packet lengthways then tied it in a knot and flicked one end across his lips. "From the station, I mean."

"Nae idea – we kin ask somewan, or buy a map or somethin'."

The absent JCB rucksack pushed itself into his mind: the absent Maxie was a shadow at the back of his head, company for the dull ache. "How much money we got left?"

A hand into the pocket of Adidas warm-up pants. "The change fae the tickets, less whit ah spent at the buffet..."

Danny stared at the out-stretched palm.

"...eleven pound forty six pee." Fingers curling around coins and notes.

He levered himself off the wall. Under the rugby-shirt,

delicate silver-coloured links brushed a nipple. Lowering his head, Danny groped for the chain's catch. "We could sell..."

"Aye, right!" Snort. "*Crimewatch* is nationwide, 'member? Mebbe ah look like somethin' aff *Babylon 5* noo, but that thing's..." A hand on his neck, shoving the chain back beneath rugby shirt. "...whit did the polis-wuman say aboot it?"

Danny frowned. "Distinctive and highly unusual." The voice was etched on his brain. He sank back against the wall, trapping bitten fingers.

They made no escape-attempt.

He rubbed himself against ragged flesh.

The train was slowing. The fingers moved lower.

Arching his back, Danny rested an elbow on an white-striped shoulder. Fingertips rubbed the waistband of his jeans. He glanced right.

Fields became trees and trees became houses. More houses.

The train slowed further.

A spiky black head leant against his. Danny smiled.

Glasgow: five hundred miles away.

Last night: five hundred light years away.

Different city. Different people...

A pale hand fingered the slender length around his neck.

...who didn't matter. Who didn't exist.

Low snort. "Ah thought ye liked it." Gentle tug.

"I do!"

"You were gonny sell it."

"Only to give us...money." Danny dragged his eyes from blocks of concrete flats and stared into a frowning face...

...which cracked into a grin. Then the fingers on his waist were poking and he was elbowing in the direction of a laughing face and the fingers were tickling and Glasgow was even further away.

Chapter Nineteen

Fourth phone-call.

Fourth ten-pee. Danny stuck a finger in one ear, blocking out a tannoyed message behind. He asked the same question for the fourth time.

A different question in return. "Are you a relative?"

"Er, yes..." Danny tugged the fabric of an Adidas warm-up top.

Kel spun round.

Danny held the receiver between them. The voice from Glasgow Royal Infirmary's A&E department desk talked on:

"Mr Kelston is recovering well. After surgery, he was transferred to Ward 16, Male Surgical. Visiting-times are between..."

"Thanks." Danny replaced the received and stared at the bruised face opposite. "Happy?"

Pink skin flushed pink around a greenish cheekbone. Wordless nod. Kel shrugged the Head bag higher on a white-striped shoulder. "You gonny phone yours?"

Danny frowned, eyes scanning beyond the spiky-haired figure to the station concourse.

Bigger.

Shinier.

Noisier...

...even at half-seven in the morning. Fingers tightened around one remaining ten pee. "And tell them what?" His parents were the last thing on his mind. Danny refocused on an ebony-topped face.

A shrug. "That's ye're okay – they might be worried." Head cocked.

Danny scowled. They'd be worried that he was missing something important at school...

...that he'd lost his Wrangler jacket and hadn't finished his homework. He leant against the public telephone and stared past a white-striped arm. Something tingled at the back of his mind. He pushed it away, walked towards the

Underground sign.

They had to change. Three times.

Nothing went where it said it went. All the stations looked alike and everyone was walking the opposite way.

Tunnels blurred into other tunnels. His feet hurt. Steep escalators carried them ever downwards. Steeper stairwells spiralled back up. His legs hurt.

They got on a train.

They got off after one stop.

They got on another train.

They got lost.

On another platform, Kel stopped four different people, received four blank stares.

Danny watched the back of four different heads merge into the sea of skulls. Then he was shouting over tannoys and asthmatic doors and Kel was pulling him down another tunnel past a guy with a guitar and an arrow marked Westbound pointing the other way. His head hurt.

On the sixth train he pressed a hot forehead against a cool steel pole and stared into greylight.

Then daylight.

His eyes hurt. He closed them. A voice in his ear:

"Baker Street...wis that no' a song?"

Danny gripped the pole and tried to stay upright. Tangled maps of coloured lines writhed on his eyelids.

The train stopped. Bodies pushed past him. Another hand gripped beside his. The voice in his ear again:

"Paddington – like the bear, eh?"

Danny squeezed his eyes more tightly shut. The train moved off. His head hurt worse than ever. A gentle nudge:

"C'mon..."

Eyelids eased apart. He stared through a window at rows of tower-blocks, then surveyed the rest of the train.

Emptier.

Head bag on knees, Kel was lounging over three seats. A nail-bitten hand patted a fourth.

He pulled his fingers free from the steel pole and sat down.

222

Kel snatched an abandoned newspaper from the opposite row of seats. Bitten-fingers flicking.

Danny stared back at the tower-blocks. They shrank into multi-storey car-parks.

The doors opened...

Two black guys in green overalls got on.

...closed. A Royal Oak sign passed without comment. Danny glanced at a tabloid-obscured head then twisted round to check the tangle of coloured lines above it.

Westbourne Park was next.

Beyond, vibrant swirls bloomed on concrete walls. The grafitti was bigger, brighter. In Glasgow, people wrote their names in stark, unmistakable letters. Down here, intricately-painted designs exploded, words unreadable amidst neon colours. A splayed knee nudged his:

"Nothin' in the paper."

Danny glanced left.

Kel was rolling up the tabloid, tapping it off the edge of the seat.

He frowned: more people watched *Crimewatch* than read newspapers. Danny examined the pale face beneath the ebony hair.

Luminous green eyes on his.

Jordan...the police...the police...Jordan...

"Whit ye think they're daein'?"

He was trying not to. Danny rubbed the side of his head and looked away.

Beyond the window, parallel tarmac lines snaked upwards then dipped down. He focused on a small green car and followed its progress.

Jordan...the police...the police...Jordan...

...Maxie...

Vaguely curious. "Wonder who else saw it?"

Danny's heart lurched. Witnesses...

...his mind rewound to a strobing blue ambulance-light and a huddle of mumbling neighbours. Then the ambulancemen, one of whom had got a good look at...

"Think a lotta folk recognised me?" Less-vaguely curious.

223

The parallel lines diverged. The small green car disappeared. His neck switchbacked left, mouth opening. A frown.

Grin. "Wonder if onywan we ken phoned in?" Grin widening. "Christ, ah bet there's an announcement at assembly this mornin', eh?" Nail-bitten fingers through ebony spikes, then laced behind head. Adidas-clad legs stretched out, crossed at ankles. "The polis'll be there – mebbe that wee community-polis wi' the specs – an' auld Cooper'll be standin' beside him oan the stage..." Face contorted, voice sinking to a parody-bass. "Now, ah'm sure you all seen that hooligan Michael Kelston oan television last night..."

The sides of his frown twitched upwards. The imitation was spot-on.

"...so if any of you..." Mimicry wavering. "...gutless wankers ken where he might be, tell this nice polis-man an' he'll write it doon in his nice notebook." A trainered foot kicked his.

Danny kicked back, not wanting to think about what else Mr Cooper might say. His mind strayed onto the positive: no-one had any idea they'd been on the train...

Maxie's huge body squeezed itself into what was left of his mind, followed by tanned handsome features.

...no-one who would tell the police.

The parody-face remained fixed. "There's also...the mattera yon swotty wee poof Daniel MacIntyre..."

The frown re-solidified. The change unregistered. Mock-bass charging on:

"...who's wanted fur missin'-oot a comma in wanna his essays. The...Punctuation Polis ur investigatin' further an'..."

Danny kicked an ankle. Hard.

"Ow, ya...!" Imitation disintegrating. "Whit wis that fur?"

Danny scowled. He looked up from the floor and met two pairs of curious dark eyes on the seats opposite.

"Whit?"

"Don't use that word." Danny dragged his eyes from the

half-smiling faces of the men in the green overalls.

"Whit word?"

Danny looked back at the floor. "You know what word I mean..."

"Swotty?" Snigger.

Something twisted inside him. "Very funny..." An elbow in his ribs:

"Thought you said it wis jist a word? Sticks an' stones can break ma bones, but words..."

Hurt too. Most of all from a mouth he wanted to feel against his. Danny chewed his bottom lip. "I know. I did. It is." Hs own lies trapped him. "Forget it..."

"Naw, ah'll no' forget it..."

Bitten fingers grabbing his arm. Danny flinched. The train was slowing.

"Bent-boay, bum-boy, cunt...jist words..." Green eyes glared into his. "...so it disney matter!"

His own phrase parroted back to him. Danny tried to look away. Couldn't. He tried to answer. His own lies wrapped themselves around his throat. "It matters..." Danny wrenched an answer free. His chest tightened. "...when the person who says it matters." The grip on his arm relaxing:

"Whit auld Cooper says matters?" Disbelieving.

The train stopped. Danny pulled away and walked towards opening doors. "No, he doesn't matter."

Jordan.

The platinum chain...

...words – just words. Footsteps behind. An arm slung around his shoulder:

"That's whit ah thought!" Triumphant. Then teasing. "Ye can be affy weird sometimes, you can."

Danny stepped from the train and looked left.

The bruises had faded to a grey/green, freckles starting to grow back. Brighter green was scanning the platform. Lank tufts of matt-black stuck up from the pale face, a dozen two-inch exclamation marks.

Danny frowned. "Least I've got a decent hair-cut!" He moved towards a sign marked 'Exit'. Anguished snort behind:

225

"Ye said it looked okay!"

"I lied!" He darted away from a low flying Head bag.

Resentment fled and they were running along the platform, tossing tickets into an empty cubicle with a Tickets sign above it and out onto a street full of kids in Adidas warm-ups suits and Cat rucksacks.

Kel was gnawing at a forefinger.

Danny stared from an expressionless face to a red front door and back again. He nodded to a small white button.

More gnawing.

Danny re-read the name-plate. He raised his eyes to a large satellite dish. Another bell was ringing in the distance.

A school bell.

He looked at his watch – quarter to nine – then the red door then the expressionless face.

"You dae it, eh?" Words through gnawing – the first words since they'd arrived outside the brick, two storey house, ten minutes ago.

Danny's finger hovered, then pressed.

More ringing. Other ringing.

At his side, Kel had lowered the Head bag from a white-striped shoulder and was nudging it with the toe of a trainer.

Danny listened to the echo of a ring, ears straining. He glanced at Kel, then pressed again.

Again the echo.

"What if your mum's...not in? Does she work?"

A shrug at his side. "Nae idea..."

He leant his finger against the white doorbell and kept it there...

"Hold on – I'm comin'!"

...until a voice from inside pulled his finger away. He smiled encouragingly at the pale, freckled face...

...then the red door opened and he was looking at another freckled face.

Skin less pale. Scarlet, shoulder length-hair. Bob-cut. Green eyes. Blue cardigan. Baggy black sweatpants and

226

bare feet. One hand on the side of the door. "Yes? What is it?" Impatient. Un-Scottish-sounding.

Danny stared at the other hand, and the small, coffee-coloured fist gripped in paler fingers.

"What do you want?" Harassed-impatient.

He looked away from the chubby, smiling child in denim jumpsuit. Eyes flicked between two less-happy faces. He waited for Kel to say something.

Silence. Then: "Michael?" Semi-lipsticked lips moving upwards.

Snort. "Naw – This is Yer Life an' ah've forgotten ma big rid book!"

"What are you doing here?" Half-laugh. "And what...have ye done to your hair?"

"No' like it?"

"Ah didn't recognise you." Three-quarters-laugh. "Why didn't you phone and...?"

"Spur o' the moment thing – this is Danny."

Bright green eyes continued to focus on others. "Michael, ah..."

Softer voice. "An' who's this?" The sound of knees cracking. A crouching Kel extend a bitten finger.

The coffee-coloured boy shrank back behind a sweatshirted thigh.

Bitten finger wiggled. "Whit's your name?"

A gurgling giggle.

"Say hello to your...big brother, Anthony." Mrs Rodgers swept the chubby, denimed child into her arms.

Gurgling face buried in blue cardigan folds.

The sound of a police-siren behind. Danny flinched.

Kel stood up, head cocked to beyond the red front door. "Ony danger o' comin' in?"

Shadow of a laugh. Mrs Rodgers moved back. Kel was still wiggling a finger at the gurgling, giggling face as Danny picked up the Head bag and followed them past the red front door.

Anthony charged around, baby-walker wheels impacting off kitchen-units.

Danny sat at a wooden table. The sounds of morning television seeped punctuated the noise of frying.

Opposite, Kel stared at a cardiganned back.

"Half-term up there?"

"Aye, that's right."

More morning television. Then:

"Two eggs fur you, Danny?"

He jumped. "Yes, thanks..." He followed narrowed green eyes, watching the holes they made in the back of a blue cardigan.

Which turned. Two plates extended, placed on the table. Kel's eyes moved with the gesture.

Danny looked at his breakfast, then the pale face...

...another face now focused plate-wards. He groped for a smile. "Thanks, Mrs Kelston...er, Rodgers."

Brief nod. "You've grown, Michael – it wasn't jist the..."

"Did ye expect me tae git smaller?"

Self-conscious laugh. "No, ah jist mean..." Words tailing away.

The baby-walker impacted with Danny's then the leg of the table.

A gurgle. A wheeled frame expertly manoeuvred free.

"How long can ye stay?"

Danny raised his eyes to where Kel was shovelling food into his mouth.

Chewing snort. "Wantin' ridda me already?"

"Of course not!" Said too quickly.

Danny lifted a knife and sawed at a fried egg. It was over-cooked but easier to cut than the atmosphere.

"It's just...ah've got work in an hour and..." Too apologetic. "...got tae take Anthony to the child-minder and..."

"Don't let me stop ye – ah kin see ye've got mair important things tae dae."

"Just gimme a minute tae get myself organised..." Hint of an accent. An irate gurgle as chubby denim-covered legs were extricated from the baby-walker's sling. Hesitation at the door. Sounds of door opening. Seconds later, another opening in the distance. And closing.

228

Danny looked up.

Kel was still eating. Eyes resolutely on plate.

"Your mum seems okay..."

Munching snort. "You don't ken her."

"Well, neither do you – not after...." How long? They were sitting in a kitchen eating a breakfast cooked by a virtual stranger.

"Some things never change!" Munching laugh.

Danny stared at the crown of a lowered ebony head, then glanced around. "Nice place..." Eyes took in recently-installed units, a spotless fridge and the polished wooden floor beneath it. He paused at a screen with two newsreaders he didn't recognise. "...they've got cable TV."

"Aye, an' double-glazin' an' central-heatin' an' a fuckin' livin'-flame gas fire tae, ah bet!" Words igniting from nowhere.

Danny dragged his eyes from the two newsreaders he didn't recognise: fifteen Priestview Road had all that – except the cable: all the new houses did.

"Never fuckin' shut up aboot livin'-flame gas fires!" A smear of egg-yoke decorated Kel's plate. Bitten fingers pushing it away. "Sittin' here in her nice hoose wi' her nice new man an' her nice new accent – we wurney guid enough fur her!" Green eyes flicked up.

He winced at the pale face.

"Wan wee...bad patch an' she's away – Christ, everywan wis gettin' laid-aff..." Green eyes focused past him. "It wis jist tempray. Somethin' widda come up – we wur nearly at the toppa the housin' list, tae. Jist a matter o' time..."

The voice was different. Older. The woman in the blue cardigan had left...he did the arithmetic...five years ago?

"...okay, it wisney easy fur her – ah could see that. Wisney easy fur me either..."

The words were different. Danny's stomach flipped.

"...ah wis doin' ma best, but ma best wisney guid enough fur her – nothin' wis ever guid enough fur her! There wur nae jobs – there's still nae jobs! Think ah liked her goin' oot tae work? Think ah liked askin' her fur money?" Kel was on his feet, shouting at the wall.

229

Danny stared.

Then lower words. A finger jammed into mouth. "We dinny need her, son – dae we?" Mumbling. "We can manage jist fine on our ain." Tears streamed down the pale face.

Danny's stomach was jumping. He stood up, bumped against the table.

Kel continued to stare at the wall. Green eyes blazed.

Inches away, he reached out a hand. Fingers contacted with a rigid shoulder. Which tensed further...

...and swung upwards, bitten fingers clenched. "Lea' me alain, ya wee...!"

"Kel!" Danny's hand shot out. He gripped a wrist, stopping the fist mind-air as it crashed down towards his face. "Kel!"

Another white-striped arm rose to follow the first.

He seized it, pinning a wrist to the side of a furious body.

Wild green eyes stared blankly into his face.

Wrists quivered in his palms, sending shock-waves up his arms. "Kel...Kel..." Like calling a dog back from somewhere it shouldn't be.

Wild green eyes refocusing, lips slumping from sneer into a limp 'o'.

A pale forehead hit his shoulder. Danny loosened his grip, wrapping arms around a suddenly boneless body.

Shivers leak from a trembling scalp into his palm. Then huge breaths sucked into lungs, expanding the chest against his.

Danny stared beyond, stroking matt-black hair and waiting for the breathing to return to normal.

Eventually it did. Hands hung limply against his thighs. The rugby shirt was damp against his shoulder. An ebony head raised. Throat clearing. Words spoken to the floor between them. "Ah widney huv hit ye."

"I know." He didn't. "'S'okay..." It wasn't...

...and it was. Danny's hand eased itself from thick dark hair. It lingered on the back of a bristly neck.

Half-laugh. Head slowly raised.

He watched its progress.

Ginger lashes remain low. "Ah dunno why ah..."

"Doesn't matter." Kel's breath brushed the side of his face. Then a bang. And a voice:

"Didn't mean tae be so long, I..." Apologetic.

Then the kitchen door was opening and Kel was widening the distance between them.

"Oh! Sorry!" Surprise.

Danny stared at the confused face. His own flushed scarlet. He turned away, hands grabbing plates.

"How auld's...Anthony?" Voice from the other side of the room.

Danny wrenched at a tap.

More surprise. "Fourteen months..." Then grateful for the neutral ground. "Eats like a horse!" Self-conscious laugh. Then: "It's good to see ye, Michael – ah didn't know if you were getting my letters, if you'd...moved or..."

"Ah got'em."

Danny rinsed one plate, then the other. Behind, the stilted conversation staggered on.

"You've...grown so much – ah can't believe how much you've grown."

"Aye, that's me – the human bean-pole."

Half-laugh.

Danny sighed: he shouldn't be here – this was private, personal.

"How's school?"

"Fine."

"How's...?" Unable to say the name.

Unable to tell the truth. "He's fine."

Pause, then: "What happened to your face – is that a bruise?"

Danny continued to wash already-spotless plates, braced for another untruth.

It didn't come. "Aye, it's a bruise. Matches the wan oan his knuckles."

Danny waited for a response. The lack of one prickled the hair on the back of his neck. He turned off the tap and wiped hands on jeans. "Er, can I use your...?" The request

231

froze on his lips.

Large droplets made their way down Mrs Rodgers' face, leaving make-upless tracks.

Kel's hands were deep in pockets. Green eyes focused on the floor.

Danny stood motionless. He didn't know what to do, say or think. Thirty seconds later his legs made their way to the door and he was looking for the toilet.

Chapter Twenty

When he got back, Kel was lounging back in a chair. Adidas-ed legs hung over the edge of the table.

The TV was louder.

Danny leant against the edge of a work-top.

Grin. Over the sound of the TV: "Found the bog, then?"

Danny nodded, eyes scanning.

Answer to an unasked question. "She's away tae work – we've got the place tae oorselves 'til..." Nod upwards. Scowl. "...he gets up, 'boot twelve-ish."

"Oh. Okay." He didn't know what else to say. Life should have a rewind button. Danny refocused on the grinning face.

"She says we can stay as lang as we like." Off-hand. Face refocused on the TV.

He fiddled with the edge of the worktop. "What does your mum do?" The magazine programme on the TV had broken for the ten o'clock news.

"She's a nurse..." Snort.

Danny fumbled for another subject.

"...looks efter other folk, nae problem, but when it comes tae her ain kid she..."

"Want to go out?"

Green eyes stared at him. "Oot...where?"

Danny shrugged. "For a...walk or something..." He wandered over to the TV sat, leant an arm on it. "We could go and see the...Tower of London."

Where they once took murderers.

Maxie...

...Danny closed his eyes. The newsreader's voice swam around his head like a goldfish. Then a hoot:

"Notch!"

His eyes sprang open. Words vibrated up from beneath his fingers:

"...an unidentified man is today recovering in Northampton General Hospital after apparently falling from a train. Although suffering extensive bruising and a

233

broken arm, a spokesman for Northampton General told this programme earlier, he is in a satisfactory condition and lucky to be alive..."

Another hoot. "Telt ye that paddin' oan the big bastard wid help!"

Danny darted in front of the TV. Like Maxie, the item was gone before he'd worked out what was happening.

The news-reader was smiling. "...and on the subject of luck, residents of the Millfield housing-estate, south of Northampton woke up this morning to an unexpected windfall – literally. Several thousand pounds have already been recovered from trees and bushes at the foot of their gardens. Police are baffled by the money..."

Danny sank to a crouch, watching the outside broadcast footage. Up a ladder, a frantic woman in a pink housecoat was plucking pink, purple and brown foliage from the branches of a leafless tree.

"...which appears to be a mixture of Scottish and English currency, and are exploring the possibility that the notes are part of a consignment destined for removal from circulation and therefore..." Smug shuffling of papers. "...non-negotiable. Sorry, Millfield!"

Danny sat down on the parquet floor.

Satisfactory condition...

Satisfactory condition...

...lucky to be alive.

Alive...

The screen returned to an intense-looking couple on a leather couch.

He stared at them, unseeing. Then white-striped legs were twitching in front of his face:

"Removal fae circulation, ma arse!"

His eyes tracked up the warm-up suit.

Frowning. "That's oor money!"

Something rushed from his brain, spangling in his veins. Danny bounded to his feet. "Maxie's okay!"

The frown remained.

Spangling exploded into a shower of pounding light. "He's okay! He's okay!" An arm around his neck:

234

"Stop shoutin', eh? Ye'll wake him up..."

The laugh evened into a broad grin which refused to move. Danny ducked free of the arm. Beyond a double-glazed window the sky was bluer, colours louder. Sparkling conversation from the TV glittered in his ears.

The future was brighter, the present was wonderful and the past had disappeared. Danny beamed into a still-frowning face. "He's okay – Maxie's okay..."

Full lips softening into a smile. Nail-bitten fingers lightly slapping his face. "Aye..."

Danny grabbed a pale wrist, twisted it to his mouth and kissed the inside. The gesture was automatic, unthinking.

Inappropriate.

The warmth of Kel's skin lingered on his lips. The arm wrenched away.

Silence. Then:

"We should celebrate, or somethin'!" White striped legs striding around the kitchen.

Danny leant back against a work-unit, bathed in a hot glow of last-minute reprieve. The spangling zipped through his body. Toes curled, fingertips pulsed...

...groin throbbed. His face flushed.

The blush noted. Snigger. "Weird, eh?"

He focused on eyes which flicked from the front of his jeans and glinted more than usual. Molten lava rushed through his veins.

Less of a snigger. "Ma knob's been like iron, tae – ever since we goat on the train. Must be an...excitement thing, eh? Aw' that dashin' aboot an' stuff." Nail-bitten fingers re-adjusting the front of white-stripped warm-up pants. "Blood rush."

Danny watched the process. He didn't care about the cause. He wanted his hand where Kel's was.

He wanted to stand behind Kel, rubbing the front of his jeans against the baggy seat of white-striped Adidas and feeling Kel's knob twitch under his fingers. He wanted to be in Kel, on Kel – all over Kel. He wanted...

"Wanna see if there's onythin' tae eat? They eggs jist made me hungrier."

His gaze refocused on the back of an ebony head.

Kel was peering into the fridge. Snort. "Christ, whit dae they live oan, doon here?" Turning.

Danny stared.

One hand held a cling-film-covered bowl of salad. The bitten fingers of another gripped a saucer of what might have been cheese: he wasn't sure what it was now.

Lip curling. "Jeez, this is disgustin'!"

Danny giggled. "Are there any potatoes? We could make..."

"Notch!" Plates shoved back in fridge. Cupboard doors wrenched open. "You luck ower there." Cupboard doors shut. Moving on. "An' keep an eye oot fur a chip-pan."

Then he was on his knees, rummaging through other cupboards, the head of another hunger pushing at the waistband of his underwear.

A transparent container of sea salt and a bottle containing a dark liquid and a leaf sat on the table.

Danny raised another chip, blew on it.

Kel was turning the pages of Thursday's *Evening Standard*. Pen bobbed between teeth. "Whit's commis mean?"

Danny's eyes moved from the horoscopes. "Commis?"

"Aye, there's masses o' ads fur commis chefs – that a qualification?"

Danny bit the chip. "I don't know – sounds something to do with...commissioning. Maybe it's a style of cooking." He chewed: Kel made a great chip. "Like chinese?"

"Oh, right." A bitten-finger edging downwards. "There's masses here fur Chinese cooks tae, but ye gotta speak Cantonese – where's Canton?"

"It's not a place – it's the language Chinese people speak." Danny took another chip.

Sigh. "Aw' the wans that get tae work in restaurants, looks like." Page turned. Pen removed from between teeth. Kel grabbed a handful of chips, rammed them in his mouth. Pause, mid chew. "These taste funny."

"Nice, though." He nodded to the bottle with the leaf in

it. "Different vinegar..."

The bottle registered. Green eyes narrowing. "Somewan's dropped somethin' in it!"

"It's...basalmic – the leaf's meant to be there."

Disbelieving look. "You sure?"

"It gives flavour, I think."

Chewing re-commenced. Thoughtful mastication. "Aye – it's nice, sorta...sweet." Slow head-shake. "Canny see it catchin' oan in Royston, but."

Danny left the last chip and dragged the newspaper to his side of the table.

A sparse scattering of red-circled ads.

He peered, then paused, gaze lingering on a tiny ad in the Employment General. "You're not phoning them..." Eyes raised. "...are you?"

Licking finger tips. "Who?"

Danny glanced back at a red circle. "The...male-and-female-escorts-wanted people."

Snort. "They're 'boot the ainly wans who dinny want experience."

He squinted at minuscule print. "They also want over-eighteens only."

"So? Ah git intae pubs nae problem."

Danny looked up. "You know what escort means?"

"'Course!" Worldly shrug. "Ah gotta dress up an' go wi' auld women tae restaurants an' stuff..."

He thought about the ads in the 'Escort' section of the magazines no longer under the carpet in his room.

"...an' ah git extra if they want me tae fuck them."

The word made him shiver. Danny blinked.

Grin. "Nae sweat!"

Danny shivered again.

Shrug. "Same as fuckin' lassies, 'cept they're gonny be a bit looser cos they're aulder an' had kids an' that."

He stared down at the newspaper.

Snigger. "You've never fucked a lassie, huv ye?"

The unmissable implication filled his brain. The idea of Kel with girls made his stomach lurch.

"It's...different fae whit ye think it's gonny be..."

237

He didn't want to think. He didn't want to hear.

"...no' onythin' like wanking..."

He tried to close his ears.

"...it's aw' wet an' warm an' they're aw' soft an' they jist lie there an'..." Running out of adjectives.

Through the thudding of his heart, ears strained for more. Danny dragged his eyes from newsprint.

Self-conscious grin. "Well, Andrea Clark an' Linda Wilson did."

"You..." He couldn't say the word. "...Linda Wilson?" She sat beside him in Biology.

Nonchalant shrug. "Aye – but this wis years ago – before she went aw' snotty an' started hangin' around wi' the fuckin' rugby-team." Words tinged with resentment.

Danny hauled his mind back to other red circles and the search for employment. "Well, what about...?"

"You could gie'em a ring tae." Grin. "Nae experience necessary, so ye'd be okay."

His brain went into orbit.

"Money fur auld rope – bet it's mainly evenin' work, so you could dae it efter school. Meals are included, ah bet; that wid save us spendin' money oan food an' stuff. Ye'd still huv time tae dae homework..." Focused stare. "...or ye could dae... the guys that want escorted – they gotta eat tae."

His chest tightened. His brain soared back to the tiled room, and the only guy he wanted to be with and what he wanted to do with him.

Hoot. "Or we could dae the women thegether – like a team!"

He was visualising a posh hotel room. Danny stared down at himself and Kel, naked, standing each side of a large bed on which someone with Linda Wilson's face and someone else's body lay sprawling. "No, I..."

"Aw, come on – it wid be a laugh!" A hand ruffled his hair.

"No!" Danny moved away.

Irritated snort. "Who ye savin' it fur?"

The lie was out before he could stop it. "Not saving it for

anyone." Danny chewed his bottom lip. "I just don't want to..." He looked up into a frowning face. "...sleep around."

"Whit's the big deal?" Another snort. "Christ, it's jist ...knobs intae holes."

"I know..." His face flushed. "...but when I...do, I want it to be special." His first time...

'...bin workin' wi' Jordan fur nearly a year...'

...not Kel's first time.

Derisive hoot. "Special?" Laughing. "Wanna hear how special it can be?"

His ears didn't want to know: his groin was back in the tiled room with the bubbling jacuzzi, longing for details.

"Round the backa the garages at Cranhill Park – ah came before ma knob got onywhere near her cunt!" More laughing.

His chest tightened. "What about your first time with Jordan?"

Shreds of a fraying laugh stretched then snapped somewhere above him. Kel grabbed the Head bag and loping towards the door. "C'mon an' we'll dump oor stuff – she said we could huv the bedroom on the top flair."

Danny sighed at the sudden onset of tidiness, and followed.

The house was tall but thin – three storeys, two rooms per storey.

On the first landing, a ebony head poked through an open then nodding at a closed door. Whisper: "That must be her man's room, so keep yer voice doon, eh?"

Danny tightened his lips and moved on up polished wooden stairs. He tried to visualise Kel with some faceless girl, coming all over warm-up pants before he'd even done anything. Then Kel-on-the-bed-thing, in the tiled room, the head of a softening knob sticky with milky sap.

He turned a bend in the stairs and found himself in the middle of a wide, open-plan space.

Kel had thrown the Head bag onto a double bed with no legs and was standing in front of a large, curtainless window. "Notch view – come an' look!"

239

Danny's trainers squeaked on more polished wood. He stared past a three-striped shoulder over a hundred slate roofs. Beyond, the same tarmac snake he's seen on the train slithered wetly between buildings.

"Whit direction's the Tower o' London?"

Danny was still taking in the panorama. "East, I think – beside Tower Bridge." He scanned: which direction was east? "Look for water."

One trainered foot onto the window ledge. Bitten fingers grabbing a curtain-rail. Swaying.

Danny braced his hand against the small of an Adidas-ed back. "See any?"

Sigh. "No' a fuckin' drop!"

His eyes were drawn downwards to the street below. A sign read All Saints Road, W11: if this was west, east must be...

"Water! Ower by the motorway..."

"That's north – the Thames shouldn't be up there..."

"Well, it is!" A hand hauled him onto the window-ledge. One bitten finger pointed to a trickle of gray-blue just visible on the far side of the tarmac snake.

Danny narrowed his eyes. "That's not the Thames – it's too wee. Looks like a...canal."

Snort. "Mebbe it starts aff wee, an' other rivers an' stuff run intae it later oan – like the Clyde?"

In the distance, a siren howled. Danny flinched, then relaxed: London, like Glasgow, had as many ambulances as police-cars. "No, it's the the wrong place – and it's definitely too wee.

Disappointed. "If that's no' the Thames, where is it?" Trying to turn.

Nail-bitten fingers grabbing his shoulder for balance. Danny wobbled.

A bell rang. Loudly. Two floors below.

He wobbled more violently, eyes flicking left and down to the street below.

A car...

Another ring.

...a police car.

240

Silence.

The hand on his shoulder regripped.

Danny lost his balance, toppling from the ledge. He heard the third and fourth rings over Kel's giggles.

"All right, all right..."

A deep, unfamiliar voice cut the giggles short.

Footsteps.

More ringing.

He looked from the edge of the stairs to the window-ledge.

Kel's head turned slowly from the window. The face was a mask. Trainered feet landed squeakily on polished wood.

More footsteps. And more ringing.

More deep, irate complaints.

Then the sound of a door opening and they were both crouching around the top of the stairwell, ears aimed down.

Two voices rang in his head, sucked up through a conduit of polished wood:

"Mr Desmond Rodgers?"

Sleepy irritation. "So the door says."

"DC Lynne, Mr Rodgers – this is WPC Mandelson. Your wife is Mrs Margaret Rodgers, formerly Mrs Margaret Kelston?

Less sleepy. "Yeah – what's happened?" More worry than irritation.

"Nothing's happened, Mr Rodgers. We'd like a word with your wife."

Worry melting back into irritation. "She's at work – what's this about?"

Danny's fingers gripped the edge of a polished wooden floor. Desmond Rodgers' voice was a deep sing-song. The police officer's jarred, an unwanted refrain. Under it all, Kel's breathing.

"It's in connection with her son. We..."

"Anthony? Something's happened to...?"

"No, Mr Rodgers..." Patient. "...Michael."

Confused. "Who?"

241

More patient. "Michael Kelston – your wife's son, from her first marriage?"

The irritation returning. "He doesn't live here."

"We're aware of that, sir – has your wife heard from Michael recently?"

Irritation growing. "No she hasn't!" Interest waning. "Listen, I'm on split-shifts – I need my..."

"Where is your wife, Mr Rodgers?"

"At work."

"She works...?"

"Hammersmith – Charing Cross Hospital." Irritation twisting into curiosity. "What's he done?"

"I'd be grateful if you could ask your wife to give us a ring if Michael does get in touch, Mr Rodgers."

"What's he done?"

"Just ask Mrs Rodgers to ring if she hears anything, sir."

Pause.

Danny's right foot cramped beneath him. He flexed his ankle, biting back a yell. At his side, Kel was motionless.

"Yeah, okay."

"Thank you, Mr Rodgers – sorry for waking you."

Then a door closing.

Danny massaged a trainered arch. He strained for the sounds of feet on stairs. Outside, a car engine turned over.

No footsteps.

Movement at his side. His eyes swerved left.

Kel was flattening himself against the floor, ebony head slowly leaning into the stairwell.

The cramp had subsided to a sharp stab. Danny crawled forward, risking a glimpse downwards.

Three floors below, a tall, black man in a tartan dressing-gown was standing beside a telephone table, scrutinising a small white card.

Danny stared at the top of a crew-cut head.

The white card placed on the telephone table, Desmond Rodgers walked from the hall into the kitchen.

Two hours later he left the house, wearing the same green overalls as the two guys on the Underground. At the third-floor window, a voice in his ear:

"Thank fuck – ah need a piss!" Trainered feet slapping on polished floor, then polished stairs.

Danny followed. The last one hundred and twenty minutes of silence had thrown up an equal number of thoughts.

Only two were worth bothering with: were they going to stay and, if not, where were they going to go?

He jogged down wooden steps.

The bathroom door was open. Sound of pissing.

He leant against the door-frame, staring at a hunched, white-striped shoulders. His mind read over liquid splatters:

"Ah'll tell her ah ran away..." Snort. "...like mother, like son, eh?"

"What about...him?"

"Who him?" One shoulder shaking. Then a flush. Kel turned.

"Mr Rodgers."

Shrug. "Her problem." Then a smile. "Wanna go find the Tower o' London noo?" Tap turned on, hands washed.

Danny's brain was back with one hundred and eighteen fruitless thoughts: it hadn't taken the police long to track them down – but the police tried everywhere, and it seemed so obvious now that, if not actually staying with her, someone who was implicated in a robbery and had just shot his father might at least contact his mother.

"Eh?" Shout over hand-washing.

Were they watching the house? Were they questioning the lucky-to-be-alive Maxie? Danny frowned: no, Maxie wouldn't say anything...

His heart hammered.

...at least to the police.

"Ground control tae Major Dan – come in, Major Dan!"

Danny blinked.

Kel grinned at him. "Tower o' London, then?" Eyes to cabinet above sink. "Hey, he uses Kurous!" Bottle snatched. A squirt into wet hands. Jaw lightly slapped.

A sweet smell invade his nose. The bathroom became

the safest place on earth. "I don't think we should go out until we...have to – just in case we..."

"Christ, ah keep thinkin' that's somewan else!" Half-laugh. Pinking, freckled face turned from the mirror above the sink. Towel grabbed.,

Danny stared. Maybe the hair made a difference – maybe the police expected a red head on his own, not an ebony one with a blond. Maybe...

The decision was made for him. Hoot. "Okay, ye had yer chance – we stay, make mair chips an' check-oot the cable."

Chapter Twentyone

Voices...

...the guy trying to sell him a hand-crafted, limited-edition musical jewellery box stopped, mid-rant.

A woman shouted in what sounded like Spanish but could have been Portuguese.

On the couch, Danny raised a heavy eyelid.

On the floor, a white furry rug. On the rug, Kel. Doo-dah gripped, pointed. Snort. "Fuck, where's Sky News? Ah had it a minute ago..."

A snatch of English.

A snatch of American-accented English...

...more of the Spanish/Portuguese. Danny eased another eyelid open.

The TV chopped channel. Black-and-white images merged into colour then bled back into monochrome. A man talked at a woman. The woman twisted a handkerchief between her hands and stared at a wet pavement...

...the guy with the jewellery-box was repeating an 0891 telephone number.

Danny rubbed an eye. "Turn it down a bit."

Ebony head swivelling. "Decided tae join the land o' the livin'?" Pupils glinting.

"I wasn't asleep." Maybe his body had been...

A grin. "Ye were – ah asked twice if ye wur awake an' ye didney answer!"

...his mind had replayed bits of a well-known film with various endings:

The police coming back.

Desmond Rodgers coming back. Finding them.

Desmond Rodgers coming back. Finding them. Dragging them to the nearest police-station.

Desmond Rodgers coming back. Himself and Kel barricading the door. Going upstairs to the open-plan room with the bed with no legs, which was now tiled and had a jacuzzi. Himself and Kel on the bed. Lying on their sides.

245

Kel...

"Ye canny remember whit number Sky News wis, can ye?" Hopeful. Doo-dah peered at.

The request blew fragments of dream from his brain. Danny edged upright. "Turn it down!"

"Nae need tae shout." Shouting. Doo-dah aimed.

He stared past the ebony head to a mute face with a still-moving mouth.

They had to talk.

They had to plan.

They had to work-out what they were going to do when...

"Ah phoned." Ebony head turning.

He blinked. "You phoned...?" The male-and-female-escorts ad shimmered in his mind.

Smug smile. *"Crimewatch."* Smile widening. "The lines wur closed, but they put me through tae the polis in Edinburgh."

His mind shuddered to a halt.

"Don't ye wanna ken whit ah telt'em?"

His mouth opened. Nothing came out.

"Ah said ah'd seen the guy in the programme wi' the red hair at Stranrar, gettin' oan the two o'clock ferry tae Belfast – ah ken there's a two o'clock wan cos ah phoned them first tae, check. Guid, eh?"

Danny tried to form words.

"That'll make the polis think we're no' in the country ony mair, so they'll stop lookin' here fur us." Grin. "They asked ma name, but ah said ah wis a businessman an' ah didney wanna git involved but it wis definitely the guy wi' the red hair." Thoughtful pause. "They asked whit he wis wearin', so ah made somethin' up."

Danny's head turned slowly towards the hall. "You phoned from here?"

Snort behind. "Think ah'm daft? Used the wan at the bottom o' the street."

His eyes brushed the wall-clock: quarter past four. "Did you do...one-four-one?"

"Whit's that?"

"Call-blocking..." He focused on the clock-face. No-one – businessman or otherwise – could get from Stranrar to London in two hours.

"Ah..." Shadow of doubt. Then shadow shortening. "...but even if they trace it, it's jist a phone-box."

Danny turned away from the clock. Just a phone-box.

In a street. In London – the destination of a train from which a Glasgow man fell?

The city where Kel's mother lived?

Just a phone-box: just a...coincidence?

He stared at the confused face, then looked back at the clock: they wouldn't be here long anyway – not when Mr Rodgers told Mrs Rodgers about the police-visit, and Mrs Rodgers added that to Kel's explanation of their presence and... "Let's just go." He swung his legs onto a polished floor.

"Go where?" Scowl.

"Anywhere!" He paused inches from the door. Then Kel was standing beside him:

"Haud on til it gets dark, eh?"

Dark, light: it made little difference. Danny walked into the hall. A white card shone up at him from the telephone table.

White card seized. "This whit ye're worried aboot?" White card waved.

Danny chewed his lip: that, and everything else – including an unnecessary phone-call.

"Nae problem – she'll tell him whit ah tell her, an' he'll believe her." Trying to sound convinced.

At the foot of the stairs, he turned.

Bitten fingers flicking the edge of the white card. Ginger lashes lowered. "Ah canny jist leave." Finger gnawed. "There's stuff ah need tae..." A trainered toe nudging the side of a polished stair. Sentence unfinished.

Danny stared. Five years of stuff. He remembered the cuttable atmosphere in the kitchen earlier – and the words which came from Kel's mouth via five years' worth of resentment from another mouth...

The fingers gnawed. "It'll no' take long." Studiedly

247

casual. "Since we're here onyway..."

Dark would be better, less conspicuous. He thought about the just-under-eight-pounds they had left, wondering if it was enough for a hostel.

Then Kel was looking up at him through lowered lashes and Danny was walking back into the living-room and trying to relocate Sky News.

"Eh?"

Danny wanted to leave the room again. He couldn't tear his eyes from the pale face.

Collected, fed and watered, Anthony was baby-walkering around again. Margaret Rodgers had arrived back thirty minutes ago and was still in the blue cardigan...

Action-replay of this morning. Inaction-replay.

... now over a blue and white uniform. Now kneeling on the white furry rug. Not moving. Staring.

"They no' huv abortions back then or somethin'?" Voice calm.

On the couch beside him, rage trembled up from an white-striped thigh.

"Michael, ah..."

"Oh, ah get it." Ebony head nodding, mock-understanding. "They gie ye a hoose if ye huv a kid."

Anthony bumped into the side of the sofa, giggled and staggered away.

Danny focused on the chubby figure.

"Took ye ten years tae work-oot it wisney the kinda hoose ye wanted, so ye packed yer bags, found another guy an' had another kid an' got..." Forced laugh.

Anthony wandered over to his mother. Automatic, cardiganned arms lifting a giggling bundle from the baby walker.

"...another hoose!" Snort. "Ye did guid, hen – took ye a while, but ye managed it."

"Oh, Michael..."

Anthony struggled and gurgled in blue cardiganned arms.

"...it wasn't like that. Ah..."

248

"Whit wis it like, then?" Another shiver. Then standing. Shouting. "Wis it me? Did ye no' like...?"

A strangled cry. Then a roar. Blue-cardiganned arms hugging the crying Anthony.

Danny looked up at Kel.

Green eyes stared straight ahead. A pale, bitten hand reaching out towards the back of a curly black head. Then withdrawing. Low, desperate words over subsiding roars. "Ye didney wanna leave – he wis knockin' lumps oota ye..." Eyes focused on mother and child. "...an' ye couldney stand it ony mair..." Desperation increasing. Voice lower. "Ye wurney thinkin' straight: ye didney huv time tae get me fae school an' ye wur gonny come back fur me but ye..." Words whispered. The remnant of a thumb-nail torn with teeth. "Ye didney want tae leave, but ye..." Words fading.

Danny's chest was tight. He stared into a face he'd never seen before. In the background, Anthony's cries had reverted to less discontented gurgles.

"Oh, ah wanted to." Margaret Rodgers stood up and began to pace slowly. "Couldn't wait!"

Danny recognised the motion. Not the words.

"Ah can't lie to you, Michael..." Patting the back of a denim jumpsuit. "Lied to myself for ten years: happy wife, proud mother – everyone liked me when ah lied." Turning, words into the side of a curly black head. "But it wisney working – it had never worked. When Arch...your dad lost his job and ah went back to Ruchill part-time, it worked even less." Turning back, words fainter. "Ah was twenty six, Michael. Each time ah got back from the hospital, your dad was further away from me. So the odd shift turned into doubles – part-time turned into full..."

Disbelieving. "Ye didney need tae work – we woulda managed. A mother's place is..."

"Christ, ye sound so like him!" Pacing stopped. Margaret Rodgers paused at the edge of a chair, lowing the softly snuffling shape onto a cushion. Other cushions arranged around an almost-asleep Anthony.

Danny looked at Kel.

Pale face flushed pink.

He looked away.

Margaret Rodgers perched on the arm of the chair. Sad smile at the floor. "Ye probably canny hate me more than ye already dae, so ah'll no' lie tae ye."

Danny dragged his eyes from one freckled face and stared up at another. Words in the background:

"You wur the last thing on my mind, Michael – you were part of the lies. If ah'd thought about you, ah couldney huv left. So ah didney think about ye." Pause. "Sound like a real bitch, don't ah? That's whit they aw' said – the neighbours, ma friends...the court..."

Danny began to count freckles.

"...abandoned ma kid – went from perfect wife and mother tae the maist despised wuman on earth. But that didn't matter, because ah wis finally tellin' the truth – no' so much tae them, but tae me..."

The words hovered around his head, releasing tiny bombs of information into his brain. Danny watched pink skin pale beneath freckle number eighteen with every detonation.

"Ah wanted nice...things. Ah wanted oota Cranhill so much it hurt. Ah couldney be somethin' ah wisney, ony mair – ah wis...rottin' away, inside." Sigh. "Can ye understand that, Michael?"

An atomic device went off inside Danny's head. Eyes whirled round from the freckle-count.

Kel's mum's face was unnaturally calm. White shoes clacked dully across the white furry rug. "Can ye understand whit it's like tae pit oan an act, month efter month – year efter year?" Difficult words...

...aftershocks reverberated in Danny's heart. He could hear the sound of Kel's breath.

"Ah gave ye up, Michael – ah hate masel' fur that mair than you ever can, but at least ah ken who ah am noo, an' ah can live wi' that person." Pause. "Maist o' the time."

Danny watched a carefully-manicured hand come to rest on a white-striped shoulder. He watched it allowed to remain there.

250

"Noo, are ye gonny to tell me whit you an'..." Head slowly turning. "...Danny are doin' here?"

He flinched under a perceptive green gaze.

Half-laugh. Eyes returning to the freckled face. "Ah'm the last person ye'd visit through choice!"

Danny frowned.

Silence.

Another half-laugh. "Come on – ye've no' killed anyone, huv ye?"

Danny remembered the half-agreed story. He opened his mouth. Words tumbling from other lips:

"Naw, ah didney kill him – it wis jist a graze. The polis think ah robbed a supermarket. Ma picture wis oan *Crimewatch*, cos o' the platinum chain, an' the twenty K fell oot the train along wi' Big Maxie an' Danny hurt his heid an'..." Pausing for breath.

Sceptical smile. Then concern. Turning. "Let me see."

Danny shrank back. "It's okay, really..." Hand to the small lump at the back of his skull.

Then fingers were parting his hair, gently probing. In the background:

"...the polis wur here, when ye wur oot – yer man talked tae them. They wur lookin' fur..."

Words in his ear:

"Whit's really happened – you two run away?" Fingers continued to probe.

Danny listened to the truth and half-lied. "Yes – ow!"

"Sorry – that's a nasty lump." Fingers moving from scalp. "Ye should get it looked at." Sigh.

Danny moved back.

Yards away, Kel had stopped talking. Frowning eyes.

Mrs Rodgers sat on the arm of a chair. Eyes from a fading bruise on a pale cheekbone to Danny. "Did Archie thump you tae?"

Danny winced. "No." The truth sounded more like a lie than the lies had.

"You phone yer parents, let them know you're okay." Eyes back to Kel. "Michael, we'll work somethin' oot – move ye down here, or something. Ah've been trying to

251

get him all day – he's no' answerin' the phone." Lips tightening. "But he'll have to answer a visit from the police, when ah..."

"He's in the hospital – an' the polis already ken, cos he'll have telt them whit happened."

Low panic. "What did happen, Michael?"

Danny looked beyond a blue-cardiganned figure and caught a green eye. He tried a reassuring smile. It faltered miles from his mouth.

A ginger slug raised.

Danny nodded. He walked over to where Kel was sitting and stood behind the couch. Parallel with his chest, an ebony head began to move.

Anthony was sleeping, oblivious.

In the kitchen, Mrs Rodgers was preparing a meal. Noisily.

Danny looked at Kel.

Leaning over the edge of the cot, bitten fingers gently stroked a black curl.

"We should have told her about Jordan, too."

Bitten fingers paused. "She disney need tae ken aboot that."

Danny sighed: more half-truths. "But we...?"

"If we'd telt her aboot Jordan..." Words slow and measured, staring at one child and talking to another. "...we'd huv tae tell her aboot Maxie an'...." Stroking recommenced. "...that gets really complicated."

And involved more than an accidental wounding and possession of stolen money. Danny stared at a smudge of fading hair-dye on the back of Kel's neck.

"Think we luck like each other?"

Danny smiled. Even with the ebony hair, Kel and his mum were similar: the pacing, the way the green eyes darted and roved. Similar, but different – Margaret Rodgers was a further-on version of Kel. "Yeah, but she doesn't bite her nails."

Low snort. "Ah don't mean her – me an' Tony here." Fingers moving from the black curl. Kel raised his head.

252

Danny laughed. "Not really – he looks like...his dad."
Self-evident.

Kel didn't smile. Green eyes focused somewhere in middle distance.

Danny wondered what he was thinking about. Then distant bangings from the kitchen dragged him back to his own brain. "What do you think she'll decide?" The semi-confession had ended, fifteen minutes ago, with her request for 'time to think.'

"Disney usually huv a problem wi' decisions!" Kel moved from the cot and leant against the wall.

Danny moved to beside the lounging figure. "We should go – it's not fair on her, putting her in..."

"Naw!" Hiss. "She fuckin' owes me! Wan night..."

A gnawed finger trembled in front of Danny's face.

"...wan night, fur five years – she fuckin' owes me that much!"

On the other side of the room, low snuffling.

Danny glanced at a re-settling Anthony, edging towards the door. "But it's not just up to her, is it?"

Kel stared at him.

On cue, the sound of an opening, then closing door at the far end of the hall explained further. Danny watched the back of a green-overalled shape make its way into the kitchen, then nodded upstairs.

Sigh. "Aye, lea'em tae it."

Life was waiting in other rooms for other people to discuss and make decisions around them.

At the top of the house, Danny lay on the bed, chin resting on palm.

Kel was unpacking the Head bag, flapping creases from crease-resistant warm-up suits and draping them over a high-backed chair.

Danny watched the process. His mind rewound. Two hours earlier, Des Rodgers had stood where Kel stood now:

"Tomorrow. First thing." Wide, sombre face.

Danny couldn't take his eyes of Des Rodgers' mouth. Broad, purple lips spreading around very white teeth. The

Liverpool accent hadn't been as noticeable when he'd answered the door, that afternoon.

Wry smile. "Running away never solved anything. Only so far you can run. Sometime, ya gotta stop."

Danny replayed the conversation and watched Kel.

Then they'd all gone downstairs and eaten something with salad. No questions, just general chat.

About school.

About work.

Danny had glanced at Kel, noticed Des Rodgers doing the same to Kel's mum.

No questions...asked. He and Des had talked to fill the spaces, which wasn't easy since there was little common ground. So he asked questions. Danny remembered the sound of his own voice rambling on about balsamic vinegar.

Des had trained as a chef before he'd been laid off.

Then Kel stopped staring at his plate and joined in.

Commis was explained.

He'd dried dishes while Margaret Rodgers washed and Kel and Des discussed the merits of qualifications over on-the-job experience.

They'd watched television until Des had to go to bed – he was on earlies, from tomorrow onwards.

The whole thing had been so normal it felt abnormal.

After he'd shaken Danny's hand and done a palm-slapping routine with Kel, abnormality had returned.

On the other side of the room, unpacking continued. A crumpled mass of dark green fabric hauled free.

He stared at the John Rocha. It hadn't fared as well as the warm-up suits.

"Seems okay, eh?" First words in a while.

Danny blinked. "Bit crumpled, but an iron'll..."

"No' the suit..." Head cocked to the stairwell. "... Des." Jacket and trousers carefully laid over the creaseless pile.

"Oh...yes." A tee-shirted figure threw itself onto the bed beside him:

"Must be aw' right, bein' black..."

An arm grabbed him in a mock neck-lock. Danny

wriggled free. From downstairs, the sound of one door closing, then another opening and doing the same told him Kel's mum had gone to bed too. The arm re-grabbed:

"Tarentino's black guys are notch..."

Danny gave up struggling and leant back against the tee-shirted body. "There weren't any in *Reservoir Dogs*..."

Snort. Mock-pummel of a shoulder.

Danny winced.

"Aye, but Travolta's side-kick wis black in *Pulp Fiction* , an' the big baldy-heid-honcho guy wis black...."

Danny shivered, remembered finger-viewing the scene with Bruce Willis in the basement.

"...an' there's Jackie Whit's-her-face, in his new wan – the air-hostess."

Danny giggled. "Des isn't an air-hostess or a..." Jordan's handsome, whiter face circled in his mind. "...drug-dealer."

Hoot. "'Course no'!"

The arm pulled him back further. Kel's heart pounded against Danny's spine.

"Ah'm jist sayin' Des is...followin' in the great tradition o' notch black guys!" The grip slackened.

Danny twisted round.

Kel was lying beneath him, one skinny arm behind an ebony head. "Aye?"

Danny raised his chest from a tee-shirted one, moving weight to his hips. "Yes, I suppose so – but they're not real." Hardness from the pocket of Adidas warm-up pants pressed up into his thigh.

Grin. "Aye, they're no' real, right enough!"

The hardness bucked up against him. Danny frowned. "I mean they're...made up – Tarentino's ones." His body pushed down, rubbing against the hardness.

Snort. "So? Musta bin based oan...somewan – like the folk in your books."

"Suppose so..." Danny gave up. He moved, groin brushing a humped outline...

...a too-hard humped outline. He shrank back...

Shoulders braced, bitten fingers plunged into pocket.

...then jumped as a darker object clanked onto polished

255

wood at the side of the bed.

Then Kel was undressing and Danny was doing the same.

Chapter Twentytwo

Big bed, lots of space.

Danny lay on his back in the middle. The platinum chain was a slack, clammy hoop around his neck. A muscle thrummed in his right thigh. He ignored both.

Inches away, Kel twisted and turned, eventually settling into a face-down-arms-pinned-under-chest-position. Ebony hair spiked up from a pale blue pillow around paler skin.

Danny stared at the side of a snub nose and one translucent lid – he couldn't see the other eye.

They should talk.

They should talk about tomorrow.

Ginger lashes fluttered in the half dark, came to rest above a shadowed cheekbone. A snuffle.

Beneath the duvet, a leg threw itself over his. Danny's knob twitched against his stomach. He edged away from the flailing thigh at his balls and re-focused on the ceiling.

Another snuffle. The limb settled. A bony knee pressing against the inside of his legs.

He concentrated upwards. One hand moving to finger the platinum chain. The other lay damp against a pale blue sheet.

Light moved across a recently-plastered surface in broad tapering beams, narrowing off to pencil width then disappearing down the wall in stunted zig-zags.

Too high for car headlights – plane lights? The double-glazed window kept out all sound.

He followed the sweeps with his eyes, mind moving back to Des Rodgers' words, then forward to tomorrow.

The police would understand. It was just a matter of explaining...

A thick bank of white flowed effortlessly across the ceiling. More snuffling at his side. An arm brushed his shoulder. Danny watched the light. A shimmer coursed over his balls.

...how it had all started, how Kel was only trying to make Lennox stop...

The arm settled. An elbow grazed his wrist. Danny's balls clenched.

...and how everything that had happened after that, had happened because of that...

Another light-wave broke against cornicing, rippling over the smooth surface. The platinum chain was an itching noose against his skin.

...and it was really all his fault: he should have burnt the money and the gun with their clothes. He should have made sure everything connected with that night was destroyed.

No chain, no CCTV footage, no ambulance at fifteen Priestview Road, no need to run...

A handsome face projected itself onto the ceiling. Danny blinked.

What if none of it had happened?

What if Jordan's mobile hadn't rung?

What if...?

The knee against his thigh shifted higher. Breath on the side of his face. Sweat cooled on his balls.

Jordan.

The tiled room.

Another low bed. Another...

Fingers tightened around the platinum chain.

Cross-currents of light swam towards each other. He waited for the swirling eddy which would form when they met and drag him down into...

The breath on his face paused, then blasted his skin.

Danny shivered.

"Christ, ah'm fuckin' wired." Another sigh. "An' it's boilin' in here!" Harsh, irritated whisper.

Danny's eyes flicked from the maelstrom of light to the body beside his.

"Double or quits?" The leg moved. The arm moved. Kel lay on his back, pale face zebra-striped by receding white beams. One hand tucked behind an ebony head.

Danny watched the peaks and troughs in the duvet, made by movement of the other. His knob pulsed in parallel. "I...can't – don't feel like it." Limp, lame lies.

Sigh. "Well, geeza paira knickers or somethin' fae the floor, eh?" Low voice. Bare feet kicking at the padded quilt.

Cool air brushed his body. Skin flushed with heat. Danny watched bitten fingers curl loosely amidst springy ginger whorls. A fine sheen of sweat slicked pale chest and stomach.

The duvet lay in folds around their feet. His mouth was dry. He moved onto his side, then remembered the silver-coloured packet in the back pocket of his jeans. He lunged over the side of the bed, fingers groping in shadow for discarded clothes. And finding them.

Shallow breathing seeped into his ears. Knob dragged across rumpled sheet then thigh as he turned back.

Kel was sprawling, eyes focused upwards. Curled fingers tugged furiously.

The sight sparked off shivers in his groin, erecting the hair on the back of his neck. "Hold on..." His voice was a hoarse whisper. Fingers fumbled with cardboard packaging, tearing and wrenching. One then two foil-wrapped rectangles freed. Kneeling, he ripped frantically. The mattress trembled beneath him. "Use a condom – it's...less messy."

Nail bitten fingers pausing. Narrowed eyes, then: "Pit it oan me, eh?" Words tight.

Danny crawled across the mattress. One foil-wrapped rectangle between teeth. The other squirmed and writhed in his fingers.

Kel was gripping the base of his knob. The length of flesh stuck up perpendicular from a pale stomach.

Blood drained from Danny's face, racing lower and taking all thoughts of tomorrow with it. Kneeling on a now-still mattress, he leaned over, positioned the tip of the condom above a tiny droplet of clear liquid then began to unroll the dense pink ring.

A long sigh.

His fingers shook. Other fingers moved from beneath his. Sharp ginger springiness brushed his knuckle. Then warm hairy slackness.

The pink ring was less dense now. Kel's knob glistened

259

stripy in light from broad, overhead beams.

Danny's hand remained there, thumb easing the last millimetres of rubber into place. Quivers spread from the encased shaft into his fingers. He glanced right.

A unicorn's horn of ebony hair stuck up from a creased forehead. Green eyes stared at him out of a pale face.

His knob twitched. He wondered how long Kel had been watching.

Low, breathless laugh. "Learn this wee trick fae wanna yer books?"

The flesh in his fist twitched. Danny frowned, remembering his mother's assumptions. Then the flesh slipped from his grip and Kel's mother's words swam in his head.

Nail bitten fingers plucked a still-wrapped rectangle from between his lips:

"Ye want wan tae?"

Danny could only nod.

Kel had moved further along the bed and was sitting up, knees raised. The horn of hair flopped down over a brow now creased in concentration. "C'mere, then..." Bitten fingers tearing at foil-wrapping.

Danny moved between mattress-planted bare feet. He sat back on his heels, eyes circling between his, Kel's knob and the pink ring between them.

They'd sat like this, dozens of times.

They'd wanked each other, dozens of times.

Alone, in his room, he'd stroked himself through latex and felt the drag of two moving skins.

The prospect of Kel sheathing his knob made cold fingers clench inside him...

...then real fingers gripped him and his mind stopped working. Easing up onto knees, Danny braced one hand against the wall behind a lowered head. His other hand rested on a hunched shoulder. Fingers tightened on pale skin as other fingers moved awkwardly.

Whispered irritation. "Fuckin' fiddle, this is – ah canny see whit ah'm doin'..."

Danny tried to speak. Couldn't. He stared down into the

260

darkness between his legs.

Bright light.

The tiled room.

Watching Kel crouch between muscular thighs – watching Jordan watch deft fingers unfurl a length of latex along Jordan's big, veined knob.

Ragged skin caught in the descending condom. Anxious breathing joined the thump of his heart and the lubricated slither of stretching rubber.

The slender chain hung slack between them, swaying slightly.

Danny bit his lip. Each halting pull shot jabs of longing up his length. Fingers tightened on a hunched shoulder. The air swelled with two sets of breathing...

...and no words.

No jokes.

No laughing comments.

No mention of timing or rule-breaking.

Kel's thumb grazed his balls...

...like he'd watched it graze Jordan's.

The urge came from nowhere. Thighs hit heels. Danny released the wall and the shoulder, grabbing in the darkness. One fist found another latexed length and the fingers of his left hand were on the back of Kel's neck...

...and Kel's hand was gripping his thigh and Danny's mouth was wet and trembling on surprised lips.

They fell sideways.

Danny held on. His nose bumped against a chin. Pink fullness slipped away. As his head hit the mattress he searched for and found them again.

A second froze itself. Kel's lips were dry. His mouth was open and damp...

Danny blinked at closed eyelids.

...and motionless. Terror churned in his stomach.

He tried to imagine Jordan kissing Kel...

...the way he'd imagined his own mouth clamped to full, grinning lips for so many months.

And failed.

Terror rose into panic. He'd stopped breathing – Kel had

stopped breathing. A fist was tightening around the root of his knob, mirroring the clench in his chest. Remnants of nails dug into his thigh. A hundred miles away, Danny felt the pain.

Then the moment unfroze itself and Kel was breathing again...

...and leaping from the bed. "Ah telt ye – nae poof stuff!" The voice cracked, anger erupting through breathlessness. Sounds of unsteady feet thudding on polished wood.

The feel of Kel's mouth was imprinted on his. Unable to look away, Danny watched car-headlight sweep past the thin, naked body at the window. Fingers tightened around a sloughed-off, latex skin. Kel's condom cooled in his fist.

Furious breathing filled his head.

An apology hovered in his throat. Danny ran his tongue around the inside of his mouth and tasted Kel.

The pale body was a dark outline, framed by window panelling. Head lowered, long fingers gripped the sill.

A rapid pulse sprinted in his cheek. Danny shook cooling latex from his hand, swung legs over the side of the bed. His eyes never left the dark outline.

Slope shoulders hunched.

Danny stood up. The platinum chain hung down his back, tight against his neck. "Why not?" The whisper hurt his throat.

Slope shoulders remained hunched.

He stared at the long line of Kel's spine. The question split the semi-dried crust at the corners of his mouth. Stomach lurched. The distance between the edge of the bed and the window stretched from feet into yards. Then miles...

...hundreds of miles.

Back to the playground. Big Frank's sneering tones echoed in his head...

...joined by another, more educated voice from a white tiled room with a bubbling jacuzzi. Low, rasping words from the window:

"Cos ah'm no' a fuckin' poof, that's why..."

Dry lips tilted further downwards. The imprint of Kel's

mouth on his was stronger than ever.

"...an' neither ur you!"

He scowled. Another voice joined the chorus in his head – a female, red-headed voice. Feet hit cold wood. Danny walked slowly towards the window.

Shoulders almost meeting ears.

He stopped a foot away, staring at the nape of Kel's neck. "Okay."

Snort. "Okay...whit?"

His eyes moved to the fading outline of a bruise on the inside of a goose-fleshed thigh. "Okay, you're not a..." The words stuck in his throat. Danny spat it free. "...poof! I'm not a poof- no poofs around here!"

Ebony head slowly turning. Bitten fingers releasing window sill.

Danny took a step back.

Freckled face drenched in shadow. A rigid hand pushed a lock of matt-black hair from a furrowed forehead. "

He could feel eyes boring into his. Danny waited for Kel to say something – anything.

Shadowed eyes continued to stare.

Ice drenched his skin. Reflected from below, twin beams of light crossed the wall somewhere behind him. Then paused, illuminating the face inches from his.

Kel's bottom lip was slightly swollen. A bitten finger rubbed the shiny surface...

...then a yawn stretched the full lips tighter than ever.

Danny forced a laugh. The sound lingered, too loud.

The beams moved away. "Well ah'm glad we finally goat that sorted oot!" A pale, naked body brushed past him. "'Night..."

Danny flinched. "Goodnight..." He stood there, waiting until Kel was back in bed.

Ten minutes later He took his place at the opposite side of the mattress. A salty-sweet smell filled his head, mixing with the faint odour of 'Ebony' and the scent of fabric-conditioned sheets.

It did nothing to improve the sour taste in his mouth.

263

Running...

...down narrow streets lined with people. Big Frank's big leering mouth hurling words. Other, scowling faces, one eye apiece. Snatching hands.

Running beside Kel, legs pumping like pistons.

Snatching hands seized the collar of his rugby shirt.

Danny twisted away from a ferret face, grabbing Kel just before a ringed hand did.

Then swerving into another narrow street. Flanked by men in uniform. Danny saw his father's face and ran faster. Kel was sprinting in front, weaving in and out between clumps of arms and helmets. Sirens. Behind. In front.

Danny rolled across the bonnet of a white car with pink stripes. He fell.

Bitten fingers seized the collar of his rugby shirt and hauled him on.

More sirens.

More streets...

...tiled streets, filled with plants and bubbling sounds. His bare feet slapped against the smooth surface. He stared at the back of a red head. Kel's hair flew behind like wings. Then they were soaring above a sea of handsome tanned faces. Somewhere below, Maxie was waving.

Then everyone was waving. Sirens became bells. Church bells. Danny grabbed Kel's hand, soaring upwards. They laughed, staring down at the waving crowd. Air-currents caressed his skin. Danny held Kel's hand more tightly and flew higher.

More ringing.

Everything was blue. Kel's hair fanned out around his head. Full lips smiled, moving towards his.

Danny opened his mouth.

The ringing changed...

...Kel's hair flopped around bony shoulders.

Poof-stuff.

Poof-stuff.

Poof-stuff.

An inch short of the kiss, fingers released his and Kel plummeted earthwards to a forest of naked Jordans...

Ringing.

Danny hovered there, one hand stretched down towards the falling figure.

The ringing was distant...

Below, Kel was an orange-headed dot on a flesh-coloured surface.

...fading.

Banging...

...then he was falling too and someone was crying.

More banging.

Danny's eyelids shot open.

The bangings solidified to dull thumps. Then a voice:

"Maggie? Lemme in, hen!" More banging.

Through sticky lids, he watched Kel scrabble on the floor for clothes and tried to shake the dream away. It refused to budge.

Voices drifted up from below: one angry and male, the other scared, female. Anthony was wailing.

"Maggie? Come on, hen..."

Footsteps and the sound of a door unlocking. Danny caught a snatch of a curse, which was obliterated by more banging. Then thumps. Uneven thumps.

Kel was struggling into warm-up pants and grabbing tee-shirt.

More voices. Male/female. Anthony's howls punctuated words Danny couldn't hear.

The uneven thumps turned into uneven footsteps. On the stairs. Closer. From the floor below:

"Michael? Ah ken ye're here!"

Danny's stomach lurched. He tried to make sense of the voice. No sense to be made. He fumbled for the bedside light.

An orange glow flooded the large space.

Kel was pulling the Adidas warm-up top over his head. The face emerging from beneath black fabric was a light grey colour. Full lips set in a hard line. One nail-bitten hand was back in the side pocket of the Adidas warm-up pants.

Behind the uneven footsteps, a faster, more nimble tread.

265

Not fast enough...

...his eyes jolted towards the top of the stairwell.

A tousled black head. Face scarlet with exertion. Two large, nail-bitten hands gripped the sides of a pair of aluminium crutches. Archie Kelston laboured up the last two steps.

Danny shrank back.

Kel moved forward.

Breathless laugh. "Ye've done it this time, Michael son." The figure tucked both crutches under one arm and leant against a wall, chest heaving. Narrowed eyes spotting Danny. "An' you? Half o' Glasgow thinks you've topped yersel'!" One hand wiping sweat from forehead. Then another laugh.

Footsteps dragged Danny's eyes from the glowering face. He stared beyond to where Des Rodgers had appeared, holding a baseball-bat:

"Get outta here!"

A bitten hand waved casually. "Ah've nae quarrel wi' you, pal – here tae see ma boy..."

Then Des was in the room, waving the bat and Archie Kelston was trying to light a bent cigarette and Kel was grabbing Danny's arm and hurling clothes at him.

Chapter Twentythree

"Whit the hell ye done tae yer hair?"

Danny tried to dress, eyes flicking between three players on a stage.

Pyjama-bottomed and bare chested, Des stood at the head of the stairs. Baseball bat lowering. Eyes narrowing. Somewhere below, Anthony's crying was less violent.

Kel gnawed a forefinger. "Ye're okay, then?"

Danny stared at the bulge in the back pocket of Adidas warm-up pants.

"Aye – nae thanks tae you, but." Archie Kelston had staggered into the chair by the window. Crutches leant against polished wood. Bitten fingers gripping a crumpled cigarette. "Ye shouldney be playin' wi' guns, Michael."

Danny's gaze moved from a belt which wouldn't fasten to a stiff denimed leg thrusting out from the chair.

"Ah didney mean tae..."

"Ah ken, son." Cigarette ash flicked onto polished wood. Non-belligerent, almost regretful tone. "Ah telt the police it wis kids wantin' tae rob me." Tone hardening. "Ah telt that fuck-heid Burns ah didney ken where you were, an' ah didney care."

Danny's fingers shook, struggling with trainer laces.

"Ony chance o' a wee refreshment, pal?" Flushed, sweating face now focused towards the stair-head.

Des was leaning on the baseball bat.

Choking laugh. "A vodka wid slip doon great – nae free booze oan that fuckin' plane, an' ah widney gie'em the prices fur they miniatures!"

Danny lurched to his feet, moved to where Kel was still gnawing.

"Lager?" Reluctant.

"No' got onythin' stronger?"

"There's some whiskey, somewhere..."

"That'll dae nicely, pal." Broad palms rubbed together.

Des's eyes scanned a bruised, freckled face.

White-striped shrug.

Then the sound of descending bare feet on polished wood.

A sigh.

Danny watched bitten fingertips extinguish the glowing end of the cigarette.

Kel's voice ripped through sizzling. "How did Jordan... seem?"

Hoarse laugh. "How dae ye think? The skinny fella wi' the stitched rat face that wis wi' him didney look very happy either."

Danny slumped against the wall.

A set of smouldering eyes bored into him. "An' you – ah've goat a bone tae pick wi' you!" Archie Kelston lit another cigarette and levered himself out of the chair.

Danny tried to merge with the wall.

"You tell yer parents ma boay here wis giein' you a hard time at school?" Cigarette held dart-like.

"Whit?"

"No!" Danny stared at the glowing tip. A hand grabbed his arm. He shook it away, eyes directed towards the creased, once-more belligerent face. "I didn't tell them anything..."

Sceptical. "So how come ah'm gettin' phone-calls fae heid-masters an' social workers an' fuck kens whit?"

The hand regripped.

Danny looked at a confused, bruised face. He sighed. "Frank and Gibby got my duffle-bag – I...er...jumped on him and Mr Cooper caught us fighting." More words rushed from between his lips. "But I didn't say anything – Cooper got the wrong end of the stick. I told him you had nothing to do with..." The words he'd actually uttered circled then collided with each other in his head.

One ginger slug raised. "You took-oan Big Frank?"

Danny's throat was dry.

Grin. "Wish ah'd fuckin' seen that – whit happen?"

Danny opened his mouth. Archie Kelston was in there first:

"Yer ma thought ye'd topped yersel' causa some note ye left, son – but ye wur alive oan Thursday night, an' ah ken it wis you phoned the hospital, yesterday mornin'. Ah telt yer parents ma boay an' their boay ur pals, an' that Michael's a guid boay – he widney bully onywan..." Wince. Hand rubbing leg. "...fuckin' hellish shot, though, but ah shouldney complain aboot that, ah suppose." Sigh. Tousled head flicking towards stairwell. "Where's her man wi' that whiskey?"

Then Kel was asking other questions. Danny concentrated on Archie Kelston's hurried answers:

Friday morning, after he'd been released from hospital, the police had questioned him for three hours, on his son's whereabouts. They already knew about this address. Half way through the interrogation, he's been asked about any relatives in Belfast. Then about the supermarket robbery in Balerno:

"Is it Burns' money, son?"

An Ebony head shook slowly. "Lennox's – the wan ah shot?"

Nod. Frown. "So how come Burns is efter...?" Words tailing away. Wince. Leg rub. Frowning realisation. "Ah shouldda broke both yer legs before ye put wanna mine oota action – mebbe that widda keep ye away fae that fuck-heid!"

Kel flinched.

"Ye're way oota yer depth, Michael – Jordan Burns is wired tae the fuckin' moon..."

Footsteps on the stairs.

Angry voice lowered. "But ah dinny need tae tell you that, eh? Listen..." Head lowered. "Ah ken a guy can clean that money fur us – takes twenny five percent, but it's worth it tae..."

"It's gone." Danny stared at the floor.

Pause. Then: "Whit's he mean?"

"The money – it's gone. Fell oot the train wi' big Maxie."

He refocused on a disbelieving frown:

"Ye mean ah came aw' this way fur nothin'?" Smouldering eyes flicked between two faces.

"Aye – wasted journey, dad..." Kel walked to the window chair and began to fold a more-crumpled-than-ever John Rocha.

Danny listened to the sound of creases smoothed.

A sigh. Then: "Whit ye gonny dae, son?"

He waited for Kel to say something.

Sound of folding continued.

Danny frowned. "We're going to the police tomorrow – I'll tell them what happened and..."

"Ye'll tell nae-wan nothin'!"

Danny blinked. "I thought...?"

"Aye, you thought – ye're eyeways thinkin'!" John Rocha stuffed into Head bag, swiftly followed by two warm-up suits. Zipping. "'S'aw' right fur you..." Kel spun round, green eyes blazing. "You'll git a slap oan the wrist. Ah'll dae ten years – an' that's efter Jordan's finished wi' me!" Pale jaw rigid. "You wanna go tae the polis, you fuckin' go!"

Danny stared at the scowling mouth and remembered what it felt like against his. Voice from the stairwell:

"Michael, your mother wants..."

"She can fuckin' want, then!"

Kel's eyes were boring into him. People were talking in the background. Danny didn't hear them. He stared back at the bruised, confused face...

...then turned away and lifted his jacket from the floor.

Kel was hoisting the Head bag over a white-striped shoulder, striding towards the stairwell.

Danny followed.

Des was standing by the bed, holding a half bottle of Teachers and glaring at Archie Kelston.

One crutch waved for emphasis in a conversation Danny had lost track of. At the bottom of the stairs:

"Michael..."

He hung back.

Bitten fingers paused on the door handle.

"...look efter yourself, son."

Snort. "Ah've had plenty o' practice doin' that, thanks!"

Then they were outside, jogging down a dimly lit street.

After fifteen minutes, Danny slowed to a breathless trot.

270

Coins rattled in his pocket. He fished them out, counting in darkness.

Three pounds and thirty four pence – unless Kel had any money. He closed his hand around the money, tried to imagine the conversation between his parents and Archie Kelston.

And failed.

In front, an ebony head bobbed purposefully, increasing its lead.

Danny sprinted, fell in step beside it: he had to phone home – had to tell them he was okay and that Kel had nothing to do with anything.

Green eyes narrowed, Kel stared straight ahead.

He scanned for a phone-box. An illuminated red circle loomed ahead. Another Underground station. An open Underground station.

Kel slowed to a brisk walk, striding on past.

Danny had to run to keep up. "Where are we going?" The first words in twenty minutes, directed at the side of a frowning face.

The answer came an hour later, when Danny's legs were lead and his eyes were watering too much to see street signs.

Pale face peering up narrow road.

"Where are we going?" Danny grabbed a white-striped arm, dragging its owner to a halt.

"We need tae find somewhere tae sleep – we need tae get aff the streets an'..."

"That's a station." He tugged towards black letters on an illuminated white rectangle. "We can...pretend we're waiting for a train." Pupils the size of full stops stared at him.

Frown. "That's no' very permanent – we need a...base, til we can git oorsels sorted-oot."

Danny pulled harder. "We can talk about it, inside..." An icy wind ripped through his thin jacket. It chilled less than the eyes did.

Then they were jogging up dirty concrete steps towards glass doors.

271

Euston was almost as busy as it had been the previous morning.

In the all-night Burger King, Danny bought one large coffee from someone who looked younger than he did. He wove his way past huddles of people at tables to a white-striped huddle and a Head bag.

Beyond the fast-food concession, station workers swept the concourse with yard-long brushes. A pair of figures in black trousers, hats and radios sauntered between the activity.

He sat down beside the hunched figure, de-lidding the coffee. The smell was warm and vaguely reassuring.

Ebony head slowly tilting upwards.

Danny held out the polystyrene container.

Bitten fingers closed around the cup.

He talked as Kel drank.

Three people asked them for money.

Four offered to sell them *The Big Issue.*

Two women in head-scarves wanted to know if they knew the true way to God.

A girl with bleached blond hair wouldn't believe they didn't want to buy dope.

"Well?"

A guy in a baseball cap had been watching them for the past half an hour, as had a woman in a leather coat and hair that looked like Kel's used to.

Danny pulled the platinum chain from under his rugby shirt and fingered it. "What do you think?"

On the opposite side of the table, Kel was finishing the last of the cold coffee. And nodding. "We try them aw'?"

"Yes – if it's casual-work, they won't care about national insurance numbers and stuff like that. Cash-in-hand."

More nodding. Bitten fingers broke off sections of empty coffee-container.

Danny stared through glass to where one of the floor-sweepers was handing over a pound coin to one of the people who'd approached them, half an hour ago. "That's only if *The Big Issue* thing doesn't work out – but it should.

It's... designed for people like us."

People who couldn't take the chance of being seen on the streets? Danny sighed.

Bitten fingers tore the polystyrene cup into sections. Still nodding. "So what do we dae noo, Mr Five Highers?"

Danny met the eyes of the guy in the baseball cap again.

Beyond, two girls in body-warmers were draped over each other and a pair of proper rucksacks.

A frown tugged at lips sore from talking. The eyes beneath the brim of the baseball cap were both functioning, but it was too much of a risk. Danny stared at a neat mountain of polystyrene debris. He stood up.

So did the man in the baseball cap.

Danny's legs wobbled. He sat down again.

Curious. "Whit is it?"

Danny focused on the destroyed cup. "There's a guy over there – he's been watching us for ages. I don't know if he's..."

"Him in the Ducks' cap?"

"Don't look!" Danny shivered, raised his eyes.

"Clocked him when we came in." The back of an ebony head was beckoning beyond. Low words. "Lea' this tae me."

Danny watched, throat tightening.

Seconds later, the guy with the baseball cap was standing at their table.

Kel lounged back against the window.

Danny fiddled with a section of ruined coffee-container and waited for someone to say something.

No-one did. He could hear the man's breathing.

He risked a glance sideways to the thighs of dark denim.

Dark denim moving away.

A trainered foot brushed his on its way past. Danny's eyes shot up.

Kel thrust the Head bag at him. Bitten fingers stroked the chain around his neck.

Then he was watching white-striped legs lope across the concourse in the wake of the baseball-capped man.

"You Scottish, pet?"

Danny wrenched his eyes from where he'd last seen Kel and swallowed. "Irish."

The woman with the red hair was sitting opposite.

He waited for her to ask for money or offer to save his soul.

"Couldn't help overhearing your conversation." Long, matching finger nails lighting a cigarette.

Danny considered embroidering the lie, then thought the better of it.

Heavily made-up eyes scrutinised him. "How old are you?"

He frowned. "Eighteen."

"Aye..." Laughing exhale. "And about as Irish as Edinburgh rock!"

His skin reddened. Danny looked back to the Kel-less space. It was now occupied by the two police officers. He looked away.

"What do they call you, pet?" Another exhale.

He stared through a haze of smoke, wanting to get up and walk away. He knew he couldn't. He focused on the little cracks of red which bled from her lips.

"Ina." Scarlet-tipped fingers extended across the table.

He took the hand. "Danny." Her palm was warm. The grip was solid.

A low, cracking voice. "Oh Danny-boy, the pipes, the pipes are..." Laugh. "First Irish song that came to mind?" Cigarette clenched between red lips.

"No, it really is Danny – Daniel."

She let go his hand. "That's better – you looked like you were under a death sentence, when you were talking to your friend."

Something hard wedged itself in his throat.

Silk Cut packet pushed towards him.

Danny shook his head.

"Bad habit, right enough." Cigarette crushed in silver foil ashtray, another lit. "Just in?"

He looked at Ina's face and tried to make sense of the question.

274

Large blue eyes narrowed through blue/grey smoke. They didn't match the hair on the head which nodded towards the bag.

"Oh...yes."

Slow nod. "Got any money?"

Danny grabbed the Head bag and stood up. "No, sorry." Preamble different, message the same. He'd wait for Kel outside. Scarlet-tipped fingers on his arm. A laugh:

"Park yer arse back down, pet..."

Danny's face matched the nails. He remained on his feet. "I've got to go and find Ke...my friend."

Lower, more insistent voice. "Sit down – you want the cops over here?" The fingers squeezed.

His eyes flicked to where two hatted figures were still sauntering. The seat of his jeans hit moulded plastic.

Blue/grey exhale. The fingers patted, then moved away.

Danny focused on a section of folded flesh beneath Ina's chin.

"Left home?"

The flesh wobbled when she spoke. Danny nodded.

"And you've got no money?" A mole wriggled on the folded flesh.

Danny stared at it. "About four pounds...but Kel and me are going to..."

"Kel's your friend – the kid with the bad dye-job?"

His mind flashed to the reason Kel's hair no longer looked like Ina's. He pushed the past away and tried to concentrate on the future. "Yes – we're going to go round the burger-chains tomorrow, see if they're taking on casual workers if we can't get to sell *The Big Issue* and..."

"Slow down, pet."

Danny's eyes left the mole and settled on thickly lashed eyes. Deep creases fanned out from corners.

Ina cocked her head. "Got somewhere to stay?"

Danny sighed.

Thickly-lashed eyes to wrist. "That's my break nearly over..." Frown. Scarlet-tipped fingers into the pocket of the leather coat.

He stared at the white, printed rectangle on the table

between them.

"If you and your friend can get twenty quid together, this place is okay – and they do weekly-rates. It's just round the corner..."

Danny plucked at the card.

"...and if the worst comes to the worse, come anyway – but make it after six. Room sixteen."

He read the card. Why was she doing this? He raised eyes from the table to hers.

"I've a boy back in Middlesborough older than you!" His mind was read. "Don't hang around here, pet..."

Beneath the table, legs edged past his.

"...an' if I don't see you again, good luck with *The Big Issue*." Scarlet-tipped fingers ruffled his hair.

Danny covered the card with his palm. "Er...thanks.

Then he was staring across the concourse, watching a chubby, leather-coated woman collide with a loping, ebony-haired shape.

"Six Christopher Place – The Belgrove Hotel." Under street-lit rain, he held out the card and stared at five brandished, English ten pound notes.

Snort. "There's a Belgrove Hotel in Glasgow – fuckin' doss-hoose!"

"This is twenty pounds a night – that's not doss-house prices." Water splashed off the white rectangle. "It'll be... nice." Danny wiped it with a wet hand. He stared up and down the Adidas-clad body, wanting to ask about the fifty pounds.

"Whit you lookin' at?" Money thrust back into pockets.

"Nothing." Eyes faltered...

...on the curved bulge in the front of white-striped warm-up pants. Danny flinched. "Did you...mug that guy?"

"Didney huv tae..." Laugh. "Fuckin' thing fell oot ma pocket when he wis suckin' me aff, did it no'?"

Danny's stomach lurched.

Kel eased the dark shape of the gun from folds of darker fabric and replaced it in the back pocket of the warm-up

276

pants. "Gied him a hellova fright – ah telt him it wis ainly fur... protection, but he insisted oan the money aw' the same." Collar of jacket turned up. "C'mon, then – ah don't wanna get fuckin' soaked again!" A hand tugging at his arm.

He wanted to ask where they'd...done it.

He wanted to know what a man's mouth on your knob felt like...

The hand tugged harder.

...he hoisted the Head bag further over his shoulder and stumbled up a dark street.

He wanted to know why Kel would let complete strangers suck his knob for money but turned away every time he offered to do it free.

The hotel was grotty, but not that grotty. And warm. He switched on the bedside light, extinguished the overhead one.

Kel was opening the drawers of a small chest, looking inside.

"Told you it would okay." His eyes glazed a notice, pinned to the wall above the bed.

'No cooking in rooms.

No alcohol in rooms.

No animals in rooms.'

Snort. "Bet there's bugs!" Drawer closed, wardrobe opened.

Danny sat on the side of the bed. "No there's not..."

Peering into wardrobe. "These kinda pits ur eyeways crawlin'."

Danny tried a laugh. "...but if there are, they'll not be in there!"

Snort. Wardrobe door closing. Then a pause. "Whit wis the woman's name – the wan telt ye aboot here?"

"Ina." The heat in the room turned his eyelids into pound-weights. Blood sped through his veins at the thought of lying beside Kel again.

Thin arms wriggling out of white-striped sleeves. Sniffing. Snub-nose wrinkling. "Ah fuckin' stink, man –

wonder where the bogs are." Yawn.

Danny nodded to a small wash-hand basin on the far side of the room.

Sigh. "Ah suppose that'll have tae dae..."

A tee-shirt hurled past his face, landed inches away. Danny looked at his wrist: three forty five. His body was somewhere beyond tiredness.

Rummaging in the Head bag. Plastic-encased toothbrush, soap and shampoo produced.

Soft humming.

A hand on his shoulder.

Danny looked up.

Kel was pealing off socks.

He stared at an arc of shadow beneath a pale arm. A pause in the humming:

"You got ony stuff ye want washed, we can dry it..." Ebony head nodded to an ancient radiator.

"Oh...okay." Danny watched the arc of shadow dip and rise.

The hand removed itself. Toiletries collected form the bed, along with two pairs of socks and corresponding underwear. Sigh. "Git a move oan, eh?"

Danny dragged his eyes from the bare chested and footed figure and began to undress.

Chapter Twentyfour

The sheets were nylon and itchy. Damp air drifted over
from an ancient radiator draped with socks and knickers.

Danny scratched at his thigh. His body wanted to sleep
and never wake up. His mind itched more than his leg.

Sounds of rough fabric on on soft skin.

Danny stared through warm darkness.

Inches away, Kel changed position for the eighth time.

A leg threw itself across his.

He flinched. A snuffle near his shoulder. Then:

"You awake?"

"Mmm...?" He tried to sound sleepy.

A still-damp head against his arm. "It wis nice o' that
wuman tae tell you aboot this place."

"Mmm..."

"Whit wis her name again?"

"Ina."

"Aye, Ina." Kel turned onto his stomach.

Danny tried to ignore the way his blood was rushing
downwards. Pause, then:

"It's gonny be okay, eh?"

Warmth from Kel's hair seeped through skin into bone.
Danny turned towards a face he couldn't see. "Yes..." The
thigh slid from his, settling somewhere around his knee:

"Aye..." Contented-sounding. "London's a big place.
Millions o' people. We're jist another two. We'll get joabs –
you're still goin' back tae school, but – an' we can stay here
'til we git enough money thegether tae rent a flat or
somethin'."

A length of hard flesh which wasn't his twitched against
his thigh. "Yes..." Danny moved onto his side.

"Hey, mebbe if there's time the morra, we can go an' see
the Tower o' London, eh?"

Danny lowered his chin, rubbing it against still-damp
hair. "Yes..."

"Aye..."

The syllable vibrated against his collarbones.

279

"...it's gonny be okay..."

An elbow brushed his stomach. Bitten, water-wrinkled fingers played with the platinum chain. Danny flinched.

The fingers stopped playing. An arm flopped over his hip. "We'll git an early start, eh? Git up early an' plan it aw' oot."

He felt each word as it hit his skin. "Yes..."

"We can go tae the station fur breakfast."

One arm had gone to sleep.

"Mebbe say thanks tae yon Ina, fur tellin' you aboot this place."

The other lay rigid against a mirroring groin. Prickly nylon erected every hair on his body.

"Should we mebbe phone roon' the burger-places? That wid be cheaper than walkin' it."

Danny closed his eyes.

A snuffle. "You asleep?"

He opened his mouth against still-damp hair, breathing in the smell of soap, drying underwear and the scent of his own discomfort.

Sigh, then: "'Night, Danny...."

London on a Saturday was Glasgow city centre multiplied by a hundred.

Advantages sank into disadvantages.

Too busy. Too noisy. Too big.

Few of the people who handled job applications were available. Those who were told them to apply in writing.

The first *Big Issue* office was closed.

They couldn't find the second.

In dusky light, Danny looked away from a street sign. "We're in the wrong place." His head hurt.

"How kin it be the wrang place?" Snort. "Said Greenwood Road in the phone-book – this is Greenwood Road." The toe of a far-from-shiny-shoe kicked at a wall.

Danny peered at the *A to Z*. "I told you, back where we had to change." Tiny print strobed in front of his eyes and made his head hurt more. "There's more than one Greenwood Road."

"Whit they doin' huvin' mair than wan?"

Danny ignored the question. "This is...E13 – we should be in E8."

Another snort. "Why didn't ye say so?" Another kick.

Danny stared at the rumpled John Rocha. "I did – I said E8!"

"Naw, ye didney..."Foot raised, Ebony head shaking slowly. "Ye jist said..."

"Back at..." He tried to remember the name of the Underground station. "...back where we changed, remember? I said there were five Greenwood Roads and we were looking for Greenwood Road, E Eight."

Bitten fingers grabbed the *A to Z*, snapped it shut. "Well, thirteen's ainly five away fae eight..." Book shoved into pocket. "It'll be aroon' here somewhere." Green eyes scanning the darkening streets.

Danny slumped against the wall. "It could be miles away – in a different...zone." He was hungry.

"Well, ye shouldda thought o' that, when ye jist said..."

"I said eight – I definitely said eight." Danny stared at the pavement. He needed a shower.

"Well, ah didney hear ye!"

Danny raised his eyes. "Give me the map." He levered himself off the wall and walked closer to the street-light.

The kicking resumed. "It's fuckin' useless, that thing – you go an' ask somewan where E-eight is."

Danny leant against the lamp-post. He was sick of asking people. Most didn't even stop. The rest either didn't know or stared at them then reluctantly gave long, complicated directions which didn't match anything on the map. His forehead was throbbing. The back of his left trainer had rubbed his heel raw. "There's no-one around to ask."

The kicking increased.

Danny stared at the growing heap of crumbling masonry around Kel's foot.

He'd no real idea where they were.

The battery in his watch had run down, and he didn't know if the office would be open, even if they found it.

Kel stopped kicking and turned.

Danny stared at a lowered face:

"We'll go back tae the Underground station, luck at the map again an'..."

"How much we got left?"

Hand thrust into pocket, then withdrawn. Content of palm surveyed.

Danny moved from the lamp-post's reassuring solidness and walked over.

Only one note, and that looked like a tenner – the afternoon had cost a fortune. Achieved nothing. He looked away from the collection of coins.

"Twenty four pounds an'..."

"If we'd bought the travel-passes like I wanted to, it would have been much cheaper and..."

"Willya shut up an' let me finish a fuckin' sentence!"

Danny stared. "Don't take it out on me!"

"Take whit oot on you – the fact you've goat us fuckin' loast?"

"We're not lost!"

"We fuckin' are! If we'd done like ah wanted tae, an' jist phoned roon', it widda bin cheaper than yer fuckin' travel passes an' we widney huv wasted money oan this!" *A to Z* wrenched from pocket, hurled onto the pavement.

Danny stared at the sprawling book. "If you'd been listening when I said E-eight, we might have got here in time!"

"Ah wis listening'! Ye didney..."

"You were not! You were going on and on about the fucking Tower of London!"

"You wur the wan that wanted tae go in the..."

"But not today!" Danny clenched his fists. "Today was for getting jobs!"

Their voices echoed in the dark road.

Danny frowned into a flushed face.

Bitten fingers shoved into pockets. "Listen, ah..."

"We agreed! We need money – we can go to the Tower of London any time!"

"Ye're daein' it again." The gruff voice dropped in volume.

"Doing what?" Danny watched his breath condense. He was still shouting.

"No' lettin' me finish whit ah'm sayin'."

He scowled. "Okay, what is it?" Irritation jangled every nerve in his body.

Shrug. "Disney matter noo."

Nails dug into the palms of his hands. "No, come on – let's hear this...pearl of wisdom." He crouched, picked up the *A to Z*.

Beneath dark green fabric, rigid shoulders tensed further.

Frustration twisted in his stomach. Danny stared at millimetres of lighter hair on the crown of a lowered head.

Silence drowned out their shouts.

Danny narrowed his eyes. "I think we should cut our losses and go back to the hotel – we've still got tomorrow." They had barely enough money for another night.

A mumble.

Danny frowned. "What?"

"They'll definitely be closed oan Sundays – *The Big Issue* oaffices. The Greenwood Road wan's probably closed the day, tae."

He rolled the *A to Z* into a tube. Part of him had known that for hours. Another part wanted to keep looking, because it was at least doing something – and when they were doing something, it was easier not to think. "I know, but there's masses of burger-places we've not tried – we can do those tomorrow..." The words were out before he could stop them. "...on travel-passes."

Muffled snort.

He looked away from the rigid figure and tried to get his bearings.

They walked in silence towards Plaistow underground station.

He'd stopped feeling hungry hours ago.

At about the same time they'd stopped talking.

Back in the hotel, Danny handed over twenty pounds for another night.

283

Two hours later he asked the woman behind the desk for the phone-book again. His legs were heavy on the stairs towards their room.

Kel was checking the washing. Again.

Danny removed pencil from pocket, took off his jacket. He sat down on the unmade bed and opened the phone-book beside a dog-eared *A to Z*.

Sounds in the background told him Kel was opening drawers. Again.

He longed for the sound of a voice.

It came an hour later, after a knock:

"You awake, pet?" Husky words.

Danny glanced from a list of Pizza-Hut addresses to the door, then the chair on the far side of the room.

Kel stopped fiddling with his hair. Narrowed green eyes.

Danny got up from the bed. "Yes..." He continued to look at Kel, mouthing a name.

Green eyes looked away. Fingers resumed fiddling.

Opening the door, Danny stared at the crinkly face. The red hair was now stacked on top of Ina's head.

She was wearing the leather coat again, holding a Burger-King tray. Balanced on top, two burgers and three polystyrene cups. Smile. "Thought I'd take my break back here..." Tray held out.

Danny took it, moving aside as she tottered into the room:

"Christ, these damn things pinch!"

He closed the door, placing the tray on the bed where Ina was now rubbing scarlet-nailed toes:

"Hello, pet – you're...what is it – Kel?"

Bitten fingers paused, mid fiddle. Curt, ebonied nod.

The smell of the burgers brought his appetite back. Kel's lack of words brought the past three hours back. Danny managed a smile for Ina, lifting one of the burgers. "Thanks – we were just going out to eat..." He started to half it.

"No..." Words from the bed. Coffee-lid prized off with scarlet finger nails. "...I've got my waistline to think about, pet. He looks like he could do with feeding-up!" Stacked-

284

head nod to the slouching figure in the chair.

Danny sat down. He held out a wrapped package to Kel.

Ina was lighting a cigarette, looking around. "How did the job-hunting go?" Eyes to the phone-book on the bed.

"We're going to try again tomorrow..." Danny continued to extend the burger.

Bitten fingers were fiddling again.

"Good – that's good, pet..."

Something in the voice made him turn from a lowered head.

Little red cracks leaked outwards from pursed lips. Crinkly eyes stared at him. Long drag on the cigarette.

Fingers took the burger from his, picking up on the something too:

"Whit is it?"

The first three words in three hours sent ripples of panic up and down his spine.

Ina's frown increased, directed over his shoulder. "Someone's been askin' about you and Danny, pet." The red mouth left a matching stain on the polystyrene cup.

Voice from behind. "Polis?"

The stack of red hair shook. "They were there earlier." Another drag on the cigarette. "This was a bloke with an accent a bit like yours."

Danny's fingers pressed into the burger.

"When wis this?"

Danny's fingers pressed harder.

"'Bout an hour ago."

"Where?"

Mushy warmth crept over fingernails. Something thumped in his ears.

"Under the bridge up at Kings Cross – asking all the lads, he was. I thought maybe he was someone's da, or someone's man at first. None of the lads was saying anything, but I thought you two should know..."

The thumping in his ears obliterated another one word question from behind...

...and Ina's husky answer.

Jordan.

285

Danny stared at greasy burger smears. He took a napkin from the tray and wiped his fingers.

Jordan.

He stared down at stained whiteness. The thump echoed down from his ears and trembled over his body. His eyes were wet and cold in the warm room.

Jordan.

"You okay, pet?"

Another voice, very close. "Aye, he's fine – thanks fur tellin' us, an'...thanks fur the burgers."

Jordan.

Wetness drip onto the stained napkin and spread outwards.

Movement on the bed.

On the periphery of blurring vision, a pair of bare legs stood up. "You sure you're okay?"

Danny staggered to his feet. "Yes, I'm fine." His voice sounded very far away. Then someone was hugging him:

"Take care, pet...."

The smell of make-up and cheap deodorant caught in his throat. The leather arms tight. Too tight. They squeezed the thumping back into his chest and made his eyes hurt.

Then the arms were gone and he could hear Kel talking to Ina somewhere in the direction of the door.

The phone-book and *A to Z* blurred.

A door opened.

A door closed.

He raised his eyes from jumbled names and pages of streets. He sniffed.

Inches away, a freckled face.

Danny's throat was tight. The thumping moved up into his gullet, emerging as a sob. Then other arms were around his shoulders:

"Oh, man...don't cry..."

The thumps split into bullets of breath, exploding from his open mouth onto Kel's neck. Danny gripped a warm waist. Hands stroked his back:

"Jesus, don't..."

He couldn't breathe. He tried to speak. The sobs only

286

increased.

"It'll be okay..."

It wouldn't.

"We'll...get oota London, eh?"

They couldn't.

"The morra, eh? We'll...hitch-hike – there's Burger Kings everywhere, no' jist in cities..."

Danny clung to the skinny body and tried to breathe through his nose.

Jordan was everywhere.

Where Jordan wasn't, the police were.

Breathless words close to his ear:

"Oh, man, ah'm sorry aboot the day – ye did say E eight, but ah wis gettin' tired an' fed-up an' ah jist wanted tae git it ower wi' an'..."

"I'm...sorry...I...shouted at you..." Danny gripped the back of the warm-up pants. The sobs were easing. The thumping was a dull pulse in his stomach.

Half-laugh. "'S'okay..." Bitten fingers stroked the back of his neck, easing under the platinum chain. Lips brushed his ear. "...everythin's okay, Danny..."

The pulse moved lower.

He gulped in air.

Bitten fingers rubbed the small of his back. Other wetness met tears drying on his jaw.

He raised his head.

Wetness moved back to his ear.

A pulse throbbed in his groin. Danny scowled. Not now. He turned his head, opened mouth to...

...then warm palms were holding his face and Kel's lips were on his.

Danny moaned, twisting the waistband of the warm-up pants. His mouth remained open. Every muscle froze.

The movement was slow, unrushed...

Danny stared at an expression he hadn't seen before.

...against his top lip, the sides then down.

His stomach flipped over.

Kel was making noises somewhere at the back of his throat.

The sounds vibrated through warm palms and tingled in Danny's ears. He stared at lowered lids, watching the way blond lashes fluttered against freckled skin.

Kel sucked his bottom lip into his mouth, running a warm tongue along the dry inside. The tongue swept his bottom teeth.

Danny shuddered.

The pressure was light. Gentle.

Danny's groin was tight and hot. Fingers uncurled from the warm-up pants and gripped tee-shirted shoulders. Drying areas around his mouth became wet again. He closed his eyes, hips moving instinctively against other hips.

Then hardness was grinding back against him and light, gentle pressure solidified into another grinding.

Two sets of eyes opened.

Kel thrust his tongue into Danny's mouth, sealing the gasp with dry lips and a moan of his own.

Fingers tangled in his hair, gripping the back of his neck and tilting his head. Danny lips were pressed back so hard it hurt. Fragile flesh met the hardness of his front teeth...

...then other teeth glanced off his and Kel's arm was around his neck, a tongue was exploring his mouth and his ears were full of the sound of the kiss.

His stomach flipped over. Danny tried to return the pressure.

A skinny body prevented any movement in any direction. Kel was rigid against him, crushing the breath from his lungs. A double-heart hammered onto his ribs.

Two tongues touched.

Danny gasped into a wet mouth.

Grabbing a handful of ebony hair, he pulled the pale face closer.

He was choking on saliva.

He couldn't breathe...

...he couldn't care less.

Low growls from deep in Kel's throat vibrated downwards and resounded across every link of a wet platinum chain into Danny's nipples.

288

The urgency knocked his brain out and pushed him off his feet. Danny clung on, gnawing at Kel's mouth and trying to suck a wet tongue down his throat.

Gravity and the force of the kiss defeated him. Maps and phone-books and burgers bounced around his head. Danny released tee-shirted shoulders. Hands plunged down then upwards.

He needed to feel skin.

He needed to know this was real.

Then the body on his rolled away and Kel was kicking off trainers.

Chapter Twentyfive

Poof-stuff...

The overhead light was still on.

In the room next door, a radio blared. Danny moved onto his knees and tried to identify the song from the bass-line.

Green eyes gazed down between them. A thumb gnawed to bleeding caressed a swollen length of flesh.

Danny flinched at the touch and concentrated on the bass-line.

Lips brushed his forehead...

Poof-stuff.

...then Kel was moving back, ebony hair lowering.

Lips nuzzled.

Danny laid shaking hands on two pale shoulder-blades. The bass-line blurred under drums.

The nuzzling moved down his length.

Heels hit thighs. Danny slumped backwards.

Bitten fingers eased his knees apart. Wet warmth stroked his balls.

Poof-stuff.

A spiky black head rested on his thigh. Two hands gripped his knob. Danny slumped forward, pressing his face to the base of a nobbly spine.

A gasp against his groin.

Danny kicked legs free, hands reaching down to stroke the fine ginger hair on Kel's calves...

Poof-stuff.

Poof-stuff.

...then they were moving and his knob was twitching against full lips and his own lips were open against the shadow of a bruise. Danny's hips bucked forward, pressing the longing in his groin against what felt like teeth...

..then the teeth were gone and he was sliding past something tight and wet and all the pictures in all the books burst into flames.

His stomach twisted. Danny hauled hands from calves,

fumbling between slender thighs.

Three feet away, his balls impacted with the roughness of Kel's chin and something was flicking along his knob.

The twisting in his stomach moved down and back, tingling in his bowels. Hips moved by themselves, responding to the tightness in his groin and the heat of Kel's mouth.

Somewhere in the distance, muffled moaning.

Danny braced paper arms against the bed and thrust forward into wet warmth...

Poof-stuff.

Poof-stuff.

...a clutching in his chest made him pull away. Wet flesh slapped back against his stomach. On hands and knees, Danny crawled up to where Kel sprawled. He stared down at the freckled face.

A spit-smeared mouth curled somewhere between a sneer and a silent shout.

Poof-stuff.

Poof-stuff.

Green eyes all black...

Danny lifted one hand from rumpled bed-covers and covered the curving length in Kel's groin.

...mouth all shout.

On his.

In his head.

In his heart.

Then Kel broke the kiss and they were both searching scattered clothes for a silver-coloured packet.

Danny unrolled the condom over his knob and listened to the bass-line of a different song.

Kel was lying on his back, knees splayed and clasped to nipples.

He stared at the pink, crinkled hole beneath ginger tufted balls. Fingers stumbled. The sound of speedy breathing filled his ears. Holding the condom in place, he lunged forward, stabbing at the tiny orifice and trying to kiss Kel again.

A groan. "Haud oan..." Words low and hoarse. "Whit kinda idiot buys condoms an' no' lube?"

Danny frowned. Breath hissed through his teeth, swelling lungs then refusing to leave.

Kel released one knee and spat onto three fingertips.

His chest was motionless. Blood pounded in his ears, finding an distant echo against his stomach.

Hips raised, three slick fingers massaged the pink crinkled hole.

Air burst from his lungs. Knob pushed at latex. Then Danny was lying beside Kel, coating his own fingers with saliva and rubbing the wet orifice.

A moan.

Danny shivered. Something leaked into the tip of the condom. He stared at Kel's face, watching a hundred expressions wiggle across flushed, freckled skin.

A finger tip edged past rimmed wetness.

Muscle clenched, then relaxed a little.

Sensation jolted up his arm.

Kel's mouth was open, gulping.

Danny moved between the splayed thighs and eased a finger further inside. His stomach lurched, collapsing in on itself as Kel pushed down onto his hand.

A travel-sick elation broke out on his skin, flooding his body with heat and ice.

Then the ice was melting and sticky fingers were holding his knob and Kel was guiding him forward.

The friction almost made him scream.

The music had stopped. Danny concentrated on the movement of something which no longer belonged to him.

Somewhere around the second thrust he'd withdrawn too far and the condom had come off.

Somewhere around the fourth Kel had stopped grabbing covers and started grabbing him.

Somewhere around the sixth he fell backwards and stopped counting.

Kel was kneeling over him. Arms in the air. Features wet and contorted. A solid slapping sound echoed the grip on

293

his knob each time a pale torso moved forward and up, then backwards and down.

Danny watched a long length of flesh smack off tensed stomach muscles. His own body moved by itself, thrusting rhythmically off the bed and upwards into Kel.

Over the churning in his stomach and the ache in his balls and the tightness in his chest, Danny's mind was somewhere else...

No tiled rooms, no jacuzzis, no pictures in books.

No words. No poof-stuff.

...a hand gripped his, fingers lacing.

The ache increased.

Sweat poured down Kel's chest, soaking the soft ginger hair between nipples. Ebonied spikes flopped over a creased forehead. Bitten fingers were clamped around a twitching knob, hauling maniacally. Huge black pupils stared down at him.

Like Jordan...

...in reverse. Kel dominated his eyes, pale and giant-size and thrashing and thudding down onto him.

His mouth fell open. Something was rushing through his veins, gathered from every corner of his body. Spine left the bed.

Kel was an unfocused shape very close to his face. Danny's knob twitched violently. Then warmth.

Under his skin, on his chest, face...

...and something deep inside Kel was trying to push him out.

The second time, it succeeded and he came into a dense, ginger bush.

The third time, Danny gripped slick shoulders and held on. In his ears, something erupted. Inside Kel, a fist of heat and wetness clamped around him, holding more than his burning knob.

Kel collapsed forward, mumbling into the pillow.

Muscle was paper, torn into shreds. Danny pressed his face into the back of a sweating, heaving neck.

A leg curled back over his. More breathless mumbling.

His mouth closed around pink skin. "What?"

Soaking ebony head turning sideways. "Stay in me..."

Danny tried to answer. His mouth wouldn't close.

Then Kel moved both legs and Danny was slipping between them, nipples and the platinum chain pressing against the damp skin on the wet back.

Kel was on the second burger.

Danny watched through a daze of exhaustion. A crusty scum cracked on his lips. He couldn't stop smiling.

Burger held out.

"No thanks..." His mouth hurt, twisted out of shape.

A grin. "Whit's wrang wi' your face?" Shiny chin wiped on the back of hand.

He wriggled up the bed and rested head on one crossed thigh. "Nothing – nothing at all."

Greasy fingers played with his hair. "Fuck, ah'm starvin' – sure ye dinny want a bit of this?" Munching. "They're no' bad..."

His stomach was mush. He'd never eat again. Danny shook his head and felt his brain rattle. Twining one arm beneath the raised knee, he stroked the inside of a pale thigh. "Kel, I love you." The words came from a thousand books and what was left of his mind.

Fingers paused.

A cold shiver swept his body.

"How come?" The fingers moved away.

His mouth was dry. Throat barren of answers. "Didn't you ...like it?" The question came from nowhere, sprinting into his head.

"Like whit?"

Danny stared at the soft, sticky folds of skin hooding the head of Kel's knob. "What we did." The responding laugh made him feel worse:

"Oh, that?" Fingers ruffled his hair. "Aye, it wis great." Abstracted.

He searched behind the sentence. Beneath his face, the thigh moved. Danny clung on.

"Pity we didney time it – you musta gone thirty-five

minutes at least, that second time."

Danny frowned. Bitten fingers gripped under his arms, hauling him up. He gazed into glowing eyes:

"Wis it..." Curious. "...like in they books o' yours?" Thumbs stroked his nipples.

Danny's heart melted and dripped down his ribs. "It was better – wonderful! I love being inside you when you come, I love kissing you, I love when you touch my knob, I love holding you, I love..." Words ground to a halt. Hands slipped from his chest.

Kel was chewing the side of his thumb. "'S jist fuckin', man."

"No..." Danny gripped a bony wrist, dragged the thumb from the full mouth. "...I made love to you – we made love! That's not just... fucking."

"Makin' love, fuckin', shaggin' ma arse..." Wrist wrenched away, gnawing resumed. "...suckin' me aff – it's aw' jist words fur knobs intae holes..."

Bits of his heart dribbled away. "No, it's not." He groped for reasons. "It's..." Found none. "...just not."

A ginger slug slid up a furrowed brow. "Man, fur somewan doin' five Highers, ye can be affy stupid, sometimes."

Green eyes bored into him.

Danny looked away.

A sigh.

A hand on his shoulder. Danny flinched.

"Ken whit ah like maist?"

The question made him refocus. He peered into an alien face. "Tell me what you like – please! You should have told me before we..."

"When we jist...dae stuff thegether." Kel was staring into the distance. "Watching vids, goin' tae see films, talkin'..." Something like a smile twitched at the corners of saliva-stained lips. "Even when you're goin' oan an' oan aboot they fuckin' books, ah like it."

Danny blinked. "You can do that with..." Big Frank, Gibby, Le Coq Sportif. "...anyone." He corrected himself. "Apart from the book-discussions, I mean."

296

"Ah like..." Pupils telescoped. "...jist bein' wi' ye. Ah dinny care whit we dae, really, lang as ah'm daein' it wi' you..." Eyes still focused on something Danny couldn't see, ears unhearing. "An' ah like the way you wanna dae well at school, an' ah...like that you're gonny go tae university." Smile.

Danny listened to the longest single speech Kel had ever made.

"Ainly other person ah ken's been tae university's Jordan..."

The name was an icicle into afterglow.

"...an' ah'm almost glad ah crossed him, cos if ah hudney, ah widda missed...aw' this." Words further away.

Danny frowned. "All...what?" The last three days were a nightmare...

Ina's words swayed drunkenly in his mind.

...which showed no sign of ending.

A laugh. A different laugh. An un-Kel-like laugh. "Nothin' – forget it!" Pupils expanding into focus. Then a naked figure bounded from the bed and loped to the radiator. "These ur dry ..." Socks and knickers folded, laid on the back of the chair.

Danny tried to move. Someone had attached sandbags to his ankles. He slithered up the mattress, easing tired limbs between nylon. The sheet was sandpaper against his sore knob.

"Want the light aff?"

The bed stank of them. Danny inhaled lungfuls. The action pushed every doubt and reservation from his mind.

Jordan didn't matter.

None of it mattered.

All that mattered was right here. Right now.

"Yeah..."

The room plunged into darkness. Another body slipped between staticky fabric and into his arms. Danny rubbed gooseflesh from skinny biceps.

A snuffle. A shiver. A thigh draped itself over his. Arms wrapped themselves around his waist. And squeezed. "Thanks."

He manoeuvred a hand under the warming shape. "You did like it, then?"

Soft snort. "No' fur that – fur...stayin' wi' me. It's no' your problem."

A frown edged through a haze of bliss.

Lennox.

Hurting his arm...

...Kel making him stop.

Fingers tracked spine knobbles. "We're in this...together, remember?"

Together.

Together.

Together.

A wriggle. Then: "Aye."

Danny rested his head against another. "I do love you, you know..."

All that mattered was right here. Right now.

"Aye..." The word brushed the side of his face.

"...and it's going to be okay..."

"Aye." The brush was softer.

"We can hitch-hike, get an early start..."

"Mmm..."

Danny tightened his grip. "Brighton, maybe. It sounds nice – or Dover. Bet there's lots of work down there, with the Channel Tunnel and everything..." And another continent, thirty minutes away.

"Aye..." Barely audible.

A hand on the top of his head pushed it lower. Danny smiled, resting his face on Kel's shoulder. London was too obvious, anyway – and too expensive. "The coast will be cheaper – there's bound to be bed-and-breakfast places, and maybe we can..."

"Danny?"

The word was in his hair.

"What?" He shifted position, cuddling in closer.

"Gonny fuckin' shut up and go tae sleep?"

"Sorry..." He smiled. He'd never speak again, if that's what Kel wanted.

A snort against his right temple. The sound slumped

into a soft laugh.

Danny eased away from a razor hip-bone before the arm beneath Kel beat him to sleep.

Breath was warm on his neck, knees pressed behind his and soft hairiness lay against the crack of his arse.

Heat...

...on his face. Danny drifted up from a dream in which Kel was kissing his forehead and saying something he couldn't hear. Opening his eyes, he squinted into sunshine and smiled. The movement cracked dry lips. Danny groaned, moving back against the shape still curled around his.

The shape moved with him.

Danny turned his head. He stared at the bank of pillows then scanned the sun-streaked room. Even the wallpaper looked better. Brighter.

The toiletries-bag was gone.

He snuggled back down into Kel-scented warmth and wondered if the tiny shower cubicle at the end of the hall would hold two.

Sleep-scummed eyes focused on the chair in front of the window.

One pair of socks and his green stripy underpants. The sight made his stomach flip over and his burning knob twitch. His body was tired and energised at the same time.

An early start.

He didn't want to move...

...eyelids came together and the smell of last night pulled him back down.

Knocking woke him up.

Loud knocking.

Danny crawled from the bed in a tangle of sheets.

More knocking.

Fingers hovered inches above the handle. Then a voice:

"All rooms must be vacated by noon, for cleaning – okay?"

"Er...okay, thanks..." Relief tingled on his skin. He sat

down on the bed.

The toiletries-bag was still missing.

And the Head bag.

His eyes moved around the room. Really looking.

Nothing...

...then something. On the bedside table, the maps and the phone-book. Below a pencil. And a sheet of paper.

He grabbed the note.

Kel's neat hand-writing wobbled:

Phone your mum and dad. They will come and get you.
Sorry about everything.
love,
Kel

Heart thundering, he re-read the words.

No Brighton.

No jobs in fast-food chains.

No hitch-hiking.

No money...

...his eyes moved to a small pile of coins at the side of the lamp.

Jordan.

Danny's chest tightened.

Jordan.

He looked back at the note, clutching the nylon sheet against icy skin. One finger traced the second last word on the cheap note-pad they'd bought in the newsagents' round the corner.

Then he was thrusting arms and legs into clothes and trying to remember if the *A to Z* showed motorways.

Ina gave him five pounds and another hug.

The Jubilee Line ended at somewhere called Stanmore. Danny turned five times to say something to someone who was no longer with him.

A guy with a lorry full of beds took him as far as Long Eaton, said Danny wasn't very chatty.

Two miles outside Nottingham a guy in a red car and a

white suit talked non-stop and played Garth Brookes all the way to Huddersfield. Danny rubbed dull silver links between sweating fingers and stared through the windscreen. In the Dewsbury service station, a woman driving a Rentokil van was only going as far as Southwaite. She lectured him on the dangers of hitch-hiking and told him about how she'd hitched round Europe when she was his age.

The Rentokil van stopped at every motorway service-area on the M62.

Danny stared at blue rectangular signs which said 'The North' and wondered how far Southwaite was from Glasgow.

If he could get there first he could...

...the service station straddled six lanes of motorway, a white concrete giant in fading afternoon light. In a car-park crammed with lorries and container trucks, Danny shaded his eyes from the sinking sun and watched the woman from the Rentokil van stride towards the restaurant with another armful of air-freshener refills.

Another sinking, in his stomach. Last night was a sticky memory inside newly-washed underpants.

Last night was hazy, dazy words he'd heard but barely listened to.

'No' your problem...'

'No' your problem...'

Two honks of a horn made him jump. Danny turned, one limp hand raised to the woman in the Rentokil van as she negotiated between a reversing Marks and Spencer lorry and a coach of children. He watched her number plate fade southwards, staring the space the van left...

...another, Kel-sized space expanded inside him. Danny turned from six lanes of flashing cars and walked to where a small man with a bobble hat was climbing out of the cab of the M & S lorry.

He had to wait an hour – something to do with statutory rest-periods. The man with the bobble hat had offered him a cup of tea.

The next two drivers he approached were going to Edinburgh.

A third wasn't allowed to carry passengers.

Beside the pay-phones, Danny peered at a map.

Southwaite wasn't far from Carlisle...

..which wasn't far from Glasgow. Really. An hour and a half on the train.

He turned, wading through a torrent of laughing kids. Staring through plate glass at dozens of lowered, eating heads, Danny twisted the platinum chain between his fingers and tried to will time to pass faster.

Food-smells drifted out from the opening-then-closing restaurant door. The sound of a fruit-machine sang over engine-noises.

He pressed the side of his hot face to plate glass.

He watched the bobble-hatted driver pay for another cup of tea and saunter back to his table.

Sweat condensed on cool glass.

At another table.

Alone...

...matt tufts stuck up from the back of another lowered head. Set on a pair of hunched, John Rocha-covered shoulders.

Chapter Twentysix

"Whit you doin' here?"

He looked away from a frown of irritation and ignored the question. "Newcastle's just across a bit – I saw it on the map. It's a port – boats go to...Norway, Denmark. We can..."

"You phoned yer mum an' dad?" Weary irritation.

"...stowaway on a boat – a cargo-boat. It'll be easy, and..."

"Ye huvney, huv ye?" The sound of chair-legs scraping. "Well, ah'll fuckin' phone'em an'..."

"Don't..." Danny reached across the table, grabbed a John Rocha-ed sleeve. He pulled the figure back down. Grip tightened on rumpled fabric.

A sigh. Kel seized, up-ended a salt-container.

Danny watched one gnawed index-finger push spirals of formica into tiny white grains. "...don't go." Chest tightened.

The finger swirled. "Ah've goat tae – ah never shouldda left."

Danny released the sleeve and gripped the edge of a hard, plastic seat. "Why?" It didn't make sense – they had plans, options. "Why do you have to go...back?"

"Cos aw' ah ever dae is run fae stuff..." Bitten flesh circled one way, then the other. "...an' drag other folk wi' me."

He flinched. "I came because I wanted to – because we're in this together..."

"No' we're no', Danny..." Eyes raised from the table-top.

Green gazed into blue.

"...five fuckin' Highers an' he still disney get it!" Green rolling ceilingwards.

"Get what?" He scowled.

"When ah go back, that'll be the end o' it." Calm. Expressionless.

Danny shivered. Green-flecked irises floated in front of his eyes.

The end?

Coldness seeped into his bones. He looked away from the eyes and stared at the table.

"The slate'll be wiped clean, see?" A finger drew an X over the spirals. "Fur both o' us – Jordan disney hold a grudge."

Others weren't as magnanimous. Danny watched the arms of the X broaden to obliterate salty curls. Grainy CCTV-footage replayed itself in his brain. "What about the police?"

The finger paused. "Jordan'll see me aw' right – he looks efter his ain. Maxie's went fae strength-tae-strength."

His nose was running. Danny wiped it on the back of a hot hand. "And what about..." He frowned into the uncreased face. "...me?"

Sigh. "Aye, ah ken – we need tae git your story straight." Salty fingers through Ebonied hair. Thoughtful pause. Then: "Everywan seems tae think ye ran away, cos ye wur gettin' battered at school. Let'em keep thinkin' that, eh?"

A cool hand lightly slapped his cheek. Danny ducked away. "I mean, what about...us?"

The face was lineless. Paler. Younger...

...apart from dark, smudgy shadows under the burning eyes.

The question ignored. "Gie yer mum a ring..." Head nodded backwards towards the pay-phones. "...say ye slept rough fur the weekend." Half-laugh. "Ye look like that's whit ye've done onyway."

One hand groped for the platinum chain. The events of a week ago circled in his head.

Only a week.

Only seven days...

...it felt like years. Had passed in minutes.

Pleased-sounding. "Aye, that's whit tae dae. They'll move ye, ah bet – transfer ye tae some other, nicer school. Nae-wan kens we hung aroon' thegether, so nae-wan'll make ony connection between..."

"I'm coming with you." The words by-passed his brain.

"No ye're no'!"

Danny's nails grated against the edge of the hard, plastic chair. A conversation over-heard from behind a toilet door zoomed back to him, punctuated by rasping sobs and bloody paper-towels. "I can...take you to the hospital afterwards – I won't say anything, and then I'll...go home." He stared into the pale face.

Kel was gnawing his thumb. Green eyes squinted sceptically upwards from beneath ginger lashes.

Danny fumbled for further justifications. "I want to make sure Maxie's all right."

Scepticism hardened into undisguised doubt.

He groped further. "And I want to...apologise to Jordan for all the trouble we've caused."

Snort. "No' thinkin' o' tryin' tae talk him oota it, are ye?"

"Of course not!" Jordan was the last thing on his mind.

"'S'ainly an eye, efter aw'..." Dismissive hand through hair. "... ah'll wear shades – or wanna they notch leather-patch joabs. Could be a loat worse – there's a guy in Paisley collects balls. But he's a fuckin' animal."

Danny winced. "I just want to make sure you get...medical attention, when it's over."

Hand pausing. The sounds of clattering dishes and low conversation seeped into to fill the thoughtful silence.

Danny chewed his lip.

"Ye'll go home, efterwards?"

Afterwards was a vanishing-point on a constantly-shifting horizon. He nodded.

"Promise?"

He nodded more vigorously.

Resigned sigh. "Don't suppose ah could fuckin' stop ye, onyway – how the hell did ye ken ah'd be here, by the way?"

Danny smiled. "Kismet." Beneath the table, a foot kicked:

Low, hissing words. "No' here – no' in front o' aw' these folk!"

Danny kicked back. "It means...fate – destiny."

A leg wriggled away. "Read that in wanna yer books, tae?"

305

"Still want that lift, lad?"

Danny looked up.

The man with the bobble hat was leaning against Kel's chair.

He found a smile. "Er...yes – have you got room for someone else?"

The M74 was an unending line of striped traffic-cones and red tail-lights.

In the lorry's dark cab a John Rocha-ed thigh pressed against his, had been doing so for the last two hours. Through semi-lowered lids Danny read another Road Works Ahead sign and listened to a discussion of World Cup qualifying matches.

On the dashboard, green luminous figures said nineteen thirty eight.

Warmth pulled at his eye-lids. Danny blinked, refocused on green luminous digits.

He had to stay awake.

Sleep tugged more insistently.

"...we did okay against Lithuania, but..."

Good-natured chuckle. "Monkeys with boots on."

"Ye wurney sayin' that last year, when they equalised two minutes intae extra time!"

"Friendly, lad – the boys were saving themselves."

Snort. "Aye, so's Belgium could run rings roon' them a month later!"

The conversation drifted away. Danny's head lolled sideways, contacting with a John Rocha-ed shoulder. Shining green numbers changed before his eyes...

...then disappeared.

He had to stay awake.

He had to feel every second, remember each moment.

He concentrated on Kel's gruff voice, ignoring the words and just listening to the sound.

They'd crawled past the turn-off for Strathaven half an hour ago. Glasgow was creeping towards them.

Danny wrenched his eyes open, staring past the dashboard clock into darkness ahead.

306

Lead-like lids rebelled and showed him another darkness.

The engine tone became higher.

A jolt, then the tone evened off and the lorry speeded up.

The top of a bony shoulder was pushing through padding and digging into his cheekbone. Danny revelled in the discomfort, swaying with the motion of the lorry. Distant voices:

"Your mate's out for the count!"

Low laugh.

The shoulder moved. Danny's head slipped, then landed further down the John Rocha. Ragged fingers eased him back into position. The weight of a casually-slung arm draped itself behind his neck:

"Aye, he's hud a busy weekend – an' fitba'-talk eyeways sends him tae sleep."

Somewhere in the distance, the driver changed gear. "Yeah, he didn't strike me as the football-type."

"He...reads a loat." Vaguely-apologetic.

Fighting exhaustion, a frown formed on lips too tired to move.

"I like a good book – gives me something to do on my breaks, apart from eat." Chuckle. "Richard LaPlante, Eric Lustbader ..." Another gear-change. "...now there's something to get your teeth into!"

"Either o' them write...*Babycakes*?" Vaguely-curious.

The word wrenched him consciouswards.

"No, lad – that was..." Pause. "...what the hell's that fella's name?"

"Armistead Maupin." The words were a croak. The arm tightened around his shoulder:

"Thought you were sleepin'?" Soft laugh.

Danny's eyes opened. "Just dozing." The lorry was stationary. Beyond the windscreen, he recognised the outskirts of Hamilton.

"Yeah, Armistead Maupin – writes a good story..."

A bobble-hatted face poked past the John Rocha-ed shape:

307

"...read *Sure of You*?"

"No, just *Tales of the City*."

The bobble-hatted head nodded. "Saw it on Channel Four – the book was better..." Hand-brake released. The lorry moved off. "That Mrs Madrigal was a case, eh?"

Danny hauled himself upright, leaning back against Kel's arm. "I liked her." He rubbed his eyes.

"Great old bird. Just a bit...unexpected."

"Yes, the end was a surprise..." In the dark, bitten fingers played with his hair:

"How come – whit did she do?" Less-vaguely curious.

Chuckle. "That would give it away!" Gear-changing. The lorry increased speed.

Danny squinted left into darkness. "I've got it, at home – you can borrow it, if you want."

Studiedly off-hand. "Aye, ah might dae that." The arm removed itself. Kel leant forward. "Where ur we?"

The question dragged his mind back to their destination. Danny's chest tightened.

"Baillieston – the M8's coming up. Where you two want off?"

Ribs dug into his skin. "Anywhere..." A foot moved beside his:

"As close tae the city centre as ye go, pal."

Bobble-hatted nod. "I need to break soon anyway – get in another couple of chapters of Lustbader. Read any of him, lad?"

Danny shook his head, eyes focused through the window.

Fifteen minutes later he knew the plot of *Floating Cities*.

A blackened church spire flick past. His heart sank.

He turned his face away from the new houses. Stomach lurched as the lorry dipped into the Townhead slip road.

Ten minutes after that, the driver was hauling a book from below four figures which read twenty one fifteen and they were jumping from the cab.

"Jordan? Let us in, eh?"

JB's was in darkness.

Kel peered through metal slats, fist thumping. "Jordan? Maxie? Onywan?"

Danny staggered from the wet, trembling shutter. Hope surged in his stomach, undigested and warm...

"Roon' the back – the deliveries' door." Kel bounded down the steps, swerving right.

...and premature. By the time he'd caught up with the sprinting figure, a shineless shoe was kicking the bottom of a double door:

"C'moan – open up!"

The shout scythed through driving rain.

Danny shivered, hefting the Head bag over his shoulder. "They're closed – he's not there. Let's just go..." Where?

"He's in there..." Kick. "He's..." Metal-framed wood shuddered under the assault. "...eyeways..." Foot drawn back. "...here oan..." Another shudder. "...Sundays – Jordan?" Voice heavy with effort. "Man, see if we've gotta go aw' the way oot tae his place ah'll..." A final kick.

"We'll come back tomorrow..." The tiled room and a bubbling jacuzzi limped into his mind. Danny hugged himself. "...or we can phone and..."

"Whit's goin' oan oot there?" Words from beyond metal-framed wood. "Whit ye want?"

"It's me, Pat – gonny get Jordan?"

Silence, then: "Kel?"

Danny heard the surprise in the muffled voice.

"Aye, tell Jordan ah..."

Double doors swung outwards, unwelcoming arms.

Danny blinked in bright light.

The eye-pad was gone. In its place, a puffy, weeping hole.

Something kicked him in the stomach. Danny glanced right.

Kel stood blank-eyed, long arms hanging loose from sloping shoulders. No smile. No frown. No expression at all. A slightly breathless voice from behind Pat's silhouette:

"What on earth have you done to your hair?"

Then Pat moved out of the way and Danny was staring at a handsome figure in scoop-neck vest and shorts.

Jordan had been upstairs, working-out. He smelled of sweat and something else. "You shouldn't have lied to me." No surprise. Just disappointment.

"Ah ken.

"And you shouldn't have run – it never helps."

"Ah ken – ah'm sorry."

"I was worried about you – and you too, Danny."

He looked away from Jordan's muscular form and moved closer to a slope-shouldered shape.

"London's a dangerous city, full of all sorts of dangerous people, boys..." Tinged with sadness. "...our mutual friend Lennox, included."

He focused on book-shelves. Blurring spines danced in front of his eyes. He'd forgotten about Mr Lennox.

"Why, Kel?" Vaguely curious.

Danny stiffened.

"Why...whit?"

"Why did you shoot Lennox?" Vaguely amused.

"He wis gettin' rough wi' Danny." Matter-of-fact.

"Hmm..."

His body was rigid.

"...I'll enjoy hearing the whole story...afterwards. Beats me how you got him from way up there into the Clyde. For the moment..." Pause.

Danny waited for more words. They didn't come. He looked to where ringless fingers extended, palm up.

Kel shoved a hand into pocket, placing a dull heavy object on top of smooth skin.

Jordan's fingers closed around the weapon, trapping the pale hand. "What do you need with a gun?" Mildly reprimanding.

Danny watched ringless tighten over bitten fingers.

"You ever see me with a gun?" A well-manicured index finger stroked the back of a bruised knuckle. "Do you?"

"Naw, Jordan." The words tighter than the grip.

"Guns can be traced..." Pressure increasing. "...guns can go off when you don't mean them to..."

Skin turning white around a bruised knuckle.

"...and hurt people."

Danny's eyes moved from Kel's twisting hand to where a thick muscle pulsed in a sweat-sheened arm.

"Guns are for mugs – and wee boys with big ideas." The grip easing. "But you know that now, don't you?"

Danny heard the hiss of released breath:

"Aye, Jordan. Sorry, Jordan."

Relaxed strides to the other side of the desk. Drawer opened. Weapon inside. Drawer closing silently.

Kel was grimacing, curling and uncurling crushed fingers.

"Maxwell's recovering nicely, by the way..."

Sweat trickled from one arm pit. He refocused from the figure in shorts, who was now perching easily on the edge of the desk.

Towel from around neck, underarms casually wiped. "...he knows what happened on the train was an accident, Danny..."

A trickle of sweat cooled into a snow-trail.

"...and the rest will do him good – he's been working too hard, anyway."

Danny stared at the sweat-matted hair on the broad chest. The snow-trail turned to liquid, flushing over his face.

"You acted out of loyalty – I admire that." Towel back around neck. "Wrong acts for the right reasons are always to be praised."

He shivered.

"Loyalty, freely given, is a wonderful thing, Danny..." Muscular legs eased themselves from the edge of the desk. Feet stopped, an inch away.

His body was rigid.

A still-warm hand slipped beneath the collar of his rugby shirt. "I knew this wasn't silver..." The slender chain weaving between soft fingers. A tug.

Danny watched a platinum chain join the gun. His neck felt naked. The skin around his nipples could still feel the imprint of Jordan's hand.

"He'll buy you more, don't worry – he'll buy you a hundred." Something like a smile.

Danny risked a glance at Kel.

No finger-gnawing.

No hands in pockets.

Arms still hung loosely from now-straight shoulders.

Eyes directly carpetwards.

Danny's throat was a desert. He had to say something.

"I knew you'd come back – you're a lot of things, Kel, but you're not stupid." Something like a laugh. "A wee bit wilful, perhaps, but you did the right thing, in the end, and that's what counts. You know where your loyalty is and you..."

"I made him lie."

"Shut it, willya?"

Furious eyes on his face. Danny stared straight ahead. "I made him – it was my idea. He didn't cross you – I did, so you should..."

"Fuckin' shut it, willya?" Hiss tinged with panic.

Danny glared at Kel. "No, you shut it! If anyone's to blame in all this, it's me – if I hadn't...over-reacted to what Lennox did, you wouldn't have shot him, and you wouldn't have had to lie about what happened and we..."

Genuine laugh. "Both of you shut it!"

A well-muscled arm draped itself over his shoulder. Danny flinched.

The other arm around damp John Rocha, Jordan walked to one of the leather sofas. "Let's all just calm down. Kel knows the score, Danny – it's business, nothing personal. You've seen it done, haven't you?"

Ebonied nod.

"It doesn't hurt – that's not what it's about. A little messy, but no major arteries are involved and the optic nerve has few pain-receptors. I'll book a taxi, you can take him to the Royal and..."

The door opened.

Jordan spun round, taking them with him. "I said I didn't want to be interrupted!"

Something crumbled in his chest. A wet, rodent face peered at him from above the zipped neck of a leather jacket:

312

"They're here?" Large hand wiping rain from forehead.
"Why the fuck did ye no' gimme a ring?" Lennox moved
into the room. "Ah've got an airmy combin' London fur
them!"

Danny tried not to look at the ragged line of stitches
flaring from above the right eyebrow into a section of
shaved scalp.

"I'll take care of this – they're my boys."

A muscular arm tightened around his shoulder.

Ferrety frown. "Aye, well it wis ma money an' ma
fuckin' heid!" Fingers to forehead stitches.

Danny's eyes flicked between a calm and a furious face.
The muscular arm released him.

Jordan moved forward. "I said I'll take care of this." A
edge to the voice.

Danny shivered.

Lennox was unzipping the leather jacket, shaking rain
from soft folds. "Christ, we're no' jist talkin' face here,
Burns – ah'm twenty K doon. Whit ye gonny dae aboot
that?"

"An unfortunate accident – a misunderstanding."
Another muscular arm continued to shadow the rigid
shoulders of crumpled John Rocha. "You're sorry, aren't
you, Kel?"

Stilted nod.

"Aye, well sorry's no' guid enough." Frown. Hand into
the pocket of the leather jacket.

Eyes swivelled to where a John Rocha-ed form was now
leaning against a muscular shoulder. Ringless fingers
stroked the back of a lowered, ebonied head:

"Want him?" The handsome face turned slowly. Fingers
continued to stroke:

"Want both of them?"

Danny's heart shrivelled under a penetrating gaze.

"Aye, ah want'em..."

The words were a blow on top of a bruise.

"...an' if ye wanna continue tae dae business wi' me,
ye'll hand'em over."

The weapon Lennox eased from his jacket looked

different from Kel's: more compact, blacker. Newer. Placed on the desk beside the complicated telephone, it drew his eyes like a road-accident.

"Call it a...gesture o' goodwill. There's another twenty K, jist a phone-call away an' ah kin take aw' the H ye can supply, Burns. East meets west: we'll divvie up Scotland between us. Whit dae ye say?"

Silence.

Danny's eyes scanned the room. The door was too far away, even if he was able to move. Then:

"This money clean?"

"Passed the doorstep challenge months ago!"

"And you can take as much as I can supply?"

Ferrety-smirk. "An' whitever else ye wanna pit ma way – ah've goat the..." Weasel-like laugh. "...contract fur Saughton an' Peterheid jails, an' there's boays workin' oan a screw at Cornton Vale."

The words meant little. The tone freed his feet from the floor. Danny sleep-walked to where Jordan was raising an ebonied head. The voice was low:

"Business..."

Hard lips planted soft kiss on a freckled brow:

"...you understand, don't you?"

"Aye, Jordan."

A dark head turned away from the Ebonied one. Blue, pin-pricked eyes nailed his:

"Danny..." Muscular shoulders shrugged slowly. Something like regret. An immaculately-manicured finger stroked the side of his face. "I had such plans..."

The touch was cool. He flinched, drawing back and bumping into Kel. Bitten fingers scrabbled for his.

"Not on my premises." The voice was cold. "And I don't want any debris left lying around."

Bitten fingers linked with his. Danny held on.

"Nae bother." Ferrety laugh. "Ah ken jist the place..." Sounds of re-zipping, and something oily and new replaced within folds of leather. "...thanks tae this pair."

"I don't want to know – I can have...five kilos by Wednesday."

"Geez a bell. Man-tae-man, this time? Nae room fur error?"

Danny listened as conversation continue around them. He looked at Kel.

Freckles stood out on an ashen face. Then full lips were moving. "The chain – gie Danny his chain back, eh?"

Soft laugh. "Don't suppose it matters now…" Drawer-opening sounds. Something soft and slender and cool and broken forced into his fingers.

Danny's fist closed around it and he was sleep-walking again.

Chapter Twentyseven

Rain.

Mud.

The Iceland security lights.

Lurching stomach...

Action-replay in reverse.

...only this time Lennox was on his feet. Behind. With the gun.

Danny stumbled down the steep incline, slipping on the remnants of a torn bin-liner. Wild lilac whipped at his face.

Inches in front, Kel was silent. Pale skin orange under sodium. The hair and the John Rocha blended with the night.

At the bottom of the slope, he slipped again. Danny's face impacted with something hard. Bitten fingers gripped his arm:

"You okay?"

The first words since they'd left JB's. Knees inches from his face. Danny grabbed them. "I'm..." Scared wasn't the word. The cold, empty feeling in his chest was beyond terror.

Bitten fingers squeezed. Arm around his shoulder. Lower words. "Run – ah'll jump oan him an' you run."

A memory of bouncing up and down on a carpet which refused to bend squeezed into his jumbled mind. Danny almost laughed...

...then a claw grip clamped around his other wrist, hauling him upright. He tried to wrench his hand free.

Lennox held on, fingers digging in.

Danny yelped, staggered forward towards the outline of excavation equipment.

"Lea' him alain." Slow anger.

Ferrety laugh. "Change the CD, eh?"

"It wis me shot ye – jist let him go, eh?"

Twisting pressure on his wrist halted the stagger:

"Wisney guid enough fur ye, posh-boay, eh?" Breath hissed through clenched teeth. The claw-like grip twisted higher.

Danny pitched forward on tip-toe. He tried to make sense of the words:

"Ye'll take it fae Burns, but no' fae me?"

Something other than rain was leaking from red soreness above one eye. Something nippy.

"Eh?" The grip jerked sharply.

He howled through the pain, staring at a pair of unshiny shoes which walked crab-like at his side.

"Don't..."

Kel's voice made his chest tighten.

"...don't hurt him."

Danny swallowed the sensation of stretching in his right arm. He stumbled on. The side of his trainer hit off something flat and metallic. He gazed at the rusting tripod.

The grip dragged him back and up.

Feet trailed on wet ground. His wrist was going to snap.

"Move it."

The instruction made no sense. He raised his head.

The gun flicked on the periphery of blurring vision. Lennox motioned a crouching Kel towards the flat metal plate which covered the shaft for the new drains.

'...debris...debris...'

"Go on – push it oot the way."

A grating sound. His eyelids squeezed themselves shut against it. He could smell new leather, wet metal and the meaty scent of Lennox's sweat. Beneath the scrape of metal on stone, the gulp of his own breath and a heavier rasp echoed in his ears.

"C'moan – pit yer back intae it!"

Danny lurched forward. "I can help if you..."

"You stay where ye are."

The grip on his wrist hauled his hand up between his shoulder-blades. Danny's feet left the ground. Legs flailing, eyelids shot open.

Hard warmth brushed the bottom of his spine.

Trainer soles thudded into muddy grass. One arm flapped for balance. Head flicked away from where Kel was heaving at the metal plate. Danny craned his neck over one shoulder.

318

Ferret-features contorted by impatience...

...or something else. His arm was numb. Rasping breath tingled on his ear. Danny took a step back.

The direction of the movement was unexpected. Claw-like grip loosening. Narrowed eyes darted to his.

Warm hardness rubbed against the back seam of jeans. Danny inhaled sharply. He looked away, focusing on red roots on the crown of an invisible head.

A week ago.

Wrestling on the same ground. Another hardness in the front of another body...

...the hardness of a 120 gun.

Breath left his lungs painfully.

This was no gun...

"Noo c'mere." Words static, interrupting others unspoken.

More flicking on the edge of his vision. In the opposite direction:

"Ah said c'mere!"

Kel's pale face was motionless.

A curved outline dug into the seat of his jeans. Maxie's words reeled back to him:

'...yon closet-case fae Edinburgh...'

'...yon closet-case fae Edinburgh...'

Then his free hand was on the back of a damp thigh.

Stroking.

Muscle flinched under his palm. The breath in his ear vanished for what seemed like hours, then blasted the side of his face.

Danny's fingers tightened around wet fabric. "Can I...have a last request?"

Kel walked unsteadily around the metal plate, closing the distance between them.

Weaselly wheeze. "A whit?" Less static.

Kel stopped an inch away. Green met blue.

"A last request."

The grip on his wrist increased. Another wheezing laugh. Words tuning in. "Well, ah huveny goat ony fags, if that's whit ye..."

319

"Before you...do it..." Stroking. "...we could..." His heart stopped. Close to his ear:

"Ah, Jesus!" Impatient wheeze, tinged with disgust...

...and something else.

The grip on his wrist twisted. The pain was somewhere miles away. Danny stared into black pin-pricks. They grew to tennis balls. Another, lower voice:

"Ainly wan thing's worse than dyin', an' that's...no' even huvin' lived."

The words thundered in his ears. Danny leant back against the curved outline in the crotch of Lennox's trousers.

Fingers met around his wrist...

...then the grip was pushing instead of pulling.

Danny twirl-stumbled outwards into the dark. Lennox's voice twisted after him. A soaking John Rocha-ed shoulder impacted with his...

...then was wrenched away. Unzipping tore into his ears. Words minus static:

"Take it oot..." Low wheeze.

"Fuck aff!"

Danny landed heavily, scrabbling one-handed.

"Dae it, bum-boay – dae it afore ah ram this..."

Flicking on the edge of his vision.

"...up posh-boay's arse an' make ye watch me pull the trigger!" Words tingled with anticipation.

Danny stared at two pairs of muddy feet.

"...take it oot an'..." Words fading into a sigh.

The thunder in his ears exploded miles away. Then he was wrenched upright and twirling back to where bitten fingers held Lennox's knob.

"...git yours oot, posh-boay..." Hoarse.

The pressure on his wrist slackened. Danny's non-numb hand groped towards the front of his jeans. Fingers wouldn't work...

...then other wet knuckles knocked his away and Lennox was fumbling inside his underpants.

The gun's cold wetness brushed his stomach. Eyes skittered to where bitten fingers loosely held a fat length of veined flesh.

Hoarse, wheezing words. "Pit it in yer mooth, you." A hand moved from his soft knob.

Danny stood motionless. A clumsy hand dragged at the waistband of his jeans. Cold rain spiked off goose-fleshed thighs and the hand was pushing his rugby shirt up towards nipples.

"Yeah...oh yeah...fuckin' posh-boay..."

Desperate fingertips pulled at delicate skin, twisting and pinching.

Rasping mumbles.

Danny couldn't stop gulping.

The crown of an ebonied head bobbed level with Lennox's groin.

Under increasingly heavy rain, his eyes were dry, mouth drier.

The movement of a palm grazed his chest. Fingers swept up, rubbing pit hair between sweating fingers and staining the skin of his upper arm. "Ye like it, dain't ye?"

Danny bit his lip.

"Dain't ye?" Pit hair tugged.

"Yes..."

Kel was a dark lump. Bitten fingers gripped the thigh of water-darkened trousers for balance. Another set curled around the root of the fat veined length.

The sweating, staining hand was back at his nipples, rubbing and wrenching.

'...yon closet-case...'

'...yon closet-case...'

His chest was on fire. The shiver began around his ankles. It shimmered upwards into calves, thighs and over the groping hand which had now returned to his flexing knob. Knees buckled. A wheeze in his ear:

"Show me yer arse, posh-boay..." Almost a plea.

Heat flushed over his face.

"...turn roon' an' show me yer arse." Less than a whisper.

The hand moved down between his legs, rough fingers nipping his balls. Danny yelped, turned.

321

Between another set of legs, bobbing had stopped.

"Get it back in yer mooth, bum-boay!" Sudden rage.

Mid turn, a beam from distant security lights glanced off the weapon as it sped down towards the side of an ebonied head.

Adrenalin joined with the spreading blush and returned the circulation to a numb arm. He lunged upwards, fingers closing around a broad wrist and dragging it left.

Something hit him in the stomach.

Danny gasped and held on, his other hand gouging at wet fingers. He took a step forward. Jeans manacled his ankles. He hobbled then fell forward as something launched itself on top of him. Arm tingling, he tried to push it away...

...everything blurred in a mass of thrashing arms and laboured breath. He clenched his teeth, trying to wrench the gun from fingers curled in concrete. His other hand was trapped somewhere in the middle of writhing bodies. Teeth met tongue. Iron in his mouth.

Through the wet soup of sliding limbs, he realised he was lying on top of Lennox, and Kel was on top of him.

Seconds later, everything was reversed. Danny's head hit the remnants of a melted Irn Bru bottle and a leathered forearm was pressing against his windpipe. Light flashed in front of his eyes. Gasping for air, he inhaled through an open mouth.

Above, Kel was hauling at handfuls of leather.

Pressure on his windpipe easing. Shoulders reared up from the ground. Teeth sank into soft, wet hide...

...then a roar. Other blood in his mouth.

Bitten fingers raked past his face.

A knee thrust between his legs. The light flashed red, then yellow. Instinct tried to free the trapped limb and shield his burning groin.

He rolled, knees jerking upwards. Through a mist of pain, his arm lengthened until the hand on Lennox's wrist was miles away, limp and useless.

Then fingers thrust between then and the trapped hand was curling around springy softness and Danny was twisting and someone was screaming.

Miles away, index finger slipped through what felt like a ring. His knuckle rebelled, then twitched spasmodically.

A thud. Another twitch, on top of him...

...and a smell. Knuckle tightened.

The second shot was less muffled. The smell was worse. Danny uncurled wet fingers from around Lennox's fat, non-throbbing knob and crawled out from beneath the limp body.

He tried to pull-up jeans.

Fingers rebelled, curled into claws.

When he finally managed it and got to his feet, something dark and warm dangled from a swollen knuckle.

Two sets of eyes stared groundwards.

A shineless, mud-caked shoe kicked at the kidney area.

Nothing.

An ebonied head lowered. Nose wiped on the back of free hand. Breathless rasp. "You wur right..." Nod towards the underside of the fetal shape. "...they dae git stiffies."

Danny shook his hand. The gun refused to leave his finger. His eyes refused to leave the pale length jutting up from dark, rain-splattered trousers.

"Don't suppose ye've goat a pound coin?"

Words tore his eyes away from Lennox's hard-on. He stared up beyond Iceland to the chain of streets lights along the Parade. One blinked red, breaking the circuit.

"Well, Mr Five Highers?" The voice was different. Not laughing.

Danny turned back, peering into a mud-splattered face.

Green examined him. A frown. "Ye've hurt yer heid..."

A bitten finger gently stroked an area he couldn't see. The gesture wrenched his brain into gear. "I'll phone the police."

The fingers paused. One ginger slug raised. "Aye, very funny. Whit...?"

"Self-defence..." He raised his arm, staring at the dangling weapon. "He was going to kill us."

"Ah ken, but..."

323

"We tell the police everything – it's the only way."

The ginger slug sloped back down the pale face. A sigh. "Everythin'?"

Danny lowered his arm, nodded. The gun brushed the side of his knee.

Kel was peering at the curled outline on the ground. Another sigh. "Jordan'll go spare..."

An ebonied head soft against his shoulder.

Danny kissed the top of it and stepped over Lennox towards Townmill Road.

Chapter Twentyeight

They made him take an Aids test.

They took him to see a psychiatrist, who talked about 'repressed memory' and 'emotional damage'.

"Ah'm sorry..."

So long ago. Something happening to someone else. Three months had passed since they'd walked into Baird Street police station.

'The Beast Escapes Justice!' The headline screamed at him. Danny stared at the grainy colour photograph which dominated the front page of *The Record*.

"...he wis guid tae me, an' ah ken it's daft but ah'm still sorry he's deid."

Danny blinked at newsprint.

Two prosecutions, running concurrently.

Two deaths: one on the waste-ground, November twelvth...

He speed-read the few sentences around the photograph of the handsome face, then turned to page two.

...details of the second threw themselves at him:

'While on remand at HMP Barlinnie, awaiting the outcome of a trial for drugs and other offences...Jordan Burns...later died in Glasgow Royal Infirmary...self-inflicted wounds to the throat...the sentencing of Michael Kelston – Burns the Beast's fifteen year old lover – and his sixteen year old school friend Daniel MacIntyre, for the manslaughter of William Lennox, is expected to take place today the High Court.'

"Eyeways said he'd never dae time again..." Half an inch of cropped, scarlet hair stuck up like a halo around the freckled face.

A thinner face.

Green eyes shone dully, the skin underneath smudged darker.

"...an' he meant it."

Danny thought about other dull eyes and the handsome face he'd avoided for the three, preceeding days.

He'd given his statement in court, a week ago. Following evidence recovered from a search of the tiled room, two separate prosecutions merged into one and Jordan became a series of unsavoury attributes from the mouths of Archie Kelston, police officers, girls with orange faces and loose-lipped men with one eye.

Only one pair of lips had remained loyal.

Danny frowned. "Will you say...what she wants you to now?" He glanced beyond the figure in the dry-cleaned John Rocha to where Kel's solicitor was chatting with the guy from the Outreach Unit. "It might help your case – duress."

"Whit?"

"Means he...pressurised you."

A halo-ed head shook slowly. "Jordan never hurt me – he never made me dae...onythin' ah didney wanna dae."

"He gave us to Lennox!"

"Ah ken, but that wis business – that wis wrang..." Snort. "Did ah no' say aw' that tae the lawyers?"

Kel had been as co-operative as he'd been, concerning the drugs and the money: their joint statements, plus names, dates and places supplied by Kel had resulted in Jordan's and half a dozen other arrests for countless offences. Danny looked back at the headline then closed the newspaper: why wasn't anyone interested in that any more? A foot nudged his:

"Christ, ye luck aboot twelve!"

"They made me wear it." He wrenched at the tie around his neck.

Make a good impression.

Emphasize your age.

'Undue influence...

...first offence.'

Head slumped back against the wall behind. Danny stared up at the ceiling.

"Nervous?"

"No..." Beyond nerves. He scrutinised tiny grey fault-lines. "You?"

Snort. "Nae sweat – jist wish they'd git oan wi' it."

326

"Me too." Danny peered at a section of discoloured white.

"Ye'll git aff wi' it: school-uniform, exams comin' up, clean record..." Voice featureless.

Veins of plaster cracked and spidered in front of his eyes. Danny focused on a rusted light-fitment and searched flat words for peaks of hidden meaning. "My barrister said it could go either way."

"Naw, ye will – nice boay like you?" An attempt at a laugh.

An elbow in his ribs dragged his eyes down:

Halo-ed head cocked to the other side of the room. "She reckons ah kid get as little as eighteen months – less, if the judge takes ma key-worker's an' the psychiatric report intae account."

The legal words were strange, alien. Unoptimistic. "That's good."

Eighteen months...

He was doomed to speak in two-word sentences. Danny stared at the pale-than-usual face: more alien than the legal terms.

...on top of three.

Pale hand smoothing non-existent creases from a sleeve. "How's things at hame, onyway?"

Danny scowled. The first condition of his bail was a twenty-four hour parental presence. His mum had stopped teaching.

"They giein' ye a hard time?"

Three hours of shouting and one of pleading had let him wait in here, rather than with them, this morning. Danny reached under the collar of his shirt to fiddle with something which had been impounded months ago. "Not really..." Fingers slipped away.

"That's guid."

Narrowed green eyes flicked around the walls.

His stomach lurched. "What's the... hostel like?"

Slope-shouldered shrug. "'S'okay." Shadowed eyes elsewhere.

"That's good..." He didn't want to know. "...I'm glad."

He wasn't.

He wanted it to be as much of a prison as his house was.

He wanted the guy from the Outreach Unit and everyone else in the hostel to look at Kel the way his parents looked at him.

He wanted Kel to be as miserable as he was...

A frown bisected the pale, freckled face.

...and he didn't. His stomach folded in on itself. Eyes darted to the other side of the room. The solicitor and the guy from the Outreach Unit were still chatting. "Kel, I..." One hand strayed towards sticking-plastered fingers...

...then Kel was on his feet. "Jist wish they'd fuckin' hurry up an' git it ower wi'!" Pale palms rubbed together.

Danny watched the pacing. Hand dropped. Fingers tightened on the thighs of school trousers.

Eighteen months...

...buzzing in his ears. "I'll come and visit you."

"No ye'll no'." Pace. "Ye'll git...oan wi' yer life." More pacing. "Ye'll go tae yer new school..." Speeding up. "...make new pals..." A halo-ed head twisted downwards. Words aimed at the floor. "...git yersel' a nice wee boayfriend an' that'll be that!"

Danny's heart lurched.

The door opened.

Four heads turned towards it.

Then his heart collided with the pit of his stomach and a white-shirted police-officer was beckoning them through.

Chapter Twentynine

The corridor beside the row of already-full cells smelled of piss and ancient vomit. At the far end, two police-officers eyed them warily. Somewhere beyond a scored, iron door a loud, angry voice sang 'Flower of Scotland'.

Two years...

...the school-uniform had backfired. The small, sitting man in the wig had gone on and on about 'lack of parental responsibility' and 'out of control youth'.

A John Rocha-ed knee bobbed convulsively beside his. Over angry singing, more words from the courtroom buzzed in his ears.

Two years...

...'irresponsible...age no defence...academic record and good background only exacerbating...'

The knee bobbed more vigorously.

His stomach was a large cold mass. The small, wigged man had added another six to Kel's sentence, for contempt.

"Yer solicitor'll appeal..."

Danny stared from ancient, cracked tiles to the rigid metal bracelet which secured a thin wrist to his.

"...that wuman fae the newspapers said it wis a...parody o' justice – mebbe they'll campaign fur us!"

Danny flinched.

"...Free the Royston Two – or the Royston Wan an' the Dennistoun Wan, eh?"

His mind was back on the waste-ground. With Lennox. He could still hear the desperation in the wheezing voice. 'Flower of Scotland' blared in his ears and drowned it out. Beneath drunken words:

"Ah shoulda kept ma fuckin' mooth shut in there."

Exhale.

He inhaled sweet/sour breath. Calling the judge a stupid fuckhead wasn't exactly helpful.

A tug on his wrist.

Sticking-plastered fingers scratched a ginger slug. "Danny?"

"What?"

Small voice. "Ah'm fuckin' terrified."

The rigid cuff slid down beneath the cuff of the blazer and dug into his arm. The three word sentence healed every cut made by every lie the voice had ever told. Another three words hovered at the back of Danny's throat. "I know." He didn't feel scared...

...felt like closing the covers of a book he'd failed to understand.

Empty.

Confused...

...frustrated.

The hand returned to the bench between them. "Jordan couldny handle the jail – man, if he couldny handle it, how ur we gonny?"

We...

We...

We...

The large cold mass twisted. Danny looked up from their cuffed wrists.

Freckled stood out on ashen skin. Green eyes glowed from beneath ginger lashes.

Sticking-plastered fingers slid between his. Another hand on his cheek.

Danny blinked.

Green eyes glowed into his. "Still love me?"

The large cold mass melted into something hot and liquid. "I don't know what that...means anymore."

Snort. Soft finger tips rubbed his knuckles, then squeezed once. "Jist words, eh? Like aw' the other words..."

Three months of isolation seeped into the squeeze. Danny stared into pupils the size of footballs. Fingers returned the pressure and dissolved an equal span of loneliness. "Just words, but..."

Then lips were moving gently on his and 'Flower of Scotland' floated away.